SUDDENLY THE SMILE FROZE ON HER LIPS

It was as though a giant vise had taken hold of her heart. Zaccheo was still speaking though she had no idea what he was saying. All she knew was that she was looking straight into Laurence McAllister's eyes. He was standing at the other side of the room, just in front of the bay window, but for the moment, as though by some extraordinary preordination, a space had opened in the crowd between them. Kirsten felt she might be swaying, that her entire body might be dissolving. Not even for a moment had she forgotten how incredibly handsome he was, how compelling his eyes, nor how physical his presence, but neither for a moment had she expected that seeing him again would affect her so profoundly. Suddenly the blood was beginning to pound through her ears and her chest felt so tight she was unable to breathe. So many memories were passing before her eyes, so much love, so much passion, and so many promises. This man had once been her whole life, she had loved him so much and even now, looking at him, she felt as though he was still hers. They had meant so much to each other, how could they be apart?

ALSO BY SUSAN LEWIS

A Class Apart

Dance While You Can

Stolen Beginnings

Obsession

Available from HarperPaperbacks

BETRAYAL

SUSAN LEWIS

HarperPaperbacks
A Division of HarperCollins*Publishers*

This is a work of fiction. The characters, incidents, and dialogues are products of the author's imagination and are not to be construed as real. Any resemblance to actual events or persons, living or dead, is entirely coincidental.

HarperPaperbacks *A Division of* HarperCollins*Publishers*
10 East 53rd Street, New York, N.Y. 10022

A hardcover edition of this book was published in 1994 by William Heinemann Ltd. under the title *Vengeance*.

Cover photograph by Herman Estevez

First HarperPaperbacks printing: September 1994

Printed in the United States of America

10 9 8 7 6 5 4 3 2 1

For an absent friend

Acknowledgments

I SHOULD LIKE TO EXPRESS MY THANKS TO ALL THOSE who helped me in New Orleans, especially Carrie Jo Martina at the Richelieu Hotel, Little Joe Catalanotto of Independent Studios, Danny, whose guidance and friendship was greatly appreciated, Sergeant Wayne H. Cooper of the New Orleans Police Department, and Dr. Paul Wagner of Honey Island.

On a personal as well as professional level I thank my editor, Helen Fraser, for her invaluable support.

My love and thanks go also to my cousin Karen Shields and to my friends Lesley Morgan, Bridget Anderson, Barbara Thorn, Pat Cockram and, of course, Denise Hastie who were with me throughout the writing of this book and so much more. Most especially of all though, I should like to thank Carl and Brenda Clump, they know why.

VENGEANCE IS MINE, SAID THE LORD; BUT WHY WAIT for the Almighty when He had given her the power to seek it for herself. So vengeance would be hers. She would use the mightiest of her weapons; she would expose the temptress and watch her squirm in the spotlight of degradation and contempt until she was spurned by those she loved, ridiculed and scorned by those she knew, and damned by all. She would pay for taking that which was not hers; she would learn, slowly and painfully, that she would never have that which she wanted: love, friendship, trust. For her there would be nothing, not even death. There would be only a living hell, an interminable journey of suffering and a timeless reaping of her own iniquity.

CHAPTER ONE

"HONESTLY, I'M NOT INTERESTED," JANE SAID.

"What do you mean, you're not interested! He's got heaps of money, oodles of charm, a flashy car . . . What is it he drives, Laurence?" Pippa asked, turning to her husband.

"God knows," Laurence murmured, not taking his eyes from the morning paper as he sipped his coffee.

"Well, it's a smart one," Pippa said forcefully. "And he dresses rather snazzily, you've got to admit that."

"I've only seen him once." Jane giggled, the color in her normally pallid cheeks deepening. "And he didn't notice me at all. So please, Pippa, don't say anything to him." And in an attempt to end this embarrassing conversation Jane, too, picked up a newspaper.

"Hmm," Pippa grunted, "I suppose he is a bit full of himself; men like that often take some time to notice anyone else. But we could work on it."

Jane reached across the breakfast table to Tom, Pippa and Laurence's three-year-old son, trying to extract a soggy piece of toast from his hand. For a moment Pippa watched her, a vague and unpalatable feeling of revulsion injecting itself into the otherwise genuine fondness she felt for the girl. Pippa wasn't too sure why, but for some reason she felt almost as responsible for Jane's welfare as she did for Tom's. And feeling responsible wasn't something Pippa particularly enjoyed. Laurence was much better at it. Still, there wasn't a bad bone to be found in Jane's scrawny little body, which, to Pippa's mind, made her about as dull as it made her irritating. But as Tom quite simply adored her, almost as much as Jane did Tom, Pippa considered herself extremely fortunate in having such a perfect nanny.

Catching Pippa watching her, Jane gave one of her annoyingly self-conscious giggles. Pippa bit down hard on her irritation. Jane had been with them for over three years now and still Pippa hadn't managed to break her of that infuriating habit. Still, Pippa reminded herself, she mustn't concentrate on Jane's shortcomings; in fact why should she concentrate on Jane at all when she had so much else to think about.

Realizing she was temporarily off the hook, Jane picked up her tea and turned another page of the newspaper. She loved breakfast time when the whole family, and she counted herself as one of the family now, sat down together in the basement kitchen of their Kensington home, idling away the first half hour of the day where the mouth-watering smells of toast and freshly ground coffee filled the cluttered room. As usual the radio was playing, though this morning it could barely be heard above the frantic chattering of the birds coming through the open French windows and Tom's cheerful little conversation with his imaginary friend. Despite having spent all his short life in England, Tom had almost as pronounced an American accent as his father did and at times as colorful a vocabulary, which only a few moments ago he had been reprimanded for.

"Laurence! You must know someone we could invite along for Jane," Pippa suddenly declared, coming out of her reverie. "What about that researcher of yours? He's single, isn't he?"

"Oh, Pippa, stop it, please!" Jane groaned. "I don't want to meet anyone, honestly."

"But a girl's got to have some fun," Pippa protested. "It's not normal to shut yourself away like you do with only Tom for company."

Jane broke into a toothy smile as Tom's huge blue eyes gazed up at her waiting to see what she would say. "What are we going to do with Mummy?" she said to him. "How do we get her to take no for an answer?"

"If I were you," Laurence said, leaning back in his chair and reaching out to stroke the back of Pippa's neck, "I'd just tell her to mind her own business."

Jane watched as Pippa turned to Laurence. She could no longer see Pippa's face, but Laurence's she could as he gazed into Pippa's eyes, and for just a second or two Jane felt like an intruder. She turned to Tom who was now wheeling his toy train around his breakfast dish while mashing an eggshell with a spoon.

As she started to clean him up she was half-listening to Pippa and Laurence as Pippa cleared the table, then weaved her way through Tom's toys to the sink while discussing her schedule for that week. Laurence stood up, waited for Jane to finish with Tom, then swung him up into his arms. Jane smiled as she watched them, loving the way Tom responded to his father. He adored Laurence and was never happier than when he was with him. Pippa could, and often did, go away for days on end, but Tom was never so fretful at her absence as he was at Laurence's. Which, in its way, was a good thing since Pippa, as a freelance editor with authors dotted all over Europe, was away a good deal more often than her film-producer husband, who, unless in production, worked mainly from home. In fact, probably because she saw so much of him, there were times when Jane wondered if she didn't know Laurence better than Pippa did. She guessed she knew more about him, at least so far as his professional life went, since he conducted so many meetings at home. Jane also knew when Laurence was being subjected to the overzealous attentions of an actress or makeup artist or female journalist, for it frequently fell to her to ward them off. As far as she knew, Laurence had never been unfaithful to Pippa, but Jane could hardly blame these women for trying, since Laurence, with his unruly mass of black hair, piercing blue eyes, and devastating smile, was quite simply the most handsome man Jane had ever set eyes on. And, at six feet three inches tall, with the hard, muscular body of an athlete and the self-mocking humor of someone at odds with his looks, he was, in Jane's book, just about perfect in every way.

Fortunately for Jane she was over her crush on him now, but it had taken some time—almost two years in fact. Now, at last, she could look at him and no longer suffer those stomach-wrenching surges of adoration and, of course, disloyalty. But even worse had been the horribly deep-rooted humiliation. She'd known throughout that miserable time that a man like Laurence McAllister would never be interested in someone like her, would probably not even notice her existence were it not for the fact that she was his son's nanny, but sadly that knowledge had done nothing to quell her feelings. Neither had the fact that he was so much older than she, almost the same age as her father.

But at last the pain was over. Jane could never be too sure exactly when it was that her feelings had changed, that the unbearably exquisite ache in her heart had ceased to be and the churning knots in her stomach at last unfurled. All she knew was that one day, about a year ago now, she had suddenly realized that she was looking at him and feeling only a very genuine affection, unencumbered by the pain of longing. It had surprised her, delighted her, and in a way disappointed her, for the buzz of excitement she'd always experienced when in the same room with him had died, leaving her feeling as drab, perhaps even drabber, than she had been before. But that didn't really matter too much, she'd told herself brightly, as long as she had Tom, this perfect child whose mischief and tempers were as like his father's as his thick, glossy black curls and heart-stoppingly blue eyes. And who could say, perhaps before much longer, he would have a little brother or sister she could dote on too.

Now, as Laurence rested Tom in the crook of his arm and he and Pippa started to discuss their plans for that day, Jane returned to the newspaper, helping herself to another slice of toast. She was on the point of biting into it when she suddenly stopped.

It was the weirdest thing. She couldn't explain it. All

she knew was that this wasn't the first time something like this had happened to her, and in its way it was quite frightening. To be able to look at someone in the newspaper and to know that that person was going to play an important, if not vital role, in her life was as bizarre as it was inexplicable. And even odder was that the person she was looking at now was Kirsten Meredith, a woman she had neither met nor, so far as she could tell, was she ever likely to meet.

"Oh, old Dermott's not laying into her again, is he?" Pippa said, coming to read over Jane's shoulder as Laurence wandered out of the kitchen. "What's he saying this time? No, I'm not sure I want to know. By the way, did you give Laurence the message that he'd called yesterday?"

"Yes," Jane said, turning up her nose.

Pippa laughed. It wasn't very often that Jane took a dislike to someone, but to Jane's dismay, Dermott Campbell had been an all too regular visitor at South Edwardes Square these past couple of years.

As Pippa turned away, Jane discreetly pushed the newspaper into the side drawer of the table. She'd read it later when there was no one around.

A few minutes later the telephone rang, and as she was the closest Jane reached out to answer it. "Oh, hello, Mrs. McAllister," she said. "Yes, Tom's right here. No, we didn't have anything special planned today. . . ." She turned to Tom. "Are you going to speak to Granny?" she asked.

"Granny Mac!" Tom whooped and shot across the room to take the phone.

The way Tom referred to Laurence's extremely elegant, rather snobbish American mother as Granny Mac never failed to amuse Jane, for it was difficult to imagine anyone who looked less like a Granny, but that Thea McAllister and her grandson were devoted to each other was beyond question. In fact, Don McAllister, Laurence's Scottish father, had retired early from the diplomatic service, leaving his post in Washington, D.C.—where Laurence had spent most of his childhood until going to the University at Oxford—to move back to London, so that he and his wife could be near their grandson.

As Tom chattered on with his grandmother and Laurence strolled back into the kitchen, Jane became aware of Pippa's mounting tension. She knew that Pippa disliked Thea McAllister and though Jane liked Thea herself, she could understand why Pippa didn't. Thea was an overbearing woman who was possessive enough of her son and grandson to make any wife and mother uncomfortable, but in Pippa's case there was more than mere discomfort. She'd only recently confided to Jane that the "damned woman" made her feel so ridiculously guilty.

"And it's not as though I've got anything to feel guilty about," Pippa had grumbled. "But whenever she looks at me I feel like she's accusing me of something."

Jane would never dream of saying so, but she, too, thought that Thea's manner toward Pippa held a certain, well, a certain sort of reproach, but then she guessed that was fairly typical in a mother-in-law and didn't really set too much store by it.

"So," Pippa said now as she stacked the breakfast things into the dishwasher, "we still haven't resolved the problem of who we are going to invite to the party for you next Saturday."

"Oh, hell, you're not back on that are you?" Laurence groaned. "Give the girl a break, why don't you?"

"Well maybe if you were to come up with some suggestions . . ." Pippa snapped.

"I'm off," Laurence said. "Some of us have work to do."

"When don't you have work to do?" Pippa remarked sourly, but Laurence didn't answer, he simply left the kitchen and ran up the stairs to his study.

To Jane's relief Pippa didn't pursue the subject of finding an escort. Instead she turned her attention to Tom, who had finished speaking to his grandmother and was trying to reach up to the TV set and turn it on.

"You'll pull the damned thing onto your head one of these days," Pippa barked, smacking his hands away.

Tom looked up at her, hugging his hands to his chest.

"And don't look at me like that," Pippa said irritably. "I've told you a thousand times, you watch too much TV and I'm not having it. Now tidy up these blasted toys before someone breaks their neck."

As Pippa turned away Tom dropped forlornly to his knees, his bottom lip starting to tremble as he fought back his tears. Quietly Jane set about helping him reload his toy box while Pippa continued to slam about the kitchen. They were all well used to these sudden mood swings of Pippa's, which usually preceded a spell away from home—and Pippa was flying to Italy the next day, would be gone until the end of the week. For all her protestations that she had nothing to feel guilty about, she obviously did feel guilty about the amount of time she spent away from Tom, and because he made her feel guilty he annoyed her. Though not half so much as Laurence seemed to lately, Jane reflected, and felt her heart sink as Pippa suddenly rounded on her, her violet eyes flashing and her pretty mouth tight with anger.

"How dare that bastard speak to me like that!" Pippa said. "Anyone would think that he was the only one around here who's got a career. Oh, but I'm forgetting, aren't I, his is the only one that matters. Mine's just a little indulgence, nothing to be taken seriously. Well I'm going to tell him just where he gets off patronizing me." Pushing Tom out of her way, she stormed up the stairs.

Picking Tom up, Jane carried him out to the garden and settled him in his swing hoping they were far enough out of earshot for him not to hear the inevitable row that was brewing. It would be over almost as soon as it began, Jane was sure, for Laurence had a way of handling Pippa that, as much as it infuriated her, Pippa could never resist. And as Jane envisaged Laurence's startled face when his indignant wife crashed into his study, she smiled fondly to herself and swung Tom up in the air.

"For Christ's sake, Pippa, just listen to yourself, will you?" Laurence sighed, throwing a pen down on his desk and turning in his chair. "You're overreacting and you know it!"

"Oh, am I? Well as it so happens I think I've got something to overreact about. You speak to me as though I'm a complete imbecile and right in front of Jane too! Then you walk out of the kitchen like Mr. Important Producer Himself and to hell with everyone else, then you've got the fucking audacity to tell me I should have knocked before I came in here. This is my home as well, in case you'd forgotten."

"All's I said was the door was shut because I didn't want to be disturbed. I still don't want to be—"

"Well tough fucking luck! I'm here now and you're going to bloody well apologize to me for the way you spoke to me just now."

Laurence shrugged, still not too sure what it was he'd said. "Okay, I apologize," he grinned. "Happy now?"

"There you go again!" Seething, Pippa threw up her hands in exasperation. "I'm not a fucking child."

"Then why don't you stop behaving like one."

"Perhaps I would if you started behaving like a husband!"

Laurence's face tightened. He knew what she was going to say next, but she sure as hell wasn't going to get any encouragement from him. Besides, they'd been over and over this these past six months, and right now he had other, more immediate things to deal with.

"It's still the same, is it?" she said, waspishly. "You're too busy to spend a little time with your wife and son. You just want to be locked away in here, undisturbed! Well, pardon me for interrupting you, but like it or not we're going to damned well have this out."

"Pippa, why don't you just go pack your suitcases and check your flight reservations."

He ducked as the book flew across the room and slammed against the wall behind him.

"Don't do that again," he said quietly.

"I want your attention, goddamn you! I want you to look at me, to listen to me . . ."

"I've listened, Pippa. I've listened and understood. You don't want us to go live in the States. So we stay here."

"We stay here because I've got a career too," she yelled. "What the hell would I do in fucking Hollywood? I hate the place, all those phoney people . . ."

"I said, we stay here."

"And now you're punishing me for it. You lock yourself away in here and don't come out from morning till midnight. Well I can't stand it, do you hear me? I can't put up with it anymore!"

"Pippa, I'm in here because I need to work. Because getting a movie off the ground in this country is next to impossible. I don't have to remind you what happened the last time, and one failure is already one too many. Now will you just quit thinking about yourself for once and leave me in peace?"

"I don't suppose for one minute you'd throw Tom out if he walked in here, would you? Oh, no, not your precious son. It's only his mother you can't tolerate."

"Because his mother should know better. And being jealous of your own son isn't healthy, Pippa."

"How can I help being jealous of him when all he has to do is bat his eyelids and you're all over him. What do *I* have to do, Laurence? What do I do to get your attention? Does Alison have this problem? Do you ignore her, too? Of course you do, but she still comes back for more, doesn't she? They all do, don't they, Laurence? We all want you and there's not enough of you to go round. So who's the one to suffer? Not your son, no, never him! Not your goddammed mother either. And certainly not your mistress. Do you listen to her when she needs to talk, or do you just fuck her? Do you do it here, in this room, when I'm not around? No, I'll bet you don't, your darling Thomas might walk in and that would never do, would it? Do you think of me when you're with her, Laurence? Do you think of her when you're with me? Or are you just thinking about your precious movies the whole time, because that's what you really get off on, isn't it? Just to think of those endless reels of celluloid gives you a hard-on like no woman ever can . . ."

Laurence sat watching her, saddened by the way she was working herself into such a frenzy but knowing there was nothing he could do to stop her—not yet anyway. She had to get it off her chest, and any minute now she would start contradicting herself, get herself into a complete confusion, and then she would cry.

This wasn't the first time she'd accused him of having an affair with Alison Fortescue, the production designer he always worked with, and though he guessed she knew it wasn't true, lately he'd had an uncomfortable feeling that she almost wished it were. But he wasn't. He loved Pippa every bit as much now as he did when they'd married, five years ago, but he was, as was she, very much aware that recently they had started to drift apart. He didn't want that to happen. Despite their occasional difficulties and Pippa's unreasonable tantrums, they were good together, they always had been, right from the start, which was why he had taken no longer than three months to propose to her. Pippa had had everything he was looking for in a woman then and still did. Perhaps, he told himself now as he watched the tears start from her eyes, he should make more of an effort to understand her, and it could be that she was right, that he did patronize her, but she sure as hell made it difficult not to sometimes.

Getting to his feet he walked across the room and closed the door. Then, taking her by the shoulders, he pressed her up against the wall and looked down into her face. Christ, there were times when she felt so frail in his hands, so vulnerable, that he was afraid he would crush the very life from her were he to give full vent to his feelings. Of course that was nonsense, but even so it had taken him a long time to get used to the fact that such a slight and delicate body could handle the overriding passions of his own. How many times over the years had he secretly searched her tender pale skin for the bruises he was sure he must have inflicted during the heightened moments of their lovemaking? And even now he could still be surprised by the flawlessness of the smooth milky flesh that covered such fragile bones when his ruthless masculinity had ceased its demands for fulfillment.

As she gazed up at him her eyes were angry and bewildered and, he realized with a sudden and painful jolt to his heart, strangely lonely.

He lowered his head, and as their lips touched his hand went behind her and brought her body hard against his.

"It's not true, is it?" she whispered. "About Alison, I mean."

"You know it's not," he said softly.

"Kiss me again, Laurence. Hold me close."

He gathered her tightly in his arms and pushed his tongue deep into her mouth. They kissed for a long time feeling their desire building to a pitch where one of them would break away and begin the ritual of lovemaking. This time Pippa was the first, and Laurence's head fell onto his arms against the wall as she slid down his body, unzipping him as she went. He looked down as she lifted his semierect penis from his jeans, then groaned as she took him into her mouth. She pushed his jeans to his knees, inserted her fingers between his legs, raked her nails over his buttocks and thighs, and tightened the grip with her mouth.

She knew how he loved this and would have brought him to climax had he not reached down for her, and pulling her to her feet he buried his tongue in her mouth. She whimpered softly as he lifted her short skirt to her waist and pressed himself to her.

After a while she whispered, "Pull my knickers down."

He heard the catch in her voice and kissed her hard. It turned her on to say it, which in its turn excited him too. He eased her panties to midthigh, the way he knew she liked it, then slid his fingers into the wispy thatch of blond hair between her legs.

"I love you," he murmured.

She pulled back to look at his face, but as he opened his eyes she caught him to her again. "Take me now," she moaned. "Put it inside me. Deep inside me."

As she stepped out of her knickers he cupped his hands under her buttocks and lifted her. Her legs circled his waist and pushing her hard against the wall he penetrated her. For a fleeting moment he was aware of her frailty again, but he pushed it from his mind. It was true that he felt less urgency with Pippa, that there wasn't, nor never had been, the overpowering intoxication of being totally submerged in a sea of feminity, but in its place was a deep and unparalleled love the likes of which no amount of lust could ever destroy.

But equally true was the fact that making love to her was no solution to their problems. He knew that Pippa would never forgive him if he made her move to the States, but if they stayed in England, his career would undoubtedly continue to suffer and maybe die altogether.

The following morning Laurence cancelled Pippa's taxi and drove her to the airport himself. Tom went along too, though Laurence wondered after a while whether it had been such a good idea to bring him. Pippa was as jittery as she always was before going away and no matter how much Laurence tried to persuade her that they would be fine for a couple of days without her, he could see that nothing was going to assuage the guilt. Their parting, when it came, was much more tender than usual and for a moment Laurence actually thought that Pippa was going to back out.

"I don't want to leave you," she said, her eyes brimming with tears. "I know it's silly, but I don't." She looked up at him then, and Laurence knew what she was going to say even before she said it.

He shook his head. "I can't do it, honey," he said softly. "I can't ask you to give it up. That has to be your decision and yours alone."

"I know," she said, attempting a smile. "Oh, God, Laurence, why do you have to be so reasonable?"

"I guess I'm just that sort of guy." He grinned. "Now, do I get a kiss?"

She leaned forward awkwardly as Tom clung to her; unlike his father he was more than ready to ask her not to go. But both Pippa and Laurence knew that within minutes of Pippa handing him over to his father, Tom would be filled with excitement at the prospect of having Laurence to himself for a few days.

"Do you have any idea just how much it makes my heart ache to look at you two together?" Pippa smiled wistfully as she put Tom down and watched him automatically reach up for his father's hand.

"Sure I do," Laurence answered. "It kind of gets to me too when I see him with you."

"I don't deserve you." Pippa smiled sadly.

"I guess you don't at that."

"Am I really so hateful?"

"Yeah, I reckon you are."

"Don't let me destroy us, Laurence."

"You think I'm gonna do that?"

"I love you."

"Yeah, I know. I love you too. We'll get through this, honey, we'll find a way, you'll see."

As he watched her walk through to the departure lounge Laurence's face was inscrutable, though deep down inside he was hurting. He was hurting because she was hurting. He sighed. Women were strange creatures, almost alien at times. Just how did a guy handle it when the woman he loved was unable to make a decision herself, when she longed for her husband to make it for her and yet would deeply resent him for doing it? Somebody answer him that for God's sake, because he sure as hell couldn't answer it himself.

He turned to the newsstand, intending to pick up a paper before heading back to London. It was almost midday and most of the morning editions had sold out, but there was one tabloid left that he would have bought had it not featured a picture of Kirsten Meredith in the top left corner. Immediately Laurence's jaw tightened. She was one woman he sure as hell didn't want to read about, didn't even want to think about, and scooping Tom up into his arms he started out to the parking lot.

CHAPTER TWO

IT WAS JUST BEFORE MIDNIGHT. THE WIND WAS PICKing up again, swelling through the narrow streets of Chelsea in an as yet gentle roar. The rain will soon follow, Kirsten thought absently to herself as she looked out of the window, but maybe tomorrow, if only for an hour, the sun might shine. How she missed the sunshine.

She was sitting alone in a pasta bar on the Fulham Road waiting for a take-away and huddled into the large raincoat that had belonged to Paul. By anyone's standards she was a beautiful woman. With her wide, slanting green eyes, impossibly sensual mouth, delicately flared nostrils, and rich, olivey skin, she was a sublime mix of the exotic and erotic. Yet when she laughed there was such a freshness, perhaps even a naïveté about her, that it never failed to affect those she was with. It never seemed to matter how she dressed for the tantalizing fullness of her figure and the superb contours of her long shapely legs were all but impossible to disguise; and despite the fact that right now a paisley silk scarf was wound tightly around her abundant coppery curls, defiant tendrils had escaped their imprisonment to rest gently yet somehow proudly against the flawless skin of her forehead and neck.

Following the quick glance through the window, Kirsten had once again bowed her head to look down at her loosely knitted fingers on the table in front of her. There were several reasons why she kept her head lowered when in public these days, and one of them was to conceal her lovely face. Although it was a face that any other woman would have been proud of, for Kirsten, it, perhaps more than anything else, was the cause of the terrible and seemingly endless pain locked so deep inside her that sometimes she wondered if it was only that which held her together now.

A wave of choking misery threatened to overwhelm her. It would be the easiest thing in the world to join hands with self-pity, to allow herself to be led to that longed for sanctuary of oblivion, to a self-inflicted end to the pain. So many times during these past weeks she had come close to giving in, to surrendering herself to the beckoning arms of release, but she hadn't. She didn't know why she was resisting it, for there was nothing here for her now, so wouldn't it be better to put an end to this intolerable, interminable farce she called her life?

Abruptly she swallowed hard and squeezing her hands tightly she forced her head up. Sometimes it was so hard to remember that she had nothing to be ashamed of, that the whole world was wrong about her, and that she had every right to hold her head high. But being the victim of a campaign so powerful and so unjust did that to a person. You started to forget your own innocence; sometimes you even reached the point of believing all the lies yourself.

Dear God, she sighed inwardly, how has this happened to me? So alone at thirty-six. No friends, no job, no anything. But maybe she could endure that if only Dermott Campbell would leave her alone. But she knew already that Campbell's campaign had hardly begun. Day after day he printed stories about her. Stories with little foundation and no mercy. And to Kirsten's dismay the other newspapers had immediately picked up on these stories, adding, of course, their own scurrilous embellishments.

She'd been a fool to come back; she should have known that Dyllis would use the might of her great newspaper empire to wreak her revenge.

Kirsten felt tears welling in her eyes at the injustice of it all. Right now all she wanted was to be able to run back to Paul, to have him make her feel safe and secure the way he had over the past five years. But there was no going back now, those wonderful days on the Côte d'Azur were over.

She and Paul Fisher hadn't had many friends on the Riviera, but they'd been happy with each other, even though Paul had tried many times to make Kirsten return to England and live a normal life. It was true that there were times when she'd wanted to, but her feelings for Paul had kept her at his side—she just couldn't bring herself to walk out on him when he loved her so much.

No one understood that because no one wanted to. All they saw was that their darling Paul Fisher, the great Shakespearean actor, the great movie actor, too, had in his old age been bewitched by the Kirstie Doll—as the media had taken to calling her—whose only ambition in life was to take him for every penny he had.

When they first went to France, Paul had done everything he could to shield them both from the press, but it hadn't been easy. The scandal was as titillating as any rag could wish for—at the age of seventy-six Paul Fisher gives up stage, screen, and wife to run off with a thirty-year-old TV producer. Not that the press ever referred to her as a producer. In fact, they'd only just stopped short of calling her a whore. No one had been interested in the truth then, and they were even less so now. What did it matter to them that she, Kirsten Meredith, had, for the first time in her life, found someone who truly cared for her, who had made her feel as though she mattered and wanted to do all he could to repair the damage of her early life? More to the point, what did they know of Paul's marriage? Of how for over twenty years he had been subjected to his wife's megalomania, had been forced every day to show his gratitude for what she did for him. She wanted nothing more from him than the glory of being married to a man who was so adored, respected, and revered by all. But Kirsten had made him happy in those last years—and to her he had been everything: friend, brother, father, and, yes, lover.

And now he was dead.

Kirsten felt the familiar tightening in her throat. God, how she missed him, and, dear God, how she longed to talk to him now, to ask him how she should handle this. It had come as no surprise that he had remembered her in his will—he'd talked about it often enough—but Kirsten had been unprepared for the fact that he had left his entire fortune in trust for her until the end of her life, at which time the staggering sum was to be split between his own three children and any that Kirsten might have. Not a single sou had gone to Dyllis, who for the past month had been giving the performance of her life as the grieving widow.

Dyllis, very cleverly, had decided not to contest the will—that may not have won her much sympathy when the whole world knew that she was richer than Croesus. Neither had she seen fit to make public the fact that her children were, in truth, beneficiaries. Instead, via the press, she had told Kirsten to keep the money, that she herself would see that Paul's children were taken care of. And if she, Kirsten, could live with her conscience, having wheedled herself into an old man's will during his years of senility, then really, what could Dyllis say?

Not surprisingly, the press went to town with this, and since, according to the press, Kirsten had no conscience, every columnist without exception was currently urging Dyllis to rethink the situation and get her children's rightful inheritance out of the money-grabbing Kirstie Doll.

What a manipulative and cunning woman Dyllis Fisher was. She had the world on her side, and no one had even thought to question her claims that Paul was senile—which of course Dyllis knew was nonsense and was also why she wasn't contesting the will. She knew she'd never win on those grounds, and there simply weren't any others. Paul had made his decision, and they all, including Kirsten, had to live by it. He had probably never dreamt of the pain it would cause her.

Suddenly Kirsten realized that she had been waiting an interminably long time for her pasta. She looked over at the counter and at that very instant the lights dimmed in the restaurant.

"Excuse me," she said to one of the waiters. "I still haven't had my take-away."

"I'm afraid it's too late for take-aways," he answered avoiding her eyes. "The chef finished an hour ago."

"But I saw you serve someone long after I'd . . ." Kirsten started to protest, but her voice trailed off. She understood perfectly. The waiter had recognized her and hadn't even bothered to put her order through.

Saying no more, Kirsten got to her feet and walked out onto the Fulham Road. It didn't matter about the food, she had no appetite anyway, but what did matter was the continued and horrible snubbing she suffered every time she ventured from the house. Dimly she wondered if Dyllis actually knew just how successful her vendetta was proving.

The cinema was just turning out, but thankfully the rain had come so most faces in the crowd were shielded by umbrellas. Nevertheless Kirsten lowered her head as she hurried to the house Paul had also left her, in Elm Park Gardens.

It was a wonderful house, much bigger than it seemed from the outside, yet every bit as cozy as the cottagelike exterior promised. There was no front garden to speak of, just a few paving slabs, and no fence or gates. At the back, however, was a beautiful and immaculately kept oval lawn with a little fountain in the middle and trees all around the high brick walls to keep it from prying eyes. Inside was a little like a maze with hidden rooms on haphazard landings with low doorways, and wooden floors strewn with aging oriental rugs, and any number of antiques and paintings.

Locking the front door behind her, Kirsten went into the sitting room, by far the largest room of the house, yet somehow the snuggest. She loved this room with its pretty marble fireplace, deep armchairs, kelim-covered sofa, and soft lighting. The endless rows of books made her think of Paul and in a way feel closer to him. How he had loved books. But then so did she, and how much reading she had done these past few weeks. It had been her only escape.

She flopped down on the sofa, unraveling the scarf from her hair and shaking out her shoulder-length curls.

"I should cry," she said aloud to herself. "I should let it all out and stop bottling it up this way. There's nothing to be afraid of or ashamed of in grieving for someone you love."

But the tears wouldn't come and she knew that it was because she dared not let go; if she did, she might never stop.

She curled up in a ball, resting her head on the cushions and hugging herself tightly. Even if she could sleep, she still wouldn't have gone to bed, lying there alone, without the comfort and warmth of Paul's body beside her. This was the hardest of all to bear.

To her dismay when the papers arrived the next morning she found a photograph of herself leaving the pasta bar. She hadn't been aware of the photographer, but that was no surprise. They followed her everywhere these days and she rarely, if ever, saw them. The accompanying story was predictably by Dermott Campbell. It was as cruel as ever as it pointed out her loneliness and the fact that even the friends she had had before she went to France could see her for what she was and had deserted her. She wondered if that were true. Had everyone really deserted her? She hadn't tried contacting anyone since her return, but then who was there to contact? There never really had been anyone she could call a friend—except Paul. And, of course, Helena. There had always been a companion though, a companion as constant, as unrelenting, and as cruel as Dyllis Fisher's revenge. Loneliness was her companion. An only child of parents who had died young, in and out of foster homes until her late teens, Kirsten had been lonely for so much of her life that she could hardly remember a time when that dull ache wasn't circling her heart. Throughout the years she had known Paul though, which were ten in all since they had been friends long before they had become lovers, there had been no ache. With Paul's help she had conquered her fear of people, of herself even, and had allowed herself to believe in happiness. She was already a successful woman by the time he came into her life, but it was he who had taught her how to enjoy her success—and most importantly of all how to trust in those who had already put their trust in her. He had made her understand and eventually believe that no one wanted to hurt her, and in time that tightly knotted fear inside her had started to unravel, so slowly at first that she had thought it would never let go. But it had and she would never forget the years that had followed when she led a normal, happy, and almost totally fulfilled life.

All she was left with now was Paul's wonderfully generous legacy, which he had hoped would give her the security she desperately needed with him gone, but which was proving Dyllis Fisher's best weapon in her vicious vendetta against Kirsten.

But she would survive it, she would have to. Just please, God, don't let Campbell ever find out about Laurence; don't let him get hold of what they had shared and twist and soil it with his lies, the way he was doing with what she had known with Paul. For what she had had with Laurence McAllister—the man whom Paul himself had so proudly introduced her to, the man whom she had loved so much that no amount of words could express it, the man who in the end had broken her completely—was something she would never want to be made public, and something that even now she didn't know if she could ever truly put behind her. . . .

CHAPTER THREE

"KIRSTIE! KIRSTIE, IS THAT YOU?"

Kirsten looked at the receiver then put it back to her ear. "Hello?" she said, cautiously.

"Kirstie! It's me! Helena! Shit, I've had one hell of a time trying to get hold of you. Why haven't you called me?"

"I thought you were in Hollywood," Kirsten answered, wondering whether or not she should believe her ears.

"I was. It didn't work out, so I'm back. Looks like we're both back."

"I don't believe it!" Kirsten suddenly started to laugh. "I was just thinking about you. God, Helena, tell me I'm not imagining this call."

"I'm right here, honey. Now, you gonna give me your address so I can come over and see you? We got one hell of a lot of catching up to do so we'd best get started. You are free I take it?"

"You bet your sweet Louisiana bum I'm free. Just get here as soon as you can. I can hardly wait to see you."

Half an hour later Helena was sitting on the other side of the kitchen table sipping the champagne Kirsten had cracked open to celebrate. Her wild, frizzy black hair, coffee-colored skin, startlingly large brown eyes, and generous mouth were so familiar and such a welcome sight that Kirsten could almost have wept with joy. Instead she laughed at the way Helena was so openly assessing her with all the frankness Kirsten remembered so well.

"Sheeit, Kirstie!" Helena exclaimed, grinning widely. "You just get more gorgeous by the year. Can't you do the decent thing and start to age, like the rest of us?"

"I'll do my best," Kirsten laughed. "But you're looking pretty terrific yourself. Something in Hollywood must have agreed with you."

"A plastic surgeon. He agreed I needed lifts and tucks and all that rubbish, so I went for it. Didn't get me any work though. In fact I've been resting, as they say, ever since the soap folded."

"No!" Kirsten gasped. "But that's over four years now. Surely you've done something in all that time."

"Nothing worth mentioning. So I'm here hoping that my favorite producer might have a l'il ol' role for her l'il ol' friend. Anything doing?"

"Give me a chance." Kirsten laughed. "I've only been back in the country a month, and it can't have escaped your notice that I'm not exactly the flavor of the month."

"No, you sure aren't," Helena agreed. "Would I be right in thinking that Dyllis Fisher is behind Campbell's campaign?"

"You would."

"God, that man's such a prick! Words escape me for

her at the moment, but never fear I'll think of some. Still, I'll have a word with Campbell if you like, see if I can persuade him to back off."

"You mean you know him?"

"Unfortunately. He had the hots for me once, well, he has the hots for anything in a skirt. But I'm telling you, honey, I'm not that desperate—not yet anyway. To tell the truth I feel insulted that he could actually believe I'd be interested in a creep like him. Still, it's the story of my life, as you well know. Why can't I ever pull the gorgeous ones like Laurence McAllister is what I want to know? Incidentally, I just got to ask, what the hell happened between you two in the end? You never did tell me. You just skipped off to France with Paul Fisher and we never heard from you again. So, come on, dish the dirt. What did the bastard do?"

"Nothing really." Kirsten smiled, looking down at her glass. "It was me. I kind of went into self-destruct."

"And good old Paul was there to help put you back together. Well, let's thank God for him anyway. Did you two ever get it together in the end?"

Kirsten nodded. "We did. Eventually."

"I knew it!" Helena cried, clapping her hands with glee. "Paul Fisher was in love with you from the day he met you, though why the hell he didn't do anything about it then beats me. Still, if anyone ever deserved his roll in the hay it was him."

"I'm glad he's not here to hear you put it like that." Kirsten grimaced. "He spent a long time getting me over the way I always used myself to, amongst other things, reward people."

Helena looked suitably chastened. "I guess you really

did have your problems back then, didn't you? There you were, just about the most successful woman in television, at least certainly the youngest to be so successful, churning out one hit show after another after another, looking for all the world like you'd really got it together and all the time you were so badly screwed up. Tell me you're all right now. Tell me you got yourself sorted."

"I'm sorted." Kirsten smiled.

"With Paul's help, I'll bet. That man is a candidate for sainthood. I guess you really miss him, don't you?" she added softly.

"Yes. But he'd be the first to tell me that life has to go on, which it does. I don't think it's going to be easy though. Getting Dermott Campbell off my back could be a start. Will you speak to him?"

"Sure I will. But I've got to tell you, Kirstie, I don't really hold out much hope. Not when Dyllis Fisher is pulling the strings. She is one powerful lady." She looked thoughtful for a moment, then lifting her eyes back to Kirsten's, she said, "Look, I've been reading all that stuff, and well, did it ever occur to you that someone is giving Campbell his information? I mean a lot of what he's writing is based on the truth. For sure there are a hell of a lot of lies, but . . ."

"Yes, it had occurred to me," Kirsten answered, "but I just can't think who it would be. Can you?"

Helena shook her head. "I mean, I guess you made plenty of enemies back when you came in to revive the soap, with all the people you fired 'n' all, but that was years ago now. I can't think anyone would hold a grudge for that long. I mean things like that happen in this business, everyone knows that. Still, we can't rule it out. Has anyone from back then been in touch with you at all?"

Kirsten shook her head. "You're the only one."

"Mmm, well I'd be careful about who does try to get in touch over the next few weeks, if I were you."

"Have you ever met anyone more careful about people than me?" Kirsten grinned.

Helena laughed. "No, I don't guess I have," she said, overemphasizing her Louisiana drawl. "But you have been known to make mistakes."

"Oh, yes, I've made plenty of them." Kirsten chuckled. "And one of them was not keeping in touch with you. So come on, let's have it, what have you really been up to all these years?"

Like most actresses Helena didn't need much encouragement to talk about herself, which she did, quite happily, for the next hour, by which time Kirsten was aching from laughing so hard.

"But I have to tell you," Helena said, "none of it was so much fun as we had back in the old days. Shit, the things we got up to. Do you remember the time when old what's-his-name, the head of drama, ordered you to fire me? Me! The star!"

"Yes, I remember it only too well," Kirsten said dryly. "And I should never have told you, going into his office the way you did and throwing his coffee over his head. You really were lucky not be fired then."

"But you saved me," Helena grinned.

"Only just. I really had to stick my neck out . . ."

"Your *neck!*" Helena cried.

"Well, all right, a bit more than that," Kirsten

conceded, "but I'd only just taken over at the time. I didn't have anything else to bargain with."

"So you really did screw him just to keep me on the series?"

"You know I did. And stop reminding me of the way I was then. . . . We all know I screwed my way to the top."

"Yeah, but no one ever denied that you were a damned good producer. Even so, you sure were hot to trot. Yeah, I know, I know, it was because of all the problems you had in your past, but Paul sure sorted that out when he came along, didn't he? Do you remember the day you met him, at that garden party? You hogged him all afternoon when the whole world was dying to speak to the great man . . ."

Kirsten smiled nostalgically. "God, yes, I remember that," she said. "I'd never felt so important in my life. There I was twenty-five years old, the producer of a dying soap opera . . ."

"Which you very successfully revived."

". . . which I revived. And there I was chatting away with the great Paul Fisher as though I'd known him all my life. God, that seems such a long time ago now."

"Do you ever wonder what might have happened to you if he hadn't come along?"

"I shudder to think. I mean, I might have continued to produce, but I don't think I'd ever have been able to have a relationship with anyone. Not the way I was. God, I was such a mess. But even Paul didn't stop me hankering for a baby. I asked him once if I could have his."

"I remember. It was why you and I went off on that

hilarious skiing trip and I ended up breaking a leg. He'd thrown you out of his flat for trying to seduce him after he'd told you no a thousand times."

Kirsten winced and laughed. "He told me I was embarrassing us both, then threw my clothes at me. . . . God that was awful. I hadn't slept with a man in three years by that time, I had no confidence at all, at least none to speak of, if anything I was terrified of any kind of involvement with anyone, and then to have Paul react like that."

"But he was right. He was too old, he was married to someone else, and you were just starting out on your career. About, if I remember rightly, to go off and produce that Hamish Fullerton drama. Real big time."

Kirsten nodded. "Paul was always right. Do you know, he cried when I went back to apologize. He was so upset by the way he had treated me. He just wanted me to meet the right man, was what he said."

"Which you did. Eventually."

"Well, I thought I did." Kirsten sighed. "And how's *your* love life?"

"About as barren as barren can get. It's not easy meeting anyone when you're my age. . . . I'll be forty-two next week, you know, and that's not a good age when you want a husband and baby and have a penchant for seventeen-year-olds. The two don't go hand in hand somehow."

"I didn't know you wanted children." Kirsten laughed.

"I don't. Well, I do. Oh, what the hell do I know. I wish though, that just for once in my life I could fall in love and have someone fall in love with me. . . . I've never really had any relationships to speak of, at least nothing like you had with Laurence."

"Yes, well," Kirsten said, her smile fading slightly, "that didn't exactly work out, did it?"

"But why?" Helena said, shaking her head incredulously. "I just don't get it. What happened back then?"

Kirsten gave a wry smile as her head tilted to one side. "He met Pippa," she answered simply.

Helena shook her head. "No. I'm not buying it," she said. "That guy was so crazy for you he'd never have looked at another woman."

"But he did. He met Pippa, fell in love, and they got married. End of story."

Helena was about to protest again but stopped herself. There was no point in trying to get anything out of Kirsten until she was ready to tell. "And how do you feel now?" she said softly. "Do you still care for him?"

Kirsten looked down at the champagne glass she had cupped between her hands. "I don't know," she answered. "It's hard to say when I haven't seen him for so long."

Again Helena was shaking her head as though she still couldn't believe, even after all this time, that Kirsten and Laurence had parted. "I remember the night you met him," she said. "I was there for that too."

"We were always there for each other in those days." Kirsten smiled.

"It was the night you won the BAFTA award, wasn't it? For that Hamish Fullerton series. And Laurence won one too, if I remember rightly. God, what a night that was for you two. A BAFTA each and love at first sight. I'll never forget the look on Paul's face when he introduced the two of you. God, talk about the proud father. Come to that I'll never forget the look on Laurence's face. He could hardly believe his eyes. You sure did look gorgeous that night, but then you always do. Did you sleep together that night, by the way, I can't remember now."

"Oh, yes." Kirsten laughed. "We slept together all right. It was the first time in my life a man had ever actually made love to me. It was also the night he told me he loved me." She laughed. "He couldn't believe he'd said it. Neither could I, come to that. It was so absurd it really made us laugh, but he swore it was true. He said he thought that things like that only ever happened in the movies."

"For most of us it does," Helena remarked. "How long were you together in the end? A year, was it?"

"Just about," Kirsten answered, her voice taking on a soft, dreamy quality as her eyes moved to the middle distance. "God, we had some crazy times. I'd never been that happy. I could hardly believe it was happening, but at the same time nothing in my life had ever seemed so real."

"So, come on tell me, what the hell went wrong?"

Kirsten shrugged and sighed. "Me. I went wrong. I thought I was over all those problems in the past, but suddenly, one day, there they were staring me right in the face again. I just couldn't believe he would continue to love me the way he did." Her eyes drew focus as she came back to the present. "And I was right," she smiled. "He didn't."

"But something must have happened. I mean, he

couldn't have stopped loving you," Helena clicked her fingers, "just like that."

"No, he didn't. I forced him to. God, it was an awful time. I just couldn't stop myself hurting him. I was so convinced he was going to leave me, I was so insecure and afraid he just didn't know what to do. He got so desperate at one point he asked Paul to speak to me, but I wouldn't even listen to Paul. Of course, I've been through enough analysis now to know that it all stemmed from the death of my parents, and the abortion I was forced to have when I was 15, but none of us realized that then. Well, I think Paul did, but like I said, I wasn't prepared to listen."

"It's still hard for me to believe that Laurence didn't stand by you. I mean if Paul knew what was going on he must have told Laurence."

"He probably did, but then Laurence met Pippa and the rest is history."

"Except that you're still not over him, are you?" Helena said gently.

"As I said earlier, it's hard to say when I haven't seen him for so long."

Helena's nerve ends were starting to prickle. She knew she'd be going right out on a limb to suggest what she was about to, but hell, why not give it a shot? After all, it could be the answer. "There's a party at his house this weekend," she said. "As it so happens I've been invited. Why don't you come along too?"

Kirsten's eyes widened in amazement. "You've got to be joking!" she cried, horribly aware of the sudden sickening dip in her stomach. "Go to Laurence's house! Helena, you're out of your mind."

"Well, it's one way of finding out how you feel about him," Helena said, still not really sure whether it was a good idea or not. "And look at it this way, everybody who's anybody will be there. Think of all the contacts you could make, contacts you're going to need if you want to get started again—I take it you are intending to start again?"

"Of course I am. But right now Laurence McAllister is just about the last person in the world I want to see. And I'll most definitely be the last person he'll want to see."

"But why would he feel that way when so—"

"He just would," Kirsten interrupted.

"Well, you're going to run into him sooner or later."

"Then let's make it later, shall we? Besides, with Paul so recently dead I'm really not up for—"

"Oh, come on, Kirstie! You and I both know that Paul would be furious to hear you using him as an excuse not to face the world. And okay, it's a tough world, tougher for you than most right now, but that's all the more reason to get out there and show them what you're made of."

A quick anger sparked in Kirsten's eyes as she met Helena's. "You're forcing me to tell you things I don't want to tell anyone," she snapped, "but this much I will tell you, perhaps then you'll drop the subject. When Laurence and I split up I had a total breakdown. I was such a mess that for the first six months I was in France I was confined to a hospital bed. I had nurses on duty twenty-four hours a day to stop me from killing myself, I put Paul through the kind of hell no one deserves to go through and it was all because of Laurence McAllister. Because of what he made me do to myself and to him. So please, Helena, don't try to make me see him again, not yet anyway. I'm still not ready for it and I don't know that I ever will be."

Helena's luminous eyes were filled with remorse as she looked back at Kirsten. "I'm sorry," she whispered. "I had no idea it had got that bad."

As the anger faded from Kirsten's eyes she reached across the table for Helena's hand. "I'm sorry too," she said. "I shouldn't have told you like that. But it's not something I particularly enjoy talking about."

"Does Laurence know?" Helena asked. "I mean about the breakdown?"

Kirsten smiled. "He more or less witnessed it, at least the start of it, though whether he realized it was a breakdown, I don't know. All he wanted was to get me out of his life, but I just couldn't let him go. I'd rather not repeat the things I did at the time. Just suffice it to say that I told him I'd get him back one day even if I had to kill Pippa to do it."

Helena giggled. "You said that? How theatrical! Did you mean it?"

"At the time, yes. I'd have done anything to get him back." She gave a sardonic grin. "Though I don't think Pippa's untimely despatch would have enhanced my chances much, do you?"

"Not much, no." Helena laughed. Then the humor was gone and she sighed deeply. "God it's such a shame things turned out that way, Kirstie," she said.

"Hmm, well, it's in the past now. He has a new life and I have one to create. So, shall we change the subject?"

"Sure. I know, what are you doing for dinner tonight? My treat, if you're free."

"Are you kidding?" Kirsten laughed. "I'm always free these days."

"It's a shame about the party," Helena said, smiling at her fondly, "but there'll be others and we were always so good at parties, weren't we?"

"Outrageous, is what I'd call it." Kirsten grinned. "And sure, there'll be others." An impish light suddenly shot to Kirsten's eyes. "Mind you," she said, "it could almost be worth going to his just to see the look on his face. God can you imagine! He'll probably think I've come to pop off Pippa. What's she like, by the way? Do you know her?"

"Not very well." Helena shrugged. "She seems an okay sort of person, I guess."

"And she and Laurence? Are they happy?"

"Oh, now that's one hell of a question. What sort of answer are you looking for?"

"How about the truth?"

"Okay, well, let's put it this way. Some would say that they're very close, and others would say that they're welded at the hip. So I guess that must mean they're happy."

"That's good," Kirsten said, feeling the warmth seep from her smile. Then clapping her hands together she said, "So, where shall we go for dinner?"

CHAPTER FOUR

WHEN PIPPA RETURNED FROM ITALY THREE DAYS later, to Laurence's surprise and delight she brought Zaccheo Marigliano with her. The Italian author, whose huge frame and booming laughter seemed to fill the entire house, was a man for whom Laurence had any amount of time. Some years ago Laurence had one of Zaccheo's books adapted for the screen; it had turned into a cult movie still earning them both royalties from all over the world. Ever since, they had been firm friends and though Zaccheo's insatiable interest in everything and everyone could be exhausting for some, for Laurence it presented an intellectual challenge he found as stimulating as he did satisfying.

"Surprise, my friend!" Zaccheo roared the moment he saw Laurence come out of his study. "It has been too long. I have missed you. I leave my Tuscan retreat to see if the rust has set into the brain after this long English winter of yours." His laughter reverberated down the hall as he clapped his arms about Laurence and hugged him.

"Wacky Zacky!" Tom whooped, and beetling past his father he ran into Zaccheo's arms squealing with delight as Zaccheo tumbled him upside down and tickled his bare belly with his beard.

Gifts seemed to spring from Zaccheo's every pocket with the same ease as profundities flowed from his pen, until finally he settled Tom on his shoulders and wrapping an arm around both Pippa and Laurence, he led them into the sitting room.

"But my, it's good to be home." He sighed, flopping onto the sofa and tipping Tom into his lap.

"Would you like some tea, Zaccheo?" Jane asked.

"Tea! What is this tea?" he demanded. "Bring me whisky, woman, then come sit on my knee and make an old man happy." He laughed long and loud since even at nearly fifty he reveled in the easy conquests he still made.

Flushing with pleasure, as she usually did at the way Zaccheo flirted with her, Jane crossed the room to the drinks cabinet and poured a generous helping of scotch into a glass, then took both the bottle and glass to Zaccheo. Though it was still just the middle of the afternoon Laurence and Pippa took a gin and tonic each, and at Zaccheo's insistence Jane and Tom sat down with them drinking Ribena which Jane was doing her best to persuade Tom was wine.

As Zaccheo's mellifluous voice rumbled on, for once Laurence's attention wasn't wholly on what the big man was saying. He was watching Pippa, whose vivid violet eyes were bright with laughter and he could see how the lovely alabaster face had, these past few days, relinquished the lines of anxiety and confusion that had troubled it before she had gone. She seemed so relaxed and, at least for the moment, at peace with herself, leaving Laurence in no doubt as to how much she loved her work. It always revived her, which was why he knew he could never take her away from it.

Catching him watching her, Pippa smiled and seeing the intimacy in her eyes Laurence felt a tightening in his heart. He badly wanted to hold her right now, to have just a few moments alone with her so that he could tell her that come what may he was going to squeeze some money out of these damned Brits in order to make his next movie. He wanted her to know that they didn't need to go to Hollywood, they could stay right here where she was happy and where he could continue to see her eyes shine that way and feel the pull of love each time she looked at him. He was going to make it work for them, somehow, and he wanted to tell her. But there would be time enough for that later.

He started to laugh then as he realized Zaccheo was taking over the plans for Saturday's party. The guest list, which had started life with no more than twenty people on it, was already up to over fifty and Zaccheo was still reeling off names. Caught up in the spirit of it Pippa was excitedly adding to them, having, Laurence guessed, completely forgotten that it was supposed to be a party for Jane.

Laurence glanced over at Jane, wondering if she minded. Probably not, he decided. If anything, knowing Jane, she would be only too happy to be relieved of the starring role.

However, it didn't seem that she was going to get away with it that lightly, for Tom suddenly piped up with, "Guess what, Zacky? Granny's cook is making a huge cake for Jane."

"Oh, Tom!" Pippa groaned. "That was supposed to be a surprise."

Tom's eyes rounded as he put a hand over his mouth and looked up at Jane.

"You're hopeless at keeping secrets," Jane told him, tickling him.

"I'm not!" Tom protested. "Daddy told me a secret and I kept that."

"And what was Daddy's secret?" Zaccheo asked, winking at Laurence.

"That he's going to take Mummy away for a weekend," Tom declared proudly.

Everyone laughed as Laurence hoisted Tom onto his lap and shook him. "You fell for it, big guy," he said, planting a kiss on his son's head, then feeling Pippa's eyes on him he looked across to where she was sitting on the sofa beside Zaccheo.

"Do you have a problem with that?" Laurence asked her.

Pippa glanced uncomfortably at Zaccheo, then back to Laurence.

Laurence grinned. "Well, for sure we're not going to go while we have a guest," he said.

Pippa looked instantly relieved and came to perch on the arm of his chair. "But we will go," she said, leaning over and kissing him. "Soon."

It was brief, so brief in fact that it barely had time to register, but an awkward silence followed. Zaccheo instantly plunged into it. "So it's going to be your birthday, Jane!" he boomed. "Twenty-one. Ah, to be twenty-one again. Now let me see, what was I doing when I was this young? Why, for sure!" he cried, slapping a hand on his thigh, "I was a-drinking the whisky and a-loving the women and a-fighting a war."

"You were never in the war." Pippa laughed.

"My whole life is one long war," he bellowed mournfully. "But we must not be talking of me, we must plan this party for Jane. Who would you like to invite, *bellezza mia?* Name any man in the world whether he be movie star, politician, or great writer like me, for I, Zaccheo Marigliano shall produce your heart's desire."

"Yes, come on, Jane," Pippa enthused, highly entertained by the shy devotion glittering in Jane's eyes as she looked at Zaccheo. "Zaccheo knows everyone, so who really gets you going?"

"I don't know." Jane giggled, blushing right to the roots of her hair. "I can't think of anyone." They all waited. Jane shrugged, looked at them all in turn, then threw out her hands helplessly. "I'm happy just to let you do the organizing."

"But you've got to choose someone," Pippa insisted.

"I know! Phillip Schofield!" Tom cried, naming his current TV favorite, then looked bemused at the way everyone exploded into laughter. "You said you liked him," he said accusingly to Jane.

"I do." She chuckled. "But I think Mummy had someone a little grander than that in mind. I know," she suddenly said, "I'll invite Tom. He can be my partner for the evening."

"Oh, Jane!" Pippa wailed. "He's going to be here anyway."

"And someone has to keep the little rascal out of mischief, don't they?" she said winking at Tom.

"What do you do with her?" Pippa sighed, going to sit back on the sofa. "Incidentally, did you invite your parents?"

Jane nodded. "I'm afraid they can't make it though, they've got some function on that night at Daddy's school."

"On your twenty-first!" Pippa cried. "Surely they can miss some stuffy old function for that."

"They're taking me out to dinner during the week," Jane assured her. "Besides, they're not really the partying types, and they'd be a bit uncomfortable amongst so many people."

Pippa let it go at that, though Jane didn't miss the way she and Laurence exchanged glances. Jane read their unspoken communication only too well: They had been expecting her parents to back out, mainly because Frank and Amy Cottle always did when Pippa and Laurence invited them over. In fact Pippa and Laurence had only ever met Jane's father for Amy Cottle had never been to the Kensington house. Jane had explained, not long after she first started with the McAllisters, that her mother was very shy and would be so overwhelmed by this wonderful house that Jane felt it better not to insist she come. The one occasion when Jane had discussed her mother with Pippa was the only time in the three years Pippa had known her that Jane had shown anything even approaching rancor. She knew Jane's science-teacher father had never forgiven her for not being a boy, but on the subject of her mother she was a closed book.

Pippa had been so surprised at what, coming from Jane, were such strong feelings, she had broached the matter with Laurence, wondering if they should try to get to the bottom of it. At first Laurence was undecided, but after giving it some thought he'd decided that Jane's personal life was her own affair. Not everyone got along with their parents, he'd said, reminding her of her fractious relationship with her own mother, "Besides which, there's not one of us who doesn't have something in our pasts we don't much want to share with anyone else."

That had been a mistake if ever he'd made one, for Jane's problem had been instantly forgotten as Pippa wanted to know exactly what it was that he didn't want to share with her. . . .

Dermott Campbell was riding high. Everyone said so, including him—probably too often, but people were as used to his immodesty as they were his vulgarity. The Kirstie Doll campaign was proving such a success that, single-handedly, he had succeeded in upping his paper's circulation by almost 20 percent in less than a month. Dyllis was almost as pleased with that as she was the damage being caused to the Doll's reputation. Campbell smirked at that; in truth there really wasn't much of a reputation left to destroy now.

He'd run his last few articles as a Teach Yourself, by Kirsten Meredith series. There was Teach Yourself How to Exploit Your Beauty, Teach Yourself Social Mountaineering, Teach Yourself How to Inherit, and Teach Yourself How to Use a Guy. That one had really got the papers flying off the stands. Sadly, Campbell's source, the woman he had fancied himself in love with a month or so ago, hadn't known Kirsten's tricks of the trade, but with the help of *The Joy of Sex* they had been easy enough to concoct. And, added to his scathing wit was, of course, the fact that the Kirstie Doll was so fucking gorgeous everyone was buying the papers just to look at her. Shit, was she an easy target!

So, everything was moving along as smoothly as a train. Trouble was every now and again it dropped him off at a station he didn't much want to be at. Meaning that for the most part he was getting carried along by the sheer momentum of the campaign, but in quiet moments he was doing some reflecting he wasn't too comfortable with, for it consistently left him with the uneasy feeling that at the journey's end, when that train was moving full pelt toward the buffers, he, Dermott Campbell, was going to be the only one on board.

However, he—and his source whom he hadn't heard from for a fortnight—were beginning to run out of material. Dyllis wasn't too bothered at this stage. After all, the general public could only take so much and the signs were that their sympathy was beginning to veer in Kirsten's direction. No, they'd relaunch the campaign once the Kirstie Doll started to venture from the house.

At that moment Campbell was standing in front of his copy-strewn desk gazing absently at the photographs of Kirsten and Helena Johnson that had been taken as they were leaving San Lorenzo's. The picture of Kirsten was pretty good, in fact, laughing the way she was made her look goddammed beautiful. His eyes moved to Helena Johnson. Now that was someone he could really fall for. . . .

Wearily he sank back into his chair, wishing the damned phones around him would stop ringing and for just five minutes everyone would stop yelling. He didn't want to admit how much all this was getting to him, and were he not so tired and so rattled by the din going on around him he wouldn't even be thinking about it. But right now he had to admit that playing the role of Mr. Big Shit wasn't anywhere near as pleasurable this time around. Maybe he'd gone soft in his old age. Maybe once a man passed forty his cutting edge became blunted by sentiment.

Pushing his fingers into his hair he rested his elbows on the desk and ignored the phone. Sometimes, at least recently, he had felt as though he were playing out his life on a stage with himself, his real self, as the sole member of the audience. His acting wasn't bad, he'd give himself credit for that, for weren't the people fawning around him again, clamoring to get into his column, wheedling their way into his esteem, laughing uproariously at his unfunny jokes just so he'd write something flattering about them? God, they disgusted him at times. But without them he'd be nothing and he sure as hell didn't want to be that again.

So, there was nothing else for it but to pull up the curtain and get out there and continue with his sublime impersonation of a man who sneered at the world and just didn't give a fuck.

"Hey, Dermott! You going to pick up that phone?" someone yelled.

"Yeah, yeah," Campbell answered, reaching across for it.

"Hello," the voice at the other end said, "is that you, Dermott?"

On hearing the woman, he just couldn't work out his feelings for he said, "Yeah, it's me."

"Good. Are you ready? I've got something for you."

"I'm ready."

"She was at San Lorenzo's—"

"Christ, tell me something I don't already know, will you?"

"Okay. But you're not going to like it."

"Try me."

It didn't take long in the telling, but by the time she had finished the blood had drained from Campbell's face. She was right, he didn't like it. He didn't like it one bit, for what she had just told him was the very thing he'd been dreading. Of course he'd known it was going to come sooner or later, but he'd been banking on it being later. By that time he might have worked out a way to handle it. For a moment or two he toyed with the idea of keeping the information from Dyllis. But if he did, his source would only wonder why he hadn't gone public with what he knew, and who could say, unlikely as it might seem, she might actually go to Dyllis herself—and that was a risk he couldn't afford to take.

So now the fun really starts, he said despondently to himself, looking down at the photographs. Then he chuckled, a dry, humorless sound that in no way cheered him even though he could see the comical side of his thoughts. He didn't need makeup for his role, neither did he need direction or even any rehearsals—all it would take was a few stiff gins and he could go out there and play the part of a complete fucking asshole. And that shouldn't be difficult; God knew he'd done it enough times before.

CHAPTER FIVE

"I JUST CAN'T BELIEVE I ALLOWED YOU TO TALK ME into this," Kirsten said, as Helena walked in through the front door, clad in so much jewelry and sequins she glittered like a Christmas tree.

"Me!" Helena cried. "It was your idea."

"I know, but I've got to blame someone. In fact, I think I've changed my mind. Let's stay here."

"Not on your life. I've been looking forward to this. Anyway, what was it that made you change your mind?"

"Some kind of mental aberration. Plus the fact that you're right, I have to face him sometime, so why not get it over with?"

"That's my girl." Helena grinned. "And I'll be right there with you."

"You'd better be. I'll just pop upstairs and get into my party frock. Help yourself to wine. There's some in the fridge."

Ten minutes later, her fingers shaking so hard she could do nothing more than fumble with her earrings, Kirsten walked into the kitchen.

"My God, you look fantastic!" Helena declared when she saw the creamy white off-the-shoulder dress clinging to Kirsten's perfect figure and which showed off her flawless olive skin in a way that made even Helena's heart skip a beat. "In fact altogether too fantastic if you ask me," Helena decided. "Those many assets shouldn't be allowed on just one woman; they should be shared out a bit. Pull that skirt up and let me check the thighs for cellulite. It might make me feel a bit better. On second thought, don't, 'cause I just know you're not going to have any."

"And neither do you." Kirsten laughed shakily. Dear God, she really was nervous.

"No, you're right. Solid as a rock these thighs," Helena said, slapping them. "Comes from clamping them round young boys' heads. Nevertheless, looking like that I should send you back upstairs to change, but I can't be bothered to wait. So come on, your carriage awaits."

"You don't think I've overdone it a bit, do you?" Kirsten said as they got into the taxi.

"It wouldn't matter what you wore, Kirsten. You'd still steal the show. But rest assured in that dress you'll knock Laurence McAllister right off his feet."

"What do you mean?" Kirsten said in a taut voice.

"Well that's why you're wearing it, isn't it?" Helena teased. "To get him eating his heart out for what he gave up?"

"Is that what you seriously think?" Kirsten demanded.

Helena laughed. "Come on, lighten up," she said. "It's

just the right sort of dress for tonight. Knock 'em dead, why not! You got it, you flaunt it!"

Kirsten wasn't at all sure she was happy with that answer either, but she should have expected no less coming from Helena. "Listen," she said, "are you sure you checked this with Pippa? I mean, I would have thought I was the last person she'd—"

"I checked it," Helena said firmly. "Now stop worrying and relax."

"What did she say?" Kirsten asked.

"She said that she reckons the press are giving you a real tough time, which they are, and that you haven't done anything to deserve it, which you haven't. She says she'd be real glad to have you at her party and that I should tell you that there'll be lots of people there you should meet."

"Does Laurence know?" Kirsten asked, feeling so sick all of a sudden that she considered asking the driver to stop.

"Who knows? Who cares? Well, yeah, sure, Pippa's bound to have told him. Besides, he's just one man, Kirstie. There's gonna be heaps of others there, you know, like writers, those people a gal like you can't function without, and you got to get started some time. Now, *stop worrying and relax.*"

The party was in full swing by the time they arrived. Kirsten's nerves were by now in such a state that her teeth were chattering. She had to be insane, she just had to be, because no one in their right mind would even consider doing what she was now. What the hell was he going to say when he saw her, but presumably he had already worked that out, because presumably Pippa *had* told him she was coming. Which, she told herself by way of comfort, must mean that he had gone some way at least to forgiving her for what she had done. . . .

As they started to press their way down the hall Kirsten was suffering from the horrible feeling that she was losing touch with herself. But perhaps it was the noise and the heady cocktail of pungent drinks and perfumed bodies making her feel that way. Or more likely, she realized, it was the fact that she was actually in Laurence McAllister's house! This Victorian mansion with its high ceilings, black-and-white chequered floor, and grand rooms belonged to him—and his wife of course. She could almost have been in a dream, for it was exactly how she had imagined it would be, and coming face to face with the reality of it was as dizzying as the madness that had made her come.

Suddenly she found herself smiling, for the voice booming from the room they were heading toward she would have known anywhere. Zaccheo Marigliano! And wasn't he doing his favorite old party trick of impersonating Pavarotti while playing the piano badly? He'd done it so often when visiting Paul's house in the south of France.

"God, he's so animal!" Helena purred, as they came to a stop at the threshold of the room, which was overflowing with guests.

Kirsten turned to her in surprise. "Who, Zaccheo? I thought you liked them in short trousers."

"Not quite, darling." Helena laughed. "Seventeen's the youngest I've had, I think twenty-three is the oldest, but for Marigliano I could be persuaded to make an exception."

Laughing, Kirsten turned to look about her. There were several faces she recognized, but for the moment she didn't quite have the courage to approach any of them. And no one, she realized sadly, looked as though they were going to acknowledge her. Several faces were turned in her direction, and she felt herself smiling awkwardly as her hand tightened on her bag. It took several seconds, perhaps even as long as a minute, for the silence to spread through the entire room, but to Kirsten, as she realized what was happening, it felt like eternity.

The sea of hostile faces suddenly started to swim before her as her heart pummeled her chest so hard her whole body seemed to vibrate with it. She was on the point of turning and running when Helena's hand gripped her arm savagely.

"It's all right," she murmured. "I'm right here with you. You can do this, Kirstie." Then in a voice brimming with laughter, she cried, "Hi, everyone. We've arrived, so *let's party!*" and she started wiggling outrageously toward the man nearest her.

As the hustle and bustle started up again Kirsten stood frozen in the doorway. She had read their expressions only too well. How did she—the Kirstie Doll who had duped their beloved Paul Fisher, the man whose memory she had defiled—have the nerve to show her face in public?

She could see people snickering behind their hands and suddenly, dressed as she was, she felt like the whore they intended her to feel. Somehow she managed to take a step toward Helena. "You're wrong, Helena," she said. "I can't do it. I'm leaving."

"The hell you are," Helena shot back. "They've got over the initial shock now, so come on, show 'em what you're made of."

"They're reading that every day in Campbell's column," Kirsten reminded her angrily. "They don't want me here, and I don't want to be here, so I'm going."

"Oh, Kirsten, how lovely to see you. I'm so glad you could come."

Kirsten turned to see a petite blond woman wearing skintight blue leggings and matching overshirt pushing a path toward her.

"I'm Pippa McAllister," Pippa said, taking Kirsten's hand and smiling up into her face. Kirsten was looking for the telltale glint of hostility, perhaps even triumph, in her eyes, but there was none. "Laurence is around somewhere," Pippa went on chattily. "Probably down in the kitchen sorting out the drinks. And you don't have one! What can I get you? I think we have just about everything."

"Well, actually I was just about to—"

"Champagne!" Helena chipped in from where she was bopping around beside them. "She adores champagne."

"Who doesn't?" Pippa laughed. "I'll get one of the waiters to go down and get you some. Now there's someone over here I've just been dying to introduce you to," and before Kirsten could object she was being dragged across the room toward a tall, slightly overweight middle-aged man with dusty-colored hair, a swarthy complexion, and whose half glasses were perched pompously on the end of his nose while he waved around a huge fat cigar.

The instant Kirsten saw him she tried to pull away from Pippa. "No," she said, "I don't think—"

"Dermott," Pippa cried, "just look who I have here." She turned to Kirsten and spoke softly so that Campbell couldn't hear. "Give it your best, Kirsten. He deserves it after what he's been doing to you," and she was gone.

How Kirsten managed to stop herself from running after Pippa she never knew, but with a supreme effort of will she made herself turn to face Campbell. His quirkily handsome face was pinched with, Kirsten thought, something like discomfort, but the arrogance was so pronounced it masked it well.

"Well, this is a surprise," he said, glancing at the woman next to him in the hope she was listening. She was. So were several others.

The last thing Kirsten wanted was a scene, which she could see was exactly what Campbell was hoping for. Well she'd be damned if she was going to give him the satisfaction, so after sweeping him from head to foot with her piercing green eyes she treated him to the sweetest smile she could muster and said, "I've frequently wondered what I would do on coming face-to-face with you, and now I find that strangely you inspire nothing in me whatsoever, except perhaps a modicum of pity." In the brief moment before she turned away she saw the surprise on his face and, just as she'd hoped, the outrage.

But clearly he recovered quickly, for as she started to walk away, she heard him sneer, "The bitch has got one hell of an ass, what do you say? She could hump it over my dick any time. Hey, Kirstie Doll," he called after her, "come on, it's got to be my turn!" and he roared with laughter.

Kirsten kept going. Burning with embarrassment and rage, she walked out of the nearest door along a deserted hall and smack bang into someone coming the other way.

"Excuse me," she mumbled, trying to get past him.

"Don't mention it," he answered. Then, "Hey, Kirsten. It is you, isn't it? It's me, David Gill. Remember me?"

"Oh, David, yes. How are you?" she said, taking the hand he was holding out.

"Great. Just great. Thanks to you."

"To me?"

"Well, you were the one who gave me my break all those years ago, weren't you? I'm writing the big stuff now, you know? Nine-o'clock slots and all that. Still jobbing, obviously, haven't got an original thought in my head. But I earn a buck or two. How about you? What are you doing with yourself these days?"

"Not very much," Kirsten answered.

"No, well, I guess it's a bit soon after Paul. I was really sorry to hear he had died. He was a great guy. Well, you don't need me to tell you that, do you? And by the way, all that crap they're writing about you in the press, well, here's one guy who's on your side."

"That's nice to know," Kirsten smiled.

"If I could," he said, "I'd stand up and speak out for you. Well, a lot of us would, but you know how it is. The Fisher woman's got a lot of clout in this town and I sure as hell don't want the poison flowing through

Campbell's pen about me. Not that anyone'd be interested to read about me, I suppose, but they'd find some way to finish me. Still, if there's anything else I can do . . ."

"It's okay," Kirsten assured him. "I'll survive."

From the look on Gill's face she could see how much he doubted that. But it was nice of him to bother saying it, not many would have, and when he suggested they go and get a drink she went with him.

As they walked into the kitchen she found herself scanning the room nervously for Laurence. Hadn't Pippa said he would probably be down here? But there was no sign of him, and Kirsten smiled wryly to herself at the relief she felt. She'd have just this one drink, then see if she couldn't get away without actually running into him.

In no time at all David had dragged her into a group who was discussing Laurence's next movie project. All of them, without exception it seemed, thought he was mad to have taken on Ruby Collins as the screenwriter.

"Dermott knows her," a woman beside Kirsten remarked. "I think he might have been the one who introduced them. Anyway, she's a Yank. Perhaps Laurence thinks she'll give him a foot into Hollywood."

"But I'm telling you, she'll crucify him. Have you met the woman?"

"No."

"She's a dipso. Can't function without gin. Now tell me, who the hell in their right mind is going to take on a writer like that when there's so much at stake?"

"Perhaps Laurence knows something the rest of you don't," Kirsten heard herself say.

The man who had spoken arched his eyebrows haughtily in her direction, then continued as if she hadn't spoken, turning his back slightly as though to ease her out of the group.

"I told him," he continued, "I said, Laurence, you're committing professional suicide taking on a project like that with a writer like Ruby. But you know what Laurence is."

"I'd have thought he'd have been only too willing to take your advice, Baz, after his last disaster," a woman with purple hair chipped in. "He can't afford another or he'll be finished."

"What's his next movie about then?" a rather dowdy middle-aged woman inquired. She had to be the wife of one of these pumped up know-it-alls, Kirsten reckoned.

"Oh, some woman who lived during the last century, went to New Orleans, became a prostitute, then got herself hanged or murdered, I can't remember which," the pompous man answered. "Pretty banal stuff, if you ask me. And period! He's out of his mind. He'll never get the finance. I told him, Laurence, I said . . ."

Kirsten stopped listening. How many conversations like this had she endured in her life, and how she detested them. Everyone thought they knew better than the producer, and everyone thought the producer was mad. Of course, should the film prove a success they'd find a way of sharing in, if not taking all of, the credit.

As she turned away her eye was caught by the childish drawings pinned to the refrigerator. Instantly her heart froze. God, she would never forget the terrible setback she had suffered when she had first found out that Laurence had a son. But that was all behind her now, she reminded herself, taking a deep breath and forcing herself to move on. Just please God don't let me come face-to-face with the child tonight.

She was on the point of leaving the kitchen when she heard someone say, "Hello there."

Kirsten turned round. "Hello," she said, wondering if she knew the woman standing at her elbow.

"Molly Forsyth," the woman said. "And you're Kirsten Meredith."

For some reason Kirsten didn't like the look of this woman. There was something shifty in her eyes, and her thin, heavily lipsticked mouth was to Kirsten's mind spiteful.

"I have to tell you," Molly said, "that I heard what Dermott Campbell said about you just now. Quite vulgar, I thought, though I imagine you're used to hearing things like that."

Kirsten simply stared at her, wondering why in the hell it was that people found it so necessary to be nasty to those they didn't even know. Then, to her dismay, she realized that the people behind her had stopped talking and were now listening to Molly Forsyth.

"I have to tell you that I told Campbell he'd be insane to hump you over his dick, as he so eloquently put it," Molly continued, "after all, there's no knowing what he might catch, is there?"

As the blood rushed to Kirsten's cheeks she heard someone behind her snigger. Her luminous green eyes were still holding Molly's showing nothing of what she was feeling inside, but for a fleeting instant it was as though she was a child again, surrounded by mocking, sneering faces who wanted to hurt her in any way they could. She almost felt herself begin to take a step back, but somehow managed to stop herself. "Do you feel better now?" she heard herself ask. "Are you glad you've got that off your chest, or is there more?"

Molly pulled down the corners of her mouth and raised her eyebrows as she glanced round at the others. "Just one question," she said sweetly, turning back to Kirsten. "While you're here wallowing in all that cream you juiced out of Fisher, do you feel at all guilty about the fact that it was you who gave him AIDS?"

It was all Kirsten could do to stop herself gasping. This was the first time she'd heard that rumor and for one blinding instant she wanted to hit that supercilious face so hard she'd knock it right into next week.

Instead she took a deep breath. "As you already know, Paul died of a heart attack," she replied. "But if it makes you happy to insult someone as profoundly as you just have me, and to soil Paul's memory into the bargain, then I can only say that right now you must be ecstatic. Now, if you'll excuse me."

She brushed past Molly Forsyth, but not before hearing David Gill say, "What's she ever done to you, Molly?"

"Obviously not what she's done to you, lovey," Molly answered with lightning wit and everyone laughed.

Kirsten would have left then and nothing nor no one would have stood in her way, except Zaccheo Marigliano. And when she saw his beaming face heading toward her as she walked into the sitting room to tell Helena she was leaving, Kirsten instantly felt tears burn the backs of her eyes. Zaccheo's felt like the first friendly face she'd seen and right now, feeling as she did, one kind word was highly likely to bring the tears flooding.

"I'm not going to say anything about Paul," he whispered in her ear as he swept her into his arms and held her tight. "It's not the time and I can see you are suffering. But no matter what they say about you or do to you, Kirstie, I am your friend. Remember that. Zaccheo, he loves all the women, but you I love most of all."

"Don't or I really shall cry." Kirsten sniffed, turning her head away so that no one in the room could see the way her eyes had filled with tears.

"But these beautiful cheeks are made for the kisses of a lover, not the tiny droplets of pain," Zaccheo's voice rumbled in her ear, and then he gave a protracted, ostentatiously romantic sigh, which made Kirsten laugh.

"By the way, thanks for going to the funeral," she said. "I know Paul would have appreciated it. And thanks for taking my flowers. She sent them back, I'm afraid."

"I know. But he knows you loved him, that's all that matters."

"You're right." She took a breath and forced herself to smile brightly. "So, what brings you to England, Signore Marigliano?"

"Pippa McAllister. She is my editor. And Laurence, of course, he is my friend. I stay here with them until the end of the week. Maybe I come to see you before I go?"

"I'd like that."

Zaccheo moved to one side then to let someone pass and as Kirsten looked across the room she saw Helena dancing with Dermott Campbell. He was holding her extremely close, too close for such fast music, Kirsten thought, but Helena didn't appear to be objecting. But, as Helena lifted her head, Kirsten smiled at the conspiratorial wink she received. Obviously Helena was over there doing her stuff in getting Campbell to back off.

Kirsten was already half-turned back to Zaccheo when suddenly the smile froze on her lips; it was as though a giant vise had taken hold of her heart. Zaccheo was still speaking though she had no idea what he was saying. All she knew was that she was looking straight into Laurence McAllister's eyes. He was standing at the other side of the room, just in front of the bay window, but for the moment, as though by some extraordinary preordination, a space had opened in the crowd between them. Kirsten felt she might be swaying, that her entire body might be dissolving. Not even for a moment had she forgotten how incredibly handsome he was, how compelling his eyes, or how physical his presence, but neither for a moment had she expected that seeing him again would affect her so profoundly. Suddenly the blood was beginning to pound through her ears and her chest felt so tight she was unable to breathe. So many memories were passing before her eyes, so much love, so much passion, and so many promises. This man had once been her whole life. She had loved him so much and even now, looking at him, she felt as though he was still hers. They had meant so much to each other, how could they be apart?

And then it was as though a smothering fog was being lifted from her senses and she realized how insane she had been to think she could handle this. She felt herself start to falter, as though a dam in her mind had been broken and everything she had suppressed for so long was rushing at her.

This can't be happening, she told herself vehemently. It just can't. She was over him, she had to be because there was simply no way there could ever be anything between them now. She was just in some kind of shock and in a few minutes she'd be herself again. The new self. The woman who could hold her head high and know that she had been through hell for this man and come out the other side. The woman who had spent the last five years learning how to come to terms with her past so that she could at last deal with all that life threw at her and survive.

Yes, that's all it was, shock, she decided with relief, and how ridiculous she was to have allowed herself to be taken in by it. She found herself smiling over at him then, a still as yet shaky calm spreading its soothing warmth through her. He smiled too, then turned his attention back to the man he was talking to.

Kirsten guessed that very soon now he'd come over to say hello. She experienced a childish sort of excitement at the prospect, felt herself start to tingle even, which almost made her laugh, and for one breathtaking moment she felt almost deliriously happy.

She carried on chatting with Zaccheo, though thankfully they were continually interrupted, for Kirsten's powers of concentration were eluding her. Unable to stop herself she kept glancing in Laurence's direction and though their eyes didn't meet again, she was certain that he was watching her too. Then Helena came to join them and when Kirsten looked up again Laurence had disappeared.

Excusing herself, Kirsten went off to find the bathroom, but as she walked out of the door, still looking back over her shoulder and laughing at something Zaccheo was saying, she collided with someone coming the other way. Before she could do anything to stop it there was Campari and soda all over the front of her dress.

"Oh, no! I'm sorry!" the girl gasped. "Oh, heavens, what can I do? Your dress, your lovely dress! I'm just so sorry, I didn't see you . . ."

"It's all right," Kirsten said, irritated but at the same time slightly amused by the girl who was clearly mortified at what she had done. "I'm sure it'll come off."

"But please, let me—" the girl stopped suddenly as she looked up into Kirsten's face. Kirsten was momentarily startled by the expression in the girl's eyes. Was it fear? shock? In a way it was like recognition. And then Kirsten remembered that of course the girl would recognize her, who wouldn't these days? And, by the look of the girl she was quite simply horrified at having come face-to-face with the infamous Kirsten Meredith. And now that she had, and had ruined an extremely expensive dress into the bargain, what was the infamous Kirstie Doll going to do? Beat her? Scream at her? Humiliate her in front of all these people?

"Really, it's all right." Kirsten smiled, closing the door behind her so that they were alone in the hall. "Please, don't worry about it. I'll send it to the cleaners. I'm sure they'll be able to sort it out."

The girl was obviously still shaken, couldn't quite bring herself to believe that there were no disastrous consequences to be faced for a simple accident, so Kirsten tried again.

"Please don't look at me like that," she said kindly. "You're making me feel like an ogre. I told you, the cleaners will sort it out."

"But what about now?" the girl said, the uncertainty at last starting to retreat from her eyes. "I mean, it's all over you. Please, come upstairs and let me see if I can sponge some of it out."

"But there's a bathroom right here," Kirsten said.

"I know, but everyone's using it. I've got my own, at the top of the house. I'm Jane, by the way, Tom's nanny. And I really am so very sorry."

"Please, just forget it," Kirsten told her. "I'll just go and—" she broke off as they heard raised voices coming from a room to one side of them. The door was slightly ajar so both Jane and Kirsten could hear every word that was being said.

"I don't care, Pippa, I don't want her in the house. I don't know what the hell got into you, inviting her here, but I want her out. And I want her out now!"

"Laurence, for God's sake, be reasonable. How can I just walk up to her and tell her she's got to go?"

"If you don't then I damned well will," he raged.

"But she's a friend of Zaccheo's."

"Zaccheo isn't the host of this party, I am. And I don't want Kirsten Meredith in my house."

"I don't see why you're getting so het up over this. It was all such a long time ago. She's probably changed . . ."

"Women like her never change. Now you heard what I said . . ."

"Oh, come on, can't you at least be generous enough to give her the benefit of the doubt? Everyone's giving her such a hard time . . ."

"Pippa, I'm not arguing about this. Now just get her out of here!"

A door slammed in the distance and Kirsten and Jane turned to face each other. Kirsten's face was ashen; Jane's was hot with embarrassment.

"Come on," Jane said, rapidly pulling herself together, and before Kirsten could object Jane was sweeping her up over the stairs.

"No, no," Kirsten protested as they reached the first landing. "Let me go. Please, I have to leave."

"But, you can't go anywhere with that stain all over you," Jane said, her shoulders hunching as she giggled nervously. "Come on, we'll go to my flat." She looked into Kirsten's face and her gray eyes shone with sympathy as she saw the very real distress in Kirsten's. "Oh dear, I'm sorry you had to hear that," Jane murmured. "It was awful. I'm sure he didn't mean it . . ."

"Just let me go, please," Kirsten mumbled. "It would be better. . . . If he finds out you've helped me . . ."

"He won't find out," Jane assured her and wondered whether Kirsten realized how hard she was shaking. So hard in fact it was doubtful she'd even make it up the stairs.

But Kirsten did know, which was why she had no choice then but to go with Jane, for the idea of disgracing herself by collapsing on the stairs was too terrible even to contemplate.

By the time they reached Jane's flat Kirsten was hardly able to stand. "It's all right," she gasped, as they went in through the door. "I'll be fine in a minute. I just need to sit down."

Holding her by the shoulders Jane led her to a small sofa and gently eased her into it. "Is there anything I can do, something I can get you?" Jane asked, her pale, freckled face taut with concern. "You look dreadful."

"No, no really. I'll be fine. It's not the first time I've had an attack like this. It'll pass, I promise." But even as Kirsten spoke a welter of huge, dry, racking sobs started to tear through her body. Oh dear God, not in three years had she had an attack like this, three years! And now here she was right back at the beginning. Vulnerable and frightened and wanting him with the same desperation she had then. But it was an illusion, she tried to tell herself. Just a bad dream come back to haunt her. If she took deep breaths, held herself straight, and squeezed her hands tightly, the way she had then, it would go away. Those three years would resurface and come to stand between her and all the hurt.

But it was no good. The indignity, the self-loathing, the desperate humiliation was coming over her in wave after relentless wave. To think that she could have been so stupid as to have come here, to have expected that he might even be pleased to see her filled her with such an excruciating shame it seemed to seep into her every pore.

It was some time before she was aware that Jane was holding her and smoothing her hair, or that she was clutching Jane in a way she only ever had Paul. "It's all right," Jane was whispering, "let it all out. Just cry, I won't let you go."

Embarrassed, Kirsten pulled away and started to fumble in her bag for a handkerchief. "I'm sorry," she said shakily. "I guess things just got the better of me, but that's no excuse to have made such an exhibition of myself."

Jane dropped to her knees in front of Kirsten and took Kirsten's hands. "You didn't make an exhibition of yourself," she said softly. "Anyone would have been hurt to hear themselves spoken about that way, and with everything else that is happening to you . . ." She trailed off and shrugged self-consciously, but still she held on to Kirsten's eyes, looking searchingly into them as though it was the most important thing in the world that she should somehow reach Kirsten.

Ordinarily so reticent with strangers, Kirsten found herself looking back and wondering what it was in this girl that had not only made her cling to her the way she had a few moments ago but had encouraged her to draw down her barriers and let the girl in. Slowly she started to shake her head and as she did Jane smiled and squeezed her hands. There was something in Jane's eyes then that seemed to reach deep down inside Kirsten as though to touch her very heart.

"I've never experienced a death so close to me, the way you have recently," Jane said, "so I can't say I know how you're feeling. But if you were as close to Mr. Fisher as I heard Zaccheo telling Pippa you were, then all I can say is that I am truly, truly sorry for what you must be going through. I just wish that there was something I could do to help."

Kirsten's heart had tightened with every word Jane uttered. It was as though Paul were speaking to her, as if somehow through this girl he was gently reminding her that it was all right to trust someone. That not everyone wanted to hurt her, and those who did only could if she, Kirsten, allowed them to. "Oh, Jane, you have helped." Kirsten laughed through her tears. "You've helped very much."

"If you want to talk I have the time," Jane assured her, then her cheeks flushed at the presumptuousness of her remark.

Kirsten smiled. "Perhaps another time," she said. "I don't want to spoil the party for you, and besides, it looks like this stain has dried in so there's no point trying to wash it off now. Maybe I'd better just go home and like I said, send it to the cleaners in the morning."

"You will let me pay for it though, won't you?"

"Certainly not," Kirsten said, standing up. "It was an accident and accidents happen."

"Then at least let me lend you something of mine to go home in. I mean you can't go out like that. It looks like someone's tried to murder you."

"Oh, Jane." Kirsten laughed. "I'd never fit into anything of yours, you're so tiny."

"I'm sure I'll be able to find something," Jane said eagerly. "It won't be as glamorous as the dress you're wearing." She looked back over her shoulder as she walked into her bedroom. "In fact it won't be anything like it at all."

In the end they managed to fix Kirsten up with a long flared skirt and a baggy sweater to conceal the unfastened waistband.

"Well, you look a bit like Cinderella after the ball," Jane remarked when Kirsten was dressed, "but it'll do."

Kirsten was watching her closely, intrigued by the sudden spurts of humor and frankness that struggled through the self-consciousness. "I guess I'd better post them back to you." Kirsten's eyes still danced at Jane's observation. "After what we heard down there in the hall tonight I don't think it'd be a very good idea for me to show up again."

"I've got an idea," Jane said suddenly as they started out of the room. "You must say no if you want to, and I won't be in the least offended if you do, but what about if I come to pick up my clothes? I have the afternoon off on Wednesday. I could come then. But, no, you'll be busy, of course you will. Perhaps you're right, you'd—"

"I won't be busy," Kirsten stopped her, "and I'd love you to come."

Jane's homely little face was beaming. "If you like," she said as they reached the door, "you can go down the fire escape."

The absurdity of it appealed to Kirsten, making her laugh. "Why not?" she said. "I don't really want to run the risk of bumping into Laurence again, so would you mind searching out Helena for me? Explain what happened and tell her I'll call her, okay?"

"See you on Wednesday then," Jane said as Kirsten stepped out onto the fire escape.

By the time Kirsten arrived home her mind was racing. She knew she wouldn't sleep and neither did she want to. She had so much to do and was eager to get started. Feeling the way she still did about Laurence was one thing, but sitting around moping about it was quite another. She had to get herself back in motion, get her career back on its feet, and the only way to do that was to start right now. She sat down at her desk and pulled out the file filled with the ideas she and Paul had discussed during those wonderfully balmy evenings in the south of France.

CHAPTER SIX

PIPPA MOANED SLEEPILY AND SNUGGLED DEEPER INTO the bed as Laurence's hand came around and cupped her breast. After a while, as he lazily teased her nipples, a smile stole across her lips. She loved to be woken this way and she gave a gentle sigh of contentment as Laurence molded his body behind hers and pressed himself against her.

"Hmm," she murmured, returning the pressure when she felt the hardness of him against the small of her back. His hand was softly caressing her stomach now, his long fingers spanning the width of her hips. She pushed her head back into his shoulder, raising her chin as he kissed her neck.

"Good morning," he whispered when she turned her mouth to his. He gave her a long and deeply erotic kiss, lowering his fingers as her legs parted.

"I'll give you two hours to stop doing that," she murmured as he began stroking her. "Oh, God," she moaned when a few minutes later she felt the tip of his penis start to push into her. She raised her arms over her head, reaching behind her to touch his face. He was taking a very long and deeply sensual time to enter her, but he couldn't reach full penetration with her in this position. Pippa moved forward, half rolling onto her stomach as Laurence lifted her hips. Then suddenly the door flew open.

"Daddy! Daddy! Wake up, Daddy! Play Humpty Dumpty!"

"I don't believe it," Pippa groaned, pushing her face into the pillow. "I just don't fucking believe it."

"Not now, soldier." Laurence laughed.

"But Daddy, you said if I came in at eight o'clock we could play Humpty Dumpty and Jane says it's eight o'clock."

Laurence glanced at the bedside clock. "It's seven thirty, Tom," he said.

"Just tell him to go," Pippa muttered angrily.

"Jane said it was eight o'clock," Tom said stubbornly, his eager little face starting to lose its smile. He hated to be sent away and sensed that he was about to be.

"You promised," he said.

"Sure I did," Laurence winked, feeling his heart tighten as he looked into his son's forlorn face, and disentangling himself from Pippa he rolled onto his back, checking that he was still covered to the waist, and swung Tom up in the air. "And a man has to stick by his promises, isn't that right?"

"Humpty Dumpty?" Tom cried, his face beaming with joy.

"Laurence, for God's sake," Pippa seethed as Laurence settled Tom onto his raised knees. "Just tell him that you don't want to do play and send him back to the bloody nursery."

Tom looked wide-eyed in his mother's direction, his tiny brow furrowed, his eyes almost afraid. Pippa just looked at him, as though challenging him to defy her.

"Let him stay," Laurence said, lifting Tom up and kissing him.

"You spoil him," Pippa grumbled as Laurence resettled Tom on his knees, but Laurence wasn't listening.

"Humpty Dumpty sat on a wall," he and Tom chorused, "Humpty Dumpty had a great . . . *fall!"* On the last word Laurence opened his legs and let Tom fall through. Laughing with delight Tom scrambled back up and Laurence began again.

Pippa kept her silence throughout three more falls, then, "Has Jane given you your breakfast yet, Tom?" she snapped.

Tom shook his head.

"Then tell her I said you can have some flakey chocolate with your cornflakes."

"Oh, yes!" Tom cried, waving triumphant fists in the air and leaping from the bed yelling for Jane.

"I guess we ought to be getting up," Laurence said, still laughing as he watched Tom go.

"That wasn't the idea," Pippa said, cuddling up to him.

"Sorry, I've got a meeting at nine," Laurence told her, and flipping back the cover he got out of bed.

"For Christ's sake! Is it too much to ask for some precious minutes of your time?"

"No more than it is to ask for precious minutes of

yours," Laurence countered, heading toward the bathroom.

"And just what the hell is that supposed to mean?"

"Work it out for yourself," he answered, and closed the bathroom door behind him.

He was already showered and halfway through shaving when the door opened and Pippa sauntered in. "Are you sulking because I haven't let you have sex for the past week?" she asked.

Briefly he met her gaze in the mirror. "No. If I were sulking I wouldn't have woken you up the way I did," he answered.

"So what's changed your mind now?"

"I told you, I've got a meeting."

Pippa eyed him angrily.

"Hey, come on." He laughed. "You're making too much of this. I told you last night . . ."

"But I notice that Tom doesn't get deprived of his share of your time," she said petulantly.

"Pippa, for heaven's sake, do we have to go through this every time? He's just a kid. He doesn't understand about meetings. Now pass me the towel, will you?"

"All right," she said as she flipped the towel over his shoulder. "I'm sorry about the way I neglected you last week . . ."

"I told you, it's not a problem."

"But obviously it is, so I'm apologizing. It's just that I can't make love when Zaccheo is in the house. He puts me all on edge—I can't concentrate on anything. But he's gone now and I want to fuck!"

"Then you're gonna have to wait." Laurence grinned.

"God, you can be so damned infuriating at times,"

Pippa seethed and flounced out of the bathroom slamming the door behind her.

When Laurence returned to the bedroom some five minutes later it was to find Pippa doing her exercises. As he dressed he watched her, slightly less amused now than he had been, for he could sense her smoldering resentment. He could do without this right now; today was going to be difficult enough as it was.

"What are your plans for today?" he asked, making an effort to diffuse the situation, but Pippa wasn't playing ball. She simply continued bending and stretching as though there were no one else in the room.

Rolling his eyes Laurence slipped his feet into his brogues, fastened his watch strap, and started out of the room.

"I've worked out what it is now," Pippa snapped. "You're still pissed off with me because I invited Kirsten Meredith here last Saturday."

"Pippa," he said, pronouncing her name with deliberation as he turned back, "I'm not pissed at you at all, but you sure as hell are at me. So come on, let's have it, what's really eating you?"

"Are you sure you have the time?" she asked sarcastically.

Laurence sighed heavily. "As a matter of fact I don't right now."

"Then book me in will you?"

"Okay, I've just about had it," he yelled. "You wanna talk, we talk right now," and slamming the door he came back to sit on the edge of the bed.

"Go to your meeting," Pippa cried. "Just go. We'll sort this out later."

As he left the room Laurence didn't see the tears glittering in Pippa's eyes; if he had he wouldn't have left.

Feeling miserable she peeled off her leotard, took a quick shower, then went downstairs to join Jane and Tom in the breakfast room. She hadn't heard the front door close and had half hoped Laurence was still there, but he wasn't.

"I take it you heard us shouting?" she said to Jane as she poured herself some coffee.

"I'm afraid so," Jane smiled awkwardly.

"Did Tom?"

Jane nodded.

Pippa looked down at her son, who was sitting on the floor at Jane's feet engrossed in winding up a clockwork toy. "It's your fault," she suddenly snapped at him. "You take up all Daddy's time and if you hadn't come into the bedroom like that this morning Daddy and I wouldn't have had an argument."

Tom's wide eyes were filling with tears as he looked up at his mother. Pippa glared back, but as his face started to crumple Jane scooped him up in her arms.

"Sssh, sssh," she said soothingly as he buried his face in her shoulder, quiet sobs jerking his little body.

"Oh, God," Pippa groaned dashing a hand through her already disheveled hair. "I'm sorry, Tom. Tom, Mummy's sorry. I shouldn't have said that. It wasn't your fault at all, it was all mine. Are you going to give Mummy a kiss now, show that we're friends?"

Tom lifted his head to look at her, his soft cheeks flushed with color, his deep blue eyes steeped in apprehension.

"I'm sorry, darling," Pippa said again. "Come to

Mummy and show me what a big boy you are by accepting my apology."

Still Tom just looked at her, but after a while he twisted in Jane's arms and leaned toward Pippa.

"I love you," Pippa said, smoothing his tousled curls and kissing him. "Mummy loves you so much, and I'm such a silly Mummy to get so angry, aren't I?"

She didn't hold him for long though before handing him back to Jane and going to sit at the table. "Oh, God, what a mess." She sighed angrily and buried her face in her hands.

"Tom, would you do something for me please?" Jane asked.

Tom nodded.

"Would you go upstairs and get your pajamas? They need washing." She put him down and watched as he reluctantly left the room. He was being sent away; he knew it and Jane knew how much it troubled him. But it was clear that Pippa wanted to talk and it was probably better that Tom didn't hear. She waited until she knew he was no longer in earshot, then went to sit down too.

"Laurence is so bloody hung up on this next movie," Pippa said, starting right in with what was on her mind. She was so used by now to having Jane as her sounding board that she simply took it for granted that Jane would want to listen.

"He eats, sleeps, and breathes the damned thing," Pippa went on. "It's coming between us, I know it is, and I just don't know how to stop it. Christ, we don't even make love anymore."

Jane's mouth twitched with an uncertain smile. "I thought that was because Zaccheo was around," she said, gently reminding Pippa that they'd been down this road just the day before.

"I thought it was," Pippa answered, "but I'm not so sure now." She lifted her head and looked Jane straight in the eye. "Tell me honestly, Jane, do you think he's having an affair?"

Jane's eyes widened. "No, not at all," she answered.

"Well, I do," Pippa declared irritably. "I mean, look at the way he behaved on Saturday. Don't you think he overreacted a bit when he found out Kirsten Meredith was here?"

Jane drew back her head in surprise. "You surely don't think he's having an affair with her, do you?"

"No. At least not yet he isn't. But give him time."

Jane spent the next few moments mulling this over in her mind. "Would I be right in thinking," she said carefully, "that Kirsten and Laurence knew each other before?"

Pippa gave a snort of derision. "Oh, yes, they knew each other all right. He was the great love of her life, or so she made out. She even threatened to kill me if he didn't give me up and go back to her. . . ."

Jane's astonishment showed. "Gosh," she said, looking down at her toast. Then returning her eyes to Pippa's she said, "So why did you invite her here on Saturday night?"

"To test him, of course. To see if he really was over her."

"You mean you thought he might not be?" Jane said incredulously.

"Well, do you think he is, behaving like that?"

"I don't really know," Jane said somewhat at a loss. "I mean on the face of it I'd say he definitely was—"

"Well, you're right," Pippa cut in, her exasperation with herself suddenly deflating her irritation. "He is over her. He has been for years and I'm just being a pain in the ass. Laurence wouldn't go near Kirsten Meredith again if she was the last woman on earth."

Jane was silent for a moment but realized that she really couldn't, or perhaps shouldn't, hold back on Pippa. "There's something I think I should tell you," she began tentatively. "Kirsten Meredith overheard what Laurence said about her on Saturday, you know, when he was telling you to get her out of the house. She was pretty upset. I know because I was with her when she overheard it. I'd spilled a drink all over her dress, you see, and was about to take her upstairs to clean up when we heard you and Laurence in the study. Anyway, I did take her upstairs in the end and she borrowed some of my clothes to go home in. I went round to collect them on Wednesday."

Pippa was staring at her. "You mean you've actually talked to Kirsten Meredith! Actually been to her house?"

Jane nodded, then to her amazement Pippa suddenly started to laugh.

"What's so funny?" Jane asked.

"What's so funny is that if Kirsten Meredith thinks she's going to get back with Laurence through you she's got to be out of her mind. He'd see through that quicker than he could see through glass, and if there's one thing Laurence can't stand it's scheming women."

Neither of them spoke for a while, but Jane watched

Pippa as the thoughts raced around in her mind. Finally Pippa smiled. "So Kirsten was upset was she?" she said.

"Well, yes, she was a bit. I mean, I suppose anyone would be, hearing themselves spoken about like that," Jane answered. She didn't know quite why she should feel the need to defend Kirsten, or why she should choose to be loyal to her, but for some reason she knew she was going to withhold the true extent of Kirsten's distress.

"Yes, I suppose you're right." Pippa sighed. "And I'm just being a cow. I don't have anything against the woman, really. Why should I? He married me, didn't he? And in actual fact I do feel genuinely sorry for what the press are doing to her. If I thought it would do any good I'd speak to Dermott myself and try to get him to stop. But you know Dermott, once he's got his teeth into something there's no stopping him. Oh, Jane, if you could see your face." She laughed. "You really don't like poor old Dermott, do you?"

"I just think it's a horrible way of earning a living," Jane said, "riding high on someone else's misery. I never have been able to work out why Laurence has him as a friend."

"They've done each other some favors in the past." Pippa chuckled. "Well, you know that. And once you get on the right side of Dermott he's not so bad, you know. He's really fond of Laurence. . . ."

"And of you," Jane said.

"Because we helped him out at a time when he was down on his luck. Still he's really making a comeback now. He should be grateful to Kirsten in fact. He might still be in the wilderness if it weren't for her. Anyway, those two don't really concern me right now. What does is Laurence. Do you know who this meeting of his is with today?"

Jane shook her head.

"Then I'll just have to look in his diary and find out, won't I? Oh, get that will you," she added as the telephone rang.

Jane reached over to the kitchen counter and lifted the receiver. As soon as she heard the voice at the other end she scowled.

"Speak of the devil," she said, holding the receiver out to Pippa. "Dermott Campbell." Jane grimaced.

It was half an hour or so later that Pippa wandered into Laurence's study and found Jane standing at the desk. "Oh, I didn't know you were in here," she said. "Were you looking for something?"

"Just these." Jane smiled, holding up two carriages from Tom's train set that Laurence had been repairing.

"I'm on my spying mission," Pippa confessed. "Where's his diary?"

"Just here," Jane answered, pulling a large leather-bound book out from underneath a script. They knew Laurence's diary well since both of them frequently acted as his secretary.

"Okay, let's see," Pippa said, flicking over the pages. "Here we are, Thursday . . . Oh shit, the meeting with Ruby Collins!"

"The writer?"

"The writer. Oh, shit and fuck and all the other vile words I can't think of right now! I was just deciding to cook dinner tonight, candles, good wine, and all the rest of it to try and make up for this morning, but he's bound to come back in a foul mood after seeing her."

"What does that say there?" Jane said, still looking at the diary. "The penciled-in name."

Pippa turned back and Jane lifted her eyes to her face as she felt Pippa tense. "Alison Fortescue," Pippa muttered.

Jane wasn't quite able to meet Pippa's gaze then, for she knew that Laurence had called Alison before leaving the house, and she also knew that Alison had been the cause of many bitter arguments between Laurence and Pippa. "It's only in pencil," she pointed out feebly.

"I'm not fooled by that, Jane, and neither are you," Pippa retorted. "It's Alison bloody Fortescue he's having an affair with and you know it as well as I do."

"No!" Jane cried. "I don't know anything. Honestly, Pippa, I don't know how you can think these things. You're accusing Laurence of so many affairs it's almost as though . . . Well, I don't know, as though you're trying to push him into one."

Pippa recognized the accusation instantly. "Is that what he's been saying to you?" she raged.

"No, no," Jane said. "But I've heard him saying it to you, and I'm beginning to think he might have a point."

"Oh, really!" Pippa responded scathingly. "Well, let me tell you something, Jane. *Never* underestimate how clever or how bloody devious Laurence can be. Because I can assure you that he's more than capable of turning a very real affair into my paranoia and sending me to the loony bin into the bargain. He damned nearly put Kirsten Meredith there five years ago!"

For a moment Jane seemed too astounded to answer. "Laurence would never do something like that," she said eventually.

"Oh, wouldn't he? Then try asking your friend Kirsten. See what she has to say."

"Well, he'd never do it intentionally," Jane said lamely.

"Oh, wouldn't he?"

Jane was already drawing breath to say no, when suddenly a vision of the way Kirsten had been on Saturday night flashed through her mind.

"I see, not so sure of yourself now," Pippa said smugly. "The trouble with you, Jane, is that just like every other woman on this damned planet you think the sun shines out of Laurence's backside. Well, believe you me it doesn't. My darling husband has plenty to hide, make no mistake about that. And he's a past master when it comes to deception. . . ."

"I'm not convinced he's having an affair with Alison," Jane said quietly.

But Pippa hadn't heard her, she'd already slammed out of the room.

CHAPTER SEVEN

DERMOTT CAMPBELL WAS SITTING AT A CORNER TABLE in Bibendum, one of London's chicest restaurants. As he sipped his gin and tonic and scanned the menu he was vaguely aware of the nerves clawing away at his appetite, and not for the first time he glanced at his watch. She was ten minutes late.

The last time he'd seen her had been at the McAllister's party, ten days ago, when he had got the hots for her all over again. She was like a witch, in appearance as well as in spirit. She seemed to have woven some kind of spell over him that had completely annihilated any interest he might have in other women. And, given the mood he was in right now, nothing was going to lessen his hopes. He was going to have that woman if it was the last thing he ever did. In fact, that very afternoon he was going to take her to his bed and fuck her so hard she'd think yesterday was tomorrow and next year was last week.

He winced. Actually, what he was really going to do was listen to what Helena had to tell him, thank her, then get up from the table and leave, because today wasn't the day even to consider trying to embark on anything else—not when the outcome was going to be a betrayal of both their best friends.

Shit. Campbell groaned inwardly as his head started to throb. For two pins he'd just get up and walk out of here before she showed. But he couldn't do that, not now. If he did, Dyllis would just give the assignment to someone else and there would be nothing Campbell could do to protect Laurence from the kind of publicity he sure as hell wouldn't want. But one way or another Laurence was going to get it, because even if nothing came of this meeting today, Campbell already knew what was going to be in his next column—Dyllis herself had already written it.

Why the hell did it have to be Laurence that the Kirstie Doll had been involved with? Campbell seethed. Why couldn't it have been someone he didn't know? That way he wouldn't be having to go through this. But it was Laurence, and what Dyllis wanted to know was exactly what was behind their breakup. And in a way Campbell could understand that. After all, whatever it was had resulted in the breakup of Dyllis's marriage.

But to be fishing around in Laurence's past like this was almost enough to make Campbell wish himself back on the scrap heap. Because, to betray a man who had done for him what Laurence had, was so repellent it defied words. For Laurence was the one—the only one—who had been there for him during that miserable, nightmare stretch in the wilderness, when Dyllis had kicked him off the paper for writing the mildest criticism of one of her kids and told him to go and dry himself out and not to come back until called.

She hadn't dispensed with his name, though, had she? No, she'd kept that all right; it sold papers. But the miserly pittance she'd paid him for the privilege hadn't been enough to keep him in gin let alone pay the mortgage. And by the time his terraced house in Clapham was repossessed, he had realized that just about any friend he'd ever had had walked out on him too. And then had started that ignominious, godforsaken trail of crashing out on pub floors, dossing on sofas at parties to which he hadn't been invited, scrounging meals from the junior hacks who'd taken pity on him, and going to the public baths to get himself clean. And even, on more occasions than he wished to recall, begging at the door of the Salvation Army for charity.

It wasn't until Laurence had got wind of his predicament that he had started to see light at the end of the tunnel. Laurence had helped him when no one else would. He had given him money, got Pippa's mother to let him use her London flat, and taken him off to a clinic to get him dried out.

And this was how he was repaying him—by drinking gin to get up the courage to betray him. No, protect him! He had to keep reminding himself of that, but it gave him small comfort.

"Mr. Campbell?"

Feigning nonchalance as his stomach clenched with nerves, Campbell reluctantly tore himself from his perusal of the menu and looked up at the waiter.

"Your guest has arrived, monsieur." The waiter smiled.

Campbell started to smile too, but as the waiter stepped to one side Campbell's eyes almost bulged from his head. His mouth opened to protest, but the shock had jammed his tongue to the back of his throat. He started to splutter, loosened his tie, tried to get up, and failed.

"Another drink for Mr. Campbell please." Kirsten smiled at the waiter as she sat down. "A mineral water for me."

The waiter left and Kirsten turned to face Campbell.

"What the fuck—?" He made to get up.

"Please sit down, Mr. Campbell," Kirsten interrupted smoothly. She held his eyes, her own so steely and intense that Campbell found himself slumping back into his chair stupefyingly cowed.

Kirsten smiled and as she did her eyes softened. "I apologize for the subterfuge," she said affably, "but under the circumstances I felt it necessary." Inside she was triumphant. Just as she'd hoped, the shock of seeing her had thrown him totally, which gave her the edge.

She waited patiently as his panicked eyes darted about the restaurant, knowing exactly what was going through his mind. The last thing in the world he would want was to be seen dining in public with Kirsten Meredith, for, were they to be recognized, it could do untold harm to his credibility. Which was why Kirsten had chosen to dress the way she had, in an exquisitely cut black linen suit with a matching wide-brimmed straw hat, both of which were guaranteed to turn heads. It was unlikely that any of Campbell's colleagues were among the other diners though, which was a little disappointing, but if Helena had asked him to meet her in any of the journalists' well-known haunts, it would have seemed mightily suspicious when she was promising to reveal all about Kirsten Meredith.

"Okay," Kirsten said at last, placing her purse on the table and folding her hands over it. "I will come straight to the point. What will it take to stop this vendetta against me?"

Campbell's eyes were livid as they regarded her across the table. He never had taken well to being tricked, particularly not when he'd always been such a master at it himself, but he had to hand it to her, she really had out-trumped him. And she was one daunting woman dressed like that, and that seemingly intractable confidence was pretty impressive too. But he had regained at least some of his composure by now and was already thinking of how he was going to make this work for him. And work it better, 'cause if Dyllis were to find out about this, which she would, she'd be expecting . . . Well, he didn't know what she'd be expecting, but he'd better come up with something. Trouble was, having prepared himself for Helena Johnson, he was in the wrong persona. He was going to have to switch, fast. He took a large mouthful of gin, and as he did the implications of her question suddenly hit him. God, he had her! He had her right in the palm of his hand already and she didn't even know it. But he'd take it slow, build up to it one step at a time, and still she wouldn't know, not until the papers hit the stands. "What's the problem?" he asked. "Don't much like having everyone know what you're really like?"

"But you don't have the first idea of what I'm really like," Kirsten answered pleasantly. "In fact, all you know is what you have manufactured yourself."

"Then sue."

"Believe you me, Mr. Campbell, I have considered it. And if it comes to it, I will."

Campbell wasn't fazed. "You want to air your dirty linen in public, then that's fine by me," he said. "It's all good copy."

"And that's all that matters, is it? You don't mind at all about what you're doing to my life, of how much damage you're causing with your lies. . . . But it would seem that attacking my reputation isn't enough. I am fully aware of who is behind the blocking of all approaches I have made to various television companies recently, so it would seem that Mrs. Fisher is out to destroy me completely. Am I right?"

You're dead right, Campbell was thinking to himself as he looked directly into her eyes. Jesus Christ, was she one beautiful woman! Still, now wasn't the time to think about that; he had a job to do. "Tell me," he said, avoiding the question, "did you think of the damage you were doing Dyllis Fisher when you ran off with her husband of forty-five years?"

Kirsten looked up at the waiter as he placed her mineral water on the table and thanked him. After taking a sip she turned back to Campbell. "Have you asked yourself why it is that Paul should have wanted to run off in the first place, Mr. Campbell? Or why it is that Mrs. Fisher is not contesting the will? Oh, I know what you've printed in your column, but there's a lot of money at stake here, and you know it. So why, do you think, is she letting it go so easily?"

The quality of that dark, husky voice was as mesmerizing as her eyes. "Because," he answered, clearing his throat, "she doesn't want her husband's name, or more particularly his senility, dragged through the courts."

"Paul wasn't senile, Mr. Campbell. He died with all his faculties intact. But if you don't want to believe me, then I suggest you talk to his doctor."

"For all I know you're giving the guy a cut."

Deciding to ignore such a contemptible remark, Kirsten simply smiled. "Dyllis Fisher isn't contesting the will, Mr. Campbell," she said, "because she doesn't want people to know the real truth of her marriage. Which they would if I decided to speak out."

"Is that some kind of a threat?" Campbell challenged, hooking an arm over the back of his chair. God, she was fascinating.

"No, just a fact."

Campbell laughed mirthlessly. "No, I'm not buying it," he said. "If Dyllis Fisher had anything to fear from you she'd never have taken you on so publicly."

"Dyllis Fisher is relying totally on my discretion because she knows she can. I would never do anything that would in any way discredit Paul's name or his memory, both of which would become subject to the distortions of the press if I decided to tell my side of the story. In other words, Mr. Campbell, I did, and still do, care far more for Paul than I do my own reputation, which you have to agree is more than can be said for Dyllis Fisher with her accusations of senility. . . ."

Campbell was shaking his head. "Nice try, but we both know why you're not taking Dyllis on and it's got sweet f.a. to do with preserving an old man's name. You're keeping quiet for one reason and one reason only, because you don't want any more sordid little secrets dug out of that shady past of yours."

Kirsten could see by the look on his face that he thought he'd hit a raw nerve. He had, but she wasn't going to give him the satisfaction of showing it. "You're right, Mr. Campbell," she said, evenly, "I have no desire to see any details of my life, sordid or otherwise, spread across the newspapers. And you're right again when you intimate that Mrs. Fisher has a great deal more power than I do. She can, and will I imagine, try her very best to see that I never work again. I assume she would deem that as some kind of victory, though quite what she stands to gain from such a victory escapes me. But it is because she is so determined to ruin me that I am appealing to you now, and not to her. When I returned to England it was to try to pick up my life and start again. This would have been difficult under any circumstances, given the length of my absence, but with this vendetta going on it is impossible. So, I want to ask you to leave me alone."

Outwardly Campbell was regarding her expectantly, as though waiting for her to continue, but his inner eye could see the Salvation Army looming. "Look," he heard himself saying, "if you're trying to elicit my support here, you might as well forget it, 'cause even if I gave it it wouldn't do you any good. If you want to call this to a halt, it's Dyllis you should be talking to."

"But you and I both know that she'd never agree to see me."

He cocked an eyebrow. "So you're asking me to mediate?"

Kirsten nodded. "In a way."

"But Kirsten, you've got nothing to bargain with. That woman wants you dead."

"That doesn't mean that you have to help her."

"It does. Believe me."

"But why?"

"It's a long story. But let me tell you this, you're better off with me handling this than you are anyone else."

"Oh, do me a favor!" Kirsten cried. "With all the lies you've—"

"Laurence is a friend of mine," he interrupted, craning his neck to look at something across the restaurant. His eyes came back to hers.

Kirsten was very still. The mention of Laurence's name was so unexpected she simply didn't know what to say.

Campbell, almost as shocked as she was at what he'd just confided, regarded her with cool, inscrutable eyes, but inside he was reeling. Shit! Holy Christ! He knew he was a sucker for a pretty face, but this was unbelievable. This woman, he knew for a fact, was still in love with Laurence. She'd befriended his nanny, she'd gone to his party—she was after breaking up his goddamned marriage—and he was sitting here like some lovelorn teenager gazing into her eyes and practically telling her he would help her!

He was about to speak when Kirsten, picking up her purse, said, "I can see that I've been wasting my time."

"I don't see what that's got to do with anything," he said, startling her as much with his non sequitur as the way he had suddenly raised his voice. "But I'll tell you what does. What does is the fact that you're not looking to get your career back on the line at all. What you're looking for is the next marriage to bust up." His voice lowered as he pushed his face toward her. "But like I said, Laurence McAllister is a friend of mine, a very close friend, and so's his wife. So you keep away from them, do you hear me?

"And as for making an appeal to my better nature," he went on before she could speak. "Don't bother because I haven't got one. But I'll tell you what. I'll take what you're offering to get me off this vendetta—but before I do I'll be wanting to see the results of a few tests, 'cause from all I've been hearing about you you've been round the block a few too many times—"

He got no further. Kirsten's movement was so swift that no one else in the restaurant could have seen it. Even Campbell didn't know it was coming until the huge stained-glass windows tilted before his eyes and a wash of gin and tonic splashed across his neck. And by the time he realized what had happened Kirsten had already left the restaurant.

CHAPTER EIGHT

EVERYONE WAS UNNERVINGLY SILENT. THE ONLY sound was that of the somber news from Bosnia issuing from the radio and the delicate clatter of cups as they were lifted or replaced in their saucers.

Laurence, Pippa, and Jane were all half-hidden behind the newspapers Campbell had just handed them; Tom, lying on a beanbag and sucking his thumb, was watching a muted cartoon on the TV.

The article they were all engrossed in was a long one, written mainly by Campbell but edited by Dyllis Fisher. Over a week had gone by since Campbell had seen Kirsten at Bibendum and in all that time he had been doing battle with Dyllis to try and stop Laurence's name going to print. He'd succeeded, this time, but even so the innuendo wasn't going to be lost on Laurence. Which was why Campbell had judged it wiser to bring the paper round himself so that he could—at least in some way—attempt to defend himself when Laurence got sight of it.

"For Christ's sake, Dermott, this is a bit strong, isn't it?" Laurence said, glancing up at him.

"Did she really offer to go to bed with you to get you to stop writing about her?" Pippa asked, obviously having reached the same point as Laurence.

"More or less," Campbell answered, running a finger under his collar as he recalled the moment it had dawned on him how he could misconstrue Kirsten's question, "What will it take to stop this vendetta?"

Laurence eyed him skeptically before returning to the paper.

Several more minutes ticked by. Campbell was watching Laurence's face, bracing himself. For a moment his eyes drifted over to Jane, but they shot quickly back to Laurence as Laurence said, "And just what the hell is this?"

Jane's head came up, and to her astonishment she found he was looking at her.

"Just what the hell is going on here?" he demanded, looking from Jane to Campbell and back again. "Would you like to explain this?" he said, turning back to the paper and reading aloud. " '. . . adopted a new ploy in befriending nannies to get close to the children before striking at the heart of the family . . .' "

"It means," Pippa said prosaically, "that Jane and Kirsten have become friends."

Laurence's expression was thunderous as he turned back to Jane. Jane's face had visibly paled.

"I thought Pippa might already have told you," she said lamely, then started as Laurence suddenly slammed down the newspaper and scooping Tom into his arms walked out of the room.

"Sorry," Pippa said to Jane. "I would have told him if I'd thought it was important. I just didn't think it was."

"Then you're a fool, Pippa," Campbell told her. "Never underestimate what lengths women like Kirsten Meredith will go to to get what they want."

"Actually, I didn't," Pippa answered. "I jumped to the same conclusion as you, but unlike you, Dermott, I knew what Laurence's response would be. Anyway, how did you find out that she and Jane were friends?"

"Let's just say a little bird told me," Campbell answered.

The door opened and Laurence came back into the room. "Okay, Dermott," he said, "just what the fuck is all this about, bringing my family into your slander campaign?"

"Actually, it was my way of trying to warn you," Campbell said, feeling a slight constriction in his throat as he lit a cigar.

"There are telephones, Dermott. If you wanted to warn me . . . For Christ's sake, do you have to smoke that thing at the breakfast table!"

"Sorry." Campbell crushed his cigar into a saucer. "I think you'd better read on," he said miserably.

A few minutes later Pippa looked at him incredulously. "She actually *admitted* to wanting Laurence back?" she gasped.

"Not in so many words, no," Campbell confessed. "But if you'd seen her face when I put it to her . . . Well, she physically attacked me for even suggesting she might have you in her sights," he added to Laurence. "Now if that isn't a case of the lady doth protest too much . . ."

"I don't suppose it occurred to you," Laurence remarked, "that you might just have deserved a thump for the way you've treated her since she was back in England?"

"Funny that she chose to do it over you, though, don't you think?" Campbell countered.

"What I think is that you pushed her too far," Laurence retorted. "And you're coming pretty close to it with me, printing stuff like this."

"There's no mention of your name," Campbell pointed out.

"Come off it, Dermott. Anyone with half a brain can work out who you're talking about."

Campbell looked at Pippa, then at Jane. "Can I speak with you alone a moment?" he said to Laurence.

Laurence turned to Pippa. She nodded.

"Look, it's Dyllis," Campbell said, as Laurence closed the study door behind them. "You know she's out to get the Kirstie Doll in any way she can . . ."

"Then let her. But tell her to keep the hell out of my life."

"I'm doing my best," Campbell said. "Believe you me, she was all for printing your name, and to be frank with you I don't think I'll be able to stop her next time."

"Next time?" Laurence said tightly.

Campbell sighed. "All I'm saying is that Dyllis is delving deep. You and Kirsten split, Paul runs off to France with Kirsten. And something happened then . . ." He trailed off as the blood drained from Laurence's face. He'd never seen him so angry.

"If you print one word of that, Dermott, then I swear you'll never set foot through my door again."

"I don't even know what it was," Campbell protested.

Laurence stared at him. "But Dyllis is trying to find out?" he said.

"Yes!"

"Shit!" Laurence seethed. He was thinking fast. "Only Kirsten, Pippa, and I know," he said. "She'll never find out."

"Okay. Keep it that way. It's not a story that can easily—" he stopped, horrified.

Laurence eyed him with disbelief. "You're lying," he said, a sudden and dangerous edge to his voice. "You know what happened. How the hell did you find out? Kirsten would never have told you. Shit! Dermott, tell me it wasn't Pippa. For God's sake tell me . . ."

"It *wasn't* Pippa," Campbell said forcefully. "I swear it, Laurence. Pippa never breathed a word."

"Then who was it?"

"Oh, come on, Laurence," Campbell said in a pained voice. "You know a journalist never reveals his sources."

Laurence turned and walked over to the window. "So what are you going to do?" he said, staring sightlessly out at the rain-spattered street.

"Nothing."

"Christ, you just can't print a story like—"

"I said, nothing," Campbell repeated, then sinking into the nearest chair he dropped his head in his hands. "I guess I understand why you hate her so much now," he said.

Laurence nodded absently. His mind was elsewhere, trying, but afraid, to light on that terrible week that had, in the end, killed it all. She thought he didn't know how much she had suffered for what she'd done, but he did.

Paul had told him. But Jesus Christ, did she have any idea how much he had suffered too? Even now he still couldn't believe she had done that to him, much less to herself. He wondered if he could ever forgive her. "You've got to know enough about her by now to know that if you go to print on this you'll break her," he said quietly.

"I know," Campbell said. "But like I said, it's not an easy story to tell . . ."

"Dyllis will find a way," Laurence said, turning back.

"But she still doesn't know what happened. And she'll never find out through me."

"What about the person who told you?"

Campbell shook his head. "I can't give any guarantees on that, but I don't honestly think there's a problem there."

"Isn't there anything you can do to get Dyllis to back off?" Laurence asked.

Dismally Campbell shook his head. "I've got no sway with the woman," he answered. "I doubt anyone has in this instance. She's out to destroy Kirsten in every way possible. Not even with all that money Kirsten's got is she going to be able to work again. I know for a fact she's considered financing herself, but no one will work with her. Dyllis will see to that. And as far as Kirsten's private life goes, Dyllis has got me over a barrel. Either I write it or I'm out. And it's better that I do it than some hack you don't even know. At least this way I can temper it a bit . . ."

"But from what I've read, from what you've said here, it sounds to me like you're gunning for Kirsten yourself."

"In a way, yes, in a way no. I don't want to see her coming between you and Pip."

Laurence laughed without humor. "Pippa and I don't need your help, Dermott. Sure, we have our problems, but it'll take a damn sight more than Kirsten Meredith to come between us."

"That's what I want to hear," Campbell said. "But the Kirstie Doll, well, she's one hell of a lady. I can see why you were so crazy for her. . . . Hell, I almost found myself falling for her. . . ."

Laurence laughed and pushed himself away from the window ledge. "That kind of misery you can well do without, my friend."

When Campbell had gone and Jane had taken Tom upstairs, Pippa and Laurence sat in the kitchen reading through Campbell's article again. When Pippa had finished she looked up to find Laurence grinning at her.

"And what's so funny?" she asked.

"Campbell. I sure as hell would have liked to be there when Kirsten clocked him one."

Pippa giggled. "Me too."

"Come here," Laurence said, pushing the paper away and sliding his chair back from the table.

Pippa went to him, and as she settled into his lap he wrapped her in his arms. "You're not worried about any of this, are you?" he said.

"Should I be?"

"You know the answer to that," he murmured sliding a hand under her sweater and gently caressing her breasts.

Pippa sighed contentedly and rested her head back on his shoulder. "Are you still sure you don't want me to come to the States with you at the end of the week?" she said after a while.

"I do want you to come," he answered, "but I thought you were going to Zaccheo's."

"I could always cancel."

Laurence laughed. "Zaccheo would never forgive me for taking you away from him."

"What about him taking me away from you? Doesn't that bother you?"

"Put like that it does," he said, squeezing her.

"I'll miss you."

"I'll miss you too."

Suddenly, for no apparent reason, Pippa's eyes filled with tears, but with her head where it was, Laurence didn't see. "What time did you get back last night?" she said after a while. "It must have been late because I didn't hear you come in."

"Almost three," Laurence answered. "Ruby's come up with some pretty amazing stuff, believe it or not. She was on a roll last night. I didn't want to do anything to . . . Hmmm," he groaned as Pippa turned his mouth to hers and pushed her tongue deep inside.

"What was that for?" he asked as she pulled away.

"For being you."

"Then how about," he murmured slipping his other hand inside her sweater, "I get another. For being me." He smiled as she turned to sit astride him pressing her groin to his. "I kind of reckon you're after something, Mrs. McAllister." He grinned.

"I could be," she said, running her fingers around his neck and up into his hair.

Thank God, he was thinking to himself, as she started to suck gently on his lips while pushing herself harder against him, that her jealousy, which had been threatening to run out of control these past few weeks, seemed to have disappeared altogether now, and even Campbell's warning that Kirsten was aiming to come between them didn't seem to have fazed her. Laurence was profoundly glad of it, for having Kirsten back in London was, for him, too close for comfort. The year they had spent together still lived all too vividly in his mind, and though he would never admit it to anyone, he knew that despite what had happened at the end he had loved Kirsten in a way he would never love any other woman. What they had shared together came only once in a lifetime, but what he had with Pippa was something he would *never* give up the way he had given up on Kirsten. In a way he was grateful to Kirsten, for she had, in coming back, reminded him just how much Pippa meant to him. For a while there, though, it had scared the hell out of him to find that he couldn't make love to Pippa. Mercifully it hadn't lasted as the past week had proved, and his love for Pippa had deepened immeasurably for the way she had handled what she must have guessed was a real problem for him. And that was why Kirsten would never be able to come between them, for Pippa's unspoken support, loyalty, and love was the very mainstay of his life.

"Hey, where are you going?" he said as Pippa drew herself up from his lap.

"To lock the door," she smiled over her shoulder. "Okay, I know you've got a meeting at the bank . . ."

"It can wait," Laurence said wryly, knowing it couldn't, but he wanted her so much right now it would just have to.

She came back and stood beside him, looking down at the bulge in his jeans.

"Take off your clothes," he whispered as he lowered his zipper. "Take them all off and come sit right here."

As he spoke Pippa's eyes fluttered closed, showing him how turned on she was. She loved to be naked while he was still dressed.

Seconds later she was astride him again, slowly lowering herself onto him while looking deep into his eyes. He held her about the hips, one thumb gently massaging her between the legs.

"What was she like in bed?" Pippa murmured.

Laurence frowned. "What?"

Pippa's head fell back and she groaned ecstatically as he reached full penetration. "Kirsten," she said. "What was she like in bed?"

"Oh, Christ, Pippa! You sure as hell pick your moments."

"Was it as good as this?" Pippa asked, bringing her head back up and gyrating her hips as she pushed her tongue into his mouth. "Do you ever think of her while you're fucking me?"

"Quit talking," he said lifting her with him as he stood up.

"You're thinking about her right now, aren't you?" Pippa said, smiling up at him as he laid her across the table. "Do you want to fuck her again, Laurence? Do you want to push it right into her the way you're pushing it into me? Oh, God, Laurence," she suddenly gasped as he pushed her knees wide and thrust into her. "Fuck me, fuck me hard. Are you thinking of her now? Can you see her? Do you want to screw her this way? She's beautiful, isn't she, Laurence? So beautiful you can't get her out of your mind. Pretend I'm her, Laurence. Fuck me as though I was her."

Laurence's eyes were closed. He wouldn't listen, he couldn't, but the turbulence in her voice was driving him crazy. He pounded into her, holding her tiny waist as her legs circled him, locking him to her.

"Can you feel her, Laurence? Can you see her? Did she ever fuck you like this? Oh my God!" she cried as suddenly he hammered into her harder than he ever had before. "Is this what you did to her?" she gasped breathlessly. "Are you with her now?"

He pulled back, rammed himself into her, pulled back, and did it again. She sobbed for more and yet more, begging him never to stop. Then suddenly the semen was spurting from him. He ground into her feeling the strength start to seep from his legs. But still it came and still he pushed into her.

"Oh, Christ!" He felt her start to come too. "Jesus Christ!" Snatching her up from the table he pressed his mouth hard against hers. "I love you. Dear God, I love you."

"Oh, Laurence, I can't stop," she sobbed, clinging to him. "I just can't stop. Hold me. Please, hold me."

His arms tightened around her as her whole body vibrated with the force of her orgasm, but his legs felt so weak he knew he couldn't stand much longer. Scooping her up, he carried her back to the chair and sat down. Their arms were still entwined, their bodies joined, and they stayed that way for a long time, just holding each other and waiting for the steady rhythm of their hearts to return.

At last Pippa lifted her head. "Are you angry with me?" she whispered.

Laurence's face was grim, though he couldn't say for sure whether he was angry or not. But what he did know was that as much as he wanted to have another child, he hoped to God Pippa hadn't conceived then. For the very last thing in the world he wanted was a child that had been conceived while in his head he was making love to Kirsten Meredith.

It had been dark for hours. So dark, so very, very dark that her eyes couldn't adjust. She lay silently and still, her shallow breathing not even disturbing the covers. She could almost be dead, she mused to herself. Lying here in the inky black silence was like lying in the swallowed cavern of a grave.

After a while she moved. Reaching out a hand she pressed the switch beside her bed. A dim, grayish glow spread a circle over the floor. As she lifted herself up, her distorted shadow loomed large across the wall. It stalked her as she moved to the door. She turned the key, locking herself in. Securing her tomb.

Very gently she eased open a drawer and lifted out the book. Such a precious book. Bound in leather, embossed in gold. As she folded back the cover a rush of air sucked at the first, transparent page. She pulled it back. A smile hovered on her lips; tears stung at her eyes.

Using her fingers she traced the outline of the photograph, as though reading braille. She closed her eyes as though to sink the memory of the face into the very depths of her mind. After a while she could hear the voice, the longed-for voice, murmuring words of comfort, of love. Pulling her elbows to her sides she felt strong, caring arms go around her. Very slowly, like a flower coming to blossom, a warm, cherished glow spread through her heart.

She opened her eyes. The face was still there, gazing up at her in the misty light.

Suddenly she closed the book. She didn't want to look at it anymore.

She tiptoed across the room and peered into the cot. Flushed, tender cheeks lying on a pillow of lace. A tiny fist clenched. Soft, downy head turned to one side. The warmth and smell of new human life. How God had blessed her with this one, unthought-for happiness.

CHAPTER NINE

IT WAS NO WONDER THAT SO MANY ARTISTS CHOSE to live in this wonderful place, Kirsten was thinking dreamily to herself, as she stood on the bougainvillea-covered terrace of Zaccheo's Tuscan home and looked out on the endless rows of olive groves sloping gently into the valley far below. The light was incredible, so soft and mysterious as it shimmered on the silvery green leaves and cast spectacular cloud shadows over the slumbering mountains. She inhaled deeply, reaching high above her head as though to open her entire body to the bracing, early morning air and thought of the last time she had stood on the terrace of this magnificent hillside villa. She smiled, relishing the memory, and looked to the sky as though turning her face to the voice that now existed only in her mind.

Hearing the gentle clatter of a tea tray, she turned to see Manuella coming onto the terrace with her breakfast. The table was already set, but only for one—Zaccheo was in Rome and Kirsten wasn't too sure when he'd be back.

He'd called her two days before to invite her here, saying he felt she should get out of England for a while, at least until things had calmed down. How he had learned about Dermott Campbell's latest attack, Kirsten wasn't sure. Maybe he had got hold of an English newspaper, or it could be that Pippa McAllister had told him. Whichever, it didn't matter, for he was right; she had needed to get away to somewhere where she could concentrate on how she was going to bring her ideas to fruition. Dyllis might be doing all she could to destroy Kirsten's attempts at a comeback, but Kirsten was simply not going to allow herself to be beaten.

A few months, perhaps even a few weeks from now, Paul's death and her inheritance would be old news. No one would want to read about it anymore. Other events would be under the spotlight and by that time she should be ready to make what she hoped, given the project she had in mind, would be quite a comeback. Meanwhile no one in the world knew where she was with the exception of Helena and Zaccheo.

She chuckled quietly to herself as she sat down at the delicate wrought-iron table and filled her cup with piping hot tea. Helena had been incensed at her coming here, had accused her of running away, and had demanded to know how they could possibly work together on Kirsten's ideas when Kirsten was so far away. It had been hard for Kirsten to stop herself laughing outright, for she knew only too well that Helena was piqued because she hadn't been invited too. Zaccheo's reputation as an expert lover was too much for Helena to resist; she was simply dying to find out for herself if it were true. Though Kirsten was sympathetic, for she herself was not impervious to Zaccheo's charm, she had explained that Zaccheo was going to be in Rome and that she was looking forward to spending some time alone.

For no apparent reason, as she bit into a succulent pastry, Jane suddenly came into her mind and with the thought came a pang of guilt. Laurence had delivered an ultimatum—either Jane stopped visiting Kirsten or Jane was fired. Hiding her own pain at the harshness of Laurence's response, Kirsten had told Jane during their brief telephone conversation that it would be for the best. Saying good-bye to Jane though was more of a wrench than Kirsten wanted to admit, for she couldn't deny that she had come to see Jane as a link to Laurence and it was a link that, as much as she despised herself for it, she just didn't want to break.

Kirsten spent the next few days ambling through the hills with her tape recorder or sitting among the ornamental palms around the swimming pool transcribing plots and breakdowns onto the portable typewriter she'd found in Zaccheo's study. The flow of ideas was like a bubbling stream, hitting obstacles but never long deterred from its purpose. It was so exhilarating to find that she still had the ability to take a simple concept and turn it into something dramatically powerful. Not that there was anything simple about the ideas she was working on now, but her confidence was riding high.

It was early in the evening on the fifth day of her visit that she finally plucked up the courage to take a swim. The clear blue water looked so utterly irresistible that even the knowledge that the spring sunshine wouldn't have warmed it much could no longer deter her. She hadn't thought to bring a swimsuit with her but didn't consider it a problem since Manuella wouldn't return to the villa for at least another hour, and she'd waved Raimondo the gardener off home a few minutes ago.

As she stepped up to the edge of the pool she could feel the thrill of the balmy air curling itself around her naked skin. Strangely it felt like a lifetime ago that she had last done this, when she and Paul had swum together each evening before going to sit on the veranda overlooking Cannes and the magnificent expanse of the Mediterranean.

Feeling as though his eyes were on her now, she positioned herself to dive. The shock of the cold water when it came was breathtaking, but she swam the length of the pool, somersaulted, and swam back again. She'd done several lengths by the time her body became acclimatized and her breathing was steady again. Rolling onto her back she floated lazily across the surface, gazing up at the rosy sky. It was like being in paradise. She laughed to herself, turning again and, using long languorous strokes, swimming several more laps of the pool. A few minutes later she was drifting aimlessly on her back again, listening to the distant sounds of the valley, when she heard a stirring in the bushes nearby. Her eyes came open and she looked across to the vast stone wall from where the noise had come just in time to see a lizard scuttle back into the undergrowth.

She relaxed, letting her arms drift from her sides as she gently moved her legs and was just deciding to do a few more lengths before going to take a shower when she heard someone say, " 'Twas not for the want of beauty he rested his eyes on the nymph, but for the want of mortality and the satiation of his dreams."

Kirsten could feel herself smiling even before he had finished. "Good evening, Zaccheo," she said still looking up at the sky. "As you can see, I wasn't exactly expecting you."

She heard him chuckle, then rolled over to look up at where he was standing on the veranda. His arms were resting on the lobelia-covered wall; his dark eyes were sparkling.

"If you were a gentleman," she said, "you'd turn your back while I climbed out of here."

Zaccheo's grin widened. "I am a gentleman, Kirsten, *bellezza mia,* but I am not a fool."

Kirsten tried and failed to suppress a smile. Then tossing back her hair she hauled herself up over the steps and having no choice but to walk toward him, for she had left her clothes on the veranda, she put her shoulders back and stalked through the garden, never taking her eyes from his as though challenging him to lower his gaze to her body. He watched her, every step of the way, until she was standing beside him, waiting for him to hand her the towel he was holding. Still their eyes were locked, then Kirsten felt her smile widening as his body started to tremble and his deep resonant laughter seemed to erupt from his very depths. His head fell back as he roared his amusement, and laughing, too, Kirsten snatched the towel from him and wrapped herself in it.

"You thought I wouldn't have the courage, didn't you?" she said, somewhat surprised that she had.

"I hoped you would," he answered, still chuckling as he ran his fingers over her face. "You are such a pleasure for my eyes, such an indulgence for my mind. Will you take an aperitif now? Or will you shower first?"

"I think," Kirsten said, "that I will take an aperitif."

"Then it will be my pleasure to serve you."

As Kirsten sank into a cushioned wicker chair she watched his enormous body move almost lithely into the sitting room. She wasn't too sure why she had chosen to take the aperitif before the shower since the cool night air was prickling her skin, but there had been something in those few moments that had made her want to remain here, unclad beneath the towel and, perhaps, still in his eyes.

When he came back he handed her a cocktail she had never tasted before and sat down on a chair facing her. Kirsten eyed him, waiting for him to speak.

"So," he said at last, "you are enjoying your stay here?"

She nodded, a tiny smile hovering about her lips.

"This is good," he said, putting his head to one side as he regarded her intently.

"It was kind of you to invite me," she said softly.

"You needed to come."

There was an ambiguity to his words that, coupled with the sleepy, knowing look in his eyes, sent a quick thrill through her veins. It was so rare that she allowed herself to flirt this way, but with Zaccheo it was almost impossible not to, even when Paul had been there, watching in silent amusement, like a father indulging his children.

"What brought you back from Rome so soon?" she asked.

The look in his eyes was answer enough, and again

Kirsten felt her pulses leap. She found herself looking at his immense hand holding the delicate glass, the jet black hair that curled over his arms, the gentle rise of his massive chest as he breathed. After a while she returned her gaze to his patrician face, the heavy beard that almost disguised the fullness of his mouth, the large nose and deep, sardonic eyes. She could see the moisture on his lips, almost feel the tension mounting through his body, and felt herself so drawn to him it was as though the shadows stealing across the veranda were merging them into one. Her chest tightened as he stood up and moved behind her, resting his hands on the back of the chair. Neither of them moved and neither of them spoke as together they looked out at the burning orange sky as the sun sank imperiously into the horizon.

Not until it had disappeared fully did he touch her, so softly that were it not for the electrifying tremor that went through her, Kirsten might not have known it.

"You are cold," he said as she shivered. He walked across the terrace to pick up a fresh towel. When he came back he lifted her hands and pulled her to her feet. As she stood, the towel covering her fell away and Kirsten made no attempt to retrieve it. She knew she was going too far, that the harmless flirtation had some time ago taken on a new momentum, but his magnetism was too strong to resist. She wanted to be naked under his gaze, to feel the cooling breath of night air whisper over her skin like the caress of his fingers. But soon she would stop, any moment now she would laugh and so would he, and that strange remoteness she was feeling from the exquisite tingling of her body would be at an end.

She bowed her head, watching the indolent movements of the towel as he began to wipe away the tiny droplets of water still glistening on her shoulders. Her breasts were aching to be touched, and when at last he brushed the velvety fabric over their fullness she felt an empyrean lightheadedness wash over her. She thought she might be swaying or trembling, but aside from the burning heat spreading through her body she was still. It was as if his hands allowed her no freedom for either movement or thought.

He moved beside her, resting one arm loosely about her shoulders as he lowered the towel from her breasts to her abdomen, caressing her tenderly with its softness until he was dabbing gently at the pearls of water clinging to her pubic hair. Then the hand resting on her shoulder came up under her chin and lifted her face to his. He looked long into her eyes, his other hand now motionless yet still touching the join of her legs. It was as though she were floating away from herself, watching herself surrender to a desire she had no power to break.

As his mouth covered hers Kirsten felt a sob shudder through her. She felt the towel slip from his fingers and pool at her feet. Then, as with one hand, he massaged her neck; with the other he cupped one magnificent breast and lightly squeezed the achingly distended nipple.

Slowly he drew her to him, lifting his head to gaze into her eyes as his hands dropped to her waist and his fingers fanned over her hips. Coasting further into a daze of overpowering longing Kirsten allowed him to push her gently back into the chair, and her heart started to pound as he once again lifted the towel and parting her knees began to stroke her inner thighs.

Desire throbbed heavily through her body. Her head fell back against the chair, her eyes were closed, and all she could hear were the tiny moans escaping her lips. The voice of caution was now no more than a remnant of a distant echo, and as he pulled her forward, resting her buttocks on the very edge of the seat before lifting her legs and opening them wide, Kirsten knew that she was going to yield to him completely.

As his tongue flickered against her she gave a startled sob of pure ecstacy. Her head rolled from side to side, her fingers snaked through his hair, and as he sucked her with his lips and probed her with his tongue she could feel herself rising on a soaring tide of impossible sensation. With his thumbs he pulled her wider apart and took that most sensitive part of her full into his mouth. Kirsten gasped, and as her head fell forward she opened her eyes and looked down to where his mass of inky black hair was resting between her thighs.

It came at her from nowhere with such ferocity and such lightning speed and clarity there was nothing she could do to stop it. Her entire body seemed to jar with the impact as the shock lashed through her. The last man to do this to her was the only man ever to have done it, and he too had black hair, he too had an expertly questing mouth and a dazzling sorcery in his fingertips. And it was he she was seeing now. It was for his body that her own was trembling, for his heat she was yearning, wanting to feel it pressing so deep inside her until she could take no more.

As though she had been struck Kirsten pulled back, knocking Zaccheo off balance as she curled her long legs into the chair. "I'm sorry," she gasped as Zaccheo looked up at her in astonishment. "Zaccheo, I'm sorry. I just can't do it."

His face darkened with fury, but as he made to get up Kirsten sprang from the chair and ran into the house.

When she reached her room she closed the door behind her and stood against it, panting for breath. But just being away from Zaccheo, removing herself from the intoxicating ambience of a Tuscan night and the potency of his Italian charm, had restored some semblance of order to her mind.

As she walked to the bed and picked up a robe her lovely face was tight with anger. Not in five years had she allowed herself to relive the full intensity of the passion she had shared with Laurence; never had she dwelled, not even for a moment, on the image of their entwined bodies, the eroticism of their games, the indescribable beauty of his nudity. It had all, every bit of it, been banished from her mind's eye until those moments with Zaccheo had tricked her so cruelly.

She stalked furiously to the bathroom, snapped on the shower, and stood under the giant rose letting the scalding water pummel her body. She was going to deal with this, she told herself vehemently. Like the love she still felt for him, the desire was going to be conquered too. How could she have been so stupid as not to have realized before that the two were inseparable? It was a brutal reflection of how stupefyingly naive she could be. Thirty-six years old, she seethed as she savagely soaped her legs, and still she didn't know how to deal with the treachery of her own mind.

But she would deal with it, and what was more she knew exactly how she was going to begin. And stepping out of the shower she picked up a towel, stalked into the bedroom, and opened up the wardrobe. Half an hour later, her hair still damp, her skin lightly perfumed, and clad in a dress that clung to every curve of her body, she turned to look at herself in the mirror. Just one glance was enough to see that she wore no underwear, and as she looked deep into her own eyes it was almost as though she could see reflected in their depths the erotic images of Zaccheo's vast body joining with hers. . . .

Helena leaned against the doorjamb of a friend's Edwardian house in Chelsea, nursing a very large vodka and feeling so thoroughly wretched as she contemplated her life that she couldn't even work up the energy to find a nice young boy to help take her mind off things. Hearing a screech coming from the garden she looked up, tried to focus on the heaving mass of nubile young bodies, and promptly wondered if she were going to be sick. Her friend Melissa Andrews was having a teenage party for her pimply faced daughter, and Helena'd said she would lend some moral support. Now she was regretting it. Being fat and over forty when you fancied men of fat and over forty was bad enough, but when you fancied the hell out of fresh-faced youths with skinny hips, barely developed muscles and inexperienced cocks it was pure torture. God, what she could teach them, could she just get her hands on them, but there was nothing doing—at least not while Melissa was around. She'd have a fit if she thought Helena was planning to corrupt the sons of her fucking bourgeois friends.

But it wasn't fair, Helena grumbled to herself as she downed the vodka in one go. There was Kirsten over there in Italy getting her brains humped out by the only man of fat and over forty Helena could conceive of screwing. Helena knew all about Kirsten's Tuscan liaison with Zaccheo as did anyone else who'd scanned the center pages of Campbell's rag, while here she was standing in a doorway like a frustrated old spinster whose only chance of fulfillment that day was to go home and masturbate.

But that wasn't true, she reminded herself miserably. There was somewhere else she could go, someone else she could turn to, and the more she had to drink the more tempted she was to give in.

She reached for the vodka again, downed another large one, then poured yet more into her glass. She could hardly believe this was happening to her, but it was, and had been for some time now. Drunk or sober she was lusting for a man whom the very sight of had always made her stomach churn. Well, maybe that was a bit strong, but she'd always loathed the man. Until recently.

Was it because she suspected he was falling for Kirsten, she asked herself dismally. Or was it because she had got so desperate now she was prepared to do anything to ease the loneliness in her life?

A faint smile started to hover over her lips. What would he say if she called him now and asked him to come to the house? Christ, what was she thinking of; she was housesitting for Kirsten while she was in Italy. How could she even consider inviting Dermott Campbell there? Would he come, she wondered. She wouldn't know unless she asked, and why the hell should Kirsten have all the fun? She'd get a real kick out of running rings round Campbell and she was more than curious to know what he was like in the sack . . .

An hour later Helena looked across the room at Campbell, sitting there in the fading light, and felt her earlier defiance recede as all the alcohol she had consumed turned her mood morose. She noticed the way his eyes looked kind of vulnerable without his glasses. There were deep lines on his brow, more pronounced because he was frowning and his mouth looked somehow smaller in the strange shadow his nose cast over it. He wasn't a handsome man, not really, but when he smiled . . .

Campbell left Kirsten's at seven the following evening. At one minute past seven there was a knock on the door.

"Jane!" Helena gasped, almost reeling. She glanced quickly down the street to see if Campbell was still anywhere in sight. "What are you doing here?" she asked.

"I came to see Kirsten," Jane answered.

"She's in Italy."

"I thought she might be back."

"No, no. Um, you'd better come in."

As they walked through to the kitchen Helena tightened the belt of her dressing gown, still reeling at the narrowness of the escape. Christ, if it had been any closer Jane and Campbell would have met on the doorstep! "Can I get you something?" she said to Jane. "Coffee? Tea?"

"No, nothing, thank you."

Helena looked at her, not quite sure what to say.

Jane shrugged, but as she tried to smile her mouth quivered and to Helena's amazement she dissolved into tears.

"What's up?" Helena asked, trying not to be revolted at how ghastly the girl looked with her red eyes and dripping nose.

"Nothing, nothing," Jane cried and fled to the bathroom.

For a while Helena stared at the door, trying to swallow her exasperation at having to deal with an emotional kid when she had so much else to think about right now. Like her feelings for Campbell and what had happened between them. It was incredible and had she not experienced it herself she'd never have believed it was possible. They had spent an entire night wrapped in each other's arms and neither one of them had made any attempt to make love. She wasn't too sure why, especially when that had been her motive for getting him over here, but if the truth be told she wouldn't have changed what did happen for the world, for it had been so long since a man had held her that way—in fact she couldn't remember ever having been held that way. Kirsten, it seemed, was the only one around here who experienced that sort of thing.

The thought of Kirsten brought a stab of dismay to her heart. The guilt she felt at what she was doing was indescribable, for the odds of Kirsten getting her life back together were stacked so heavily against her now as to make it virtually impossible. Dyllis was already proving that she more than had the means, as well as the contacts, to annihilate Kirsten's career, and Campbell's determination that Kirsten would never come between Laurence and Pippa was unshakable. But there was always Zaccheo, Helena reminded herself. A quick flare of jealousy burned in her throat. For Kirsten there was always someone. Dyllis had ordered Campbell to do all he could to destroy whatever there was between Zaccheo and Kirsten, but Helena couldn't see Zaccheo being too swayed by what was written in the press, particularly not the British press.

She started as the lock on the bathroom door snapped open. Jane had been gone so long she'd forgotten she was there.

"Are you all right?" Helena said as Jane came into the kitchen.

"I think so," Jane sniffed, dabbing at her nose with a wad of toilet paper.

"Do you want to talk about it?" Helena offered, hoping the answer would be no.

Jane's bottom lip was sucked under her teeth as she half sobbed and half tittered. Her normally lifeless eyes were glittering brightly as they darted about the kitchen, then to Helena's surprise she walked over to the draining boards and picking up a cloth started to dry the dishes. Helena watched her, vaguely amused by the fact that she seemed unaware of what she was doing. "I took Tom to Laurence's parents today," Jane said, putting the cloth back down again.

"Did you? That was nice."

Jane looked at her. "I took him there because Pippa asked me to," she said.

"Oh."

"Tom and I often go there."

"That's nice," Helena said again, feeling a growing urge to shake the girl.

"It's just that . . ." Jane's eyes filled with tears. "Well, I knew Pippa wanted me and Tom out of the way while she was packing. . . . Tom's still with his grandparents; he's staying the night. I am too. Laurence's parents are so nice to me. . . . They always make me really welcome. . . ."

"Oh. Well, I'm sure they do. Uh, are you sure you won't have a coffee?"

"No, no thanks. I went back home again just now. Pippa was already gone." Helena could see the effort going into holding back yet more tears and silently she was willing her to succeed. "I knew she was going."

The words were out before Helena could stop them. "I imagine the fact that she was packing put you on to her," she quipped.

Jane's eyes came up to hers. "You don't understand," she said. "Pippa wasn't just packing for a trip. She was packing because . . ." Her voice was so strangled over her final words that Helena wasn't too sure she'd heard right.

"What did you say?" she said.

Jane swallowed hard. "Pippa's left Laurence," she whispered.

Helena blinked.

"Oh, what shall I do? What am I going to do?" Jane sobbed, covering her face with her hands.

"Well, I don't see that there's much you can do," Helena said. "I mean, it's up to them really, isn't it?"

"But if I'd got there sooner I might have been able to stop her."

"Surely that's up to Laurence."

"But Laurence doesn't know!" Jane cried. "He's in America and he's not due home until the end of next week and I don't know whether I should ring him and tell him or just wait until he comes back. I was hoping Kirsten could tell me what to do."

Helena wasn't too sure how much Jane knew about Kirsten's feelings for Laurence, so deciding not to voice her opinion on what she thought of Jane coming to Kirsten for such advice, she said, "Look, are you sure Laurence doesn't know? I mean, she can't have just gone off without saying a word."

"She's left him a note."

"Oh, I see. Do you know where she's gone?" Helena asked, more out of curiosity than concern.

Jane nodded. "She's gone, or at least tomorrow she's going, to Italy. She's staying with her mother tonight."

"Italy?" Helena said stupidly.

Again Jane nodded. "Pippa's left Laurence for Zaccheo."

"But Kirsten's with Zaccheo," Helena said, feeling her head starting to spin. The implications of all this would have been hard to handle at the best of times, but with a hangover . . . "Does Kirsten know Pippa's on her way?" she said.

"I don't know."

"Well, I think we'd better find out, don't you?" But when Helena called Zaccheo's villa there was no reply.

CHAPTER TEN

THE EARLY MORNING MIST WAS SUSPENDED OVER THE valley, the dew glinted like tiny stars on the vivid green leaves, and the air was so fresh and exhilarating as it wafted in through the open bedroom window that it had roused Kirsten long before Zaccheo reached for her.

She adored these wonderful late spring mornings and couldn't think of anywhere in the world she would rather be than half-lying, half-sitting here in this tapestry-strewn bedroom gazing dreamily out of the windows. Her eyes fluttered closed as Zaccheo's hand slipped across her stomach. She lay very still, pretending she was still sleeping, but as he leaned over her her lips started to twitch with a smile.

Kissing her softly he went off to the bathroom.

Later that day they were going to drive to Siena where he would walk her through each chapter of his latest book. It was something Kirsten had been looking forward to ever since he'd first suggested it. She loved Italy and to be shown one of its most beautiful towns through the eyes of Zaccheo Marigliano she knew was going to be one of the most precious experiences of her life.

She had more or less decided to stay in Tuscany for another two weeks, by which time she knew she would have to return to England if only because she needed to visit the libraries to carry out her own research. Despite the all too frequent distraction of Zaccheo, her own projects were progressing, one in particular, which she was quite excited to show Helena. There was a great part in it for her, and perhaps between them they could decide on who would be best to write it.

In fact the idea of going back to England didn't fill her with as many misgivings as she might have expected. Whatever Dermott Campbell had written about her recently, or whatever he chose to write in the future, didn't bother her any more than it seemed to have bothered Zaccheo. As far as they were concerned their lives were their own affair and what anyone else chose to think was simply of no consequence. And England was going to be so much more tolerable when she knew that most weekends she would be flying over here to be with Zaccheo.

"Oh!" She laughed as Zaccheo came out of the bathroom and pulled the bedclothes off her.

"Time to be going, *cara*," he said.

"Already?" Kirsten said, sitting up. "I thought we weren't leaving until lunchtime."

"Ah!" He sighed, turning back to her, his face a burlesque of sorrow. "You misunderstand me, *cara*. It is time for you to be going, not I."

"I'm sorry?" Kirsten said.

He shrugged. "My editor, Pippa, she is arriving today. It is better that you are not here when she comes."

Kirsten could feel the muscles freezing in her face.

"But what difference does it make whether I'm here or not?" she said.

"It is better that you leave," Zaccheo answered. "Raimondo will drive you to the airport." He started to get dressed.

For the moment both Kirsten's mind and body seemed locked in paralysis, but as the shock slowly permeated her senses she felt herself start to shake with fury.

"What the hell do you mean, it's better that I go?" she seethed. "What am I, some kind of dog to be dismissed when its master becomes bored? You invited me here for as long as I wanted to be here."

"Cara, cara." He sighed, turning to face her. "You make such a drama of this when it is nothing."

"Nothing!" she yelled. "Five days and five nights of unadulterated passion and you call it nothing!"

"But what did you expect, *la mia volpe furba?* That I would change my will?"

As though she had been struck Kirsten reeled back. She hadn't read the British papers so had no idea that in calling her his wily fox, Zaccheo was quoting Campbell. But the epithet itself was almost as injurious as his remark about the will. "I don't believe you said that," she gasped. "I don't believe you could think that of me. I came here—"

"You came here, *cara,* because you believed that one way or the other it would benefit you. My fortune or Laurence McAllister. Perhaps both. But you are going to use neither his wife, nor my fortune to get what you want."

"But you invited me . . ."

"Of course. Always I have wanted to make love to you. You know that. You are a beautiful woman, what man would not want to make love to you? And you, *mia bella,* are a Venus. You make love as though you were the goddess herself, but as you see, it is not so easy to outfox Zaccheo Marigliano. I have eyes that see right through to your heart, and your heart, Kirsten Meredith, is greedy for material prizes." He lifted an eyebrow. "Maybe it is greedier still for Laurence McAllister."

Laurence was standing beside the bed staring sightlessly down at Pippa's note.

His initial disbelief had given way to a strange calm. After all, he thought distantly to himself, it seemed to fit into place now. Her accusing him of having affairs was because of the guilt she was suffering at her own affair. He winced at the sudden bolt of jealousy that lurched through his gut as in his mind's eye he saw her in Zaccheo's arms. Jesus Christ, all this time she'd wanted him to fall for someone else, because it would have made it easier for her to leave him. How long had she been planning this? How long had she been lying to him?

He leaned against the dressing table and stared down at the faint rings in the dust left by the things she had taken. Why was it only now that he was understanding all that she had done for him? Had he truly been so ignorant of the fact that it was only because of her that he had been able to handle all that happened with Kirsten? To shut it out and pretend it had never happened.

Sinking down onto the stool he buried his face in his

hands. Kirsten! Kirsten! Kirsten! He should have known that something like this would happen as soon as she came back. For weeks now it had been as though he was facing an eclipse of his own emotions and his love and need for Pippa was blinding him still to the bitter deceit of his life. Except now, and perhaps only now, he realized, there was no deceit. He loved Pippa, truly loved her.

The shock of her going made him nauseous. Did Tom know yet that she was gone? For sure he'd know she was on a trip, but had anyone told him that Mummy wasn't coming back? A surge of protective love wrapped itself around his heart, and without thinking what he was doing he took himself to Tom's room and sat down on the bed beside him.

His throat started to tighten. Where in the hell were they going to be without her? What life was there for these two guys without the woman they loved? He gazed down at the innocent, childish face and felt the defencelessness of those tender limbs and the untroubled joy of the tiny heart pierce through him like a knife. He could almost feel Tom's delight when he woke to see his Daddy watching over him. They always had had a closeness that some said was unusual for a father and son of Tom's age, and now Laurence couldn't help wondering if Pippa had deliberately pushed them together knowing that in the end they would need and console each other when she had gone.

Unable to stop himself Laurence lifted Tom into his arms and held him tightly. Drowsily Tom pushed his arms around Laurence's neck and settled his head on his shoulder. Laurence smoothed his hair, kissed him softly on the cheek and only just resisted the urge to squeeze him with the full force of his love. Pippa, he was crying inside, Dear God, Pippa, please let this be some kind of joke. Please let me open my eyes and find you sitting there, laughing at me. . . .

A few minutes later he heard Jane come into the room. He kept his head averted, not wanting her to see the tears on his cheeks.

"Dermott Campbell's on the phone," Jane said quietly.

"Tell him I'll call him back," Laurence answered gruffly. But as Jane was turning to leave he remembered that Dermott had tried to get hold of him in the States. "No," he said, "I'll take it."

Gently he handed Tom over to Jane and went into his bedroom to take the call.

"At last!" Campbell's voice boomed down the line making Laurence wince. "I've been trying to get hold of you for days. I just heard you were back so I called to tell you the latest."

"And what's that?" Laurence asked dully.

"I guess you didn't see my column at the weekend," Campbell said. "No, well, I don't suppose you would have jet-setting around the world the way you do. Incidentally, how did it go over there in LA? Anything doing?"

"It was okay," Laurence answered. He took a deep breath. "Look, Dermott, do you think we can get to the point here?"

"Sure. The point is, my friend, that the Kirstie Doll is over there in Italy getting laid by none other than Zaccheo Marigliano! And you don't need me to tell you who Marigliano's editor is. And who is Marigliano's editor married to? Are you following me, Laurence? Kirsten Meredith is trying new tactics. She's got your nanny, she's getting your best friend, next thing you know she's going to be pally-pally with your wife. So at the risk of telling you I told you so . . ."

All the time Campbell had been talking Laurence had felt a burning rage running through his veins and suddenly it erupted. "For your fucking information, Dermott," he seethed, "my wife is out there getting laid by Zaccheo Marigliano herself. So get your fucking facts straight. And get the fucking hell off my back about Kirsten Meredith or—"

"What!" Campbell gasped. "What did you say? Did I hear you right? Pippa's out there—"

"You heard me."

"You mean . . . ? Are you telling me you two . . . ? Shit, Laurence! What the hell's going on here? I thought you two . . ."

"Yeah, well you thought wrong. Seems we both did."

"Oh, Christ, Laurence, I don't know what to say. I mean, are you sure you've got this right, 'cause I'm telling you the Kirstie Doll's out there too."

"I couldn't give a fucking damn where Kirsten Meredith is," Laurence raged. "My wife's walked out on me, she's shacking up with my best friend, as you call him . . ."

"I'm coming round there," Campbell interrupted.

"Don't. I got to have some time to think about this. . . ."

"You can think about it later. Right now you need to get drunk."

"That's the last thing I need. I got a son here, remember. He needs me right now."

"He's got a nanny!"

"He's about to lose his mother, for Christ's sake! And I've got to do something to stop that happening. So stay where you are, Dermott. I'll call you when I'm ready."

He slammed down the phone and was about to turn away from the bed when his eye was caught by the note he had dropped there. He picked it up, crushing it in his fist. It wasn't over yet. Oh, no, it was a long way from over.

Like the captive of a painting, she sat immobile in her frame of solid darkness. Though her hands didn't move the silky smoothness of the photograph was cool beneath her fingertips. Little pools of light glimmered happily on the surface lending an almost ethereal quality to the beautifully expressive eyes. The warmth from her skin seemed to seep into the gloss bringing the beloved face to life. She could almost hear the laughter bubbling from the parted lips, feel the joy reflecting itself in her heart. She smiled, dreamily, but then, as her eyes closed, instead of seeing the wondrous images of the past, a shadow of fear darkened her thoughts.

Things were changing. So much was happening. Nothing was in her control. What would become of her baby? And as though sensing her distress the baby started to cry. The sound of its wails echoed through her ears, gently at first and then louder and still louder, until it was as though her mind was being lashed by the cruel shards of a punishment undeserved. She bunched her fists at the sides of her face. She had to go to it, she had to. But she couldn't. . . .

CHAPTER ELEVEN

PIPPA WAS CURLED INTO ONE CORNER OF THE HUGE leather sofa in Zaccheo's drawing room, hugging her knees to her chest as though to protect herself. Laurence was standing at the center of the room, his face as thunderous as the gathering storm outside, his very appearance a reflection of the pain she had caused him.

For the moment they had reached an impasse, but Pippa knew that the worst was far from over. Zaccheo had taken himself off somewhere, though he and Laurence had spoken before she came down from the bedroom. What they'd said she wasn't too sure, though she'd heard Laurence shouting, which had all but drowned Zaccheo's placating tones. The fact that Laurence had hit Zaccheo had been evident the moment she walked in the room—a table was on its side and broken china was scattered across the floor.

It was at that point, she imagined, that Zaccheo had decided to make himself scarce. The last thing he would want was to land himself in a fight with Laurence. Physically Zaccheo might be the larger of the two men, but

Laurence was a big man too and unquestionably the fitter. Besides, Zaccheo had a very real affection for Laurence despite the guilt that, in fact, seemed to trouble Zaccheo a lot less than it ever had Pippa. But there was no mistaking the extent to which she and Zaccheo had shattered Laurence's life, and Pippa knew that Zaccheo would feel every bit as bad about that as she did.

Earlier Laurence had asked her how long it had been going on between her and Zaccheo, and not wanting to lie to him anymore Pippa had told him. Almost two years. She had seen the way her betrayal had cut into him, could read his thoughts as clearly as if he had spoken them. He had trusted her, believed in her love as he had always believed in her fidelity. It was as though she had torn out the very roots of his life, leaving him disoriented, confused, and, yes, devastated. Her heart weighed heavily in her. She felt she might drown in remorse, yet she knew that no matter what he said, no matter how much he was suffering she wouldn't go back to him. She was where she wanted to be, where she had always, for the past two years, known she would eventually come. It had simply been a matter of choosing the right time.

Laurence had walked to the window and was now staring out at the rain-spattered garden. His whole demeanor was one of barely restrained anger, but Pippa knew he was fighting it. She longed to go to him, to lend him the comfort of her arms, but knew that would be the wrong thing to do. He had to get used to the fact that she would no longer be there for him, that his troubles were his own and that whatever the future held he must face it alone.

"What about Tom?" he said, his gruffness piercing the silence.

The pain seared Pippa's heart. "What about him?" she whispered.

Laurence spun round. "What about him?" he seethed. "He's your son, for Christ's sake! Your own flesh and blood."

"He's yours too," she said simply. And when Laurence only glared at her, she added, "He's more yours than mine. He always was," but the tears had already started in her eyes.

"Pip, please," he implored, "you love him as much as I do, so if only for his sake let's try again."

Pippa buried her face in her knees, but Laurence saw the barely perceptible shake of her head.

"I don't understand it!" he cried, slamming his fist into the wall. "I thought we really had something you and I. I thought you were happy, as happy as I was. For God's sake, why didn't you tell me if you weren't?"

"I was," Pippa choked. "I loved you, Laurence. I still do, but just not in the way I love . . ." her voice trailed off and Laurence's eyes closed as a wave of jealousy swept through him.

"But what about before I went to the States? Shit, Pippa, I thought we'd recaptured everything then. We were so close, so—"

"No!" she cried. "No, we weren't. Don't you understand what happened then? Didn't it once occur to you that it was the only time in our married life you had ever made love to me that way? That all these years I've known that you've been holding back on me, that all the time you've been crying out for her! That day proved it,

Laurence. I always knew it, but that day showed me that what you and I had was never the same as what you'd had with her. And you still crave it, Laurence. You want her every bit as much now as you ever did. It's like you're saving yourself for her. You've always said you can never forgive her, but don't you understand, Laurence, you long to forgive her. So why don't you let—"

"No!" he roared, and Pippa cowered as he stormed toward her. "You're not blaming me for this, Pippa! I'm not going to let you, do you hear me? What I had with Kirsten is over, in the past. You're the only woman I want, you always will be." In his fury he hadn't realized that Pippa hadn't even mentioned Kirsten's name, but Pippa did and she gave a sad smile as she looked up at him. "You've got to understand," he raged on, "that the only reason I ever held back was to protect you. You're so damned fragile, so precious to me, I didn't want to hurt you. . . ." Suddenly he laughed bitterly as he thought of Zaccheo. "God, what a fool I am!" he spat. "What a fucking mess I've made of everything."

"Face the truth, Laurence," Pippa said softly. "For God's sake accept it and stop torturing yourself this way." She jumped as Laurence grabbed her arm and twisted it away from her body.

"You're still doing it!" he yelled. "You're still trying to convince me—or is it yourself—that I'm in love with someone else just so you can ease your own guilt. Well it's not going to work, Pippa. I love you, I've always loved you, and nothing you or anyone else says is going to change that. You're the mother of my son—" His voice suddenly caught in his throat and he turned abruptly away. To think of Tom now was too much to bear. Yet at the same time he yearned to see that beloved little face, to hold him in his arms and let him know that nothing, just nothing in the whole damned world would ever part them.

"I left him with you because I know you'll be a much better father than I ever could be a mother," Pippa said. "But please don't think that it hasn't hurt me to do it. I love him, Laurence, believe me, I love him as much as any mother can love her child. But I'm just not up to it. I can't give him what he needs. Don't ask me why, I just can't. So I did what I thought was best for him, what I *know* to be best for him. He's your son, Laurence. He loves you and we both know that if he were given the choice he would rather be with you."

Laurence's smile was vicious. "And it would have nothing to do with the fact that he'd get in the way over here, I suppose? That Zaccheo wouldn't want a three-year-old cramping his life?"

"It's true," Pippa said calmly, "it would be difficult to have Tom here. But if I thought it was best for him, I'd have brought him."

"Over my dead body," Laurence snarled.

Pippa turned her face away, looking at but not seeing the garish painting that covered the chimney breast. All the time they had been arguing, the sky outside had been darkening and now there was very little light in the room. She wanted this to be over, she wanted him to go, but even as she thought it she felt devastated by the knowledge that it would then be over—forever—between them. Nothing in her life would ever be as difficult as this, but her conviction that she was right to have left him was absolute.

Laurence's voice suddenly punctured the silence. "Doesn't it bother you to know that he's been sleeping with Kirsten?" he snapped.

"Probably as much as it bothers you," she shot back.

"Then I take it you couldn't give a fuck," he shouted, his frustration manifesting itself in the tightness of his jaw and the clenching of his fists.

"You're wrong," she said, forcing herself to remain calm. It hadn't escaped her that for the second time in her life she was committing herself to a man who had loved Kirsten Meredith. Except, she reminded herself, Zaccheo hadn't loved Kirsten. He'd merely used her to while away the time until she, Pippa, arrived. "I do care," she went on. "But I can handle it. And shall I tell you why? Because Zaccheo hasn't lied to me about it. He's told me everything that happened between them, exactly what his feelings are for her, which is more than you've ever done, Laurence. More, I think, than you are capable of doing."

Laurence's temper exploded and before he could stop himself he had grabbed her up from the sofa and was shaking her so hard he felt he might crush her bones under his fingers. "You fool!" he groaned. "You bloody fool! You're destroying us, you're destroying everything we ever had because of some goddamned illusion. She's gone, do you hear me? Gone from my life, gone from my mind. . . . I don't have to talk about her, I don't have to tell you anything about her, because there's nothing to tell. Everything I have, everything I do, everything I am is for you. I don't feel the need to sleep with anyone else because I have all I want in you. Can Zaccheo tell you the same? Can you seriously believe he'll remain faithful to you? You know his reputation, for Christ's sake! Do you think that's going to change? Do you think you're so special you can—"

"Yes, Laurence," Zaccheo said, "she is that special."

Laurence swung around. As he did so Pippa wrenched herself free and staggered back against the sofa. Suddenly she cried out as Laurence advanced on Zaccheo. She ran after him, throwing herself between them at the very instant Laurence's fist flew through the air. It connected with the side of her head and she slumped to the floor.

Horrified, both Zaccheo and Laurence stared down at her for one moment frozen with shock. Laurence was the first to stoop, lifting her shoulders, cradling her head and frantically whispering her name.

Pippa's eyes blinked open. It was clear that the force of the blow had dazed her, but as she fought to focus on Laurence's face he felt as though his heart was being torn in two. Her expression, in those fleeting seconds before her eyes hunted around for Zaccheo, was one of profound regret and sad understanding.

"Pip, I'm sorry," he said helplessly. "Oh God, I'm so sorry."

"It's all right," she murmured, reaching a hand out to Zaccheo, who was kneeling on the other side of her. And, as she weakly strained toward him, Laurence's loss and grief expanded through his entire body.

Letting her go he eased himself back to his feet and stood staring down at them. Zaccheo was holding her now, engulfing her. He was murmuring to her in Italian, and as Pippa's fragile hand came up to stroke the wiry hair of his face Laurence had never felt more of an intruder in his life. He took a step back, hardly able to believe that it was his own wife he was watching turn to another man for comfort. His mind recoiled from the reality that their sudden togetherness showed him. This was how it would be from now on. It was this man who would hold his wife, who would love her and cherish her. It was to him she would turn for the love and laughter in her life. In his arms she would seek her happiness, and it would be for his heart that she would care.

His sense of defeat was almost crippling, but somehow Laurence managed to turn away, to walk across the room toward the door. Once again Tom's face flashed before his eyes, and as the overpowering need for his son engulfed him he felt the tears welling in his eyes. Somehow he would deal with this, somehow he would manage to hold himself together, but what about Tom? How was he ever going to explain to a three-year-old child that his Mummy had gone and was never coming back? That his Mummy just didn't love him enough to stay? But of course he would never tell Tom that.

He was already half out the door when he heard Pippa say his name. He turned back to see Zaccheo helping her to her feet.

"Laurence, I'm sorry," she whispered.

Laurence lowered his eyes and was about to walk on when she spoke again.

"I know right now you'll find this very hard to believe, but one day you'll thank me for this."

A grim smile crossed Laurence's mouth. "No, Pippa," he said, "you're wrong. And maybe one day you'll know just how wrong."

CHAPTER TWELVE

LAURENCE WOKE WITH A START, THE HAMMERING OF his heart and almost stifling breathlessness veering him away from the dizzying height of the dream. He was covered in sweat, his entire body rigid with the force of his desire. Something was digging into his side, and as he reached down to remove Tom's foot he heard himself groan at the excruciating ache in his loins.

His head fell back onto the pillows, his mind reeling with vivid recall. Only minutes before, in his dream, he had been plunging into her, holding her fullness against him, feeling the hardness of her nipples press into his chest. His hands had held the roundness of her hips, his fingers had dug into her flesh as she writhed beneath him, his mouth had sought to trap her breath, his penis had throbbed with indescribable desire. And still, in these first waking moments, his need was like a living creature. It trembled with its own pulse, shuddered with its own hunger, and gripped every fiber of his body so relentlessly that even to touch himself was to fire his craving again.

He stared into the darkness, looking at but not seeing the street lamps outside pool into the room. The light through the curtains cast strange patterns across his eyes, the sheets clung damply to his limbs, and the humid night air was suffocating.

He'd lost count now of how many nights he had woken this way, so submerged in the power of his body's need that even to move was torture. He could feel his hardness pulling ruthlessly at his groin, spreading its strength through his abdomen along his thighs and deep into his buttocks. His skin was alive with the sheer exquisiteness of it, and his sweat was like tears pushing through his pores, as though his whole body were crying in desperation for unattainable relief.

He waited, praying silently for the fire to leave him, for the soothing escape from such tension to steal through his limbs. Yet as his eyes closed he could see her again. With a will of their own his fingers moved as though to touch her, and the potency of her imagined presence gripped him anew. He wanted her, he craved her, he was a furnace of white hot need for her.

Of course he knew that all these things were magnified by the unnerving silence of the hour, that when he woke in the morning the nightmare would be all but forgotten. But lying here now, faced with the stark realities liberated by his subconscious he felt as though he were in a living hell. Yet what troubled him even more than the treacherous yearnings of his body, was the terrible conflict in his heart.

Just to think of her caused his heart to contract with feelings he had hidden from for so long he couldn't, even now, begin to face them. He turned and pulled

Tom gently against him, brushing his lips over the tender, sleep-flushed cheek that pressed against his. There was no room in his heart now for anyone but this child, his son whom he loved so much it hurt.

It had all happened such a long time ago, but he knew he would never forget that time, not as long as he lived. And even now, as he lay there in the darkness, he could feel the past embracing him, pulling him into the tortuous memories he'd tried so hard to forget.

It was two months after he'd left Kirsten for Pippa. He knew he was going back to her—he was going to end it with Pippa and go back to her. He'd made the decision even before she'd called him. He was going back because he loved her so much he couldn't live without her. He'd been on the point of calling her himself when the telephone had rung.

"Laurence," she'd said. "Laurence, it's me," and just to hear her voice, as exhausted as it was, had filled his heart so full that for a moment he'd been unable to speak.

"How are you?" he said.

For a long time there was only silence. Then in a voice so soft he barely heard her, she said, "I'm going to have a baby." And then she started to cry. "I feel so alone without you, Laurence," she sobbed. "Why can't I make myself believe you love someone else?"

"Kirsten, Kirstie, listen . . ." he said.

"You always wanted a baby so much," she went on. "You wanted to be a father, but I'm the wrong mother, aren't I?"

"No! Kirstie, listen to me—"

"Do you still want to be a father, Laurence?"

"Yes. Oh God! Look, stay right where you are, I'm coming round."

"No. Don't come. It hurts too much to see you. I just wanted to know if you wanted this baby."

"Yes, Kirsten," he said. "I want it very much."

She'd rung off then, but he'd gone immediately only to find she wasn't at home. He went to Paul's, but Paul didn't know where she was either. For three days the two of them had looked for her. Knowing how unbalanced she was, they were both frantic with worry, but no one had seen her and no one had heard from her.

She turned up on the fourth day. She was standing at the window of her apartment when he walked in, using the keys he'd never returned. He made instantly to go to her, but there was something about her that stopped him.

"I was about to call you." She smiled.

"Where have you been?" he asked. "We've been looking for you everywhere."

Her eyes were glittering in a way that sent a curl of alarm through him. "Were you worried about your baby, Laurence?" she said. "The baby with the wrong mother? Well you don't need to worry anymore. It's safe now."

He felt the color drain from his face even as the derangement contorted hers.

"I killed it, Laurence." She laughed. "I killed your baby. I had it scraped from my womb so that I have nothing left of you. But you wanted that baby, didn't you? I asked you and you said yes, you wanted it. So I killed it. I killed my baby and you made me do it."

She'd said so much more, but most of it was lost to

him now. All he really remembered was how pleased she had been at hurting him so much. Killing the baby was her revenge. She'd lost her mind, he'd known that at the time, just as he'd known that if ever she needed his help it was then, but he'd felt such bitterness, such frustration and anger that he wanted only to get as far away from her as he could. So he'd turned his back on her, returned to the calmness of his new life with Pippa and left Paul to pick up the pieces.

Now, as Tom stirred sleepily in his arms, Laurence could feel the tears on his cheeks. He knew, because he'd known for a long time now, that it was himself he couldn't forgive, not Kirsten; it was just that he hadn't been able to bring himself to face it. All these years he'd hated her for killing a baby that she had wanted even more than he had, but he hated himself more for being the cause of making her do that to herself. He knew her past, he knew what the abortion she had as a teenager had done to her, but instead of being there for her he had turned and walked away when she had needed him so desperately.

Through Paul he had learned of the depth of her suffering, and the more she had suffered the more he had hated her. She had filled his life with a guilt so consuming that there had been times he had thought it would destroy him. For years he had blamed her for a crime of which they were both guilty. But they hadn't been the only ones to pay the price; Dyllis Fisher had lost her husband and because of that Kirsten was still paying. She had nothing in her life now except the inheritance Paul had left her, whereas he, Laurence, had his son and his work.

Lifting himself carefully from the bed he went downstairs and poured himself a drink. Facing up to all these truths was neither pleasant nor easy, but he wasn't going to back away from it now.

It was as if his betrayal by Pippa had at last opened his eyes to what Kirsten had gone through. Only now could he think about what he'd had with her, in the time before . . . but no, he would not wallow in self-pity. He must find positive directions into which to channel his life now and one of the things he'd decided to do was to help Kirsten. Or at least it was partly his own decision, spurred on by the few words Zaccheo had said to him, that terrible night when he'd confronted him and Pippa in Tuscany: "You must help her, she is so special, so brave," knowing it would strike a chord with Laurence as with no other. Oh, he knew all of their motives were suspect: Zaccheo feeling uncharacteristic guilt whereas his were more complicated; misery at Pippa's leaving him turning to anger, even hate, the hate he now realized he'd once reserved for Kisten. He didn't want to think too much about that now. All he knew was that he could help Kirsten start a new life. He could do all the things for her now he should have done five years ago—except this time he couldn't love her. He could never do that again, not ever.

The question now, though, was would she let him help her? Suddenly he laughed. He knew her so well he could almost hear her response. As vulnerable and insecure as he knew she was, pride alone would make her refuse him. But he would persevere; he'd make her come work with him not only because he owed her, but because, he now realized, he wanted, maybe needed, her back in his life. It was the only way that either of them could exorcise the ghosts.

CHAPTER THIRTEEN

"LAURENCE! ARE YOU LISTENING TO ME? ARE YOU RE-ceiving me loud and clear? Good, because I don't want any misunderstandings over what I'm about to say. I'm not a charity case, and neither am I desperate, so we might just as well end this call right now."

"If you come to work for me I think we'd better get a few things straight," he said.

"Didn't you hear me, Laurence? I'm not coming to work for you. I know your ego is finding that difficult to accept, but try."

"Kirsten!"

"Don't shout at me, Laurence, I don't have a hearing problem."

"I know I'm not handling this too well, but look, I really am sorry about—"

"Forget it." And for the fifth time that day she slammed down the receiver and turned to Helena.

"That's three days he's been calling now," Helena remarked, "and I'm gonna say it again, you're going to blow it if you keep that up."

"Impossible," Kirsten answered. Then clapping a hand over her mouth she said, "Oh, sorry, did I forget to tell you? I don't want the job, I'm just enjoying myself making him suffer."

"What do you mean you don't want the job?" Helena cried. "You're hardly in a position to turn it down."

"You're beginning to sound like him," Kirsten commented.

"Kirstie! He obviously really wants you on that film and as far as I can see it that puts you at an advantage. And let me remind you again, this is a feature we're talking about. Big time."

Laughing, Kirsten flopped onto the sofa and stretched out her legs. "All right, I'll come clean," she said. "I will do it, I just think Laurence and I have a few things to iron out before I say yes. Like professionalism. I can't have him speaking to me or treating me any way he likes just because we were once lovers."

"And what about that side of things?" Helena asked carefully. "Do you think you can handle it?"

"I won't know until I try. It's not going to be easy, that's for sure."

"Maybe not for him either."

Kirsten moved restlessly. "Let's not discuss that," she said. "I wonder what Ruby Collins is like."

Helena didn't feel like telling her; Kirsten would find out soon enough what Ruby was like.

"Incidently," Kirsten said, "I called Jane this morning. She's coming over later if she can get away." She looked up. "You know, I was thinking, maybe we could try to do something about getting a little romance into her life."

"You've got enough to think about without playing Cupid for Jane." Helena laughed as she rose to look out the window at whoever was knocking on the door.

"You're right." Kirsten grimaced. "Like preparing myself for more bad publicity once Dermott Campbell finds out I'm working with Laurence. Come to think of it I wonder if Laurence has thought about that."

"Now's your chance to find out," Helena said, letting the curtain fall back into place.

"No, I don't want to discuss any of this with Jane," Kirsten said.

"It's not Jane." Helena grinned. "It's the man himself. And bearing gifts from what I could see."

Kirsten's heart did such an almighty somersault that whatever she'd been about to say never materialized.

"Well, do I let him in or don't I?" Helena laughed.

"I don't know. Let me think!" Kirsten was suddenly so agitated she didn't know whether to stand, sit, lie down, or scream. "Oh, for God's sake, let him in," she cried when he jammed his finger on the doorbell and kept it there.

As they slipped into their chairs in a dimly lit corner of the restaurant and a waiter handed them the menus, Kirsten was so nervous she knew she'd never be able to eat. However, she was going to try because tonight was the first test as to whether or not she could be around him and keep her feelings in check. If she couldn't, she would have to turn him down, but she wasn't going to allow herself to think about it too much. The enormity of what was happening would almost certainly overwhelm her if she dwelled on it.

"Okay," Laurence said, putting the menu down. "Did you choose yet?"

"I'll have the liver," Kirsten answered, folding away her menu.

"But I don't like liver," Laurence objected.

"Well it's not you who has to eat it," Kirsten declared. Then seeing the way his eyes were dancing she started to smile. Whenever they'd gone to dinner in the past she'd invariably ended up eating his food, leaving him with whatever she'd ordered. "It's okay, I'll eat it myself," she said coolly.

"Good. So, where do you want to start? We can go back over the past, say all the things—"

"No, I don't want to do that," Kirsten interrupted. "Let's just leave it where it is, shall we?"

Laurence looked at her for some time. "Okay," he said at last. "But any time you feel you—"

"No, honestly, I don't think it'll serve any purpose. We're colleagues now, not lovers. Let's operate on that level, shall we?"

He nodded slowly. "Sure," he said, glancing up as the waiter passed him the wine list. "Red or white?" he said to Kirsten.

"White."

"But you're having liver."

"I know."

"So you want red wine."

"Why did you ask me what color I want if you're going to make up my mind for me?"

"I'm not, I'm just saying—"

"Look, if it makes you happy I'll have red."

"No. You want white, you have white," and he ordered a 1979 white burgundy.

That done he sat back in his chair and surveyed her. At least that's what Kirsten thought he was doing until she realized that he was lost in thought.

"Shall I begin by telling you what ideas I've had?" she said, watching his eyes come back into focus.

He shook his head. "No. I'll begin by admitting that I've brought you here under false pretences."

Kirsten frowned. "I'm sorry," she said, her heart starting to thud. "I don't understand. I thought you wanted me on the film."

"I did," he answered, and Kirsten's heart plummeted at his use of the past tense. "I'm afraid," he went on, "there isn't going to be a film."

"What?" She waited as Laurence tasted the wine, then nodded for the waiter to pour. "Then what's all this about?" she said when the waiter had gone.

Laurence sighed heavily. "I'm not sure," he said. "I've been mulling it over in my mind all day and I reckon I've come up with a solution, but—"

"Laurence! Has Dyllis Fisher been on to you? I mean, how did she find out—"

"No, she hasn't been on to me," he interrupted. "But I guess she soon will be, unless . . ."

"Unless what? Laurence, will you please tell me what's going on."

"Willie Henderson, the director, pulled out today. He's also pulled out the money."

"But why? Did he give a reason?"

Laurence nodded. Then with a wry smile he said, "I

guess I better come clean here, 'cause if what I've got in mind is going to work you'll need to know what you're up against."

"A producer who's getting on my nerves is enough to be going on with," Kirsten remarked.

Laurence grinned, but it quickly faded. "Willie pulled out because he can't work with Ruby," he said. "I'm not going to lie to you; the lady's got a few problems."

"Show me a writer who hasn't," Kirsten remarked.

"Well, Ruby tries to solve hers in a bottle," Laurence said. "I know, show you a writer who doesn't. Trouble is, like a lot of writers, she's pretty touchy when it comes to other people putting in their ideas. And Willie just couldn't handle it. So now we're right back at the beginning, with a distribution deal providing we can raise the finance. And you and I both know we're not going to be able to do that while Dyllis Fisher is—"

"Then I'll pull out," Kirsten broke in. "I don't want you to lose this because of—"

"I had a better idea," Laurence said. "Now I want you to hear me out because it's pretty crazy, but I think, no, I know, it can work. But most of it depends on you."

Kirsten eyed him steadily. "Go on," she said.

"I want us to go into partnership for this movie," he said. "McAllister and Meredith, Meredith and McAllister, whichever way you want to play it. In other words, we form a production company and raise the money ourselves."

Kirsten blinked. "Do you mean personally?" she said.

He nodded.

"But we've got to be talking about over ten million sterling here."

"Eight. By using what capital I have, cashing in investments and mortgaging the house, I can put in close to four. I have no idea what your inheritance was—"

"My inheritance is in trust," Kirsten interrupted. "But I can always borrow against the income," she added, vaguely aware that her head was starting to spin.

"Can you raise as much as four million?"

"I don't know—until I try."

"Then you will try?"

"On the condition we dedicate *Moyna O'Malley* to Paul's memory," she answered, knowing that she was fast losing touch with reality.

"I don't have a problem with that," Laurence smiled.

They sat quietly then, toying with their food when it came and mulling things over in their minds. Kirsten could barely get herself to think straight. This was such a monumental step, not to mention risk, that for her at least it might as well be in Never-Never-Land. In fact she could hardly believe that the conversation had been so simple when what it entailed was so staggeringly complicated. But perhaps even more bewildering was this sudden about-face in Laurence. Having declared he never wanted her in his life again it seemed he was now prepared to tie her to him almost as effectively as if he were marrying her. She was about to speak when Laurence interrupted her.

"There's something else," he said.

"I haven't quite got used to the first bit yet," she said.

"I know, but I want you to consider the package I am proposing as a whole."

"I'm listening. I'm not sure I'm believing, but I'm listening."

"I don't want you to produce the movie, I want you to direct it."

Kirsten's fork clanged against her plate. "Laurence, is this some kind of a joke?" she declared. "I've never directed anything in my life, and you know it!" But despite her protest, despite the fact that he really might be playing with her, his words had already sent a tingle of excitement buzzing through her veins.

"But you and I both know that you've always wanted to direct," he said, smiling at the way her eyes were giving her away.

"But this is a feature film, Laurence. I've never even worked with thirty-five-millimeter, let alone directed it."

"I'm aware of that . . ."

"Plus the fact I've been off the scene for five years . . ."

"I know that too. But I still reckon you can do it."

"No," she said, shaking her head. "No, we have to get someone who knows what they're doing."

"Will you stop eating my food," Laurence complained. "I told you, I don't like liver."

Kirsten looked at him, nonplussed. He nodded for her to look down at his plate and only then did she realize that she'd started to reach across the table and fork up his lamb. She put her fork down and reached for her wine.

"We can discuss this as much as you like, right now," Laurence went on, "but if you'd like to take some time to think it over before we enter into negotiations . . ."

"But the crews, the budget, the cast, it's all so much

bigger than anything I've ever worked with," she protested.

"Sure. But that doesn't mean you can't handle it. And I'll be right there."

"Then why don't you direct it?"

"Because you could do it a lot better than I could. We both know you've got a real talent when it comes to the creative side of things, so why not use it where it really counts and take the credit for it?"

"Oh, God," Kirsten said, taking another gulp of her wine. He was right, this was something she had always dreamed of, but only to him and to Paul had she ever confided it. But nothing was this easy, nothing! What was she thinking of? It wouldn't be easy, it would be a damned nightmare—and she'd love every minute of it. And like he said, he'd be there, holding her hand every step of the way. . . . Her head came up.

"We'd fight," she declared. "We'd never see eye to eye . . ."

"You were prepared to take the risk if we produced together," he reminded her.

"But this is different. I'd want to shoot it my way and I know what you're like, Laurence. You'd undermine me in front of the crew—"

"The hell I would," he declared. "And since when have you not been able to stand up for yourself?"

"In a professional capacity? Never."

"Exactly. And that's what this is, a completely professional relationship."

"Partnership," she corrected.

"Does that mean you'll do it?"

"I want to give it some more thought."

"Okay. But should you agree I don't want to go public until you've arranged the loan with the bank. Get it signed and sealed first, then Dyllis won't have anyone to lean on to turn you down. And if she pressures them to call in the loan, we'll sue."

"We will?"

"We will."

Kirsten looked down at her barely touched food, still not too sure whether she was going to wake up any second and find herself back in Elm Park Gardens. "Laurence," she said, lifting her eyes back to his, "why are you doing this? I mean, does it have something to do with the past? Are you . . ."

"Everything about us is to do with the past, Kirstie," he said softly. "But as of now we're going to change that."

As she looked back at him in the flickering glow of the candlelight her heart was so full that for a moment she was afraid to speak. "Okay, then," she said, picking up her glass. "Let's drink to us and to a great future as partners."

"I guess that must mean you've done that thinking you mentioned," Laurence teased.

When he dropped her at her house later, he said, "Get a good night's sleep. You're going to need it because it's going to be one rough road from here on in."

But just how rough neither of them could ever have begun to imagine.

CHAPTER FOURTEEN

EVERYTHING SEEMED TO BE HAPPENING WITH LIGHTning speed. Neither Kirsten nor Laurence had wasted any time in contacting their banks, lawyers, and accountants, and at the offices they had taken in Windmill Street, preproduction and recruitment were already—just five weeks after their dinner—going ahead in earnest. In fact there was barely room for everyone in the six-room suite on the fourth floor of the old Victorian building.

The place was in sore need of a lick of paint, but now that schedule boards, cast and crew lists, first-draft graphics, photographs, telephone lists, and a thousand other things were finding their way onto the walls, the peeling paint was barely noticeable. Production managers, accountants, line producers, production secretaries, and location managers had all moved into the two larger offices; the casting directors and assistants were just along the hall in what had probably once been a very grand bedroom; the unit publicist and her team were next to casting, and at the end of the hall was Kirsten and Laurence's office, which adjoined a small attic-type enclave that served as a screening room and a place to receive the satellite link-ups with New Orleans when they auditioned the American cast. Their personal assistants were in the hall itself, along with four spare desks for the costume and makeup designers, stunt arrangers, and film crew to use when necessary. The drive and excitement was such that no one found time to complain about the lack of space, but if they needed more, those who could simply worked from home or took themselves off to Alison's design offices, which she had leased just around the corner in Colville Place.

Kirsten's time was split mainly between Ruby, Alison, and Jake, the director of photography. Jake, with his boyish good looks and incorrigible eye for the ladies, was someone with whom Laurence had worked in the past—as indeed were most of the team—and it was only with Jake that Kirsten had so far managed to build up a rapport. On the first two recces to Ireland, where the shoot would begin, Jake had come up with a number of ideas that so excited Kirsten she had, much to Ruby's annoyance, incorporated them into the script without consulting Ruby first. Of course it was an unforgivable and stupid thing to have done, which had not surprisingly earned Kirsten Laurence's wrath as well as Ruby's. Okay, the ideas might be good, he'd told her, but Jake was the lighting cameraman not the writer and though Kirsten might think the sun shone out of Jake's ass, she damned well better get used to the idea that any and all script changes were to be discussed with Ruby first. Suitably chastened, though extremely indignant that Laurence should speak to her that way when she knew he wouldn't with another director, Kirsten took herself off to deal with Ruby, whose protests turned out to be as loud as they were justified. But in general, Ruby's outbursts were nowhere near so frequent as Kirsten had expected them to be and when they did come, usually it was because Ruby really did believe she was right. Kirsten could only guess at how hard Laurence was working to get Ruby to accept her, though Ruby's animosity wasn't only directed at Kirsten. It seemed that any woman who was unwise enough to show an interest in Laurence was treated to Ruby's outbursts. With Laurence himself she was all smiles, hearty kisses, and pats on the head. In fact, were it not for Laurence's wry humor, coupled with his embarrassment at what he was having to endure, Ruby could quite easily have turned him into a laughing stock. But her visits to the office were mercifully rare, and on the whole the changes she was making to the script, at Kirsten's instigation, were so impressive that Kirsten would have been prepared to put up with her hostility throughout the entire movie.

However, quite unexpectedly, Kirsten managed a breakthrough of her own. It came about when she was at Ruby's flat one afternoon and happened to open a photograph album lying on the coffee table. When Ruby came into the room, toting a tray of coffee and biscuits, Kirsten hurriedly closed the album, apologizing for the intrusion. But Ruby simply set down her tray and opened the album again. Her pride in the way she had looked in her earlier years was so evident and brought about such a change in her as she gazed wistfully down at the undeniable beauty of the face that had once been hers that Kirsten was moved to ask about her life on the catwalks. Perfectly sober Ruby waxed lyrical for the entire afternoon, each photograph having its own story to tell, each memory softening the harsh lines that pinched Ruby's mouth. The sun had long since set by the time Ruby closed the album—they had done no work that day, at least not on the script—but Kirsten knew that it had been one of the most valuable days they had passed so far. Ruby even asked her to stay for a gin and tonic, prolonging her stay until the early hours of the morning. She had found Ruby's Achilles' heel and it was one she could make work for them both.

This wasn't to say that Ruby became in any way pliable, but at least the script debates that followed were no longer filled with the bitter resentment and jealousy Kirsten had encountered before. In fact, Kirsten was coming to enjoy her exchanges with Ruby, for when Ruby was sober her mind was so acute, her ideas so innovative, that it not only kept Kirsten on her toes, but served to engender a respect for Ruby that Kirsten hadn't at all thought to find. Kirsten only wished that she herself could get the same respect from the ever-expanding production team.

It wasn't that everyone was set against her, but those who really mattered were dishearteningly influenced by the things Dermott Campbell was writing in his column. Laurence rarely commented on it, but Kirsten knew that Campbell's accusations that she had managed to bewitch Laurence into giving her a position for which she was in no way qualified irritated him as much as it did her. In fact, Kirsten wasn't too sure if that was what made Laurence so moody with her. Or was it, she worried constantly, that Laurence was now regretting the rashness of persuading her to take on something that everyone else was convinced was totally beyond her.

But no matter what anyone else thought, Kirsten knew she was going to succeed. The fact that Alison and her art directors, the line producers, and production managers always took their queries or problems to Laurence when they should have been coming to her was something she was just going to have to suffer until she proved herself. Laurence invariably rerouted them to her, but their lack of cooperation was as wearing as it was infuriating. She didn't want to discuss it with Laurence because she didn't want him to think she couldn't cope. Besides, if she couldn't hack it here in the office, then what chance was she going to stand once they were out in the field? Just thank God for Jake, who not only was fully aware of what was going on, but flatly refused to tolerate it from his crew. And the support of the camera crew once they were out there was going to be as necessary as film in the camera.

There was one other person who was proving a godsend and that was Vicky, Kirsten's personal assistant. She was the only member of the team Kirsten had hired herself and in her own inimitable fashion managed to organize Kirsten's busy schedule. Like Jake, Vicky succeeded in keeping Kirsten's spirits buoyant just when she wanted to throw up her hands and scream or fall to her knees and weep. In fact Vicky, who was as pretty and lighthearted as she was efficient, had worked for Kirsten on the drama that had won Kirsten a BAFTA, so even if no one else had known Kirsten at her best, at least Vicky had. But even if the others had known Kirsten then, there was no getting away from the fact that

Kirsten's success had been in TV and that held sway with no one. Stripes had to be earned in the world of features or they were no stripes at all, and that, even more than Campbell's attacks, was what really lay at the root of the problem.

Still, it wasn't all bad, she reminded herself when she tucked herself up in bed at night. She couldn't have wished for a greater challenge and neither would she have dared to hope that her self-confidence would turn out to be her greatest ally. Things were beginning to take shape, the script was exciting everyone, and the casting, by now almost complete, was terrific. There was only one part on which she and Laurence couldn't see eye to eye and that was the part of the Irish heroine, Moyna O'Malley. Laurence wanted Anna Sage, who was, to Kirsten's mind, too young for the part and far too pretty. She had the talent to carry it off, Kirsten conceded, but she looked wrong. They'd tested her, and though the wigs, makeup, and costume had undoubtedly helped, she still didn't quite work for Kirsten. Laurence had ended up storming out of the screening room, not uttering a word, but obviously furious at her stubborness.

In fact the tension between Kirsten and Laurence was growing by the day, and Kirsten knew that it wasn't only professional disagreements that were causing it. It was the proximity they shared that seemed to be creating the real difficulties. Their office, at the back of the building, gave them the privacy they needed in order to work—which was of course precisely what they did. But all too often the need to sit closer together, or to lean over the other's shoulder as something was being explained, would create an atmosphere of such acute awareness of one another that it required a superhuman effort on Kirsten's part to keep cool. To her annoyance he seemed to sense her tension, and although it could easily make him irritable with her it could also, though rarely, bring a teasing lilt to his voice and a softness to his eyes that was in its way so intimate and so compelling it was as though he were stealing into her with all the potency of a lover.

Kirsten smiled sleepily to herself as she turned over, hugging the pillow. It was inevitable that part of her was now daring to hope that eventually they would get back together. She was exhilarated by the unsteady beats of her heart when she watched him taking charge, when she felt his presence as though he were touching her, when she heard his laughter and felt herself almost melt at the incredible intensity of his blue eyes, yet in a way she was terrified. For, as intransigent as her confidence might appear to others, she knew how reliant it was on Laurence for its strength. That in itself told her that it had been a mistake to take this on, but it was too late now to back out, not that she would have dreamed of doing so; it was just that her nervousness that he might do something to hurt her emotionally was hard to shake. She knew she was in danger of becoming paranoid, but Anna Sage's resemblance to Pippa was as unsettling as Laurence's determination to cast her. And Anna's obvious attraction to Laurence on the few occasions she and Laurence had met with her irked Kirsten in a way that only added to her unease. Laurence couldn't be ignorant of the likeness although he'd never mentioned it, not even when a couple of weeks ago Dermott Campbell had run with the headline "Kirstie Doll snubs wife look-alike." Kirsten knew that Laurence hadn't spoken to Campbell himself but had instructed the publicists to handle the situation; then he personally got on the phone to Anna to laughingly tell her not to believe everything she read in the papers and invited her to lunch to—as he put it—explain the situation. Exactly what explanation he'd given her Kirsten had no idea, and neither would she ask.

She sighed heavily as she reminded herself of how against relationships on the set Laurence was. It was small comfort. So too was the flirtation she had started up with Jake. She couldn't deny that she enjoyed the attention, almost as much as she did the sour looks it provoked from Laurence, but in truth she was doing herself no favors and she knew it. Everyone on the movie had read enough about her in the press to know that she'd slept her way to the top once, so as far as they were concerned she was doing it again. What they made of her relationship with Laurence she had no idea, but her friendship with Jake had reached Campbell's ears and so too had the arrival of Jean-Paul, the quirkily handsome Frenchman who was playing Moyna's lover and conspirator in crime. He had flown into London the previous day and spent the evening with Kirsten. If only, Kirsten thought to herself, she could get her hands on whoever was giving Campbell his information, she'd . . . she'd . . . well, she didn't know what she'd do, but whatever it was it wouldn't be pleasant.

Wearily she reached into the darkness for the ringing telephone. It was just before one in the morning she noticed on the bedside clock as she said hello.

No one answered.

"Hello," she said again, feeling her nerve ends start to prickle. Had she not been half-asleep the unease might have reached her sooner, for this wasn't the first time her telephone had rung at this hour bringing an anonymous presence into the privacy of her darkened room. "Hello," she repeated.

Still there was only silence. But someone was there; she could hear them breathing.

"Hello, who is this?" Kirsten said, her heart starting to thud as she sat up and flicked on the light.

More silence, but as she listened Kirsten thought she could make out the distant tinkling sound of music. She pressed the receiver closer to her ear. It was a gentle, comforting sound, like a musical mobile used to lull a baby to sleep.

"Hello," she said again. "Hello."

The line clicked and the whine of the dial tone replaced the silence.

A week later Kirsten was on a flight back from Dublin giving an interview to a freelance reporter who was doing a piece for *Screen International* and whose only chance of fitting herself into Kirsten's schedule was to accompany her on this flight.

"So," Kirsten was saying, "once John Rochette, that's the character Jean-Paul Feneau is playing, has successfully lured Moyna away from famine-torn Ireland—"

"But it's in Ireland that he first introduces her to prostitution, is that right?" the reporter interrupted.

"That's right." Kirsten rolled her eyes at Jake, who was sitting on the other side of the woman; she'd just been over all that had happened in Ireland. "Moyna has become a prostitute because it was the only way she got to eat. Rochette exploits that need by getting her to perform for him and his cronies, but he inadvertently manages to fall in love with her. She hates him for the way he's exploited her but can't help falling for him too. So right from the start theirs is a stormy relationship based as much on love and lust as it is on greed and hatred."

"Greed?"

"Rochette is a thief—"

"Ah, yes, but a lovable one?"

"Not at first, no," Kirsten answered, wanting to ask the woman if she ever listened to anything. "The point is he's perfectly detestable when we first meet him, and we, the audience, fall in love with him gradually, the way Moyna does."

"And that happens when they get to New Orleans?"

"Yes."

"So what takes them to New Orleans?"

"Rochette's brother, who's making quite a go of his blackmail business out there. Rochette kidnaps Moyna and takes her with him. When they get there Moyna manages to escape and loses herself in the—"

"Have you visited New Orleans yet?"

"No. But Ruby Collins, the writer, knows the town well and has made several return visits these past couple of months. The rest of us are going at the end of next week."

"I see. Okay, so Moyna loses herself . . ."

". . . and finds sanctuary with a Spanish school mistress, Conchita Sanchez. Conchita turns out to be the mayor's mistress. The mayor is one of the Rochette brother's blackmail victims, and to make a convoluted story simple, that's how Moyna once again runs into John Rochette. By now John Rochette has made himself quite at home in the seamier districts of New Orleans and is dabbling in voodoo with the priestess Marie Laveau."

"Helena Johnson is playing that role, am I right?"

"Yes."

"So will you be shooting any voodoo ceremonies?"

"Yes. Rochette gets Moyna involved in voodoo and in turn Moyna gets the young pupils from Conchita's school involved. They think the whole thing is a lark until one of the boys tells Conchita and Conchita throws Moyna out. Moyna goes back into prostitution, Rochette is her *maquereau*—"

"Her what?"

"Her pimp. Marie Laveau is her friend and together they decide that Moyna should open a brothel. Having developed a fondness for the teenage boys at Conchita's school, Moyna encourages them to visit the brothel to learn the art of love. Many of the town's prominent figures become regular clients too, which boosts the Rochettes' blackmail business, and Moyna entices rich ladies' maids to supplement their incomes by playing hostesses at the brothel. Marie Laveau quizzes the maids about their mistresses' private lives and uses the information to increase her air of mystery by telling these women their most intimate secrets as though she had read their minds. This way she also increases the number of her disciples, but really it is the young boys from Conchita's school she is after—they are the town's next generation of influential businessmen and politicians.

Remember, neither Rochette nor Moyna are educated people, so the story from their point of view is on the whole a comic one, but there is the sinister side which comes from their involvement with Marie Laveau. In fact it's not until one of the young boys is found floating in a bayou one morning and Rochette is accused of his murder that Moyna and Rochette finally realize that they're into something deeper than they can handle. They run. They're caught and taken back to New Orleans where Rochette is tried and sentenced to hang. With her girls Moyna concocts a way of getting him out of prison and they run again. They know someone is after them, but this time it appears to be only one man. Neither of them ever catch sight of him, until one morning at dawn when they are taking refuge in a deserted hut deep in the Louisiana swamplands he turns up. Rochette isn't there, he's out trying to find food. Moyna is asleep on a makeshift bed and doesn't realize until the man starts to attack her that it isn't Rochette who's come in. She struggles but to no avail. The man leaves and when Rochette returns he finds Moyna dead."

"Dead?" the reporter gasped.

"Yes. She's been strangled," Kirsten said matter-of-factly. "Rochette is hunted down. He stands trial for Moyna's murder and is once again sentenced to hang."

"So does he hang?"

"Yes."

"You mean the bad guys are going to win?"

Kirsten grinned. "You'll have to watch the film and find out, won't you?" she said, looking at Jake, who was trying very hard not to laugh, and gathering up her things she prepared to disembark.

"I thought for one minute there you were going to leave her up the garden path," Jake remarked as they left the plane and the reporter was whisked away by a publicity assistant.

"Now would I do something like that?" Kirsten said, all innocence. "Poor thing, she'd never find her way back. Anyway, what I want to know is why *I* had to tell her the story when the publicist should already have given her a press release. Telling it cold like that never works."

"So young Lisa's in for a bollocking, is she?" Jake grinned, his brown eyes dancing the challenge.

"Don't mock me," Kirsten warned. "I'll get around to sounding off one of these days, believe me—"

"Here, let me carry that," Jake interrupted, as Kirsten moved her heavy bag from one shoulder to the other.

"It's okay, I can manage," she said, but he'd already taken it from her. "Ah, such chivalry." She laughed. "You wouldn't have done that if I were a man."

"There are a lot of things I wouldn't do if you were a man," Jake responded, "and before you get on your high horse I apologize for the sexist remark. It's just that you bring out the macho beast in me."

"Well, just so long as the macho beast remembers to be a director of photography when the time is called for."

"He will. But I don't suppose he can take a beautiful woman to dinner tonight, can he, and forget for a while that he's really a DP and you're really a director."

Kirsten laughed. "Okay, why not? These past three days have been pretty grueling racing around the Irish countryside. I guess we could all do with some relaxation."

"I wasn't planning to take the whole unit," Jake objected.

"And I wasn't planning for them to come."

"Kirsten," David said, catching up with them, "could we go over the walk-on list again on the way into London?"

"Yes, of course," Kirsten said readily. She didn't mind how many times they went over it as long as he discussed it with her and not Laurence. Though it was probably only because Laurence wasn't on this recce that David was speaking to her now. Still, once they got going the pompous David was going to have no choice but to discuss things with her—and he was going to damn well listen when she spoke, jump when she said jump . . .

"Hey, what do you mean, on the way into London?" Jake suddenly cried. "My need is greater, more pressing, and since I'm more senior I get to drive her."

"Jake, for heaven's sake," Kirsten said, glancing uncomfortably at David as the three of them were swallowed up by the crowd in the arrivals hall.

"Actually, I get to drive her."

Kirsten spun around and found herself face-to-face with Laurence. "Laurence!" she gasped. "Where did you come from? I didn't know . . . You didn't say you . . ."

"I'll take that," Laurence said, taking Kirsten's bag from Jake, and without uttering another word he turned and started out of the terminal.

"If he weren't the producer I'd smack him one for the way he always cramps my style," Jake muttered.

Kirsten laughed uneasily. "Looks like we'll have to take a rain check on dinner," she said, her eyes still on Laurence.

"I'll keep you to that," Jake said, but Kirsten wasn't listening. She'd have liked to think that Laurence's foul temper stemmed from seeing her clown around with Jake, but she knew instinctively that it was nothing so trivial. In fact if it had brought him out here to the airport she could only conclude that it must be pretty serious.

"Just quit hassling me for what this is about," Laurence said, signaling and pulling from the slip road onto the M4, "and tell me about Ireland. Did you settle on Killua Castle?"

"Yes," Kirsten answered, "and I'll give you a full report as soon as you've explained why you came to the airport—"

"Did David work out yet how many days you're going to need at the castle?" Laurence interrupted, pressing his foot harder onto the accelerator and steering his black Mercedes into the fast lane.

"Twelve, I think he said—four of those will be night shoots. And before you ask, I'm going over the walk-on list with him again and the total is somewhere around one fifty. Now, will you please tell me exactly why you're in such a vile mood—"

"It can wait till we reach the office," he said with a finality that made Kirsten want to scream.

"Laurence," she said through gritted teeth, "I am not a

child and I deeply resent you turning up like this and behaving as though—"

"I wanted to be sure you didn't pick up a newspaper before I had a chance to stop you," he said, flashing his headlights so the driver in front would pull over.

Kirsten paled as she turned to look at him. "What do you mean? What's happened?"

"You can read it for yourself once we get to the office, then I'll be asking *you* for some explanations," he said, keeping his eyes straight ahead.

"Is it . . . ? Does it have something to do—"

"With the movie, yes. With you personally, no," he interrupted.

"For God's sake, Laurence, stop doing this!" she cried. "I'm not in the mood for guessing games."

"Then stop trying and talk to me about Ireland."

Some forty minutes later they walked into the office. It was past six o'clock, but there were still people around. Laurence stopped to speak to one of the accountants while Kirsten went on ahead to their office hoping to find a newspaper, but what she found instead was something she was totally unprepared for.

For several seconds she merely stood in the doorway watching the little boy who was happily tapping away on a computer keyboard. With his curly black hair, thick dark lashes, and deep blue eyes he was so like Laurence there couldn't, even for a moment, be any mistaking who he was, and for one horrible moment, as her heart contracted painfully, Kirsten wanted to run. But it wasn't only that he was such a beautiful child that was causing her to back away from him, it was the fact that she was only now realizing that Laurence had very likely been keeping him away from her deliberately. He was prepared to work with her, to support and encourage her, but she could see now what a distance he had kept from her. His son was the very core of his life and not once had he ever discussed him with Kirsten, neither had he even mentioned Tom to anyone in front of her.

She was about to slip away quietly when Tom looked up from the keyboard. For an instant he seemed frightened, as though he had been caught doing something wrong.

Kirsten smiled shakily.

Tom continued to look at her.

"Hello," she said softly.

His eyes grew wider.

"Are you Tom?" she said, her heart pounding in her ears.

He nodded, uncertainly. "This is my Daddy's," he said pointing to the keyboard.

Again Kirsten smiled but had to bite her lip to stop it from trembling. "Does Daddy know you're here?" she said.

"I came on the bus with Jane," he answered.

"And where's Jane now?"

"She's gone to the toilet. Can I ring someone up?" he asked, trying to reach the telephone.

"Please," Jane corrected him, coming in behind Kirsten.

"Please?" Tom repeated looking at Kirsten.

Kirsten nodded and walking forward handed him the receiver. "Who are you going to call?" she asked.

"My Mummy."

Again Kirsten's smile wavered. "Hello Jane," she said turning to her. "How are you?"

"Oh, I'm fine," Jane said, shrugging as awkwardly as ever. "This is Kirsten, Tom." She went over to the little boy. "I told you we might meet her today, didn't I? He wanted to see where Laurence worked," she explained to Kirsten.

Tom's eyes suddenly lit up and he was out of the chair like a shot, leaving the telephone dangling. "Daddy!" he shouted.

Laurence swept him up in his arms, turned him upside down, then raised him up to kiss him. "What are you doing here?" He laughed into Tom's up-turned face. "I thought you were going to Granny's."

"I went on a bus," Tom told him.

"Did you, now?" Laurence said, swinging him around so that he was sitting in the crook of his arm. "Was it good?"

Kirsten hardly knew what they were saying; all she could feel were Laurence's eyes on hers, as she somehow kept the smile on her face.

"Jane," Laurence said, "take Tom out into the production office, will you?"

Tom started to protest, but Laurence assured him there were lots of treats in store out there, and setting him down he stood aside as Jane led the way out, then closed the door behind them.

"Are you okay?" he said to Kirsten.

"Yeah, yes, I'm fine," she answered.

"You don't look it."

"Well, I suppose it was just . . . Well, the shock . . .

He's so like you . . ." Tears were burning so painfully in her eyes and her heart was so filled with emotion, she could barely speak.

"Hey, come on," Laurence said, putting his arm around her shoulder. "I know what's happening . . ."

"No, don't, please," Kirsten said, trying to pull herself away.

"Kirstie . . ."

"Oh, God, Laurence, it hurts so much," she sobbed.

"I know," he whispered. "I've been trying to think of the right way for you to meet him. I knew it wouldn't be easy for you. . . ."

"He's wonderful," Kirsten said, her voice muffled by his shoulder, her senses drowning in the belovedly familiar smell of him.

"Yeah, well I kind of like him." Laurence smiled, pushing her back so he could look at her.

"Oh, God, what an idiot I'm making of myself," Kirsten groaned, pulling away.

"Hey, listen," Laurence said, catching her hand, "I understand how you're feeling. And I told you, any time you want to talk about it . . ."

"No amount of talking is ever going to change what I did . . ."

"Kirstie, you've got to let it go, stop hurting yourself . . ."

"I've tried," she said, "but it's not easy. And seeing Tom . . . Oh, God, what am I saying? I'm sorry, I'll be all right in a minute."

Laurence dropped her hand, but he was aware of how the need to say more was almost choking him. Worse though was the feel of her still burning through his body. Sure he wanted her, he'd never deny that, but he didn't love her and it would be wrong of him to give her any hope in that direction when they had so much at stake here. He wished to God Jane hadn't brought Tom even though he knew that Kirsten would have had to meet him sooner or later; he'd just wanted it to be later. Having her around his son was going to be difficult to handle, for him as well as for her.

Abruptly he turned and walked out the door. He'd give her a while to collect herself while he got someone to drive Jane and Tom home. They had a pressing matter to discuss tonight, but as mad as he was about it he knew already he was going to go easier on her than he might have done if Tom hadn't shown up.

Fifteen minutes later Kirsten and Laurence were sitting at their desks with the door closed. Kirsten had by now finished reading the article about Helena in that morning's paper and was looking at Laurence, waiting for him to comment.

"Did you know?" he asked.

Kirsten nodded.

"Then don't you think you should have told me?"

"I would have if I'd thought this was going to happen," she answered.

"You realize that we'll have to pay her off and recast."

"But why? It all happened such a long time ago."

"The story's right here in today's paper," he reminded her. "And how's it going to look once we come to shoot the scenes in New Orleans, scenes that involve boys the same age, when we've got someone notorious for her affairs with boys playing the part."

Kirsten knew he was right. She also knew she didn't

have much of an argument except to say that Marie Laveau was a voodoo priestess not a pedophile. Helena's participation in scenes where young boys were procured from school was enough. With a weary irony Kirsten recalled how she had once slept with the head of drama in order to safeguard Helena's job—that wasn't going to work this time, Laurence would never be so easily coerced. But even if he could be, she was in no doubt that it would have to be someone else who did the coercing, for never had he seemed more unapproachable than he did now. It was strange how those few moments of intimacy had dissolved the barrier between them, and yet he now seemed to resent her for breaking down in front of him. And right now she was so tired and so confused all she wanted was to go home.

"I can't help wondering why this story should have broken now," she said.

"The cast list was published yesterday. With your agreement to Anna Sage I saw no reason to hold it back."

"So it would seem that Campbell has been waiting in the wings. . . . I mean, he couldn't have got that story together overnight."

"No."

"So it's not just me he's out to destroy it would seem, it's Helena too."

"It would seem that way."

"But you're prepared to put up with what he writes about me? Why not this?"

"This is different."

"So, we give in to him and fire Helena. Who will he go for next?"

"Kirsten, Helena Johnson went into a boy's boarding

school to research the role of a school mistress for a BBC play. While she was there, under total trust of the school authorities, she seduced, corrupted it says here, a fifteen-year-old pupil. Not once, not even twice, but repeatedly. She got that boy so mixed up and so crazy for her that when the authorities found out, they expelled him and he hanged himself. Now tell me, how in God's name, can you defend that when we're going to have her working with boys the same age?"

"I'm not trying to defend it, I'm just asking you to help her put her past behind her, the way you have with me."

"I am not a charity, Kirsten."

"And neither are you perfect, you supercilious bastard. Don't you think she's paid for that? How many nights do you think she's lain awake thinking about that boy and dying inside for what he did to himself? Do you honestly think she intended that to happen?"

"She was a grown woman. He was just a boy."

"So you're going to throw Helena out and let Campbell win?"

"It's not a point of letting him win. It's a point of what this is going to do to the movie. I know she's a friend of yours and I appreciate that you want to help her, but she's got to go, Kirsten."

"She's set her heart on this, Laurence. She hasn't worked in over four years—"

"I'm sorry, but I can't help that."

"But that boy's suicide happened over fifteen years ago! I know," she said with a sigh, "it's in the paper today . . ."

"And it will continue to be in the paper as long as we

keep her on. Is that what you want for her? Do you want people walking out of the movie because they're revolted at seeing her with teenage boys . . ."

"There has to be a way round it," Kirsten said helplessly.

"Well if there is let me know and I'll consider it. You've got twenty-four hours."

But the following morning when Kirsten arrived late in the office, having been to see Helena to explain that on this occasion there really was nothing she could do to save her, Laurence was waiting with the news that Helena was to stay on the cast.

". . . and he just refuses to tell me what happened to change his mind," Kirsten said to Helena that night. "I mean, it doesn't make sense. He was so dead set against it and now . . . Well, I guess we shouldn't knock it."

"I'll tell you what happened," Helena said staring down at her drink.

"You mean you've spoken to Laurence?"

Helena shook her head. "No, to Dermott Campbell. He was here last night." She gave a sad and bitter laugh. "He came to apologize, can you believe that? He actually thought I'd forgive him."

"What! Was he drunk?"

"Very." Again the same dry and cheerless laugh. "That guy has to be some kind of fruitcake to think I could ever forgive what he's done. But I can't help wondering what that makes me for going to bed with him."

Kirsten blinked, opened her mouth to speak, then closed it again. Her eyes started to hunt the shadowy room, moving over the untidy rows of paperbacks, the cheap abstract art, the old-fashioned hi-fi, the tiled grate with its gas fire. She looked back to Helena. Her head was still bowed, her hands were circled around the stem of her glass, her wiry hair sat dejectedly in a knot at the nape of her neck.

"He told me he loved me," Helena whispered as a solitary tear splashed onto the table. "How can he love me when he did what he did?"

"He used you to get to me," Kirsten answered.

"It would seem so." The desolation that emanated from Helena was almost unbearable. It was so rare to see her like this that somehow it made it seem all the more tragic.

"He called Laurence last night, from here," Helena said tonelessly. "He told Laurence that if he didn't keep me on he'd go to Dyllis Fisher with the story about how you and Laurence broke up."

"Jesus Christ," Kirsten murmured. "How on earth did he find out about that?"

"I got no idea. All I know is that Laurence told him to go to hell, but obviously Laurence has given it some more thought. . . . My guess is Laurence wants to protect you."

"More likely his investment," Kirsten joked half-heartedly.

"Yeah, that too. But he can't afford for that kind of story to be spread across the papers, at least not the way Dyllis Fisher would tell it, and with this scandal of mine too . . . Don't you see, one way or another it's all to do with children. People don't take well to horror stories about children."

"God, just what kind of a man is Dermott Campbell," Kirsten muttered. "He calls himself a friend of Laurence's, he tells you he loves you . . ."

"He's totally fucked up, that's what he is," Helena said. "Like me, I guess."

"Come on. You're not fucked up, you're just—"

"Kirsten, I went to bed with a guy who's just destroyed my career. Who's quite effectively seen to it that I can hardly show my face in the street again. If that's not fucked up then tell me what is?"

"What made you do it?"

"Loneliness, what do you think?"

"It must have been more than that."

"Yeah. I fancy him. Now that's seriously fucked up, wouldn't you say?"

Kirsten was on the point of reminding her that she'd never gone for men his age before, but under the circumstances thought better of it. "Are you seeing him again?" she asked.

"I don't know."

"Do you want to?"

"I don't know that either." She let go of her glass and dropped her head in her hands. "Oh, God, Kirstie, I've made such a mess of my life, and nothing I do seems to change it."

"You're still on the film," Kirsten reminded her gently.

Helena shook her head. "There's no way I can do it now and you know it."

"Laurence and I have already spoken to Ruby about putting a different slant on your character. There won't be any scenes with children, if that's what's bothering you."

"Isn't it what's bothering you?"

"Of course. That's why we're changing it. We want you with us, Helena."

"You might, but Laurence is being forced to accept me. I can't work like that."

"I'm going to call him," Kirsten said, getting to her feet. "I'll let him speak to you himself, because he'll put what he has to say much better than I can."

"Oh, shit, I don't think I'm up to speaking to him right now," Helena groaned. "No, no," she said as Kirsten started to dial. "I think you'd better sit down and hear the rest of it before you do that. You might change your mind."

"What do you mean, the rest of it?" Kirsten said, an uneasy sensation stealing over her.

"The rest of it is, that it was me who gave Dermott Campbell his information about your rise to the top."

"You," Kirsten said incredulously, sliding back into her chair.

"I did it to stop him printing his story about me," Helena said, her voice starting to break. "I guess you could say he blackmailed me into it. And I asked myself which was worse, that the story about James Scott came out or that your reputation got damaged. I thought you could weather the storm better than me, so, I told Campbell what he wanted to know."

"Including what I did when Laurence and I broke up?" Kirsten said, incredulous that this conversation was even happening.

"No. I swear I never told him that. I don't know who

did either. He won't tell me. But I guess keeping that to myself isn't enough to make you forgive me for doing what I did, and don't worry, I won't hold it against you if you don't."

Kirsten sat quietly for a long time going over everything in her mind. It was almost laughable really, to think that all the time she had been trying to protect herself from being hurt by Laurence she'd had just as much to fear from Helena. In a different way, of course, but what was this thing Helena had going with Campbell?

She took a sip of wine and tried to shake off the encroaching feeling of isolation. That her best friend should be responsible for the difficulties she was having now was hardly conceivable, and if it hadn't been Helena herself who was telling her, she doubted she would have believed it. But she had to ask herself, if she had been in Helena's shoes with the history of James Scott hanging over her, wouldn't she have done the same thing? She honestly didn't know the answer to that. Loyalty was something she put great store by, but with all that had happened to her, didn't she put even more by self-preservation?

"I guess it's too late to say I'm sorry," Helena croaked, and as her eyes moved from Kirsten's to a distant place in her mind Kirsten sensed the same isolation wrapping itself around Helena. She too was on the point of losing her best friend, but unlike Kirsten she had no career to turn to now, neither did she have the comfort of someone doing his best to shield her the way Laurence was shielding Kirsten.

"No, it's not too late," Kirsten said, reaching out for

Helena's hand. "We need each other, Helena. We've been through a lot together, we can weather this too."

"Oh, God," Helena gasped, swallowing hard on the lump in her throat as her fingers tightened around Kirsten's. "I don't deserve you, Kirstie."

"What you don't deserve is what Campbell's done to you," Kirsten told her. "And you don't deserve to lose the film either. Now I'm going to call Laurence and let him tell you himself what he's done today to make it possible for you to stay."

"No, you tell me."

"Okay. But remember, this is Laurence's doing, not mine. I know he was pushed into it, but he wants you for that part every bit as much as I do. I'm telling you that so you know that we're both on your side. He called a conference with the publicists this afternoon and had them draw up a draft statement for the press voicing your remorse for what happened to James Scott. Evelyn, the chief publicist, is lining up a sympathetic journalist, probably someone from a women's weekly magazine, to handle the story. It'll be done in the form of an interview, but most of what you say has already been written for you. I've read it myself. It's pretty moving and I imagine by the time Evelyn's finished, providing you stick to what she tells you, there won't be a dry eye in the house. Just before I left this evening she told me she'd been in touch with James' parents—"

"Oh, God, no," Helena groaned.

"And they told Evelyn," Kirsten continued, "that they've forgiven you. They said they couldn't go through their lives with so much hatred and bitterness, so they took the decision some time ago now to forgive you.

They were as upset as you were that the story had come out now and they're contacting Dermott Campbell's editor to ask for a printed apology for stirring up things that were best left in the past. After that, with any luck, there'll never be any mention of it again, and by the time the movie comes out hopefully most people will have forgotten. But like I said, there's going to be nothing in the film now even to suggest that the character of Marie Laveau is in any way involved in procurement. Laurence is overseeing everything; he wants to see you tomorrow before you speak to Evelyn. There's only one thing left for me to say: I don't know how you're going to take it, but I don't really have any choice but to ask for your solemn promise that you never have anything to do with Campbell again—at least not for the duration of the film."

"You have it," Helena choked through her tears. Then letting her head fall to the table and burying her face in her arms, she sobbed, "I can't believe you're doing this for me, Kirstie. I just can't believe it."

"I'm doing it," Kirsten said, "because you're my friend. And because you're a great actress. A really great actress."

CHAPTER FIFTEEN

"I CAN'T BELIEVE YOU JUST SAID THAT!" KIRSTEN yelled.

"Then I'll say it again," Laurence yelled back. "If you don't pull your finger out and give the crew proper direction, then we might just as well pack up and go home now!"

"So it's all my fault!"

"You're the fucking director!"

"Oh, is that so? And there was me thinking it was you . . . I mean, you spend more time talking to my assistants than I do . . ."

"They come to me because you're not making yourself plain. They need information to do their jobs and you're not giving it to them."

"Because they won't bloody well listen to me."

"Then make them!" he roared. "If you let them run circles round you now, then how the hell do you think you're going to cope—"

"I'll cope! I'll cope just fine, thank you very much, but would you like to tell me precisely how I deal with that pompous prat of a first assistant who *you* employed and who goes behind my back at every turn telling everyone how fucking useless I am?"

"Did it ever occur to you he might have a point?"

Kirsten's eyes blazed into his. "Do you think he has a point?" she said bitingly.

"As a matter of fact I do. You're useless at handling the crew and the crew doesn't consist only of Jake Butler, though the rest of them might be forgiven for thinking so."

"Jake is working *with* me. The others are working against me."

"Then get them on your side. Stop putting up with the way they're treating you and stand up for yourself. I'm not nurse-maiding you through this, Kirsten. I've got my own problems to deal with and I expect you to deal with yours. If you're not up to it, then I suggest you say so now before we go any further."

"Do you have any argument with my approach?"

"No."

"Do you understand what I'm trying to achieve?"

"Yes."

"Then if you understand, there doesn't seem to be any reason why everyone else doesn't, except for the fact they don't want to."

"Then fucking well make them! How many more times do I have to say it?"

"All right! All right! I'll sit every head of department down individually and go over the script with them a page at a time and—"

"Are you telling me you haven't done that already?"

"Of course I've damned well done it and I'm getting

results, it's just that it's like pulling teeth. They're all professionals, they'll come up with the goods in the end, but they're doing their utmost to undermine my confidence. Like coming here complaining to you that I've requested too many walk-ons when the size of shot warrants the number I've asked for."

"And what about costume? Janet tells me Moyna's costume is going to clash badly with the set out at the plantation house—"

"It's supposed to!" Kirsten almost screamed. "I've told her that a thousand times. The lighting's going to clash with it too, but did Jake come here whinging to you? No, he accepts what I say and if he doesn't, we discuss it between us."

"Then you'd just better find a way of working your charm on the others or you and I are going to seriously fall out."

"Well, thank you for your support, Laurence. I don't suppose it's once occurred to you to tell any of them who come creeping here to you that you might just agree with what I'm doing? Or that you understand it and can't see why they don't? I don't imagine it's even entered your head to tell any of them that *you* believe in me, that you have confidence in my ability. But no, it wouldn't have, would it, because you don't. In fact you deeply regret ever asking me—"

"Stop putting words into my mouth!" he barked.

"Words that you don't have the guts to utter because you've got—"

"Words that are bullshit and you know it. I have every confidence in you. I know you can do this, I know you're going to make a terrific movie—"

"Then maybe it's time you showed it," Kirsten said, and without another word, she turned and walked out of the room.

They were staying at the Richelieu Hotel in New Orleans, having flown in two days before for the preshoot recce. Kirsten loved what she had seen of the city: the time-worn streets and the beautiful filigree balconies, but the idea that she was in charge of capturing New Orleans on film was daunting to say the least. In fact the further into production they went the more nervous she became. And obviously it showed, or at least it had to Laurence. The row of the sort they had just had was the last thing she needed right now. More than ever she was wondering if she'd made the right decision in agreeing to direct this film.

She didn't see Laurence again until the following afternoon when Little Joe of Independent Studios, who had been setting everything up for them here for the last two months, came to drive them out to Honey Island—one of the largest of the Louisiana swamps. By then Laurence had tried several times to speak to her, to apologize for what he'd said, and though Kirsten had told him it didn't matter she had refused to discuss it on the ground that she had too much work to get through.

Jake, Alison, David, the first assistant, and Bob, the sound man, were the only ones accompanying them on the recce since it was unlikely they would use the location—it was just that Kirsten wanted to see it before making up her mind. One of the location managers had waxed lyrical about the swamp's potential as a setting for the voodoo ceremonies, but Little Joe hadn't agreed. Unless they had an endless amount of time and wanted to risk losing lives in the murky depths of the rivers and bayous, then they'd be crazy to use it, he'd told them. Already Kirsten doubted its practicality for the simple reason that traveling outside New Orleans Parish to St. Tammany was just not feasible. It was going to eat into the schedule in a way they simply couldn't afford. Apart from which, Scout Island, Joe's find in City Park was, as far as she was concerned, a perfect location for the ritual. However, for the time being she was going to keep an open mind until she had actually seen the swamp.

It was one thirty by the time they arrived at the Indian Village Landing where Dr. Wagner, the ecologist who lived on the swamp, was waiting for them with his boat, but the darkening sky made it seem more like dusk.

As they climbed aboard, seating themselves along one of the two benches that stretched back to back down the center of the boat, Kirsten gazed across the water toward the dense, towering cypress trees that, to her, already seemed to resent the intrusion. There was no sign of the sun peering through the blanket of dismal gray cloud; there was no wind either. Everything was perfectly still, even the river currents seemed eerily motionless.

Dr. Wagner handed out blankets to put over their knees and with Laurence on one side of her and Jake on the other, Kirsten folded her hands in her lap and resolved not to think any more about Laurence or what was happening between them. Their movement toward a hiatus in their personal relationship couldn't be denied, and obviously he was as aware of it as she was. Quite how or when things were going to blow up was impossible to say, but what frightened Kirsten was the lack of professionalism they were both in danger of showing. She laughed bitterly to herself at that. Laurence would never allow his feelings to get the better of him in public; it was only she who was in danger of that.

They started out downriver, traveling at quite a speed to get to the bayou the location manager had set his heart on. Half a dozen or so hunters who worked with Dr. Wagner and were just along for the ride were sitting on the bench behind them, and as the boat slowed their expert eyes began picking out the wildlife secreted in the copious profusion of tupelo gum, maple, and cypress trees that rose somberly and sinisterly from the stagnant water. As they pointed out great blue herons, nutria, signs of beaver and water turkey, Kirsten's eyes were fixed on the greasy film of brilliant green duckweed half-dreading and half-hoping to see an alligator rise from the muddied depths.

Suddenly it seemed to turn very cold. Kirsten looked up at the impenetrable sky, then slowly lowered her eyes to the gray Spanish moss hanging from the trees like the fraying tangled briar of old men's beards. They had turned into the bayou by now and the gnarled cypress knees protruding from the water made progress slow as the decaying, dying gum trees reached out toward them. They stopped for a moment to watch a racoon, high in a tree, then moved on toward the depths of the morbidly silent bayou.

Kirsten leaned forward to rest her arms on the rail. She was aware that Laurence was watching her and had moved because she no longer wanted to feel the hardness of his body next to hers. Her lips tightened as she experienced a stinging exasperation at the way their minds and bodies were in such conflict. With the one they resisted each other with a determination and defiance that the other made a total mockery of. When at last she turned to look at him, stealing herself against him, her entire heart turned over. It was impossible to read his expression, but his dark blue eyes looked so deeply into hers she felt he might be reading her mind. Neither of them smiled, they simply looked at each other, until Kirsten returned her eyes to the grim splendor of the darkening swamp.

The constriction in her throat prevented her from answering when Jake asked her a question, but as his hand slid into hers, she turned to him and managed a smile.

"You okay?" he whispered.

Kirsten nodded.

"Pretty bloody spooky out here, isn't it?" he said.

At last they reached the spot the location manager had discovered. There was no doubt in anyone's mind that, were they able to do it, the voodoo sequence would be stupendous set on this bleak little island that seemed so remote from the world. However, though they disembarked to take a look around, both Kirsten and Laurence were agreed that transporting the crew, cast, equipment, and props out here at night was not only verging on the impossible, it would be downright dangerous. Apart from the risk of someone falling into the reptile-infested swamp, there were any number of other hazards, like snakes falling from the cobwebbed density of Spanish moss, or wild boar making a sudden and unprovoked charge, or even, as unlikely as it was, the danger of coming face-to-face with a black bear.

"It's a shame," Kirsten said as she and Laurence broke

away from the group and wandered toward a tumble-down shack set back in the trees. "We could have used this for the murder sequence as well the voodoo."

Laurence smiled. "Just what I was thinking," he said.

They walked around to the back of the hut and stood for a moment looking out at the mesmerizing stillness of the crowding trees and undergrowth.

"God, it's like the end of the earth out here, isn't it?" Kirsten whispered with a shiver.

She heard Laurence laugh and turned to look up at him. His eyes were unfocused on the distance, his jaw set in a way that suggested he might be angry. She watched him for a moment or two, then was about to turn away when he said, "I want you, Kirsten. I want you very much, you know that don't you?"

She stopped, but instead of the joy she had always imagined she would feel at hearing those words she felt only anger. "And is that supposed to make everything all right?" she answered tightly. "Is that supposed to excuse the way you're treating me?"

He turned to look at her. "No," he said. "But I accept that it's a problem I have to deal with. But Jesus Christ, Kirsten, you're driving me crazy, can't you see that?"

"So what am I supposed to do, stop living?"

His eyes darkened. "Why do you have to be so damned difficult about this?" he growled.

"What do you expect me to do, throw myself at your feet and say take me, Laurence? Please, Laurence, do whatever you want with me. Well, don't hold your breath!"

As she made to walk away he grabbed her hand and

turned her back to face him. "We haven't finished this," he said savagely. "Now may not be the time, but we're going to have this out the minute we get back."

"I've got other things to do."

"Then cancel them," he said through his teeth and letting her go he turned back toward the boat.

Kirsten re-seated herself between Jake and Laurence. The emotional and physical tension between her and Laurence was already moving beyond her control and she was so damned furious with him that she felt sure the others must sense it. How dare he treat her this way, as if all he had to do was crook his finger and she'd come running? Never mind that in that moment of physical contact she had felt such a desire that it had swept through her like a fire. Just who the hell did he think he was, some kind of Lochinvar who expected a woman to drop everything just because he had the urge? Well, she'd damned well show him just what she thought of that!

An hour later they were in the hotel lobby collecting their keys.

"I'd like to see you in my room. Now," Laurence said to Kirsten, then turned away as he saw the fury flicker in her eyes. He knew she wouldn't argue while everyone was in earshot.

They rode up in the lift with the rest of the crew, neither looking at the other, though Kirsten was aware of Jake's confusion. He mouthed something to her, but she didn't catch what it was, and not wanting to encourage him she looked away. When they reached the third floor everyone got out with the exception of Kirsten and Laurence. The door closed again and they continued in silence to the fourth floor where Laurence stood back for Kirsten to walk out ahead of him.

She waited until they were in the beautifully furnished sitting room of his suite, then rounded on him. "If you think you're laying so much as one finger on me," she yelled, "then you can damned well think—"

"Jane, could you take Tom downstairs for a while please," Laurence said calmly, and Kirsten swung around to see their mystified faces staring up at her from Tom's toy corner.

Kirsten kept her head averted as Jane took Tom by the hand and led him from the room, pursing her lips to stop herself laughing.

"Try not to shout at me in front of Tom again," Laurence said when the door closed behind them.

"I didn't know he was there," Kirsten responded.

"Evidently." He strolled over to the large, open brick fireplace. "Now, you were saying, if I thought I was going to lay one finger on you . . ."

"Don't take that tone with me." She was seething. "It drives me nuts!"

"Then what tone would you like me to take?"

"None. I just want to get out of here."

Laurence watched her closely, knowing that if he had any sense left in his head he'd let her go now. But she looked so goddamned beautiful standing there trying to hide the confusion she was feeling that his desire to fold her against him was too strong. If he could just touch her, just feel her for a moment . . . But no, that was madness, he'd never be able to stop himself . . .

"Okay. Go," he said.

Kirsten's surprise showed as she eyed him suspiciously. "All right," she said, and turning away she started across the room. When she reached the door she suddenly spun round. "I thought we were going to have this out!" she declared.

Despite the turmoil inside him Laurence started to grin.

"Don't laugh like that! I'm serious, Laurence."

"So am I. You want to go, I'm not stopping you."

She glared at him and his smiled widened.

"Laurence!" she almost screamed. "Look, you're the one who *ordered* me to come here. You're the one who wanted to have this out. So, I'm waiting."

Tearing his eyes away from her Laurence turned to look out of the window. He was going to give in to this, he knew it. The strength of the desire building inside him was so demanding it was driving into his every goddamned muscle. Just this one time, then he would have it out of his system. Somewhere in the depths of his mind he knew he was crazy, that as soon as he'd done it once he'd want to do it again and again, but as he turned to look at her and saw the way her hardened nipples were pushing through her blouse the unbearable sensuousness of her reached so far inside him that he knew he was beyond reasoning with it.

He moved toward her. Kirsten watched him, rooted by the sudden power that emanated from him. It pulled so hard through her body that she daren't move for fear of what she might do. Her chest was so tight she could barely breathe, the fire between her legs becoming so intense her very soul was turning into a furnace of desire.

"You bastard," she faltered, as he reached her. "You bastard . . ." but the words were lost in his mouth as his lips came down hard on hers. He thrust her back against the door, and as he reached out to turn the key it was as though the force of his desire suddenly blazed out of control.

For a moment Kirsten was dazed, but as his tongue found hers and he jerked her against him her hands flew to his hair. He pressed his groin to hers, grinding savagely against her, then he was tearing at her blouse, pushing it down over her shoulders, ripping the buttons from her shirt and releasing her breasts.

"Laurence, no," she gasped. "No . . ."

He tore himself away. "You want me to stop?" he growled. "Are you telling me you don't want this too?"

"Yes! No . . ." She looked into his stormy face. "Oh, God," she groaned. Why couldn't she find it in her to resist him when it all felt so wrong? "Laurence hold me," she whispered. "Please, just hold me."

He drew her back into his arms, resting her head on his shoulder. The violence of his passion was still quaking in his body, frightening him almost as much as it was her. After a while he pulled back and looked down into her face. Then his hands moved back to her breasts, teasing her achingly distended nipples. Her eyes closed and her head fell back against the door.

He was still watching her as he eased first her coat then her shirt down over her shoulders. Then reaching around behind her he unclasped her bra, leaving her naked to the waist. At last he lowered his eyes to her breasts and as he did his desire caught him so hard that for a moment he thought he was going to lose control again. "Look at you," he groaned. "Jesus Christ, just look at you," and Kirsten's knees almost buckled as he took first one then the other nipple deep into his mouth.

Her head fell forward and as her hands moved into his hair, his mouth and his fingers tightened on her nipples.

After a while he drew himself up and looked down into her eyes. His lips were moist, his hands were moving to her waist. "I'm going to fuck you, Kirsten," he murmured. "I'm going to fuck you so hard . . . Do you want me inside you, Kirstie? Do you want to feel me pushing right into you?"

"You know I do," she whispered.

All the time he was talking he was pushing her leggings and her panties down over her hips. His mouth was touching hers, his voice was vibrating in her throat. Then he was kissing her again. His lips molded around hers, sucking them and biting them, his tongue sought hers circling it, drawing it into his mouth and his hands came up around her face pulling her even closer. Then he was moving to his knees, sliding her clothes down over her legs, slipping off her ankle boots, and pulling everything from her until she was totally naked.

"Oh, my God!" she gasped as he lifted her leg to his shoulder and buried his face in her. "Laurence! Oh, God, Laurence, Laurence!"

Using his tongue and his lips he teased her and toyed with her, pulling her deep into his mouth and holding her wide with his fingers. He kept doing it, harder and faster until he felt the first contractions of her orgasm. Then suddenly he was on his feet, his mouth back on hers as he stripped away his own clothes. He was so hard now he could hardly bear it. His readiness was so exquisite it was agony. He pressed her against the door, lowered his hand to his penis and guided himself through her moistness to enter her.

Kirsten clung to him, twisting her fingers in his hair and biting his neck as she felt him filling her and filling her, pushing her wider and wider, joining himself to the deepest part of her. He pulled back then pushed into her again. It felt as though he was sliding into her forever. His lips were still on hers, his hands held her buttocks, pressing her to him. Then suddenly he jerked himself into her so hard she cried out. He did it again and again.

"Oh, Laurence," she choked, lifting a leg to draw him in further. He scooped her up in his arms and carried her to the table. As he set her down he withdrew himself, turned her over, then plunged into her again. His stomach was pressed hard up against her buttocks as he repeatedly pumped himself into her.

"Is this how deep you want me?" he muttered savagely in her ear. "You want me right in you, like this?"

"Oh, my God!" she sobbed as he ground himself against her while pushing a hand beneath her to rub his fingers over the most sensitive part of her. With his other hand he grabbed her hair and pulled her head back to kiss her.

"Don't come," he growled. "Don't come yet."

"I can't help it," she gasped.

He pulled away, lifted her up and folded her in his arms. Minutes later they were on the sofa. He was kneeling in front of her, her legs were on his shoulders. Then they were on the floor, he was in her mouth, between her breasts, then back inside her. He rolled onto his back and gasping for breath she lowered herself onto him, arching her spine, pushing her breasts to his mouth. He took them, squeezing them, biting them, then suddenly his hand lashed out, slapping them hard. He slapped them again and again, watching them swing over her ribcage as she groaned and writhed in unimaginable ecstacy. Then she was riding him, pumping herself wildly up and down on him and sobbing as he circled his thumb between her legs while with his other hand he continued to slap her.

Only just did he manage to stifle her scream as the first throes of her orgasm exploded, and pushing his tongue deep into her mouth he turned her onto her back and covered her with the full length of his body.

"Hold me," he groaned. "Kirstie, hold me!"

Her arms closed around his neck as her legs tightened about his waist. He crushed his lips brutally against hers, sucking on them and drawing her tongue deep into his mouth.

It was as though every nerve in her body was alive with flaming sensation, the ruthless thrusting of his hips pushed him to her very core. The blood rushed through her veins and she gasped as another tumultuous shudder erupted around him. It was as though every part of him was inside her. Still his lips were on hers, but she could feel them tightening as his body started to convulse. His arms pushed under her shoulders, holding her tightly to him as she met each thrust of his hips with her own. He had brought her to such a pitch she might scream if he stopped even for a moment. But he didn't. He continued to drive into her, on and on, taking them both to the brink of unparallelled frenzy. She opened her legs wider and he pressed himself down on to the part of her that only seconds later caused the full intensity of her orgasm to break around him in great juddering and relentless waves as, with a turbulent groan of agony, his seed spurted wildly into her.

He pushed his face into her shoulder as the spasms racked his whole body. He felt her legs slip down over his own and pushed into her again. A quick memory flickered in his mind of the time Pippa had made him think of Kirsten while he made love to her. It was the best he had ever known with Pippa, but God help him, it had been nothing like this. Nothing had ever been like this.

It was a long time later that he lifted his head to look down into her face. He smiled when he saw how dazed she still looked and took her bruised lips gently between his own. Their bodies were still joined, the dying turbulence continuing to grip them. Then Kirsten opened her eyes and as she looked up at him his heart tightened at the lazy, sensual smile she gave him. He kissed her again and again, holding himself up on his elbows and languidly rotating his hips.

"Are you beat?" he murmured.

Kirsten looked up into his eyes, her own still clouded with the aftermath of his lovemaking. Again a smile crossed her full lips, for they were both only too aware of the way he was beginning to harden again.

"No, but you are," she whispered as he ran his thumb along her jaw.

He started to smile. Only with her had he ever achieved an erection twice like this, so it was only she who would have understood his question. He pushed his hands beneath her, holding her very close as he rolled onto his back. By now he was filling her again, responding to the way she was stretching herself across him so that he could take her swollen nipples into his mouth. He caressed them gently with his tongue, while curving his hands under her buttocks as he rocked himself languorously up and down.

It was a long, long time before either of them reached orgasm again, but this time, with their bodies entwined, their movements were consumed by a tenderness that was so transcending and in its way so much more powerful than the urgency that had taken them before. In the end it was Laurence who finished it for them both. By then Kirsten was too weakened by the force of so many emotions and so much sensation to do anything more than hold him.

They were still lying in each others' arms, their eyes closed, their breathing now steady, when the door handle rattled.

"Shit! It's Tom!" Laurence cried, sitting bolt upright.

"Oh, my God!" Kirsten gasped, somehow finding the energy to spring to her feet. "Quick, where are my clothes?"

"Daddy! Daddy!" Tom called out.

"Coming," Laurence shouted, hauling on his jeans while simultaneously stuffing his arms into his shirt.

Kirsten was laughing as she, too, frantically fought her way into her clothes.

After a delay that even Jane in her innocence would see through Laurence finally pulled open the door. "Daddy!" Tom cried, bursting into the room. "I'm going to float in a bubble and drive a crane."

"You are?" Laurence said not without irony.

"Yes. And there are lots of other things to play with too, aren't there, Jane?"

"We've just been told about the Children's Museum," Jane explained, and the way her eyes were avoiding both Kirsten's and Laurence's it was clear that she knew exactly what had been happening. "I thought I'd take Tom there tomorrow," she said.

"That'll be nice for you, Tom." Kirsten smiled, looking down at his upturned face.

"Yeah, well . . ." Laurence said.

"Um, I'd better be getting back to my room," Kirsten said, and giving Tom's hair a quick ruffle she added, "See you later," and left.

When Kirsten got back to her room, among many other messages there was one from Alison asking her if she could go out to Little Joe's and take a look at the model that had been done of the ballroom. There was a note pushed under her door from Jake telling her that if she was going out to Joe's studios, he'd like to go with her. When Kirsten called his room he answered straight away, and she told him to meet her down in the lobby in fifteen minutes. She needed to take a quick shower and collect herself after what had happened.

In fact, by the time she went downstairs to meet Jake, she was still so dazed that were it not for the way her muscles were aching she might have thought it was all a dream.

Trying to focus her mind she gazed out at the shadowy dusk and noticed the ominous patterns it cast over the passing streets. A strange feeling of unease crept down her spine, making her skin prickle. It was odd, she reflected to herself, how she hadn't really noticed it before, but there was something, well something unusual about New Orleans. It wasn't something she could put her finger on and perhaps before she'd just been too busy to notice, but now she came to think about it she wasn't at all sure she liked this place. It was peculiar the way people dressed in curious costumes when it wasn't even Mardi Gras. And though the warmth of southern hospitality couldn't be denied, that, too, now she mulled it over in her mind, made her uncomfortable. It was as though there were deep, dark depths to the city that breathed a dissolute and immoral air into the streets. As though everyone nurtured a secret and watched you with eyes that both mocked and enticed. The decaying beauty of delicate wrought-iron balconies, hidden courtyards with exotic plants and alabaster fountains, the hypnotic sounds of indolent jazz trumpets, were all like a trap set to lure the innocent into an exclusive and infernal nether world.

She turned to Jake. "Do you like it here?" she said.

"I love it," he answered without hesitation. "It's weird, but I love it. What about you?"

Kirsten shrugged. "I'm not sure," she said. "I think it frightens me."

Then suddenly she remembered that Helena came from New Orleans and for one horrible moment it seemed to create an unbridgeable gulf between them. But that was ridiculous, she told herself firmly. She knew Helena almost as well as she knew herself and there was very definitely nothing sinister about Helena.

But nevertheless with the way Laurence had been with her that afternoon and the unsettling realization that Helena was from a culture of which she, Kirsten, knew nothing, she felt as though she were drifting on the outside of a world that she could see but not touch.

God, she hated feeling this way, but suddenly her head fell forward and she started to laugh. Wasn't it the way she always felt, right deep down inside? It was called paranoia. She'd hoped that her analysis had got her over these fears, but obviously it hadn't, or at least not altogether. But she'd let her maddening insecurities destroy her and Laurence once, so she just better get herself together now because there was no way she was going to let that happen again. They'd talk later, probably over dinner, and she would allow the glow she felt inside to control the way she handled things, not the niggardly, persistent doubts that so expertly managed to submerge her in a vacuum of despicable, intolerable insecurity.

It was just after eight o'clock when Kirsten returned to the hotel alone. Jake, Alison, and several of the others had taken themselves off to K-Paul's for a Cajun dinner, but Kirsten had declined the invitation to join them. She went straight up to her room, dropped off her bag, then walked along the corridor to Laurence's suite, an impish smile twitching her lips as she envisaged the teasing intimacy in his eyes when he saw her.

"Hi," she said when Jane opened the door. "Is Laurence there?"

"Uh, no," Jane said uncomfortably. "He, um, he's gone out to a restaurant."

"Oh," Kirsten said. "Do you know where?"

"Oh, yes." Jane nodded eagerly. "I've got it written down. If you'd like to come in, I'll get it for you."

Kirsten followed Jane into the sitting room. "Did he leave a message for me?" she said.

Jane shook her head. "I don't think so. Well, not with me, he didn't."

"Who did he go to the restaurant with?" Kirsten asked, taking the piece of paper Jane was holding out.

"Ruby."

Kirsten's surprise showed. "Ruby?"

"Yes, she got here this afternoon while you were all out at the swamp."

"I didn't know she was coming," Kirsten said, unsure for the moment why it was bothering her. She lifted her eyes back to Jane's. "Did Laurence know she was coming?"

"Yes, I think so. Well, he got his assistant to go and pick her up at the airport, so he must have known."

"Then why didn't he mention it to me?"

Jane simply looked at her.

Kirsten quickly pulled herself together. "Well," she said, waving a hand toward the door. "I suppose I'd better get back. I've got a lot to do."

When the door closed behind Kirsten, Jane stood at the center of the room chewing her bottom lip. It was all very bewildering what was happening between Laurence and Kirsten—one minute they were shouting and arguing as if they'd never see eye to eye and the next they were actually making love. Jane was certain that's what they had been doing when she and Tom returned to the room earlier, but now it seemed like something had gone wrong again. Jane really wished she could be the one Kirsten turned to. But who could say, maybe one of these days Kirsten would think her special enough to confide in and then she would do everything she could to show Kirsten how very, very much she wanted her to be a part of their lives.

Ruby was in a small dingy room at the back of a house in downtown New Orleans. The room was an *oum'phor,* a voodoo temple. She was seated at a rickety wooden table beside the peristyle, the rainbow-colored post that supported the center of the corrugated roof, and over the table was a large paper napkin. The chair she was sitting on was about as uncomfortable as the method of telling her future through a goddamned coconut was ludicrous.

The voodoo priestess who looked what she was, a scrap of a girl from the streets of Paris, was sitting at the other side of the table, her stringy blond hair lit by the flickering flame of a candle, her sultry lips slightly parted as she concentrated on the patterns of coconut juice that had dripped onto the paper between them and the milky white flesh of the fruit that was now exposed. Ruby had broken the coconut herself; [it was a part of putting her identity—onto a goddamned coconut!]

Ruby was supposed to have been here a week ago for this reading, but the priestess had asked her to delay her visit. Ruby hadn't asked why. In fact she'd all but lost interest by now, but the kid had called her up this morning while the others were taking off for the airport, and since Ruby didn't have anything better to do before her own flight she'd come along.

This past week had proved a rewarding one, not that she'd managed to get to any spooky midnight rituals, in fact everyone insisted they didn't happen, but the stories she'd got out of the police, self-professed voodoo victims, street entertainers, and barroom punters had been enough to make the Kirstie Doll's hair curl. Well, it was pretty potent stuff even if she, Ruby, didn't believe half of it, and cutesy Kirstie had nearly peed her pants with excitement. Ruby grinned to herself. She kind of liked Kirsten, admired her in a way. Putting up with the surly, snobbish treatment she was getting from the high and mighty feature crew couldn't be easy, but she seemed to be handling it okay. Still, if Ruby was any judge of things, they were going to get their comeuppance once they saw rushes, 'cause if Kirsten managed to pull off the approach she was taking, they were going to end up with one hell of a movie on their hands. And that was why she admired Kirsten; instead of pulling rank on everyone now; she was going to let her work speak for itself. Pretty neat that, Ruby thought. Yeah, the Kirstie Doll was okay, she had Ruby's vote, and just so long as she stayed away from Laurence's heart they would continue to get along fine.

Ruby's heavily ringed fingers moved to her mouth to stifle a yawn. This here voodoo girl was taking an inordinate amount of time to absorb one little old coconut and Ruby was getting bored. In fact she was feeling a bit peckish but decided it might not be a good idea to take a chunk out of her own destiny. Her eyes started to roam the walls, taking in the grisly masks of staring red eyes, protruding tongues, and wolfish teeth. The sickly aroma of a sweet incense thickened the air and the strains of hypnotically monotonous pipe music drifted dreamily over the totem poles, mystical paintings, and weird collection of whammy dolls. In the corner was an old iron gate with grinning skulls impaled on its spikes. More candles burned on the altar where statuettes of saints and voodoo gods stood between bunches of garlic, gris-gris bags, and an ashtray. Ruby wasn't a religious woman by anyone's standards, but the open copy of the Bible resting incongruously on some kind of clothes horse in front of the altar wasn't something that sat too well with her. And she didn't much like the python slithering indolently about a glass tank over there either.

Her painted lips opened wide as she allowed herself a luxurious yawn. "Oh, sorry, dear," she said when the waiflike priestess looked up at her. "Kind of warm in here, don't you think?"

The girl looked at her with cold, translucent eyes. Ruby stared back curiously. The girl hadn't looked that way when she'd come in here, in fact she'd looked a happy sort of soul. . . . Shit, what kind of story was she reading in that darned coconut?

"You have many troubles in your life," the priestess said in her throaty French accent.

"Tell me about it," Ruby sighed.

"Chango, the warrior god, he speaks to me of you. Your battle is a hard one, he understands, but he does not approve of what you do."

"Is that so?" Ruby said. "Well, how about you tell old Chango that if—" she stopped as the priestess held up her hand.

"Deceit is not good," she purred. "You deceive and you will be deceived."

Ruby didn't have much to say about that. Seemed a pretty obvious sort of statement to her. Anyhow, she didn't need no spear-toting voodoo god to tell her that. And sure, she'd deceived a few people in her time. Show her someone who hadn't!

"Your deception will cause you much grief. It will bring misunderstanding . . . It will hurt someone you love." Her head came up. "Erzulie our goddess of love, speaks. She tells me you seek solace for your heart. . . . I see a baby," she said. "Legba, our chief god, he is showing me the baby."

Ruby's puffy cheeks paled slightly. "Yeah?" she said. "And which baby would that be?"

"The baby you hold in your arms."

"I don't see no baby."

"It is there, in your arms. Legba is showing me."

"I don't have no baby," Ruby insisted.

The priestess blinked at her, a vacuous look in her eyes that told Ruby she wasn't listening.

"You are surrounded by many words and many people," the girl chanted. "There is much creativity. You are a woman of great talent, but you are in danger from that talent. It will bring harm to those around you. The baby is very still. I see a child with that baby. I see more memories. . . . They are captured in a book."

Ruby was thinking of the photograph album that contained all the joy of her young life. She said nothing.

"There is a wish to be a mother, yet it cannot be. You are dominated by this desire, are surrounded by women who are ruled by the same desire. You have all made mistakes, done things you deeply regret, but a child is there for you all . . . I see the child and the baby. . . ."

"You're not making a whole lot of sense here," Ruby interrupted.

"I see death," the girl continued as if Ruby hadn't spoken. "It has already occurred, but there are three yet to come. The innocent have died and will die. . . ." The girl's voice suddenly crescendoed. "You must stop this film! You must not do it! Legba is begging you. . . ." Then as though she was being possessed from within, she choked, "The first deaths will be from smoke without fire. The third is the child. The child will die." Her eyes blazed beseechingly into Ruby's. "Please stop this film," she cried. "Don't let the child die. Don't kill the child. . . ."

"I'm not going to kill no child," Ruby protested.

"But it is there. The child will die if you do this film. They will all die. You must stop protecting those who do not need it and look to those who do, or you will be blamed."

"I don't much like the way this coconut's going," Ruby objected. "Do you figure we could try a banana?"

The girl was by now so steeped in her prophecies it seemed she couldn't stop. "You must try to understand what the spirits are telling you," she demanded, seeming to speak from somewhere behind her eyes. "There are three women: one who is very beautiful, one who is our own voodoo queen, and there is you. . . . Your lives are linked by this film. . . . And there is a man with a child. . . ."

Ruby's heart seemed to freeze over. Was she talking about Laurence's son? Was Tom the child she reckoned was going to—?

"You must curb your jealousy," the girl chuntered on.

"It will do you no good. . . . The child needs you, she needs you all. . . ."

"She?" Ruby queried with some relief.

"There is a child with a child. She lives within you. . . . Look to the very heart of you and you will see the child with a child."

Ruby's uneasiness was cracking her resolve badly. She didn't like the sound of any of this, not that she had any idea what it was about, but there were just a few too many bells ringing. . . . "Do you reckon your fella Legba there could speak plain English?" she asked.

"Memories must come from our past," the priestess warned.

"What?"

"Do not allow her to create the memories that do not exist. You must stop her."

"Who?"

"The child. She is a part of you."

"I need a gin," Ruby declared.

"The strands are so knotted it is hard to find your way through. It has all begun with one woman's desire for revenge. She is to blame, not you, but you are a part of it now. The woman no longer has control. It is slipping away from her and the path is clearing. But do not let it clear, for it will open the way to death. Stop this film and turn away from it."

"Make that a large one," Ruby grumbled.

"If you do not heed my advice you will see a castle fall. You will see the death of a woman. You will see the death of a man. Then the memories will take on reality and the baby will break into a thousand pieces. . . ."

"That's it, I'm out of here," Ruby cried, springing to her feet and almost knocking the table over.

"Then will come the death of the child. . . ." The priestess's haunted voice came after her.

CHAPTER SIXTEEN

"AND YOU'RE TELLING ME HE HASN'T MENTIONED A word about it since!" Helena cried.

"Not one," Kirsten answered, making a note next to a paragraph of stage direction.

"But you've been back here two weeks, you've got to have seen him . . ."

"Of course I've seen him. I saw him plenty of times when we were in New Orleans too. But like I said, he always makes sure someone else is around."

"Well isn't that just typical of a man!" Helena declared. "Always hiding behind someone's skirts when they can't face up to what they've done."

"As a matter of fact I haven't gone out of my way to speak to him either," Kirsten said, tucking her hair behind her ear as she flicked over a page.

"Whyever not? You can't let him get away with this, Kirstie."

Kirsten lifted her head and rested her chin on a bunched fist. "The way I see it he has got away with it. But it takes two; I wouldn't have done it if I didn't want to. In fact, I reckon he's having a far harder time over this than I am. I mean I know how *I* feel, but my guess is he just can't work out how he feels."

"Shit, listen to you, Miss Cool."

Kirsten laughed and turned back to what she was doing. "To be honest, Helena, I've hardly had time to think about it."

"But aren't you just dying to know what's really going on in his head? I know I would be."

"Well, I suppose we will have to clear the air sooner or later, so we *will* have it out and then we will continue on my terms."

"Well, I like the sound of that," Helena grinned. "Going to tell me what you're planning?"

"No. But I'll let you know once I've spoken to him. Now, can we get back to this? I want to be sure you know about the visual effects that are going into the voodoo ceremony because it's going to affect your performance. Have you met up with the effects team yet?"

"Yes, last week. Can't say I really understand all those computer graphics though."

"All right, I'll come with you next time. For now, let's go over the ritual as Ruby's written it. By the way, have you seen the designs for your costume?"

"Sure. They're terrific. I've got a first fitting next week."

"Good. I'll check with Vicky that she's put that into my schedule; I'd like to see it before Janet goes ahead and has it made. So, tell me about your meeting with Ruby yesterday. Was she any help with the ritual?"

"Yeah, a bit. She's kind of getting herself worked up

over it though. It's like . . . well, it's like she doesn't want me to do it. She keeps saying she's going to change it, but never does. If you ask me, she's having some kind of crisis."

"Hmm, you could be right," Kirsten said thoughtfully. She didn't add that Laurence had called the night before to say he was at Ruby's trying to sober her up and attempting yet again to persuade her not to pull out. "Did she say anything to you about some coconut reading?" Kirsten asked.

"Some what!" Helena laughed.

Kirsten shook her head. "It's just that she went to see some kind of fortune-teller or something after the rest of us left New Orleans and it seems to have shaken her up a bit. Anyway, where were we? Ah yes, I've got a copy of a props list here so that you can see what you'll be handling during the ceremony. Try to remember that none of it's real because it's pretty revolting."

"The goddamned python's real!" Helena reminded her.

"Yes, but you'll be trained."

"It's not me I'm worried about," Helena declared. "It's the snake."

"It'll be trained too." Kirsten laughed as she flicked through her diary, which was sitting at her elbow. "Your lessons begin while we're in Ireland," she said. "A Mr. Peterson over in Essex will be doing the coaching. Which reminds me, have you met the choreographer yet?"

"Yes," Helena said. "I've met them all."

"Well, I'm pleased to hear that," Kirsten commented.

"Seems the production managers are on the ball. I've got a meeting with the stunt arrangers tomorrow, otherwise I'd have come to dance rehearsals with you."

"And who's choreographing all the walk-ons?"

"Someone over in New Orleans. You and your choreographer will get together with them just before we shoot. Now, at the risk of asking a silly question, how *au fait* are you with the background on voodoo? Do you want any more coaching in that than what Ruby's given you?"

Helena pursed her lips thoughtfully. "No," she said. "I don't reckon so. Growing up with it's all the background I need."

"Okay." Kirsten nodded and got up to answer the phone. Helena turned back to the script with the heavily underscored lines that were hers. She knew them all by now, had learned them parrot fashion so that when Kirsten came to discuss the level of performance, she, Helena, wouldn't have to return to the book. Kirsten, of course, could recite virtually the entire dialogue by now so when she read in during individual coaching she could keep her whole attention on the actor. It was pretty cool that, Helena reflected, knowing the whole script inside out. Of course she'd known other directors who'd worked that way, but being directed by Kirsten was a whole new experience. To begin with this was the first time Helena had ever been directed by a woman. She wasn't too sure she liked it, but it was something she was working on, just like the resentment she always seemed to feel when she was around Kirsten lately. She knew that it was to do with guilt. Going behind Kirsten's back with Dermott wasn't something she was proud of, but it wasn't something she was going to stop either. She just hoped that she would never be in a position where she'd have to choose between Kirsten and Dermott. . . .

"That was Vicky doing overtime," Kirsten said, glancing at her watch as she came back into the study. "The production managers are having some problem with the schedule so they want me back over there. I guess I'd better go. We can continue this at the weekend."

"Sure," Helena said, closing up her script.

"Do you reckon you can come at me from inside Marie Laveau's skin by then?" Kirsten smiled.

"I can give it a shot," Helena answered. "But yeah, I reckon I've got her pretty well sussed now. Don't like her much, do you?"

"She gives me the creeps." Kirsten laughed. "And that's exactly what we want." She picked up her bag and started stuffing things into it as Helena went to get her coat. "You don't mind me going off like this, do you?"

Helena shrugged. "Just so long as I know you'd do it to Anna Sage."

Kirsten was about to answer, then stopped to give the question some thought. The last thing she wanted was to abuse her friendship with Helena, but Helena was right; she wouldn't have walked out on a meeting with Anna Sage. But there again she didn't spend what few social hours she had with Anna Sage.

"I'll make it up to you," she said putting an arm around Helena's shoulders. "You get my undivided attention all day Sunday. How does that sound?"

"Pretty patronizing actually," Helena remarked. "But I'll live with it," she added with a grin that faded the moment Kirsten turned to open the door.

• • •

The scissors were slipping in her fingers. It had taken so long to do this and the baby just wouldn't stop crying. So many times now she had left her table and gone to the crib in the corner, lifting the tiny body into her arms and comforting it with all the love in her heart. She had held it to her breast, stroked it and changed it and whispered her dreams in its ear. The baby was sleeping now, its fair downy lashes still moist with tears, its smooth, tender cheeks flushed with warmth. The soothing tune from a musical mobile drifted over the room.

A smile curled slowly across her lips as she glued the last picture into place. She was creating the happiness for them, for her and for her baby. They were going to have a past just like they were going to have a future. They were going to be a family—all of them. She blinked as the tears started from her eyes. This was such a beautiful photograph now. So much better than it had been before. It was right to be like this—mother, father, and two children. But of course there was the baby to go in yet, and that was why she was crying. She had no pictures of her baby.

Kirsten could hardly believe how fast the time had gone. It was now the beginning of November and they were scheduled to start shooting in less than a week. Alison and her crew were already over in Ireland preparing the castle, two line producers, two production managers, three location managers and their assistants, were over there too, setting up offices in trailers, sorting the makeup and wardrobe caravans, portable dressing rooms, honey wagons, catering facilities, and the hundred and one other things that needed to be done before everyone arrived. In the Soho offices last-minute details of artists' contracts were being attended to, the final draft of the shooting script was going to print, Jake and his crew were doing double checks on the equipment lists, and Laurence was yelling at the accountants for up-to-the-minute costings.

Kirsten was unbelievably calm. She spent every day in a hotel conference room with the cast now, going over the script in the minutest of detail and loving every minute of it. Ruby was often at cast meetings, and Kirsten frequently found her input as valuable as that of the cast themselves. Fortunately Ruby seemed to have got over whatever it was that had upset her in New Orleans, though she did appear to be drinking more heavily lately. This was something Kirsten left Laurence to handle. Only once had she staggered in drunk and it wasn't something Kirsten wanted repeated. To call her own work rubbish and to tell the actors they were all wasting their time and should cancel their contracts before something terrible happened to them was not particularly helpful.

Occasionally Jake popped into the meetings and to watch him work his charm on the cast was as entertaining as it was welcome. There was no doubt in Kirsten's mind now that everything was going to go as smoothly as these things could. The whole unit was at last starting to mellow toward her; being in no doubt now that Kirsten knew precisely what she wanted, was rarely, if ever, indecisive, and was always willing to listen had raised their confidence in her no end.

There had been a slight hiccup the week before, though, when Dermott Campbell had written an article entitled *Iniquity on the Road.* In order to avoid a libel suit Campbell hadn't come right out with his accusations, but the essence of the piece was that Laurence was having to cope with a writer who was a drunk and given to manic outbursts; a Don Juan of a DP who couldn't keep his hands off the director; a director who couldn't keep her hands off anyone and whose interpretation of turnover had little to do with a camera; a cast who had no confidence in either the director or the script; and a budget that was already fast running out. Through the unit publicist Laurence had made a short statement to the press thanking his good friend Dermott Campbell for his concern, but should he care to get his information from those in the know rather than from the mole he had planted, then he would discover that not only did he, Laurence, have a thoroughly professional team working for him, but that he had rarely had greater confidence in a director or in the success of a movie that was far from being in any financial difficulties. This was backed up by a memorandum to every member of cast and crew assuring them that the budget was in no danger of drying up and that they had his personal assurance that they would continue to be paid right up to the end of shoot. He had then, unbeknownst to Kirsten, contacted Campbell and invited him to come to the set any time he liked to gauge for himself the inaccuracy of the information he was receiving. So far Campbell had declined. Laurence was neither surprised nor sorry. He knew he was in danger of sticking his neck out too far by issuing the invitation when they hadn't even started, but he had total confidence in Kirsten's ability and knew that any problems that might arise would not be of her making—and it was Kirsten's skin Campbell was really after.

Things had settled down again now, though not even Laurence knew about the angry words that had been exchanged between Kirsten and Helena when Kirsten had asked Helena if she was still seeing Campbell. Helena had denied it so vehemently that Kirsten had believed her and apologized, but Helena was still smarting at the damned impertinence of being told whom she could and couldn't see.

CHAPTER SEVENTEEN

THE WIND WAS MEWLING LIKE A CHILD ACROSS THE stark, winter-torn plains of the Irish hillside. The storm gathered overhead in great mountains of purple-black cloud, the tall, yellowy grass bent toward the gloomy castle in the distance. The lone horseman, barely more than a silhouette, galloped across the horizon through the driving rain, his cloak billowing furiously behind him. The camera, perched on its tripod, held steady on the wide shot; the operator, with small protection from an umbrella, was being buffeted by the wind and drenched by the rain as he panned slowly with the rider taking him to the castle. Jake and Kirsten, huddled into the meager warmth of padded anoraks, moon boots, and woolen scarves, were standing together beneath their own vast umbrella, watching the shot on a tiny black-and-white screen. The rest of the crew were grouped around them, two sound booms loomed overhead sucking the howl of the storm into their headphones. Rain dripped from the peak of Kirsten's cap, pools of mud swam around her feet, but she was aware of nothing more than what was being relayed from the camera to her monitor.

At last the horseman arrived at the castle, a slight, shadowy figure in the distance. The ominous rumbling of thunder started to vibrate through the wind as he dismounted, handed the reins to a barely visible boy, and stomped into the blackness of an open door. Kirsten's fingers crossed in her pockets as her heart seemed to fill her throat. The camera held steady, there was virtually no movement now, just the boy leading the horse away and the shuddering branches of trees straining toward the castle turrets.

After a while Kirsten's eyes flicked to the script supervisor, who, checking her stopwatch, eventually raised her arm and Kirsten shouted, "Cut! Check the gate!"

She turned to Jake to find his smile as wide as hers, then she shrieked and laughed with euphoria as he scooped her up in his arms and swung her round. The first shot, after eight takes, was in the can! There was no rain on the lens, the stunt rider hadn't slipped in the mud, no one had appeared in the castle doorway—it had been perfect. . . .

"Gate's clear," Lindon, the camera operator, shouted, then joined in the round of applause as walkie-talkies crackled into life; David, the first assistant, yelled into a megaphone; and Ruby took a gulp of relief from her handbag.

"Moving on!" David was shouting. "Shot two, medium wide from the middle of the field."

"How long down here?" a voice came from the castle.

"Stay inside," David answered. "I'll let you know."

The grips moved swiftly, rolling up cables, packing

up the monitors, and removing the camera from the tripod. The sound guys pulled in their booms, disconnected them from the Nagra and saluted Laurence as he walked through the milling crowd.

Kirsten and Jake, already discussing the next shot, linked arms and started down over the hillside to the center of the field.

"Do we want Jean-Paul for this shot?" a second assistant inquired over the walkie-talkie.

Kirsten stopped and looked back over her shoulder to David.

"No," David answered, giving Kirsten the thumbs-up as he pressed the radio to his lips. "Get the stunt guy back on the horse. Not now, we're not ready yet. I'll give you the word. Put Jean-Paul on stand-by."

Kirsten smiled, then hugging Jake's arm they walked on. It was a heady experience knowing that all the information she'd spent the past months giving out had filtered through to the point that questions like that needn't concern her unless she decided upon a last-minute change. But even more intoxicating was to watch everyone zooming around, yelling to each other, heaving equipment, rigging dollies, checking schedules, moving props, organizing the action, and battling the weather all at her behest. As she watched them she was overwhelmed with emotion and knew that she had never loved Laurence more than she did in that moment for giving her this chance to fulfill a dream. She wondered if Paul could see her now, and again her heart swelled. How happy he would be to see her and Laurence working together on a movie that was going to be dedicated to his memory.

The rest of the morning and the first hours into the afternoon, until the daylight had all but disappeared, were spent doing exterior shots of the castle, a tracking shot of the thundering horses' hooves, and a close-up of Jean-Paul's face as he rode through the storm. They wrapped right on four o'clock and piled into the location buses that were taking them to the hotels, boarding houses, and bed and breakfasts in the town. Laurence drove Kirsten, Jean-Paul, and Ruby back in his rented car, and though he'd made very few comments throughout the day Kirsten could tell from his expression that he was as delighted as she was with what they had achieved.

Jane and Tom were waiting in the lobby of the country hotel in which Kirsten, Laurence, and the senior members of crew and cast were staying. Laurence scooped his son quickly into his arms, and was about to go to the desk for his key when Anna Sage stepped out of the lift.

"Laurence, darling," she sang out happily, and walking over to him she stood on tiptoe to kiss him. "I hear everything went perfectly today."

"Yeah, I guess you could say that," Laurence answered, smiling down into her girlishly pretty face. "I see you got here all right. Was your assistant there to pick you up at the airport?"

"She certainly was. Jean-Paul," she said, sliding a hand into her costar's. "How did the riding go? Ah, Kirsten, I didn't see you there. Gosh, how do you manage to look so gorgeous when you've been out in that ghastly weather all day? Still, you must be relieved to have the first day over with. Why don't we all go into the cozy little bar over there and celebrate? Do you have champagne?" she asked the receptionist. "Yes, of course you do. Oh, it's all so exciting isn't it? I can't wait to get started myself."

As she spoke her arm was snuggling its way into Laurence's and she was playfully teasing the curls away from Tom's eyes as he rested his head on Laurence's shoulder. Then suddenly breaking free she made her way to Kirsten and took her arm. "Is there anything you would like to discuss with me this evening?" she asked, walking Kirsten toward the bar. "I have someone coming over from the local newspaper later to interview me. Is there anything particular you would like me to say?"

"You'd better discuss that with the publicist," Kirsten smiled, gently detaching her arm. "Now listen, please don't think me rude, but I really have to get out of these wet clothes and into a hot bath. I'll join you later, okay?"

"Of course," Anna cried. "Of course. Can we have dinner together?"

"Absolutely," Kirsten said. "I'll come and find you around seven, okay?"

As Kirsten went to pick up her key, Ruby joined her. "Do you reckon she's gonna simper her way through the next eight weeks?" Ruby hissed in Kirsten's ear.

Kirsten turned aside to hide her smile. She didn't want to encourage Ruby, but Ruby was right; as easygoing and cooperative as Anna was, she did simper.

To Kirsten and Jake's relief the weather didn't let up for the next five days, causing them no continuity problems and lending its own inimical ambience to the scenes. There had, of course, been the odd hitch or two, there always were, but whatever obstacles, mysteries, or misunderstandings coughed themselves up they were dealt with speedily and efficiently by a crew who was by now whole-heartedly behind Kirsten. They had all of them seen rushes, borrowing the videotape that was sent over from the labs in London for Laurence and Kirsten to view until they could see the film itself in a projection theater. Anna Sage's performance was so outstanding that even Ruby was beginning to warm toward her, and Jean-Paul's indomitable charm was seeping into the camera in a way guaranteed to make any woman's heart churn.

It was on the sixth day during yet another thunderstorm that was causing all sorts of problems for the sound crew that the first major mishap occurred. It was the middle of the afternoon and Kirsten and Anna were standing together beneath the castle's bleak, bulging walls sheltering from the wind. Anna's dresser was hovering beside them, having quickly slipped a fur-lined mac over Anna's costume in order to keep her warm and holding an umbrella over them. The rest of the cast were in their trailers or snugly tucked up behind the steamy windows of the location buses, while the crew slithered about in the mud setting up for the next scene.

"I'm terribly sorry about all those takes," Anna said to Kirsten. "It's so hard keeping your head up in this wind."

"I know. But it was fine in the end," Kirsten assured her. "It was just that your dialogue kept getting muffled. We've got it now though."

"Was Laurence happy with it?"

"I imagine so," Kirsten answered, watching Jake hoist

himself up in the seat behind the camera to look through the viewfinder. "If he wasn't he'd have said."

"I just wondered because I saw him talking to you just now," Anna commented casually.

"Oh, that was about something else," Kirsten answered. She refrained from adding that as the director what she thought counted every bit as much as what Laurence thought, if not more. She didn't want in any way to show her growing irritation with Anna, for she was very much aware of the gossip flying around the unit—Jake related it to her regularly. Everyone was laying odds on how long it was going to take for Anna to get Laurence into bed. For Kirsten to give way to her feelings would only add to the speculation, and it was bad enough trying to deal with them as it was. The sudden bolts of ice-cold jealousy that lurched through her every time she saw Anna and Laurence together huddled in private conversation at the edge of the set were already affecting her concentration, though so far, thank God, no one seemed to have noticed.

Jake yelled out for her and she was just about to break away from the castle wall when a second dagger of lightning flashed down from the sky at the very instant a thunderbolt exploded into the castle keep.

"Good God!" Anna choked, clinging to Kirsten. "What's happening?"

"I don't know," Kirsten murmured, watching the scenes guys diving for cover. Suddenly she gasped. "Oh, my God! The whole tower's coming down. Quick!" and dragging Anna by the arm she all but threw her out of the way.

• • •

"Where is he? I got to speak to him. I got to speak to him now!" Ruby declared, pushing her way past Jane into Laurence's room.

"He's gone out for dinner with Jake," Jane answered, dismayed at the unmistakable whiff of alcohol that had come in with Ruby.

"Well, at least he's not off somewhere with the Simpering Sage," Ruby slurred. Her lipstick was smudged and there were dark circles under her eyes. This wasn't the first time Jane had seen her drunk, but it was the first time she was having to cope with it.

"Is there something I can do?" Jane asked. "Can I give him a message?"

"Yeah. You can tell him from me that he's got to stop this movie now," Ruby declared, blinking hard as though to clear her vision. "Have you got anything to drink here?"

"Uh, no, I don't think we have," Jane answered.

"Never mind. I've got some right here," Ruby said, delving into her bag. "That bloody French witch told me this would happen," she gasped, after taking a large mouthful. "She said, 'you'll see a castle fall.' Well it fell, didn't it? It fell and it was a goddamned miracle no one was killed. So we got to stop now before someone is."

Jane stared at her.

"Well, don't just stand there," Ruby barked, "get me a glass."

Jane hurried off to the bathroom and brought one back.

"Where's Tom?" Ruby demanded.

"Asleep."

"Well, you make sure you don't let that boy out of your sight."

The corner of Jane's mouth pursed uncertainly.

"Yeah, I know, you think I'm crazy," Ruby snorted. "Well I thought she was crazy until today. . . . Coming out with all that claptrap about castles falling, people dying, and babies smashing to bits. . . . What's she talking about, that's what I want to know? She said it was me, inside me. But I didn't do nothing to make that tower come down. . . ."

"It was a thunderbolt," Jane said lamely.

"Yeah, but was it? Oh, you can look at me anyways you like. I'm telling you that I want this movie stopped. Just tell Laurence I want to see him the minute he gets back," and with that she walked from the room, staggering slightly as she reached the door.

As their days in Ireland progressed the storms, which still showed little sign of letting up, began to take their toll on morale. Anna had suddenly assumed a nervous disposition that was as false as it was pathetic. Everyone could see through it, even Laurence, whose task it was to comfort her when she claimed that the storms or Ruby's ramblings were putting her on edge. It was Anna's way of getting Laurence to herself, and since she was the star there was little Laurence could do but appease her. However, he didn't seem to object; in fact it looked to Kirsten as if he rather enjoyed his role as the great protector. And when he wasn't with Anna he was with Ruby, mollifying her and trying to keep her off the bottle.

Fortunately, he made relatively few visits to the set and Kirsten couldn't have been in any doubt during that time how vital her own morale was to the rest of the crew. She had to contain her jealousy for their sakes even more than her own. She realized she owed it to them for they were as loyal to her now as they were dependent on her. It was only Jake who seemed to sense the cracks, and always he was there to help smooth them over. He could make her laugh when it was the last thing she felt like doing and get her enthused at a time when the wind was painfully stinging her ears and the rain was dripping down her back.

They had added a further two days to the shoot, which were going to be spent doing pick-ups and Jean Rochette's solitary amblings through the bleak Irish downs. Laurence was going on ahead to New Orleans with Ruby, Alison, Anna, and several other members of the production team.

On the day of their departure Kirsten woke up feeling particularly depressed. She tried hard all morning to shake it, and although she knew she was doing what she had to do without any problem, she couldn't help feeling angry with herself for being so damned obsessed with the fact that Laurence and Anna were going off to New Orleans together.

Just after lunch, while Laurence, assisted by Tom, was clearing out his trailer, Jane came to stand beside Kirsten at the edge of the set. It was one of the rare occasions when Kirsten wasn't standing in a group of people or shouting instructions, receiving information, blocking the cast, or viewing a prop or costume.

For several minutes she and Jane stood in the drizzling rain watching the stunt coordinator round up the stunt riders and horses in front of the castle.

Eventually Kirsten looked down at Jane and smiled. "Laurence not ready yet?" she said.

Jane shook her head. "A few more minutes he said. It all seems to be going pretty well, doesn't it?" she added nodding toward the set.

"I think so," Kirsten answered cheerily. "At least I hope so. Anyway, what about you? How are you getting along? I don't see much of you these days."

"Oh, I'm fine. Tom and I have really enjoyed ourselves here."

"I'm so glad," Kirsten said, putting her arm around her. "I've neglected you horribly these past few months, but I'll make up for it once we get to New Orleans."

As Jane walked away Laurence came to join Kirsten.

"You okay?" he said as they watched what was going on on the set.

"I'm fine. How about you?"

Laurence turned to face her. His jet-black hair, wet from the rain, was slicked back from his forehead and his face, burned by the wind, somehow made his eyes seem bluer than ever. "I'm worried about you," he said softly.

Kirsten's surprise showed. "About me, why?"

He shrugged. "I guess leaving you here to cope with all this," he said, throwing out an arm toward the set.

Kirsten's expression turned to one of irony. "You're taking the problems with you," she reminded him.

He nodded, and as his smile disappeared he looked past her toward the gloomy castle perched on the hillside.

"What're you thinking?" Kirsten asked after a while.

He didn't answer for some time and as the minutes passed his frown deepened. Then, as he looked down at her again, Kirsten had the startling and overwhelming feeling that he was about to kiss her.

She waited, meeting his gaze and silently daring him to give in to the urge she could almost feel him fighting. God, how she wanted to discard her principles and feel the hardness of him at that moment. They were so close, their lips only inches apart, their eyes locked in wordless combat, each challenging the other to give in. Kirsten shivered as the surface of her skin tingled with awareness, her hands like lead weights yearning to be lifted yet too heavy, too awkward to move. For those timeless moments it was as though they were alone on the hillside, oblivious to the commotion of the set only feet away, unaffected by the mewling cry of the wind as it wrapped around them, pushing them closer together.

"You look lovely," Laurence murmured, then suddenly his eyes closed and he groaned as though in anguish, but the groan rapidly turned to laughter, which made Kirsten laugh too. "You're doing just great, you know that?" he told her.

"Thank you," she said.

"I reckon we're gonna have our work cut out over there in New Orleans," Laurence remarked, and Kirsten knew he wasn't just referring to the film.

"Yeah, I reckon we are," she said quietly. "But I think I can handle it. What about you?"

Laurence's bottom lip came out as his eyes danced with humor. "Yeah," he nodded, "I reckon I can. But, hey, no hanging around over here. Get finished and get out there smartish, 'cause I can handle it a whole lot better when you're around."

"You can?" Kirsten teased.

Laurence laughed, then winking at her he turned toward Alison who was heading in their direction.

Kirsten went over to where the stunt coordinator was lining up the horsemen for the next shot. Jake was with him and as usual he greeted Kirsten with a resounding kiss. And as usual Kirsten chided him for his lack of respect. She listened as he explained what was happening, they changed several positions, pulled in three more horses, then after blocking the scene through, David yelled out for everyone to start setting up for a take.

Kirsten was on her way to the location caterers to get a coffee when Laurence pulled his car to a halt on the dirt track leading to the main road and waved her over. By the time she got there Tom was hanging out of the back window, holding out his arms for a kiss. Laughing, Kirsten gave him as big a hug as she could, then after uttering a few encouraging words to Anna who was sitting on the front passenger seat she turned to Laurence.

But before she could speak he said so that only she could hear, "Have a word with your friend Helena before you get to New Orleans. I want this voodoo rubbish of Ruby's knocked on the head."

"I intend to," Kirsten told him, hiding her exasperation at his ever-changing moods. His expression was as black as the thunderous clouds now and his irritation was equally as evident. Still, with Ruby Collins in the backseat and Anna Sage in the front she didn't suppose she'd be any too happy herself. "Anything else before you go, oh lord and master?" she quipped.

A flicker of amusement sparked in his eyes and Kirsten pursed her lips in a smile. The chemistry leapt between them so strongly at times it took only one word, one movement, for it to spring into life, but on this occasion Laurence turned abruptly away. "No, nothing else," he said. His eyes returned briefly to hers. "Nothing at all," he added, and as Kirsten looked down at him curiously he pressed hard on the accelerator and the car sped off.

CHAPTER EIGHTEEN

"OKAY, LET'S TAKE IT FROM THE DRIVE UP," KIRSTEN shouted, clapping her hands to try and break through the noise around her.

"Stand by for another rehearsal!" David boomed into the loud hailer. "Reset the carriage! Main cast in first positions!"

"Am I delivering my first line as I get out of the carriage or do I wait until I'm on the sidewalk?" Helena asked.

"Start speaking as your foot hits the ground," Kirsten answered. "We'll go in with your turn for a close-up on Anna. But play the scene through to the end."

"Got it," Helena said, and lifting her long drab skirts she hoisted herself back into the landau.

As the carriage was turned and led back down Decatur Street Kirsten walked over to Jake. "That sky is bothering me," she said looking up at the way the sun was threatening to burst through the cloud.

"It's bothering me too. We'll have to be quick about this or nothing's going to match."

"Did you take a look inside the carriage? Are we seeing them all right, or shall we take the roof down?"

"Which would you prefer?"

"That the roof is up."

"Then we'll make it work. Phil!" he shouted to the gaffer, and leaving Kirsten he went off to organize the lights.

"Makeup!" Kirsten called.

"Right here," an assistant answered.

"Take another look at Anna before we go for a take. Her hair's too tidy. No, don't do it now, we'll do the rehearsal first. Have you got any more of that lip salve?"

The makeup assistant handed it over. Kirsten ran it quickly over her wind-chapped lips, then moved off to talk to the sound guys.

"There's no dialogue until the carriage stops," she told them, "so we can wild track the horse's hooves."

"Danny's already over there rigging up the mike," Bob told her.

"Great. Did you get the steamboat whistles earlier?"

"Not really. Too much other noise."

"Okay, we'll get it set up for another time." She swung round as a trumpet suddenly blasted from across the street.

"David!" she yelled. "David!"

"I'm on it," he called back, and Kirsten watched him briefly as he headed off toward the street musician who had somehow broken through the police cordons. "How are we doing up there, Russell?" David shouted into his walkie-talkie.

"A few more minutes," Russell answered. "The carriage is almost here."

Kirsten stood with her hands on her hips absently watching the riggers as they greased the tracks on the pavement and checked the dolly for progress. Her mind was already leaping ahead to the scenes they would shoot that afternoon. It could be, if the sun did come out, that they would have to change the schedule and do some interiors.

"Vicky!" she shouted.

Vicky came running down the street.

"Get on to the production managers and find out what's set up over at Little Joe's studios," Kirsten said. "Once you know dig me out the scenes that correspond to the set."

"Okay. Laurence called just now, by the way. He said do you want to join him and Joe for lunch?"

"Not unless it's important." She took off her cap, ran her fingers through her hair, and made off toward her chair. "How are we doing?" she shouted to anyone within earshot.

"Nearly there," someone called back.

Kirsten perched on the edge of her canvas chair beside the script supervisor. "Remind me what we're coming off of here," she said, peering over Nicola's shoulder.

"Off the steamboat wheel," Nicola answered, moving her script so that Kirsten could get a better look.

"That's right. A mix. Steamboat wheel to carriage wheel. Great. Did you get the dialogue changes for the ballroom scenes from Ruby?"

"Yes. The cast have them too."

Kirsten nodded, put her hands behind her head, and relaxed back in her chair. Seconds later she was out of the chair again, sitting at the camera, one eye pressed to the viewfinder as it tracked down the street. Then she was running up to the carriage pulling open the door and talking to Anna.

". . . I know, it's terrific," she was saying. "Just make sure you keep your face as much in the light as you can. You look wonderful. Remember, you're going to be dignified about this. . . . You don't care what anyone else thinks. . . . But don't forget the touch of uncertainty, especially when Marie Laveau—"

"It's all right." Anna laughed. "Don't worry, I've got it. Helena is going to turn to me on her line. I thought I'd give just a split-second of hesitation before I get out."

"Great. That should do it. Keep your eyes down until you get right into close up. Do you need a mark?"

"I don't think so. We'll see after the rehearsal."

"All right!" Kirsten shouted, closing the carriage door. "Clear the street. . . . Lindon! Lindon!" she was heading toward the camera operator. "I want you to take them through the gate up to the house, tracking back along the pavement and holding those railings foreground."

"Yeah, Kirstie." He laughed. "We already discussed it."

"Did we? So we did. Okay, everyone!" she shouted. "Let's go."

Fifteen minutes later the shot was in the can, the clouds had smothered the sun, and they were setting up for another street scene.

They were ten days into the shoot in New Orleans and Kirsten was as amazed by how well it was going—mainly thanks to Little Joe and his faultless organization—as she was delighted. Every night after rushes

Laurence went out of his way to tell her how great it was all looking, the crew hung on her every word of praise, and the cast were constantly begging her to dine with them so that they could either boast about their performances or discuss their roles. Kirsten was happy to listen, encouraged them as much as she could, and was hardly able to believe the thrill she was getting from it all. It was as though she had developed a totally separate personality. Kirsten the director had now eclipsed Kirsten the woman, and were it not for the odd moment in the day when she saw Anna looking so blissfully happy as she caught sight of Laurence coming on to the set, Kirsten might have persuaded herself to believe that the two of them were not having an affair after all. But the evidence was there for all to see: and her heart seemed to clench when she saw them disappear into Anna's trailer together, or when she saw them laughing at some private joke while everyone raced about the set. It was something she would admit to no one, with the exception of Helena, and not even for a moment did the pain show through the mask of total happiness and absorption she wore. And the fact that she consistently refused Laurence's invitations to lunch or dinner was because she just couldn't stand the way he looked so damned guilty every time he set eyes on her. It was as though he felt sorry for her, and though the temptation to tell him just what he could do with his pity was almost overwhelming, she had so far managed to refrain.

On every other level she and Laurence were getting along fine. They spoke civilly to each other, even made each other laugh, but should Laurence ever look like he might be about to broach something of a more personal nature Kirsten would always make some excuse to get away.

By the beginning of the third week they were into the brothel scenes. Several of them were already in the can and had caused a great deal of ribald laughter as well as a quickening of pulses during the shooting and at the viewing of rushes. It was in the largest of the upstairs rooms in the brothel that Anna and Jean-Paul would play out their big love scene. At that moment, though, Anna was in a two-hour makeup call, having any tiny blemish the camera might pick up covered and all the relevant parts of her body highlighted. In the meantime they were shooting a scene between Jean-Paul and one of the prostitutes.

David had just called cut, and Kirsten and Laurence were laughing so hard that everyone was laughing at them as much as at what had happened. Jean-Paul had been poised to leap onto the four-poster bed where the seminaked prostitute was lying seductively in wait, while those who were in the room had collectively held their breath as she'd peeled away each layer of clothing to reveal her lavishly rouged nipples while the camera tracked slowly around the bed until it was almost behind her and could by then see Jean-Paul. With a barely perceptible nod Kirsten had given him the cue, and Jean-Paul, with all the gusto of the character he was playing, had wrenched down his trousers and lunged at the girl. Somehow though he had managed to crack his knee against the bedpost, veered off sideways, and landed in a tangled heap on the floor, his bare-bottom hidden from camera but not from the crew.

When Anna, clad only in a thin sheet, appeared on the set she crossed straight over to Laurence and knelt at his feet. The whole crew fell silent, watching her, slightly stunned by such an open display of intimacy that was turning them all into unwilling voyeurs. A couple of them sniggered and turned away, and Kirsten was glad to see that Laurence could not hide his embarrassment. She was feeling murderous. As if her own imagination weren't difficult enough to deal with, she was now being forced to face the reality of what the two of them looked like together. And when Laurence stooped down to pull Anna to her feet and Anna slipped her arms around him, Kirsten felt such a surge of jealousy as his hands brushed lightly over Anna's back that it was only Jake, who shoved the console operator aside and deftly switched the lighting to a garish, unflattering mauve, that saved her.

"Are you going to stay for the scene?" she heard Anna whisper to Laurence.

Laurence's eyes were on Anna's. From where she was standing Kirsten couldn't read his expression but she heard him say, "Do you want me to?"

Anna nodded and smiled and for one terrifying moment Kirsten thought they were going to kiss.

She turned away as Jake came up behind her. "Sit down. Don't say a word," he muttered in her ear.

Kirsten lifted her eyes to his. They had never once discussed her relationship with Laurence, but this wasn't the first time Jake had indicated that he knew how she felt. "I want to kill her," Kirsten said through clenched teeth as Lindon and the other assistants started to mount the camera on its tracks and Anna remained at Laurence's side. "Why is she doing this?" Kirsten seethed.

"To make you jealous, why do you think?"

"But she's the one who's got him."

Jake's eyebrows arched. "Is she?"

Kirsten turned away irritably. She wasn't getting into that. "Anna!" she snapped. "Can we have you on the bed, please. Flissy, could you bring something to cover Anna up while we get settled." She waited for Anna to prize herself from Laurence's side, then walked over to him. "A word, please," she said, pulling open the door.

She walked ahead of him down the stairs and into a deserted room off the main hall. "I'm sorry you've forced me to do this," she said, as he closed the door behind them. "But as the director of this film I am requesting that you are not present on the set during scenes that Anna is playing nude. That little display up there just now—"

"I apologize," he interrupted. "I forgot you were doing that scene next . . ."

"I don't care whether you forgot or not. Just please keep away from the set while we do this. Now, if you'll excuse me . . ." and sweeping past him she walked out of the room.

When Kirsten left the set that evening a thousand and one thoughts were chasing through her mind. That wasn't so unusual, it had been like that since she'd started the movie and it was almost impossible, unless engaged in something palpable, for her mind to alight on one topic for more than a few seconds at a time. As she walked along the corridor she was still thinking about a particular shot and how it was going to cut into the shots before and after—should she mix through, and if so, how many frames? Then she was thinking about lighting and how stupendously it had affected Jean-Paul's performance. The sound track played itself through her head, adding effects that were as yet only in her imagination. She thought of the composer and wondered if he should come out here. She'd speak to Laurence. Thinking of Laurence she felt a strange sort of vacuum open up inside her and again her mind was racing on to other things. She must contact Little Joe, Vicky would remind her what about. What time was she meeting with the choreographers tomorrow? How long would it take to rig the set at Scout Island? When she reached her room she checked for messages, then went downstairs to find the others. Most would have taken themselves off to a jazz club or some other exotic night spot on Bourbon Street, taking advantage of the hiatus they would have the next day before the night shoots began. Helena, Kirsten thought, seemed particularly edgy about the night shoots, but that was understandable since they were her biggest scenes. Anna fortunately had much less to do, just one scene in total, which was a godsend, for Kirsten was feeling so exhausted lately that she wasn't too sure how long she could continue on this relentless emotional seesaw.

She was wandering over to the reception desk, humming along to Fats Domino singing *Walking through New Orleans,* which was wafting out of the juke box in the bar, when she heard a burst of laughter coming from the same direction. There was no need to ask the receptionist where Helena was, she'd recognize that laugh anywhere, and turning back she walked into the darkened, smoke-filled atmosphere of the bar. It was populated by locals and a couple of the hotel staff, but there was no sign of Helena. It wasn't until Kirsten had gone deeper into the bar that she spotted her, sitting out in the conservatory, the rippling glow of pool lights reflected on the window behind her, casting her in an almost dreamlike sort of radiance.

Smiling, Kirsten started toward her then suddenly, seeing whom Helena was with, she froze. For a moment she couldn't believe her eyes, felt it surely must be some kind of trick of the light. Though she didn't move she could feel herself recoiling at what she was seeing. It wasn't so much that Helena was sitting at a table with Laurence and Anna, or the way that Laurence was draping his arm across the back of Anna's chair, though that was bad enough—it was that Dermott Campbell was at the table, too, and the four of them looked so cozy, so at ease, and so wrapped up in each other that they hadn't even seen her come into the bar.

Still laughing, Helena disappeared beneath the table to get something from her bag and at that moment Laurence happened to glance up. The instant he saw Kirsten the smile faded from his lips. He turned to follow the direction of her eyes and saw Campbell, slouched in his chair, a glass cupped in one hand, a fat cigar in the other, and a grin of unmistakable triumph curving lazily across his mouth. Quickly Laurence turned back to Kirsten, but before he could speak Kirsten had turned and walked out of the bar.

So many thoughts, so many words, so much, charging through her mind. Fear and panic, hurt and betrayal. A craziness that was permeating the very pores of her skin. She had to get away from them, get out of here, run, scream, do anything to stop the truth of what she had seen. As she rode up in the lift she took deep breaths, holding on to the rail in order to steady herself. Dear God, please don't let me have an attack now, she prayed silently. Please don't let this be happening at all. She jerked her face up to the mirror beside her, glared at herself, and willed herself to remain calm. There was no explanation in the world that could either excuse or lessen the pain of what she had seen, but she must not even look for one. She had just to get ahold of herself, remind herself of the way everyone was relying on her now to finish what she had started. She couldn't back away from it, she couldn't let them down. She wasn't going to think about what she'd seen, she wasn't even going to try to analyze what was behind it because if Helena really was still having an affair with Campbell, if Laurence knew about it and accepted it, if he'd decided now to go public about his affair with Anna, and if they were going to throw all this in her face, Kirsten just knew that she wouldn't be able to handle it.

She was fumbling her key into the door when she heard Jake calling to her from the end of the corridor.

"I've been looking all over for you," he said. "Didn't you get my message?"

"Hi!" Kirsten said brightly, swinging round to face him. "No. Nothing's wrong is it?"

He laughed. "Why should anything be wrong? I was

trying to get hold of you to see if you wanted to go to a jazz club."

"Oh, that sounds nice," Kirsten said. "Why not? Would you like to come in while I get ready? It won't take long."

Once they were inside the room Kirsten suddenly felt emotion swelling in her like a storm. She was so close to breaking she could hardly bear to look at Jake. He was always there for her, turned up just when she needed him. He never questioned her; he simply gave her his support. There was nothing devious about him; he was kind and caring and honest and straightforward. So often people took those they loved for granted. . . . She wanted Jake to know how much she appreciated all he did for her; she wanted him to understand that there was nothing she wouldn't do for him in return. She wanted him to hold her and embrace her with the kindness and warmth that came so naturally to him. She wanted to feel the strength of his arms around her, holding her physically the way his support held her mentally.

She turned to face him. Distantly she was aware of the nervousness quaking inside her, the fear that he would say no. That he was happy to flirt with her, to be there for her when she needed him, but that he was married and he loved his wife. But then he looked up from the *Lagniappe* he was flicking through and when he saw the look in Kirsten's eyes he dropped the magazine and went to her.

"Christ, Kirstie," he murmured as he folded her in his arms. "What is it?"

"I want you, Jake," she whispered. "I want you very much."

She looked up into his deep, brown eyes. His thick blond hair fell over his brow briefly touching the jet-black curves of his eyebrows. His mouth looked hard, yet inviting, the dark shadow around his jaw leant it a strength to which she could feel herself responding. As he lowered his lips to hers Kirsten's hands moved into his hair, twisting it around her fingers as she pressed herself against him.

"Are you sure about this?" he whispered.

"I'm sure," she answered, pulling his mouth back to hers.

As his hands found her breasts the memory of Laurence touching her that way flickered through her mind. She pushed it away, and lowering her hands to the buttons at the neck of her dress she started to undo them. Jake took a step back, watching her with eyes that were his, then Laurence's, then his again. Slowly she peeled off her dress until she was standing before him in her bra, her panties, and gartered stockings. Jake groaned and closed his eyes as his arms went round her again, pulling her to him as he unfastened her bra. He ran his hands over her back, stroking it, caressing it, and losing his fingers in her hair as his tongue found hers and he kissed her with a tenderness that seemed to turn her heart to liquid. This was what she had longed for from Laurence, the tenderness that would take the edge from the lust. Again she forced down the shutters in her mind and made herself think of Jake. Gently she pushed him away and pulled the straps of her bra down over her arms allowing her breasts to fall free.

"Oh, sweet Jesus," Jake murmured looking down at the most beautiful breasts he had ever seen. He reached out a hand and ran a thumb lightly over her achingly hard nipples, then suddenly he jerked her against him and buried his tongue deep in her mouth. She could feel his erection pressing against her, was aware of deep and bitter sensations pouring through her veins. As he struggled to remove his shirt Kirsten's fingers were fumbling with his zip. He lifted her hands, lowered the zip himself, and as he pulled his jeans to his knees Kirsten removed her panties.

Taking her by the waist he turned her around and laid her back on the bed. As he knelt between her legs she lifted her knees and moaned softly as he ran his hands over her inner thighs. Her eyes were closed, her head was rolling from side to side, and in her mind she was seeing Laurence, feeling his fingers stroke her, tease her and torment her. She forced her eyes open, looked up at Jake, then held her arms out to him.

"Please," she whispered, "I want you now."

He lowered his body to hers, taking her lips between his and gently rotating his hips, seeking the point of penetration. It was at that moment that the telephone rang.

"Fucking hell," Jake muttered. "Just leave it," he growled as Kirsten reached out to answer it.

The telephone kept on ringing until Kirsten reluctantly pulled herself away and turned to lift the receiver. "Hello," she murmured.

"Hi. You okay? You sound kind of sleepy."

At the sound of Laurence's voice Kirsten's heart twisted so painfully it took her breath away. Her eyes moved to Jake, who had sulkily flung himself down on the bed beside her. She looked in dismay at his erection, straining toward his navel.

"No, I'm fine," she said into the receiver.

"That's good." She could hear the smile in Laurence's voice and suddenly the need for him was so strong she could feel it filling her as though it might drown her. "What can I do for you?" she whispered.

"I'm calling to apologize for not telling you Campbell was here. I didn't know until a few minutes ago that Helena hadn't told you either."

"What's he doing here?" Kirsten mumbled, then swung her legs to the floor as Jake reached out for her breasts.

"Well, to tell you the truth," Laurence began, "I got this crazy notion in my head when we were back in England to invite him onto the set so he could see for himself how well you were doing. I thought maybe then he'd let up on you. He turned me down at the time, but he called me a couple of days ago and said he wanted to take me up on the offer. He was already here in New Orleans, so I agreed to meet with him tonight to discuss it."

"Don't you think you should have consulted me first?" Kirsten said.

"Yeah, I guess I should have . . . But Kirsten, you've been so damned unapproachable lately—"

"No one else seems to be having that problem with me, Laurence," she interrupted. "But you do what you want. You're the producer, you make the decisions."

"Kirsten, don't take it that way. Don't you see—"

"I've seen all I needed to see," Kirsten said.

"Look, for Christ's sake, I can't do anything about him being here. It's a free world, he can go wherever he wants. But I can stop him going to the set . . ."

"Don't bother. I've got nothing to hide."

"Look, Kirsten, can we talk about this? Let me come over there—"

"No! I don't want to discuss this anymore, Laurence. You know how I feel about that man, you know Dyllis Fisher won't rest until she's got me where she wants me, so you go right ahead and help them. I can't stop you."

"Kirsten! Listen to me. I'm on your side, goddammit! Maybe it's your friend Helena you should be speaking to. It was her who invited him over here."

"I'd already guessed that. I don't know what you're all playing at, Laurence, but whatever it is I just hope you're getting some kind of kick out of it."

"Kirstie, we got to get this sorted. We've got to talk, you and me . . ."

"Good night, Laurence," she said.

As she replaced the receiver Kirsten leaned forward against the bedside table, pressing a hand to her mouth.

"Hey, remember me?" Jake said, taking her shoulder and trying to pull her back onto the bed.

Kirsten turned away. "Can you go, please?" she said her voice strangled by tears. "I need to be—"

"Go? What, are you crazy?" Jake laughed.

Kirsten turned to look at him, her chest starting to heave. "Jake, I'm sorry," she whispered. "I just can't go through with it. I thought I could, but . . ."

"Hey, come on," he said. "You're not pulling that one

on me. You wanted it five minutes ago, you got me all fired up . . ."

"No, Jake!" she cried as he pulled her down onto the bed. "Jake, for God's sake! I made a mistake. I'm sorry, I didn't mean to lead you on. . . . No!" she screamed as he pushed his legs between hers.

"Listen," he growled, "you wanted my cock, now you're going to get it!"

For a moment Kirsten was so dazed she couldn't move. This couldn't be the same man who'd made love to her just a few minutes ago. The man who'd stood at her side throughout the day. . . . The man she'd thought was her friend. . . .

With a strength she hardly knew she possessed she threw him off her and leapt up from the bed. "Just go!" she shouted. "Please, just get out of here!" and before he could say anymore she ran into the bathroom and turned the key in the lock.

Seconds later she jumped as the door slammed behind him, then wrapping herself in a toweling robe she sank down onto the edge of the bath and leaned her head against the wash basin.

She was shaking so hard that when she reached out for the taps she could barely make her fingers turn them. It was her own fault, she shouldn't have done that to Jake, but she was so confused, so disoriented by all that was happening she barely knew what she was doing.

As the basin filled with icy water she splashed it over her face, taking deep breaths in an effort to calm herself. But everything was crowding in on her.

God she hated this place. She wanted to leave, to get as far away from it as she could. Nothing was normal here; people behaved in strange, uncharacteristic ways. . . . Everyone around her was changing. . . . She didn't have it in her to cope with this. . . .

Dry, racking sobs convulsed her body as she thought of Helena and Campbell. The deceit was almost as hard to bear as Laurence's love for Anna.

She squeezed her eyes tightly and pressed her hands to her face as though to block out the gathering faces that seemed to be closing in on her. Ruby, with her fears of insanity; Jake, whose gentleness had suddenly turned to violence; Helena, whose friendship was as false as her word; Laurence . . . Dear God, Laurence. . . . How maliciously the memory of his hands touching Anna's body tortured her mind, yet how desperately she yearned to feel his arms around her now, soothing the pain, trying to take it from her. She needed him so much, yet she could feel herself reaching into darkness. He wasn't there. None of them were there. She was alone, so terrifyingly, bewilderingly alone. . . .

CHAPTER NINETEEN

AS KIRSTEN WALKED THROUGH THE DARKNESS TOward the cavernous opening in the trees of Scout Island she was looking at the curving sweep of the branches that reached across the top of the clearing. Shafts of bright light were shooting upward through the entwining foliage, a chill wind swaying the shadows. "Have enough branches been chopped away for the camera to see through?" Kirsten was asking David.

"Yep. The crane is already rigged. You can go up and take a look as soon as you're ready."

"Okay. What about the other cameras?"

"They're being set up now. The operators seem to know their stuff. I'll introduce you."

"All right," Kirsten said, wincing as Ruby tightened the grip on her arm.

"Shit, just take a look at all this," Ruby said, her eyes steeped in awe as they entered the clearing where electricians, props men, sound guys, cameramen, and their myriad assistants were busily setting up for the big scene, the voodoo ceremony that was the climax of

Moyna O'Malley's story. The atmosphere was electric, excitement reverberated through every voice that yelled out, exhilaration and exuberance flowed like a magnetic force through the misty night air. In the flooding beam of working lights everyone hefted and carried, threw and caught, climbed and jumped, spun cables, laid tracks, mounted cameras and rigged booms. Alison and her two art directors were at the altar, which towered magnificently toward the roof of knotted branches. They were supervising the last-minute decoration, but already the altar was so impressive as to arrest Kirsten in her tracks. As she gazed up at the gargoyle faces, the fiercely protruding tongues, wolfishly bared teeth, and chillingly obscene emblems of *loa* worship, she felt a tingling inside that seemed to spread to every part of her body. She could feel herself smiling as her heart thudded with profound admiration at the effect Alison had created, yet at the same time she was aware of her bitter resentment that all this energy would have to be put on hold while they moved to the other set for Anna's scene. Laurence had called earlier that day to ask her to bring forward Anna's scene as she had a migraine. Kirsten was not happy about it and agreed only with very bad grace.

"Is the other set being made ready?" she asked David, biting hard on her anger.

"Yes. But the camera boys are waiting to hear from you where you want them to do this shot on Helena before we go over there."

"Okay. Get them to put it there, slightly off center," she said, pointing to where the graphics team was carving cabalistic signs in the thick ashes strewn over the ground in front of the altar.

As David disappeared into the crowd Ruby said, "I'm going to get me a coffee. Want one?"

"No, thanks," Kirsten answered, wondering where, in all this mayhem, she might find Jake. She experienced a quick pang of nerves at the prospect of seeing him, but knew the quicker she got it over with the better. A sound assistant raced up to her, hooked a set of headphones around her neck, and clipped a battery to her belt.

"Monitor's over on the left side," he told her, waving an arm in the general direction of where some of the cast were already beginning to gather.

Kirsten thanked him and made her way toward Jean-Paul, stepping to one side as a handful of scenes men carried a massive, grisly-looking totem pole toward the altar. In the distance Kirsten could see the working lights of the other set. The solitary house with its gray stone walls, narrow windows, and decrepit roof was, as far as she could see, just perfect and Alison was right: They'd achieve a much higher degree of sinisterness by putting it in the midst of the looming shadows of this mist-shrouded island. But dammit, it needed the dawn!

She turned back at the general gasp of wonder that went up as simultaneously the working lights went off and the thickly colored hue of vermilion and ocher lamps beamed shafts of eddying light onto the altar.

"The man is a genius, no?" Jean-Paul whispered in Kirsten's ear as Jake waved a hand for the electricians to revert back to working lights.

Kirsten turned to Jean-Paul and gave a startled scream as she came face-to-face with the glittering red eyes of a demon's mask.

Jean-Paul laughed, and lowering the mask he planted a kiss on each of Kirsten's cheeks. "So, how are you feeling?" he said. "Please tell me you are as nervous as I—it might make me feel a little better."

"As nervous as hell." Kirsten laughed.

They talked quietly together for a while, going over the notes she had given Jean-Paul during their discussions, until David came running over to tell her that Helena was ready and should he ask her to come onto the set?

"Just give me a moment," she said, catching Jake by the arm as he passed.

"It's looking fantastic," she told him.

"You ain't seen nothing yet," he smiled, looking down into her eyes. "I owe you an apology," he said softly.

"I owe you one too."

Jake's head tilted to one side as his eyes creased in a smile. "What do you say we put it down to a moment of madness and go back to the way we were?" he said.

Kirsten lifted a hand and touched his arm. "Let's do that," she whispered.

"Hey," he said, lifting her troubled face to the light. "It's going to be great. We're all rooting for you, you know."

"Thanks." Kirsten smiled.

"So how about we get this show on the road?"

"Okay." She laughed. "You know about the change in schedule?"

"I do. I imagine you're pretty pissed off about it."

"That's an understatement," Kirsten remarked. "Anyway, how far are you off here?"

"We're about ready for a rehearsal."

"All right, David," she said, turning back to where he was still hovering. "Bring Helena on. Who's giving her an eyeline?"

"I think Anna's doing it herself," David answered, "but I'll check. Do we want any of the extras?"

"No."

A frantic string of messages started up over the walkie-talkies then, calling for Helena, for Anna, for makeup, continuity, and costume.

Kirsten looked around for Jean-Paul again, but he was gone and suddenly her heart tightened as she saw Laurence at the other side of the set. He was standing beside Ruby, who was hanging on to his arm as he talked to the choreographer. Kirsten averted her eyes. How was he feeling right now, she wondered. Was he nervous, like everyone else, or was he, as she suspected, quietly confident that all would go according to plan? Well, it just damned well better, she seethed to herself, because if it didn't . . . But she didn't want to think about that. She had somehow to control her anger and make this debacle of a revised schedule work.

She started across the clearing as Helena, in the full costume of a high priestess of voodoo, stalked majestically onto the set to a round of applause. Kirsten smiled fondly. No matter what was going on between them personally, tonight was Helena's night and Kirsten was going to do all she could to make it special for her. This, of all the scenes, was the one in which Helena was the absolute star, for Marie Laveau, as the great *mambo* of the idolatrous ritual, was to conduct the pagan ceremony of sacrilege and sacrifice.

"Okay, let's have first positions," Kirsten called out to David, as she reached Helena's side. "We'll start blocking through. You look amazing," she told Helena.

Helena grinned and Kirsten gave a gasp of laughter as her heart almost skipped a beat. Helena's own teeth were covered by another larger set that was cracked, blackened, and blood-stained. And whatever the makeup artist had used to bring out the color of Helena's eyes was equally chilling. As Helena moved into the light they sparked and flashed like flames. For the moment there was no expression in them, except perhaps a touch of anxiety as Helena began psyching herself up for the performance. The darkened skin of her face was painted with jagged red scars, her eyes were thickly rimmed with white grease. Her hair was combed viciously back from her face, heightening the harsh bones of her cheeks. Her lips were blood red, so too were her finger nails. Beneath the somber black cape whose collar sat high and stiff behind her head was a glittering gold-and-silver robe, cut so low that the dark circles of her nipples were almost visible.

She stepped in behind the altar. Anna Sage appeared and though she cooed her appreciation of the way Helena looked, Kirsten could see it was an effort. Maybe the headache wasn't a sham after all; she looked dreadfully pale.

"I'm sorry about this change," Anna said to Kirsten. "I hope I'm not being too much of a nuisance. It's not often I get these migraines, but I do from time to time. I suppose it's the pressure of—"

"It's all right," Kirsten said cutting her off. "I understand. And you don't have to be here for the eyeline, you know, your stand-in can do it."

"No, it's okay. I'd rather do it myself. It wouldn't be fair on Helena otherwise."

Kirsten looked at her. Anna always did her own eyelines and was extremely grateful when the others did theirs. It was much easier, she maintained, to get the level of performance right when you were playing to the real person. "Jean-Paul's around somewhere," Kirsten said. "If you find David he'll take you to your positions. There's no hurry, though; we'll be a while blocking this through."

As Anna went off, Kirsten turned back and watched Helena going over her moves with the choreographer. All around them people were starting to gather, as fascinated by the set as they were by Helena.

At last, having watched an entire rehearsal through the viewfinder while the focus puller rehearsed his own performance, and having decided to use the camera on the crane for the end of the sequence, Kirsten jumped down from the camera seat and walked over to where Laurence was standing at his monitor, his hands resting on the back of Ruby's chair.

"What do you think?" she said, failing to disguise her irritation.

He nodded. "I think it's going to be great."

"Any notes?"

"None."

"Okay, set up for a take!" Kirsten shouted.

"You still mad about this change of schedule?" Laurence said, though Kirsten barely heard him above the noise that had started up.

"Laurence!" she answered, raising her voice to be heard. "I want to shoot the whole scene now, complete with zombies, nude dancers, sacrifices, and offerings, the way it was planned." This veering away from the climax was getting her angrier by the minute and she knew that even Helena's single performance, which was going to be stunning, wouldn't get her worked up to the pitch of excitement she and everyone else had been heading toward. "So, yes, I'm still mad," she went on. "And I'm standing by what I said. If we haven't finished by the time the sun comes up then I want another night shoot and that's going to double the cost of what we've already laid out." In other words that was the price they would have to pay for his pandering to Anna's headaches. She didn't say that of course, but the words lay there unspoken between them.

A few minutes later she was back at the altar with Helena. "How are you feeling?" she asked, shielding her eyes from the dazzling lights.

"Okay," Helena answered. "Happy with what you've seen?"

"Happy. I know you're holding back for the rehearsal, but when it comes to the take I want you to go for it. I mean really go for it."

"Don't worry, I will."

"Okay. Why don't you go and sit down for a while?" Kirsten said, as the set decorators hovered around lighting candles and incense and adding the finishing touches to the props.

"No, I'll stay here," Helena said, looking down at the

python as it was laid out in front of her. "Hi there, little Dermott," she said, running her fingers down its back.

Kirsten burst out laughing in spite of herself.

Helena grinned. "You'll have to excuse us, 'cause little Dermott and me have got to have a bit of a chat before we go for a take."

Leaving Helena to it Kirsten strolled to the edge of the set, wincing when she passed David as he yelled, "Let's have a bit of quiet, please!"

She was leaning against a tree just a couple of feet from the set watching the chaos taking shape when she heard a rustling behind her. She turned to see who it was, but there was nobody there except those who were working on the tumbledown house, but that was too far distant to have accounted for the noise she'd heard. Suddenly all her senses were alert as she peered into the darkness and listened. Somebody was there; she could hear them breathing and she was about to yell to one of the burly electricians when to her amazement she saw Tom totter out from behind some bushes and into the light.

"Tom!" she gasped, running forward. "What on earth are you doing here?" Quickly she hoisted him up in her arms, wrapping her coat around him to cover his pajamas. "Does Daddy know you're here?" she said.

"Daddy's up there," he said, pointing to where Laurence was leaning on a balustrade of the camera platform looking down at the set.

"Yes, but does he know you're down here?"

Tom shook his head solemnly, then to Kirsten's dismay a single tear rolled from the corner of his eye.

"Oh, what is it, honey?" she said, hugging him to her. "Did something frighten you?"

She felt him shake his head and held him more tightly as his tiny arms gripped her neck.

"Then what is it, sweetheart? Do you want to see Daddy?"

"Yes," Tom said, his little voice choked with tears.

"Oh, come on then, let's go and see if we can get him to come down."

As she walked toward the camera platform Kirsten lifted her walkie-talkie in order to speak to Laurence, but she got no further than pressing the button when Jane suddenly came racing out of the darkness.

"Oh, thank God," she gasped. "I've been looking all over for him. I just popped out to get myself a coffee and when I got back he was gone. He was fast asleep when I left." She was breathless and shaking so hard that Kirsten didn't immediately hand Tom over.

"Honestly, it gave me the fright of my life," Jane went on. "God, if anything had happened to him—he might have wandered off anywhere, fallen into the river . . ."

"But he didn't," Kirsten said soothingly. "He's right here and quite safe, aren't you, soldier?"

"Jane," he whimpered, and letting go of Kirsten he held his arms out for Jane. "I want my Daddy," he said, trying very hard not to cry.

Jane looked anxiously at Kirsten. Obviously Laurence would be furious if he discovered Tom had been out here while all this was going on, though what Kirsten wanted to know was why Jane and Tom weren't back at the hotel.

"Tom wanted to sleep in the trailer tonight," Jane explained. "Laurence said he could, providing he didn't set foot outside."

"Then you'd better get him back there pretty quick," Kirsten told her, "before Laurence sees either of you."

"Yes, yes, you're right," Jane said, glancing nervously toward the stretch of forbidding darkness between the set and the trailers.

Kirsten called out to the third assistant and told him to escort Jane and Tom back to their trailer. "And whatever you do, Jane," she cautioned, "make sure you lock the door next time you want a coffee."

"Oh, I will, I will," Jane assured her. "I'm sorry, really. Oh, gosh, I wish we could go back to the hotel. I don't like it out here at all."

For some reason Jane's nervousness seemed to incite Kirsten's and suddenly Kirsten remembered Ruby's fear that the child in her reading was Tom—that he was in some sort of danger. It wasn't that Kirsten believed it, but there was no harm in being extra careful while they were out here in the dead of night. "If I were you," she said to Jane, "I'd lock yourselves in when you get back." Then to the third assistant she added, "Ask the security guards to keep an eye on the trailers."

She watched until the three of them had disappeared into the shadows, then turning back to the set she called out to David. "How are we doing over there?"

"Couple more minutes," Jake shouted back as he watched the console operator making final adjustments to the lighting.

At last the cameras started to roll. A feverish silence descended over the set as a harsh red light beamed down on the altar.

Everyone was still.

"Shot five hundred, take one," the clapper loader announced, slamming the board together.

Kirsten waited for him to settle. David moved quietly across the front of the crowd that had gathered. Kirsten looked at Jake and as Jake touched the console operator's shoulder, fluid motions of warmly glowing lights began rippling over the altar. Helena's face was a study of unholy, transcendent rapture.

Kirsten raised a hand. The sound man hit the playback machine, and a tattoo of dense, sonorous beats throbbed into the night. A few seconds later, slowly, rhythmically, Helena's body started to sway as she lifted her face toward the canopy of gnarled and mist-shrouded foliage overhead. Undulating streams of light touched her, painting her with a sleazy saturation of lurid color, as the leafy shadows cast strange and ungodly images over her writhing body.

"Papa Legba, ouvrez la barrière pour nous passer," she chanted, the turbulent emotion of her husky voice blending with the hypnotic monotony of the drums. *"Papa Legba, ouvrez la barrière pour nous passer,"* she repeated. Her head fell back, her arms spread her cloak like wings, and before her on the altar the slithering blood python moved sluggishly over the objects of tribute. At last her hands closed around the creature's succulent flesh, her fingers fanning the circles of its body as her thumbs lifted the pointed face to her own. "Damballah, Damballah," she intoned. Suddenly she jerked the snake upward as her head dipped and the drums thundered into a terrible rhythm. She coiled the snake over her shoulders and began a blood-curdling liturgy to the

ancestors. And as her body writhed, jerked, and vibrated to the diabolical rhythm and as the python curled itself lovingly about her, the gathering before her watched, spellbound.

The power emanating from her was mesmerizing. Kirsten had seen Helena rehearse this dance on countless occasions and always she had felt the strength of her performance, but that was nothing compared to what was happening to her now. It was as though the mounting frenzy of Helena's writhings was becoming a force of its own, moving with the mist throughout the set and invading the very soul of all those present. Kirsten could feel the pummeling rhythm of the drums as though their every beat were being thrummed upon her heart.

Then suddenly the drums stopped, cutting the air with silence.

Kirsten tensed as sparks of yellowy green light exploded from the portals of the altar. Helena was lying across it, the snake grasped between her legs, its head poised over her face, its flickering tongue lashing toward her. Then suddenly she was upright and as her eyes blazed across the set toward the spot where Anna was secreted, a piercing and spine-chillingly demented scream flew through the night. A tremor of unease coasted through Kirsten's stomach at the evil that seemed to seep from the frozen expression on Helena's face even as her heart swelled at the extraordinary power of the performance.

"Hold it! Hold it!" Kirsten shouted. "Nobody move!"

The crane, which had been holding a close-up of Helena's face, swooped down to the altar like a ravenous vulture, taking fast moving pans of the grisly objects, until finally it rose back into the darkness and Kirsten yelled, "Cut! Check the gates."

Breathless, Helena turned to Kirsten. Kirsten looked back. With the exception of those checking cameras, no one moved. Not until both assistants had given the all clear did Kirsten allow herself to smile. As she did the relief that came into Helena's eyes turned Kirsten's smile to laughter.

"It was brilliant!" she cried, waving her fists in the air. "Absolutely, fucking brilliant!" and running over to Helena she threw her arms around her and the two of them danced around the altar, as everyone else started to applaud.

Kirsten broke free when she saw Laurence coming toward her.

"Do you want to do another for cover?" he said.

What Kirsten wanted was to go right ahead with the full drama of the scene, but there was no point in arguing with him now. "Yes, I suppose we ought," she said, "but that was perfect for me."

Laurence nodded, then turned as they heard someone running up behind them.

"Laurence, Kirsten," Kelly, one of the design assistants, gasped. "I think one of you'd better come. Anna Sage is having hysterics over there. Ruby's gone off her head or something and Jean-Paul's threatening to do them both an injury if they don't shut up!"

Kirsten and Laurence followed Kelly around the edge of the set where the technicians were getting ready for another take, past the animal handlers who were already being organized for the cutaways, to the clump of trees where Anna, as Moyna O'Malley, had positioned herself to give Helena the eyeline.

The moment she saw Laurence Anna ran toward him, her arms outstretched, her whole body racked with sobs. "Get that woman away from me!" she choked. "She's mad! She's insane! Get her away from me!"

"What the hell is going on?" Laurence demanded as he wrapped Anna in his arms, wincing as Ruby cackled with laughter. "For Christ's sake, pull yourself together, Ruby!" he shouted.

But Ruby just gripped her sides and let out another wail of mirth.

Kirsten went to her, took her by the shoulders, and shook her. She coughed so hard it was making her retch.

"She's done it again," Anna sobbed into Laurence's shoulder. "She's trying to frighten me with all that witchcraft stuff. . . . She's off her head, I know she is, but—"

"It's not me doing the scary bits," Ruby wheezed. "It's her!" She was pointing at Helena. "That look—you saw that look she gave her at the end. . . . Stupid bitch thought it was for real. Thought an evil spell was being cast on her. . . ."

"Stop it!" Kirsten shouted, so appalled at the way Ruby was speaking to Anna she wanted to slap her as much for that as for coming onto the set drunk. "Get Anna to her trailer, someone!" she snapped, glaring at Laurence. "David! David! Where are you?"

"Right behind you," he answered.

"Get someone to take care of Ruby," Kirsten muttered

under her breath. "Lock her in my trailer if you have to, and don't let her out until she's sobered up."

"I'm sorry," Anna was wailing. "I'm so sorry. I didn't mean to cause a fuss—"

"Laurence," Kirsten interrupted. "Could I have a word, please?"

The two of them walked farther into the woods out of earshot. "Please do whatever you have to do to calm her down," she said, "then get her into makeup. We'll do her scene now."

"What? Are you saying you're going to de-rig the camera before—"

"That's precisely what I'm saying. I don't need another take on Helena, we'll have her well covered on the wider shots, and I want Anna's scene done and her out of here before I do something one of us might regret."

An hour later everyone was over at the other set on the banks of the bayou. The frayed tempers of earlier had abated, though Kirsten was fully aware that the tension and excitement Helena had created was ebbing too. She should have had this scene put back to another day when it could have been done the way she wanted it, and had Anna not gone to Laurence with her request then, that was precisely what Kirsten would have done. As it was she'd allowed her feelings to cloud her judgment. It was the first time she'd done it, and it couldn't have happened over a more critical situation.

As the crew milled around setting props, dry-ice machines, lamps, and cables, Kirsten watched the riggers haul the dolly into the house. The air was dank; there was a strong smell of mildew mingling with the chemical solution of the dry ice and the bitter aroma rising from the brackish water of the bayou. Moisture dripped from the trees, night creatures rustled, scurried, squawked, and chirped but could barely be heard over the din of the crew. Kirsten looked up at the impenetrable sky where a thin sliver of the moon emerged from a bank of cloud and inwardly vented her frustration on a god who probably wasn't even listening.

After what seemed an interminable amount of time they were ready to shoot. The rehearsals had coughed up all kinds of problems, though Anna seemed remarkably well recovered which, perversely, irritated Kirsten even more. Still, at least the technical hitches had been dealt with and now it just remained for Kirsten to return to her chair while makeup did their finishing touches. However, she continued to stand over Anna, who was sitting on the makeshift bed baring her neck to the makeup artist, going over some last-minute notes. The room, which was lit with a hot, purplish, red light, was horribly claustrophobic with its low ceiling and stone walls coated in moss, and there was barely enough space for the bed and the camera mounted on the dolly. The floor was strewn with straw, the single window was boarded up, and a small cannister of dry ice in the corner puffed thin wisps of mist around the ragged blankets on the bed.

Having gone over what was to happen Kirsten went out into the swirling mist to look for Laurence.

Tucked in behind the monitors, unnoticed so far by anyone except Helena, Ruby sat swaying around on a canvas chair, so drunk she wasn't any too sure where she was. How she'd managed to get herself there was a mystery Helena wasn't interested in solving as she moved alongside Ruby, planting herself in such a way that Kirsten probably wouldn't notice her. Then she beckoned to one of the riggers to come and fill out the blockade. They were so close to a take now that the last thing either Anna or Kirsten needed was Ruby throwing a tantrum as she was escorted from the set.

Helena could see Kirsten and Laurence exchanging what looked like heated words at the door of the house, then both of them went inside. A few seconds later the makeup girl came out, then the camera operator squeezed in, checking the connections on cables, for he was doing this scene by remote control since once the camera started to move there would be no room for him.

The whole atmosphere had a strange surreal quality about it, Helena was thinking to herself. It was as though they were all taking part in some kind of silent movie. Lips were moving, but it was as though no sound were coming out. But there was sound; it just seemed, oddly, to be coming from a long way off.

She shivered, drew her cloak tighter around her, and continued to watch as everyone moved about the set. After a while Kirsten and Laurence came out of the house, parted at the door, and went to their monitors.

Kirsten looked around, found the actor whose hands and back were to be featured in the scene, walked him to the house, then gave a nod to the props man.

"Okay," she said, rubbing her hands together as she returned to her monitor. "Let's do it."

As everyone moved into position she squeezed Helena's arm as it linked through hers. "This isn't going to work," she muttered. "The light's all wrong, I want the door to open and close in shot, for Christ's sake we have to see the guy come in. Shit!" she suddenly seethed. "If it had been anyone else but Anna I'd have thought this through better. But now look what's happening. We've got two hundred or more extras lined up for the ritual, we've got all the animals on stand-by, the makeup artists have slogged their guts out . . . I know it's childish, Helena, but I want to cry. I've been looking forward to that ritual—it's the biggest challenge of the entire film—and now that spoiled, pampered little cow has ruined it. Isn't it enough that she has Laurence? Why does she have to fuck this up for me too?"

"She hasn't fucked it up," Helena said comfortingly. "We'll do it. And it'll be great, you'll see."

"No!" Kirsten suddenly cried, hearing the continuity girl give the wrong instructions to the props guy. "All we want for now is the end of the struggle—the hands leaving the throat, the retreating figure, and a few seconds hold on Anna's face. Ask Jake can we do it with the door open to get the guy out?"

"Sure we can," Jake answered, having heard the question. "Just give me a minute and I'll sort it."

Kirsten nodded. "God, this is taking forever," she said to Helena, and as she glanced at her watch her heart sank. "Just look at the time! We'll never—"

"Kirsten! Kirsten!" Anna's voice came from inside the house.

"What is it?" Kirsten said, pushing her way inside.

"Could we just go over this again, please? If John here is going out of the door . . ."

Kirsten turned to John. "You pause at the door—we'll

give you a mark. Give the camera time to pan back to Anna, then go out of the door. It'll already be open and as you come out it'll be the cue for props to activate the mist. Then close the door behind you."

"Thank you." Anna smiled.

It was another ten minutes before the clapper loader ran into position, raising a thumb as the script supervisor called out the shot number; David had a final few words with the actors; and Laurence went to stand beside Jake at the monitor positioned just in front of Kirsten's.

"Okay, turn over," Kirsten said, as David cleared shot and came out of the house.

"Camera's rolling."

"Shot five hundred and one, take one."

Kirsten peered down at her monitor. After a moment or two she looked up and was just drawing breath to call action when Ruby keeled over and landed with a thud on the grass.

Despite herself Kirsten giggled. So too did Helena, but as one of the runners made to help Ruby up, Kirsten said, "Leave her!" Then turning back to her monitor she looked at it again for several moments before saying, "Okay, and . . . action!"

Her eyes were fixed on the tiny screen as the frantic buzz of swamp life came over her headphones together with the muted sounds of the struggle going on inside the house. Immediately she made a mental note that the sound perspective was wrong. A dark figure was looming over Anna, his hands gripping her throat, his knee pressing hard into her chest. Anna's eyes were twin pools of panicked terror as she tried to fight him off, but slowly, and alarmingly convincingly, as his fingers dug deeper into her delicate flesh, she began to relinquish the life from her body. The camera pulled back as the figure turned toward it, cloaking the screen in an unsteady movement of black. The camera moved with him to the door, still nothing more definable on the monitors than the sharp glint of a buckle. Just before the door the figure turned to look at the body on the bed. The camera panned with his gaze, registering the purple swellings on the neck, the blackened lips, and faintly fluttering eyelids. A thick cloud of morning mist billowed in the draft from the closing door. Then, at the last minute Anna remembered that her eyes should be open, bulging, still steeped in terror, and as her eyelids flew open Kirsten groaned.

"Cut!" she yelled, striding out from behind the monitor. "Set up for another. Makeup!"

"On my way," Trudie called, already heading toward the house.

"Too heavy on the mist," Kirsten shouted to the props man as she went to speak to sound while the makeup girl sorted out Anna. Behind her, Helena was prodding Ruby with her foot, but the only response she got was a depleted groan. Laurence was wandering off the set, deep in conversation with one of the production managers. Everyone else was re-setting.

Suddenly a scream came from inside the house. For a moment everyone froze. Then spinning round Kirsten started toward the house, Jake close on her heels. They burst in through the door to find the makeup girl backing toward them, her hand clamped over her mouth. Kirsten's eyes shot to Anna as the makeup girl stumbled into her. Kirsten shoved her aside and ran to the bed.

"What is it? What's happening?" Jake cried, kneeling beside Kirsten.

Kirsten lifted Anna's shoulders and began shaking her. Jake got to work wrenching open the neck of her shirt.

"Anna! Anna!" Kirsten cried, slapping her face.

"Get the nurse!" Jake yelled.

Two props guys hefted the bed away from the wall and one of them threw himself into the narrow gap to start the kiss of life.

"Laurence! Somebody get Laurence!" Kirsten shouted.

"I'm right here," he answered, coming in through the door.

He pushed his way to the bed and took over the mouth to mouth, keeping frantically at it until the nurse arrived. Immediately she pushed Laurence aside and laid her ear on Anna's chest.

Kirsten stood beside Laurence, looking down at the determined ministrations of the nurse. Inside Kirsten was screaming with fury and frustration. Nobody spoke, there was no room to move, the only activity was the astonishing performance being played out on the narrow bed.

"Get an ambulance," Kirsten muttered to anyone who was listening as the nurse pushed violently at Anna's heart. "Get it now!"

There was a scuffle at the door as someone ran off. A few seconds later the nurse turned to look up at Kirsten.

The blood drained from Kirsten's face as she turned to Laurence, her eyes wide with confusion and shock. Then they both looked back at the nurse whose face was pinched with distress.

CHAPTER TWENTY

WITHIN TWENTY-FOUR HOURS THE NEW ORLEANS POlice Department had set up an investigation headquarters on the first floor of the hotel. Anna's body had been taken to the coroner's office, but as yet no one knew when the results of the postmortem would be made known. Which, as Laurence remarked to Kirsten, made it odd that the police were so keen to begin interviewing. Laurence had been in touch with the chief of police, but all he had been told was that the day record from the coroner's office had stated that the cause of death at this stage was unknown. Now the forensic pathologist was awaiting a toxicology report from the state laboratory.

For a while it was as though the entire crew had gone into shock; no one spoke other than in hushed tones, and their faces were ashen masks of confusion, stupefied disbelief, or in some cases distinct discomfort. The support actor who had taken part in the strangulation scene was under sedation, the shock had been too much for him to handle and his protestations of innocence, until quieted, had served perhaps more than anything else to fan the flames of morbid speculation. So far no one had actually voiced the suspicion that Anna's death was unnatural. Instead they were tentatively suggesting that perhaps the tension had affected her brain and a blood vessel had burst. Or that maybe she had had a heart attack, but it wasn't long before some started to wonder if the rumor that she had overdosed just before the scene because Laurence had ended their relationship was true. And quite soon another kind of postmortem was taking place behind the closed doors of the hotel bedrooms where many were asking, even conjecturing, as to who might have the strongest motive for killing Anna Sage.

A copy of the rushes had been sent to the police, and out at Little Joe's, Kirsten and Laurence played and replayed the scene to try and work out what might have happened. There was no doubt in either of their minds, mainly because of the way Anna had opened her eyes, that until the moment the door had closed she was still alive. And in the thirty or so seconds that had followed, no one had entered the house. So, as far as they could see there simply wasn't any question of there having been any kind of foul play.

As the days passed and still no news of the cause of death was forthcoming, the tension began building to such a pitch that it was as though a ticking bomb had been flung into their midst.

It was in the middle of the morning, three days after Anna's death, that Jane came to Kirsten's room looking even paler than usual to tell Kirsten about the interrogation she had just undergone.

"They didn't actually come right out and say it," she said wringing her hands as she gazed down at the floor, "but they gave me the impression that they think Anna was murdered."

"But for God's sake, how could she have been?" Kirsten snapped. "We were all there, we were watching the monitors—the only one who had a chance to do anything was the actor, and since Anna didn't die of strangulation—"

"But how do you know she didn't?" Alison, who was sitting on the bed, interrupted.

"Okay, I'm assuming. But if she had, they'd have established that by now and there'd be no question as to what kind of inquiry this is. Anyway, what kind of things were they asking you, Jane?"

"Well," Jane began hesitantly, "they were asking me about Laurence mainly and what his relationship was with Anna. No, first of all they wanted to know if I had any idea who might hate Anna enough to want to . . . Um, how did they put it? Um, I think they said 'harm her in any way.' That was when I thought that there might be more to it than they were saying."

"What did you tell them?" Kirsten asked, feeling the muscles in her face starting to numb.

"I said that I didn't think anyone hated her that much. Then they wanted to know if I knew anything about how she got the part."

"What!" Kirsten cried. "Why on earth were they asking *you* that question?"

Jane shrugged, her pale gray eyes moving from Kirsten to Alison and back again.

"What else did they say?" Alison prompted.

Apprehension leapt into Jane's eyes as her gaze flickered uncertainly toward Alison before she said, "They asked me what I knew about Laurence's relationship with you, Kirsten."

"But what the hell's that got to do with anything?" Kirsten cried.

"I don't know," Jane answered miserably.

"So what did you say?"

"I said that you had been his girlfriend once, a long time ago, but that now you were just friends—and colleagues . . ."

Suddenly there was a frantic knocking on the door. Kirsten yanked it open to find Helena in just about as bad a state as Jane.

"They've just had me in there again," Helena cried, stalking into the room. "They kept asking me about the Marie Laveau scene I'd just done!"

"But they can't seriously believe that Anna was killed by some kind of voodoo." Kirsten declared, then quickly moved to Helena as Helena covered her face with her hands.

"If you ask me they still don't know how she did die," Helena choked. "Shit! This is some kind of nightmare. I mean we were all sitting there watching so it can't be murder. It's impossible! We'd have seen it happen."

"Unless it *was* something to do with voodoo," Jane said in a tremulous whisper.

Kirsten shot a daggered look at her, but they all fell silent as they looked at each other in appalled disbelief. It was clear that none of them wanted to believe it, but if the police had introduced the subject into their inquiries, then they obviously weren't ruling out the possibility.

"Have they spoken to Ruby?" Kirsten asked hoarsely.

"She went in just after I came out," Helena answered. "She's in a terrible state. Well, you've seen her. She can't even speak she's so horrified. . . . She just keeps mumbling about that fucking coconut."

Kirsten's hand suddenly slammed down on the table. "This is ridiculous!" she shouted. She started toward the door. "I'm going to see Laurence."

"He's down in the production office with the accountants," Jane told her.

Kirsten pulled a face. "Yes, I'll bet he is. Jesus Christ, this is going to finish us."

An hour later Laurence, Kirsten, and the production managers were in Laurence's room when Jane opened the door and ushered Ruby in. She was badly shaken, her fleshy face so pinched with distress that Laurence sat her down and poured her a stiff drink as the production managers left.

"They think I did it," Ruby mumbled. "They think I killed the stupid bitch."

Kirsten and Laurence looked at each other. "Nobody killed her," Laurence said, going to sit with Ruby. "Okay, we don't know how she died, but that doesn't mean someone killed her." Again he glanced at Kirsten, then putting an arm about Ruby he said, "Start at the beginning. Exactly what did they say to you?"

"They reckon I killed her," Ruby mumbled again. "They reckon I did it. I know they do." It was evident from the look in her eyes that she was so dazed she couldn't even think.

"Oh, God." Kirsten sighed. "Until we know how Anna died this is just going to get worse. Haven't they told you anything, Laurence?"

He shook his head as the telephone started to ring. "They haven't spoken to me at all today. Get that, will you?" he said to Jane.

"Kirsten, it's for you," Jane said, holding out the receiver.

It was Helena. Could Kirsten come to her room quick?

"What is it?" Kirsten asked as she closed Helena's door behind her.

"I've got to warn you about this," Helena said. "The crew are gossiping . . ." She put a hand to her head. "Oh, shit, Kirstie, I hardly know how to tell you this. . . . Dermott's with the police now; he's going to tell them everything he knows about you and Laurence—"

"Oh, God!" Kirsten cried, clasping her hands to her head. She started to pace the room, so caught in the rapid tangling of her thoughts that not one of them seemed to make sense. "You don't suppose . . ." she began, then groaned as she covered her face with her hands. "Campbell couldn't have fixed this to make it look like it was me, could he?" she said. "You don't think—"

"I don't know," Helena said, going to put an arm around her. "He was out at the set—"

"I didn't see him," Kirsten snapped.

"Neither did I. But he was there, apparently. At least for some of the time. But look, we don't know it was murder yet, and besides, how the hell could he have done it?"

"God knows, but it's one hell of a coincidence, isn't it, that Anna should die while he's here? And it's well and truly fucked up the film, hasn't it? That's what Dyllis

Fisher wanted." Her eyes came up to Helena's and suddenly she couldn't believe how dense she was being. "Helena," she said softly. "Helena, please tell me that you had nothing to do with this."

"No! I swear it!" Helena cried. "I swear on my mother's life he never once even mentioned anything like this. Jesus Christ, if he had I'd have told you straight away . . ."

"But let's face it, Helena, I've got as good a motive as anyone to want to be rid of Anna and he knows it."

"Yes," Helena muttered. "And I'm afraid the police'll know that by now too."

Panic suddenly flared in Kirsten's chest. But no, she wouldn't give in to it. She'd done nothing. She had no reason to be afraid. She just had to remain calm. She hadn't liked Anna it was true, and yes she was in love with Laurence, but neither of those facts was enough to prove that she had killed anyone. For God's sake, how could anyone prove it when she'd done nothing? "I have to speak to Laurence," she said and getting up from the chair she all but ran into the corridor.

However, when she reached Laurence's room it was to discover that the police had sent for him ten minutes before.

Kirsten was waiting outside when Laurence finally left the investigation room. She'd received a telephone call only minutes before to ask her to report to the police officer stationed outside.

"How did it go?" she whispered, as Laurence closed the door behind him.

Laurence's face was drawn with tension. "They still won't admit this is a murder investigation," he said, "but it sure as hell seems like one to me. The strange thing is, though, they still seem to be considering suicide as an option. They wanted to know everything about my relationship with Anna—and was it true that I'd ended it the evening she died."

"And did you?" Kirsten asked.

"Miss Meredith?"

Kirsten looked up to see a policewoman standing at the open door.

"Could you come in now, please?" she said.

Feeling as though she were moving through some kind of nightmare, Kirsten walked into the dingy room. Seated behind the file- and ash-strewn desk were the two homicide detectives, Greengage and Kowski, who had interviewed her the night Anna died. The policewoman who had come to the door held out a chair for her to sit down, then went to position herself on the window ledge.

The balding, long-faced man, Kowski, whom Kirsten knew to be the more senior of the detectives, was engrossed in whatever it was he was reading; the other offered Kirsten a cigarette.

She shook her head and inwardly willed herself to contain her fear and not be intimidated by the air of antagonism she could already feel closing in around her.

"Okay," Kowski drawled in his pronounced Kentucky accent. He lifted his head and bared his yellow teeth in a grin that was so carnivorous Kirsten almost shuddered. "I just been going over your statement here, ma'am," he said. "It's all pretty straightforward, but our further inquiries mean that there are a couple more things we need to ask you. They're kind of personal, but I'm sure you're keen to tell us all we need to know."

Kirsten watched him, saying nothing.

His eyes flicked toward the other detective, then leaning back in his chair he stuffed his hands into his trouser pockets. "Is it true that you once threatened to kill Mr. McAllister's wife, ma'am?"

Kirsten felt almost dizzied by the smooth matter-of-factness of the question. "Not quite," she answered sounding far steadier than she felt. "They weren't married at the time, so it was his girlfriend I threatened to kill."

"And why was that?"

"Because I was in love with Mr. McAllister."

"Did you ever do anything about this here threat? I mean, did you try to carry it out'n'all? Before you answer that, ma'am, I gotta tell you these things are real easy to check out."

"Please go right ahead and check," Kirsten said tightly. "I did nothing to endanger Pippa's life and nor would I."

"But you did threaten her life?"

"I was mentally unstable at the time," Kirsten said bluntly, and knew immediately she shouldn't have. However, it was too late now, and, she kept reminding herself, she had nothing to hide.

"Would you be considering yourself mentally stable now?" Kowski inquired.

"Yes, I would."

"Even though Mr. McAllister has recently been engaged in an affair with the deceased?"

Kirsten merely looked at him.

"You did know about Mr. McAllister's relationship with the deceased, didn't you, ma'am?"

"Yes, I knew about it."

"Were you jealous, ma'am? Jealous enough to want her dead?"

Kirsten flinched as the words hit her.

"Would I be right in thinking that you didn't want Miss Sage on your movie?" Kowski said. "That you opposed her casting because of her resemblance to Mr. McAllister's wife?"

"It had nothing to do with her looking like Pippa," Kirsten said. "I just didn't think she was old enough for the part, but I was wrong. She's worked out very well."

Kowski pursed his lips and let his chin fall onto his chest. "I would be right in thinking, ma'am, wouldn't I, that you still have feelings for Mr. McAllister?" he said eventually.

"You would," Kirsten answered.

"And would Mr. McAllister be returning those feelings?"

"I'm afraid you'll have to ask him that question."

"But in your opinion . . ."

"Not anymore, no. I thought he did, but it seems I was wrong."

"Hmm. I guess it's kind of difficult to swallow that, him dumping on you twice the way he did."

"Yes, it is difficult, but not so difficult I'd kill because of it," Kirsten hissed, as Kowski made to interrupt her.

Kowski's head tilted to one side as he smirked, then getting up he walked around the desk and came to perch in front of her. Kirsten could smell the musky odor of his stale cologne and the tobacco on his breath. "Do you know anything about poison, Miss Meredith?" Kowski asked. "I mean in the context of your job you've got to have come across a lot of things the average person don't ever see. Would poison be one of them?"

Kirsten felt her skin starting to prickle. "No," she answered. Then lifting her head to look him right in the face, she said, "Are you saying that Anna was poisoned?"

Kowski turned to look at the policewoman. "Was the deceased poisoned?" he repeated, as though mulling the question over to himself. His strangely elongated face came round to look at Kirsten again. "Is there any reason you can think of as to why Miss Sage might have taken her own life, ma'am?" he asked.

Kirsten shook her head. "None that I know of."

"Do you recall where Mr. McAllister was at the moment of death?"

"I'm not sure at what moment Anna died," Kirsten answered. "But during the scene, Laurence was at his monitor, just in front of me, and afterward we were both in the house."

"Was Miss Collins with you?"

"In body, yes. She passed out drunk just as we were going for a take."

Kowski's bottom lip jutted forward. "Is Miss Collins usually as drunk as all that?" he wondered.

"Sometimes, yes."

"You know that Miss Collins believes there is some kind of curse on her?" His voice was so imbued with mockery Kirsten almost felt herself blush.

She nodded. "Yes, I know, but I've never taken it seriously."

"Why?"

"Because I don't believe in that sort of thing."

"No." Kowski sighed, getting to his feet. "Neither do we. But someone around here sure wants us to believe it. And you got to admit, ma'am, there's something of a mystery here."

"Yes, there is. But I don't believe that anyone killed Anna. I have no idea how she died, assumedly you don't either or you'd have told us by now."

"She didn't die from no voodoo curse, Miss Meredith," Kowski said.

"Then how did she die?"

"Now that's what we're still trying to find out." Kowski lifted a foot onto the corner of her chair and rested an elbow on his knee. "Let's go back to the beginning, shall we? Just how did you come to be working on this movie?"

The interrogation went on, hour after hour, so many questions, so many suppositions and so many oblique accusations that Kirsten's head was spinning so hard she was losing the ability to think straight. They gave her water, offered her cigarettes, shouted at her, consoled her, threatened her, sympathized with her, did everything they could to wear her down. It was as though their mocking southern accents were tangible things wrapping themselves around her, hauling in every word, then twisting it, bending it, stretching it, enmeshing her in so much doubt that she could barely even be sure of her own name. Over and over she reminded herself that she just had to keep to the truth, but Kowski was running her round in such circles she finally started to lose track of even that.

At last one clear thought erupted through the chaos in her mind. "I want a lawyer," she cried. "You shouldn't be questioning me like this without a lawyer present."

"Do you need a lawyer, Miss Meredith?"

Kirsten was so exhausted she could feel herself brinking on frightened tears. "Yes, when you're accusing me of murder, I do."

"But no one's accused you."

"Not directly, but you're insinuating it."

"Was there a murder?"

"No! I don't know."

"Is there anything you want to tell us?"

"I've told you everything. You know my movements from the very start of the shoot, you know I was there when she died—"

"In fact you watched her die."

"I didn't know she was dying!"

"Someone must have. *If* it was murder."

"That's it, you don't know! So why are you putting me through this? I haven't done anything. All I know is what I've told you. And if it is murder, then I've been set up—"

"Set up!" Kowski pounced on it.

Kirsten recoiled sharply. "Yes, set up," she cried. "There's a vendetta . . . a woman in England . . . she wants to ruin me."

Kowski looked at Greengage and grinned. "Dermott Campbell's employer?" he said.

"Yes," Kirsten answered, her eyes darting between them. "Dyllis Fisher hates me. She wants to destroy me . . ."

Kowski waved a dismissive hand. "We've heard the

background from Mr. Campbell, but I gotta tell you, Miss Meredith, neither Mrs. Fisher nor Mr. Campbell are possible suspects here—"

"Why not? She'd like nothing more than to see me in prison."

Kowski's lips pursed thoughtfully as once again he turned to Greengage.

"I want a lawyer," Kirsten repeated.

"Yeah, I reckon you could need one," Kowski remarked, looking up as the door opened. He took an envelope from the uniformed officer who'd come in and nodded toward the policewoman who walked to the telephone and started to dial.

Kirsten watched as Kowski read, dreadful images of a future in a Louisiana State prison for something she hadn't even done racing so fast through her mind she was almost choking on her panic. Then, just as the policewoman was making contact with someone on the other end of the line, Kowski's hand came up. Immediately the policewoman cut the connection.

"Okay, Miss Meredith," he said, "you can go."

Kirsten's eyes flew open. "You mean . . . ? Are you saying . . . ?"

"I'm telling you you can go."

"So you don't think I killed her?"

"Not unless you want to tell me different."

Dumbly Kirsten shook her head. She was already halfway to the door before it occurred to her that what Kowski had read could have been the toxicologist's report. She turned back.

"Yeah," Kowski answered, "that's what it is right

enough. It would appear, Miss Meredith, that your star died a natural death."

Kirsten's confusion was evident. "What do you mean? Did she have a heart attack or something?"

He looked down at the report in his hand. "It says right here that she died of natural causes."

"Natural causes?" Kirsten echoed.

"That's what it says. So either you got some genius at work here or we all got to start believing in voodoo curses."

Kirsten stiffened. "So you still think it was murder?"

He grinned. "I think she died a natural death, is what I think. But what your crew are gonna think and how much convincing they're gonna take is another matter altogether," and with that he and his fellow officers roared with laughter.

CHAPTER TWENTY-ONE

HER FINGERS FRANTICALLY TURNED THE PAGES OF THE album, revealing all the faces of the people she had made a part of her life. Her eyes were feverish; tremors of passion rippled through her heart. The baby was screaming, but it didn't matter. She'd let the baby scream because she had to look at her pictures.

There was Laurence as a child. Or was it Tom? They were so alike. But it had to be Laurence because the picture was old and in black and white. How she loved Laurence. How she had longed for him. But she had him now, he was hers, or he would be soon and he would be everything to her she wanted him to be. They would be so happy together, all of them. No one was going to stand in the way now. The memories were almost complete; she had all the pictures . . .

Her eyes misted over, a smile trembled her lips as she gazed down at the photo of the wedding. Laurence was so tall and handsome . . . Pippa wasn't there anymore, she should never have been there, so using her scissors she'd got rid of Pippa.

She smoothed her fingers lovingly over the sharp edges of the picture, then turned the page, her body quaking with excitement as she saw the most exquisite portrait of them all. She had made such a good job of this one. . . . There she was as a baby in the arms of her mother while her father looked dotingly down on them both. There was such a thing as a happy family; she knew it because she had it—at least soon she would have it.

A spasm of fear suddenly clutched at her mind, jerking her head upward. Dermott Campbell was going to spoil it. He was writing things that weren't true. But how was he going to prove there had been a murder when even the police said there hadn't been? A brittle laugh burst from her lips. Dermott Campbell hadn't even managed to bring the film to its knees, though he probably thought he had. But she knew differently. She knew that they'd be shooting again right after Christmas, because, of course, Anna's death had been due to natural causes so the insurance company was going to pay out . . .

Anna's death! The two words clashed together inside her head. Frenzied colors exploded before her eyes. She'd done it. She'd taken a human life and now it was as though she had stepped from her skin into a world of endless chaos and terror. Her heart thudded a strident beat, pumping cowardly dread to her veins, discord and violence to her thoughts. She had killed once and knew if she had to she'd do it again. A muscle in her cheek began to twitch. She crushed it with her hand. Her fingers were rigid, crooked like claws. She was gasping for breath, so afraid of herself she could feel it lapping at the shores of her sanity. She pushed the album away, pressed her hands to her ears. The baby was screaming, screaming, screaming. . . . The tide was drawing closer, she was drowning in the screams. . . .

Ten days had gone by since they'd returned from New Orleans and the planning of the reshoot was already underway in earnest. As far as Kirsten could see they were all going to be working right up to the last minute on Christmas Eve, after which Laurence had declared that everyone should take a week off and begin again in the New Year, preparing to film by the middle of January. The part of Moyna O'Malley had already been recast. Elizabeth Bradley, an actress with whom Kirsten had worked before, was taking over the role, though not until she had been given all the details of Anna's death did Elizabeth agree to take it on. Kirsten understood completely; with all that was still being bandied about in the press it was only natural that Elizabeth would want to hear firsthand what had happened. So, Kirsten and Laurence had taken Elizabeth to dinner and told her all she wanted to know. Just like everyone else Elizabeth was fascinated by the mystery of Anna's death, though, knowing Kirsten she didn't consider, even for a moment, that there was an iota of truth in the oblique accusations that Kirsten was responsible.

It was becoming extremely difficult now for Kirsten to show her face in public. How Campbell managed to get so many pictures of her laughing to splash across his newspaper Kirsten didn't know, but seeing her so happy less than a year after Paul Fisher's death, six months after Laurence's wife had left him, and a mere couple of weeks after the mysterious demise of her rival made it—at least the way Campbell told it—seem as though she was so ruthless and dangerous in her schemings that nothing, least of all the sanctity of human life, was going to stand in the way of whatever Kirsten Meredith wanted.

For Kirsten it was like reading about a stranger, someone who had stolen her identity and was using it with such malicious and harmful intent she was as frightened by it as she was bewildered. She just couldn't come to terms with the fact that anyone could believe she was the monster being portrayed in the press, and neither could she understand what route her life was taking to have made her the victim of such injustice and prejudice. Her lawyers had applied for an injunction against Campbell's newspaper now, but it wasn't likely to be granted until after Christmas. In the meantime, the libelous allegations continued and so too did the serving of writs. In fact getting into a legal battle with Dermott Campbell and Dyllis Fisher was just about the last thing Kirsten wanted, for it was earning her even more publicity, but Laurence had insisted that she had no alternative.

Right now she and Laurence were in the festively decorated production office going over the revised schedule with the production managers. All around them phones were ringing, computers were printing out, faxes were coming in, and people were yelling to each other for information. A number of the scenes from the original shoot were still usable, so too were shots within scenes, so this time round the planning of the schedule was a good deal more complicated than the last. Plus the fact that they were faced with almost insurmountable problems over the weather.

"So what you're suggesting," Kirsten said to Melvin, the chief production manager, "is that when we return to New Orleans we go straight out to the plantation house and do those scenes first?"

Melvin nodded. "If we don't," he told her, "then we're going to run smack bang into the middle of Mardi Gras."

"Yes, of course," Kirsten said, casting an eye over the Polaroid photographs of Oak Alley, the plantation house they had selected for the shoot. She felt a pleasing lift in her heart at the prospect of filming there. It was such a magnificent house and was—at least so far as the shoot was concerned—still virgin territory. "What do you think, Laurence?" she said turning to him.

"Sounds sensible to me," he answered, taking the Polaroids from her.

"Have you discussed this with Little Joe?" Kirsten asked Melvin, perching on the edge of his desk and stretching her legs out to rest them on his chair. "Can he get us the equipment and crew we need during Mardi Gras?"

"He thinks so," Melvin answered. "He's getting back to me sometime later this week. I can't see Joe letting us down though. My guess is if he can't get what we want locally, he'll hire in from Hollywood."

"Don't let him do that until you've spoken to me," Laurence interjected. "In fact don't book anything over there yet. Just put a provisional hold on it. The same goes for the flights."

"I think, taking Mardi Gras into consideration," Melvin said, "that we'll have to be more positive than that."

"Just speak to me first," Laurence repeated, trying not to show his discomfort at how closely Kirsten was watching him. He handed back the photographs, staring sightlessly down at her legs in their long black boots and skintight jodhpurs. Then, avoiding her eyes, he turned toward their office.

"If you ask me he's having an enthusiasm failure," Melvin remarked to Kirsten. "You don't think he's going to pull the plugs, do you?"

"No," Kirsten answered, sounding more confident than she felt. "He's just being cautious."

"Well he's making everyone pretty edgy lately. I mean, if he is going to pull out, we need to know, 'cause some of us are turning down other work."

"He's not going to pull out," Kirsten assured him. "He's just got a lot on his mind. Now, where were we?"

For the next hour or so they went over the schedule in the minutest of detail until Melvin complained he was starving and wanted to go and join the others for lunch.

When he'd gone Kirsten wandered toward her own office, trying to decide whether or not she really wanted to go in. She knew Ruby was there and she wasn't too comfortable in Ruby's company lately—not since Ruby had got God. Actually, there were times when it was quite amusing, but being told constantly to repent of her sins was becoming a little wearing, particularly when Kirsten wasn't too sure whether or not it was some kind of accusation. Still, at least Ruby's counseling with a priest seemed to have cured her of her coconut ravings and, to a certain extent, her dependence on gin.

At last she opened the door to her office and found Ruby there alone, studying her Bible. She looked up as Kirsten came in and immediately made the sign of the cross.

"I wish you wouldn't do that," Kirsten complained.

" 'Seek ye the Lord while he may be found, call ye upon him while he is near,' " Ruby advised her.

"Okay," Kirsten said, sitting down at her desk. "Where's Laurence?"

"In the screening room," Ruby answered, then putting her hands together she bowed her head and started to mumble.

"Ruby, aren't you taking this just a bit too far?" Kirsten groaned.

"You can't ever go too far down the road to our Lord," Ruby told her. "And I'm saying a prayer for you here, Kirsten."

"Well that's very kind of you," Kirsten said, "but it's a bit distracting."

Neither of them spoke for some time then, as Kirsten began checking through her script to make sure there were no shots missing from the schedule, and Ruby returned to her Bible. In the end, aware of the way Ruby kept glancing over at her, Kirsten looked up.

"Do you have something on your mind?" she said.

"As a matter of fact, I do," Ruby answered, popping a Nicorette gum into her mouth. She sat back in Laurence's chair, resting her elbows on the arms and knitting her fingers across her chest. " 'Forgetting those things which are behind, and reaching forth unto those which are before, I press towards the mark,' " she said somberly.

Kirsten sighed and waited.

Ruby nodded. " 'Learn to be silent. Let your quiet mind listen and absorb,' " she counseled. "Pythagoras said that," she added informatively.

"Did he?" Kirsten said. "Well, I'm listening."

For a moment Ruby gazed mournfully across at her, then summoning a smile brimming with heartfelt compassion, she said, "The Lord has counseled me to speak. There are things Laurence don't want to say, so I'm gonna do it for him. Hell, someone's got to. But Kirstie, my child, if you'd had the good sense to pull out of this movie the minute we left New Orleans I wouldn't have to be saying this at all."

Kirsten watched her, tightlipped.

"Look, honey," Ruby said, her voice sugary sweet. "Laurence and I, we were working on this movie long before you came on the scene. You know that. It means a lot to us . . ."

"And it doesn't to me?"

"Ah, ah," Ruby said, raising a hand. "Remember, 'listen and absorb.' But sure, I guess the movie does mean something to you too, but for the wrong reasons. You put your dough in to get Laurence, the whole world knows that. Well, you gotta know by now that that ain't gonna happen. Not even with poor Anna out of the way are you gonna get him."

"Was that some kind of accusation?" Kirsten snapped.

Ruby looked blank. Then, "Oh, I see what you're getting at. No, I know there are those who reckon you were behind that terrible event," she said, crossing herself, "but not me." She shrugged. "But you've read all that stuff in the press and what I'm asking here is that you think about Laurence. This is his movie. He wants to shoot it but he can't get the insurance cover this time round. Now why do you suppose that is?"

"Why don't you tell me, Ruby?"

"Okay. Something real weird happened that day on the set, we all know that, and you were there. Now I'm not saying you did it, I'm not saying that at all, but remember Kirsten, one day you will have to answer to the Lord. But He is a merciful Lord . . . Anyways, even if you didn't kill the woman yourself someone's done it and made it look like you. That don't bode well for going out into the field with you on board again, now does it?"

"Nobody killed Anna, she died of natural causes," Kirsten reminded her, trying to ignore the horrible unease that gripped her.

"Of course, God rest her soul. All's I'm saying is what other people think. Now Laurence, he don't want to fire you, he's afraid you'll pull out your dough if he does, but, well," she shrugged, "I guess you're getting my drift."

Kirsten was, only too well. And in truth didn't she already know it herself? It was just that she hadn't wanted to face it. Of course they couldn't go on with her, not when the press was doing what they were, for who in their right mind was going to be prepared to take a risk on something like that happening again?

Kirsten left the office early that day, saying she wanted to work from home where there would be fewer interruptions. As she left, her smiles and encouragement were as bright as always; no one would have guessed what was going on in her heart. She was trying very hard not to think of how fond she had become of them all, of how she had started to look upon them as her family, for she couldn't bear to think how much she was going to miss them, how empty her days were going to be without their laughter and support.

By the time she arrived home she was so choked with tears that the door was barely shut behind her before she broke down completely. It seemed that every time she felt she was at last getting somewhere a cruel twist in fate was waiting round the corner to snatch it all away. She was misjudged, maligned, and made to feel an outcast no matter what she did. She had never claimed to be perfect, but never had she set out to hurt someone the way Dyllis Fisher was hurting her. Dyllis Fisher, the woman who hid behind her empire, never showing her face, but making sure that the power she wielded lanced to the very core.

Still wearing her coat, Kirsten went into the sitting room and picked up a photograph of Paul. As she gazed down at his smiling face so full of kindness and humor, she knew that no matter what, she could never regret the years she had spent with him. She just wished he was there now to help her through what she knew already was going to be another crisis in her life. Resentment swelled within her. A few months ago if someone had told her that she'd have to deal with all that she had—the rejection and hostility of a production team, the perversity of Laurence's behavior, the watching of him with another woman, the horrible suspicion that she had contrived to murder that woman—she'd never have believed she could do it. But somehow she had. Somewhere, deep down inside she had found a strength she hadn't known she possessed and in her own way she had been pulling through. But she could feel that strength ebbing away from her now, disappearing into a terrible gulf that was swallowing everything that mattered in her life. Her career, her friends, and whatever it was that she still felt for Laurence.

She so desperately felt the need to speak to someone now. She wished, more than anything, that it could be Laurence, but how could it be when she could only begin to imagine how bitterly he must regret ever having asked her to work with him. His last film hadn't done well at the box office and he just couldn't afford another failure. They were crazy, both of them, ever to have thought they could stand up to Dyllis Fisher, but was it that that was really bothering Laurence now, or was it that he just couldn't be sure whether or not she had had anything to do with Anna's death? As the frustration and anger surged through her Kirsten pressed her hands to her head. It seemed insane that anyone should even suspect her of being responsible for doing something like that, but that Laurence could was so horrible she just couldn't bear it.

Feeling herself being submerged by waves of desperation she thought of calling Helena, but since returning from New Orleans they had hardly seen each other. As she thought about that, Kirsten could feel her heart contracting. She had been so busy she hadn't made any time for Helena even though she had known that Helena was having a rough time over Dermott. Despising the man as much as she did, Kirsten had found it difficult to sympathize, so how could she expect Helena to be there for her now?

Covering her face with her hands she turned to the wall and cried as though her heart would break. She was so afraid of the loneliness, so tired of the battle, but knew that both were closing in on her again and there was nothing she could do to stop it.

Then suddenly, for no reason, she thought of Jane. Shy, nervous little Jane, who had told her that if ever there was anything she could do for her she only had to say. A welter of emotion flowed through her as Kirsten remembered those words, yet she knew that she couldn't burden Jane with her problems, especially not when Jane was so close to Laurence. Besides, what could Jane do? What could any of them do? She had to let go, to take stock of her life again, and sort out for herself where she went now. But first she had to speak to Laurence. There was a partnership to dissolve, finances to rearrange, as well as a handover to another director. And as the enormity of it all pressed itself into her heart she could feel the dread starting to consume her.

A yellowy warm light from the fringed lamps filled the cluttered family room with a seasonal glow. Multicolored fairy lights lit up the gaily decorated Christmas tree in the corner, and from somewhere else in the house came the distant sound of Tom's little tape recorder playing "Away in a Manger." In the old stone hearth a log fire crackled and hissed, adding an old-fashioned feeling to the sleepy mood of the dark winter night.

At that moment Laurence had his back turned so Kirsten couldn't see his face. He was setting out cups on a tray while the coffee percolated in the corner of the kitchen. Kirsten was sitting at the table, swallowing hard on the emotions rising in her heart. Despite the languor of the atmosphere there was a restlessness inside her that made her want to run, to get as far from him as she could, yet she knew that the moment she walked out the door all the pain she had locked inside would be released.

She averted her eyes and gazed up at the gently swaying Christmas trimmings. Knowing that this was probably the last time she would see him was like feeling a part of herself die. But outwardly she remained calm, fully prepared to stand by what she'd said five minutes ago, and though she longed to hear him say he didn't want her to go she knew, from his silence, that he wasn't going to.

She turned to watch him as he came toward her with the tray and felt her heart turn over at the way his dark, handsome face was so taut with concentration. Catching her watching him and seeing her expression, he gave a sardonic lift to his eyebrows.

"You warm enough?" he said, his voice low and sonorous as though not wanting to disturb the restful ambience of the room.

She nodded. "Yes, thanks," she answered, the tone of her voice matching his.

He didn't speak again until he had poured the coffee, not asking how she took hers because of course he knew. Then at last, holding his cup in both hands, his elbows resting on the table, he said, "I'm not accepting your resignation—"

"Laurence, be sensible," she interrupted, her voice still low yet mercifully steady. Dear God, was he really going to stand by her? But even if he was, she couldn't let him. "You and I both know," she went on, "that my involvement is what's preventing you getting cover—"

"Bullshit," he said softly.

"Laurence, please listen . . ."

"No, you listen. I'm not letting you walk out on me now. I don't give a fuck about Dyllis Fisher and her vendetta. You're the one who's made this movie work. It's as much a part of you now as it is of either me or Ruby—and if you listen to that woman again—"

"She told you she'd spoken to me?"

"She told me. And I told her what I'm telling you now. That I make the decisions around here as to who's hired and fired. And I am not firing you, neither am I accepting your resignation."

"I'm not pulling out my investment," Kirsten said, lifting her cup, then replacing it without drinking. "So you don't have to worry about that."

"I'm not. I know you won't pull out, because I know you won't let me down. And neither am I going to let you down. I'll get the insurance and we'll start over . . ."

Kirsten was shaking her head. "For your own sake, and for mine too, I have to leave. It's the only way to stop this press speculation, it'll give Dyllis Fisher what she wants and like I said, the insurance companies . . ." For a moment her voice faltered, but swallowing hard she made herself go on. "I'll wind things up as neatly as I can so that there won't be too much of a problem for whoever takes over, and after that—other than a return on my investment—" she smiled, "I want no further involvement. Now, that's my final word on the subject, so please, don't let's argue."

As she lifted her coffee to her lips she was aware of how searching his eyes were as they swept over her face. She didn't know how much longer she could hold on, but she was willing herself not to break down in front of him. She had no idea what he was thinking or what he was going to say next, but she knew that whatever it was her resolve was absolute. She wasn't going to change her mind and right now that was all that mattered.

Laurence continued to look at her, silently, almost wonderingly. In the shimmering soft light she looked so unbelievably lovely and so heartrendingly vulnerable. He knew her so well it was easy for him to see through her bravado. He knew too that she believed in it, that she thought her inner strength would support her, and maybe, at least for a while, it would. But he wasn't going to let her go through this alone. This time he was going to be there for her. He wanted so much to tell her he loved her. How he had never stopped loving her, that ever since the first night they'd met, the night they had both won their first BAFTAs, he had been incapable of loving anyone else. But how was he going to explain all that he had done since, when he hardly understood it himself? Why was it that he had fought so hard to keep her out of his life when she was all he had ever wanted? Why had he married Pippa knowing that it would break Kirsten's heart, when all the time, despite what she had done, it had been Kirsten he wanted? How could he have allowed anger to have governed his life that way? He knew what pain he had caused her, he knew it so well because it had been there for him too. It had all but destroyed Kirsten, and who could say, perhaps in a way it had destroyed him too.

What a lie he had lived these past six years, and how many people he had hurt. And he'd gone on and on hurting, Pippa, Kirsten, Anna, until it was almost as though he couldn't stop. Yet Kirsten was the only one who mattered. All he had ever cared about was her and she, because of his shameful inability to face up to his mistakes and his feelings, had been the one he had hurt the most. Making love to her that day had been like re-awakening his soul and if he'd been honest with himself then, he'd have admitted that a part of her lived inside him just as a part of him lived inside her. Perhaps if Pippa hadn't called him right after and mocked him, taunting him with his inability to face his own emotions, he wouldn't have done what he had. Godammit, why had he been so desperate to prove Pippa wrong? What the hell did it matter what she thought? Kirsten was all that mattered and the love they shared that neither of them would ever be able to defeat.

He didn't want to defeat it now, he wanted to give in to it, to take her in his arms and feel her against him, moving into him as though their very souls were joined. He wanted to feel the luxuriant softness of her hair sliding through his fingers, to feel her lips moving beneath his. He wanted to feel the beat of her heart, the warmth of her skin, the unbelievable depth of her love.

He watched the gentle rise and fall of her breasts as she breathed and felt an overpowering need to touch her. He was afraid, he knew that, afraid of the resolve still glittering in her eyes. Her life was being torn apart by one woman's rabid jealousy, and so far she had struggled with it alone, but now he was going to help her. He had to make her go on with this film; she had to have a sense of purpose and a chance to succeed in the face of all that was being pitched against her. He owed her that, but how in God's name was he going to do it, when she was right, he couldn't get the cover they needed because of her?

His heart turned over as she lowered her head, trying to escape his scrutiny.

"Kirsten," he said softly, and as his hand covered hers Kirsten's eyes closed.

"No, Laurence," she said, her voice strangled by the tears in her throat.

"Kirstie, look at me, please."

"I can't," she murmured pulling her hand free.

"I love you," he whispered.

"Oh, God, don't say that!" she cried, covering her face with her hands. "Please don't say it! No, Laurence," she choked as he took her by the shoulders.

"Kirsten, listen to me, please," he said. "About Anna. Let me tell you about Anna."

"No! I don't want to hear it. Laurence, please," she sobbed as he tried to take her hand again. "Can't you see how hard this is for me? I just can't let you go on hurting me. . . ."

"Darling, I'm not going to hurt you. I love you. . . ."

"But for how long, Laurence? For tonight, while you're feeling lonely? For the next week, the next month, until you find someone else. . . . No! It's over between us, Laurence. It was over six years ago. I've never really been able to make myself believe that, but I do now. So I'm leaving. I'm saying good-bye, because I can't keep pretending that one day you'll be there for me when in my heart I know I can't trust you anymore."

"Kirsten, come back!" he cried, leaping to his feet as she ran to the door, but as she dashed down the front steps he stayed where he was, letting her go because he knew that right now he had to. Nothing he said tonight was going to get through to her; she had set herself against him and, dear God, after the way he had treated her who could blame her for that? But there had to be something he could do, there had to be an answer for them somewhere.

CHAPTER TWENTY-TWO

DESPITE HER RESOLVE OF THAT NIGHT, OVER THE NEXT few days Kirsten found herself hoping beyond hope that Laurence would call. She wanted more than anything else in the world to hear him persuade her to believe he loved her, to know that she meant so much to him he was prepared to do anything to get her back. But as the days passed and still he didn't call, she knew that she had finally to admit that he wasn't going to.

She'd spoken briefly on the phone to Helena just before Helena went to spend Christmas in Scotland where she and Dermott were going to give it another go. Kirsten knew that Helena felt horribly torn between her and Dermott Campbell, but it seemed now that Helena had made her choice. Kirsten guessed that was why Helena hadn't made much of an effort to be in touch with her lately, and she couldn't help wondering if Helena's decision might have been different if she knew what was going on in Kirsten's life right now. But Kirsten wasn't into emotional blackmail, which was why she hadn't told her. In the end they had wished each other a

Happy Christmas and made a tentative arrangement to meet up in the New Year.

On Christmas morning Kirsten got out of bed early and went downstairs to light the fire. She already knew how she was going to spend the day and in a perverse sort of way was almost looking forward to it. She flicked on the TV, hummed gently along with the Christmas carols as she padded about the place in her dressing gown and slippers, knowing that come what may she wasn't going to let herself get down. It didn't matter that she was alone; self-pity was no companion for a Christmas day, especially when her sitting room was by now filled with glittering cards, all from the cast and crew of *Moyna O'Malley*. Alison had gone so far as to enclose a note telling her what a dream she was to work for even though she was as stubborn as a mule, and how much everyone was looking forward to starting afresh in the New Year. Obviously Laurence hadn't told any of them yet, and Kirsten wondered if maybe that task shouldn't actually fall to her. Whether it should or shouldn't she wasn't going to think about it today.

After tidying up the magazines and newspapers she had left strewn across the coffee table, she went into the kitchen and gave a wry laugh when she saw the turkey through the glass door of the oven. It was huge. But she hadn't wanted anyone in the supermarket to know that she was spending Christmas alone so she had stuffed her trolley full to the brim with the things she'd watched other people buy.

Still humming along tunelessly she turned on the oven, poured herself a glass of champagne, and went back to the sitting room to open the three gifts tucked neatly under the tree. One had come through the post from Helena, and Jane had put two more into her bag the night she was at Laurence's.

When she opened the first she felt a lump rising in her throat. It was a beautifully framed photograph of her and Helena looking so happy on the set in New Orleans. She turned the tag over to read the message. "For a very special friend, all my love, Helena."

The second gift was a book from Jane. It was all about Hollywood, and the inscription inside read: "May all your dreams come true." Kirsten smiled as she recalled a conversation she'd had with Laurence after their first week of shoot when they were so excited they'd talked about taking over Hollywood. Jane had been there at the time and had obviously remembered.

Her third gift was from Tom and when she saw the little gris-gris bag to ward off bad luck that he had obviously made himself her emotions rose so close to the surface that she got briskly to her feet, stoked up the fire, and went to check on the turkey.

Around midday, having showered and changed into a pair of silk pajamas and matching robe, she found herself standing at the window watching a family party in the house opposite sit down to their turkey dinner. They were all wearing paper hats and looked so happy that Kirsten wandered over to the Christmas tree, tugged on each end of a cracker, and took out a hat for herself. After putting it on she read the motto: Always Look on the Bright Side of Life. She burst out laughing even as she groaned at the corniness. Then catching sight of herself in the mirror, with her bright yellow hat and chaotic hair, she knew that she wasn't going to be able to ward off the terrible, agonizing loneliness much longer. Quickly she poured herself another glass of champagne and went to baste the turkey.

Quite what time it was when she drifted off to sleep Kirsten couldn't say, but before she did she had managed to eat part of her lunch and finish the entire bottle of champagne. Vaguely she remembered holding an imaginary conversation with Paul over the dining table, but she had no idea now what it had been about. Obviously she had cried herself to sleep. Her eyes hurt, hardly wanted to be prized open, and her whole body ached. However, that could be because she'd fallen asleep in the chair.

She looked around the room. What time was it? It was dark outside, the fire had gone out, and the routine action-adventure film was on the TV. Oh, God, isn't Christmas over yet, she groaned? It was hard work entertaining herself when all she really wanted to do was howl like a baby and give in to her self-pity.

It was only when the doorbell sounded again that she realized what it was that had woken her. Wearily she pulled herself up and went to find the packet of cigarettes she always kept for the old lady next door, who was continually running out.

Raking her hands through her hair and tightening the belt of her dressing gown she went to the door, wondering whether or not to invite the old lady in. Deciding she would, she put on a welcoming smile and pulled open the door.

Almost instantly her smile froze. She had to blink

several times before she could actually register who was standing there, his face almost lost in shadow, the shoulders of his black overcoat spattered with rain.

"Laurence?" she said, uncertainly.

"Were you expecting someone else?" he said, his eyes narrowing with irony.

"Uh, no." Her hand flew to her hair. "Oh God, I look like a nightmare."

"Yeah, I've seen you better." He grinned. He looked past her down the hall. "Do I get to come in?"

Still somewhat dazed, she stood back for him to pass her, then followed him into the sitting room.

"Where's Tom?" she asked, feeling her heart starting to pound as he turned to look at her.

"With Pippa."

"In Italy?"

He shook his head. "With Pippa's parents. I would have come earlier, but he kicked up a bit. He didn't want to go. . . ."

For a moment or two Kirsten was at a loss and glanced nervously about the room. "Uh, can I get you a drink?" she offered.

"Hmm. Sounds good. Have you got any more of that?"

Kirsten followed his eyes to the empty bottle of champagne. "I expect I can find another," she said, pursing her lips in a smile.

"You do that."

When she came back with a new bottle and two fresh glasses Laurence was still standing where she had left him, his hands in his trouser pockets, his coat bunched behind him as he gazed thoughtfully down at the TV.

Kirsten's heart wrenched in such a way that it made her feel dizzy.

"I'll open it," he said as she picked up the bottle of champagne.

Kirsten handed it to him and for a brief moment their eyes met.

"Okay," he said when both glasses were full.

Kirsten took one, then felt herself turn weak as he put a finger under her chin, lifting her face so that she was looking at him, and said, "Merry Christmas."

"Merry Christmas," she whispered.

They drank, then Laurence turned to look at the dead fire. "I reckon we could do with that going again," he said.

Kirsten watched him as he started to pile on the kindling. His movements were deft and quick despite the heavy bulk of his coat. Should she ask him to take it off, she wondered. "Laurence?" she said.

"Hmm?"

"Laurence, I don't understand. . . . Why are you here?"

"To give you a Christmas present, of course," he said, as though she should already have known that. He continued with the fire until the flames were roaring up the chimney, then standing up again he put a hand inside his overcoat and pulled out an envelope.

Kirsten took it, watching him closely and wondering why his eyes were dancing the way they were. As she tore it open he took off his coat and threw it across a chair. All the time he was watching her as she read what she'd taken from the envelope, waiting for her reaction.

Finally Kirsten looked up. Her smile was a little

shaky but she managed to say, "Congratulations. I'm really pleased for you. I told you you'd get it if I was out of the way."

"I got it," Laurence said, taking the insurance documents from her and throwing them onto the table, "without telling them that you'd resigned. So now, would you like to make my Christmas by withdrawing the resignation?"

Kirsten looked at him for a long time before lowering her eyes and searching through the flickering fire-lit shadows as though to find the words she needed to say. He waited, but in the end, when she continued to say nothing, he reached for her hand.

Before she could stop herself Kirsten snatched it away. "No," she said. "I can't. You don't understand, Laurence. I can't go on with it—"

"Darling . . ."

She closed her eyes tightly. "Laurence, don't call me that. We said, at the beginning, that ours was to be a professional relationship. Well, we both know that we've failed at that, but don't you see, I can't go back into it the way things are. You frighten me, Laurence. It's so easy for you to hurt me and as much as I want to do the film—"

He made to take her in his arms but she backed away.

"No, Laurence. I know what you're going to say, but you'll walk out on me again, I know it, and I just can't bear for that to happen . . ."

"Kirstie, listen to me for a moment. . . ."

Her eyes were flashing as they came up to meet his. "I love you, Laurence, I want you so much you've got no idea what it's doing to me . . . But I told you, I can't trust you anymore . . . No, Laurence, don't touch me! Laurence, don't!" she cried as he pulled her into his arms.

"At least give me the chance to explain," he said. "Then if you tell me to go I'll walk out of here and never try to see you again."

She despised herself for being so helpless in his arms, but the feel of him was crushing her resolve, and the temptation to give in was overpowering. Nevertheless, she managed to push him away and moved to the other side of the sofa. "I'll listen," she said, "but I don't want you to touch me. I want you to stay right where you are . . . Laurence!" she cried, as he started toward her.

Laughing, he threw up his hands. "Okay, okay," he said. "I'm rooted to the spot. Now, are you going to turn off the TV?"

For a second or two she eyed him suspiciously, then reaching behind her she fumbled around on the mantelpiece to find the remote control. The room fell into silence and suddenly realizing how cozy and intimate it was with just the soft glow of a reading lamp and the firelight, Kirsten moved to the door and switched on the overhead light.

Laurence was still smiling, but then, as she turned back to him, the challenge clear in her eyes, his smile melted away and he wiped a hand over the dark stubble on his chin.

Kirsten waited, staying right where she was at the door. How desperately she wanted to return to his arms, but too much had happened, too many times in the past he had let her down. She couldn't take that risk again.

"Hell, I hardly know where to begin," he said, lifting his head to look at her.

Kirsten said nothing.

He sighed. "Dammit, Kirstie, can we at least sit down?"

She waved an arm toward the sofa but remained where she was.

"I guess I should tell you about Anna," he said, sinking into the feather-filled cushions.

Still Kirsten was silent as his eyes returned to hers as though asking her if he should go on.

"I wasn't in love with her," he said. "Christ, I can't even say I liked her very much, but she came on to me so strong, and . . . Hell, I slept with her to try and prove to myself that it was just a woman I wanted. Any woman. That it wasn't you I was getting so screwed up over, it was just the need for sex. I guess I knew I was still in love with you, but godammit I didn't want to admit it. If I did, then I'd have to admit to all the other mistakes I'd made and I just didn't have the guts to face up to them."

"When was the first time you slept with her?" Kirsten asked after a pause.

"The first night we were in New Orleans. There I was back in the room where we'd made love. . . . Jesus Christ, I couldn't get you out of my mind. It was driving me insane seeing you day after day and wanting you so badly—"

"Don't lie!" she cried.

"I'm not lying, for God's sake! I thought I had convinced myself I was over you, Kirsten. Hell, I couldn't handle the fact that you could have so much damned power over me. I hated you for that. It drove me so crazy I hardly knew what was happening to me. My whole fucking life has been a mess since we broke up. . . . My marriage failed, my career . . ."

"But you walked out on me, Laurence!" Kirsten cried. "You had a choice. You could have stayed but you left. You turned your back on me . . ."

"And you'll never know how much I've hated myself for that. I know you're not responsible for what you did to the baby. I screwed you up so bad you just didn't know what you were doing. I realize now I had started seeing you as my nemesis, someone who would stalk me for the rest of my life. But it's not you who's my nemesis, it's me. It's all the guilt I've got inside for what I did to you. Shit, it's taken me a long time to understand it, to realize that I'm still punishing myself for letting you down the way I did. It's been like I was on fire. I had to have the release. . . . Every time with Anna I thought about you. . . ." He lifted his head and looked long into her eyes. "I despise myself for my weakness almost as much as I do for my mistakes. I know I've hurt you real bad, Kirsten, but I've got to ask if you can forgive me. I know I don't deserve it and I wouldn't blame you if you told me to get the hell out of your life and never come back. But if you love me as much as you say you do, if you want me the way I want you . . ."

"Why did you go on sleeping with her if you felt the way you did about me?" Kirsten said.

"I didn't see I had any choice. She was the star, for Christ's sake. If I upset her I'd upset the entire movie. And she was jealous as hell of you. She must have sensed the way I felt about you and besides, at the time, at least at first, I thought it was what I wanted. I thought if I kept on sleeping with her I'd get over you. Jesus, I was a mess. Then there was Pippa . . ."

"Pippa?"

"Yes. She called me that night, right after we'd made love. She went on and on about how weak I was for not facing up to the way I felt about you. She got me so mad—"

"Pippa knew how you felt about me?" Kirsten said incredulously.

"Sure, she knew. And she's been at me about it ever since she left. I wanted to prove her wrong. I wanted to make her suffer for the way she'd walked out on Tom. . . . I wanted . . . Oh, God, how the hell do I know what I wanted when I've fucked everything up the way I have." He smiled wryly, but Kirsten could see the pain in his eyes. "I remember you asking me once, a long time ago, if I'd give you another chance. Well, it looks like the tables have turned, 'cause it's me asking you now if you'll give me another chance. I love you so goddamned much . . ."

But Kirsten was shaking her head. "No, Laurence," she said, only a very slight tremor in her voice. "I can't do it. I want to believe you, I want to so much, but—No, don't touch me, please!" she cried, pressing herself to the wall as he got up.

"You're going to deny us both something we want more than anything else?" he said.

Kirsten looked at him, feeling as though she might choke on the turmoil inside her. In her heart she knew she couldn't resist him, that all she'd ever wanted in the world was standing right here in front of her, but tearing her eyes from his she pushed herself away from the wall and walking over to the window she pulled the curtains. It was a long time before she turned back and even longer before she spoke again. "What time do you have to leave?" she said softly.

"I don't. Unless you want me to."

Endless minutes ticked by. Her eyes moved to the fire as it shifted and sighed. "If you stay," she said still staring into the flames, "I want you just to hold me. I don't want any more than that—at least not yet."

As he folded her into his arms he didn't even attempt to kiss her, he just pulled her close, stroking her hair and gently rocking her from side to side. After a while Kirsten drew her head back and looked up into his eyes. He smiled and ran his fingers over her cheek. She turned to kiss his hand. It all felt so right, so perfect and so natural, but still the fear wouldn't go away.

"How's about we just sit here and talk?" he said, taking her hands and pulling her down beside him on the sofa.

For a while they did, until, almost without thinking, Kirsten leaned toward him, resting her head on his shoulder. His arms came up to hold her, one hand found its way beneath her hair and gently caressed her neck. After a while Kirsten lifted her face and as he looked down, his mouth barely an inch from hers, she lifted a hand to his cheek and pulled his lips to hers.

As he turned her to hold her tighter against him her arms circled his neck and her fingers moved into his hair. She felt his tongue push gently into her mouth and the smell of him, the feel of him, the very taste of him was curling deep into her body. She groaned and clung to him even tighter as his hands found her breasts, but then, as though suddenly realizing what he was doing, he pulled abruptly away.

"I'm sorry," he mumbled. "Shit, I didn't mean to do that. I got carried away." His eyes came to hers and he smiled. "This is kind of hard for me, Kirstie," he said, "when I feel the way I do about you, but it won't happen again, I swear it, not until you're ready."

Kirsten was gazing up at him, taking in every line and every shade of his hypnotic blue eyes. She lifted a hand and ran her thumb gently over his lips, then pulling herself from his arms she got up from the sofa and went to turn off the light.

When she returned she stood in front of him. He looked up at her and she smiled at the confusion in his eyes. She held them with her own as her fingers untied the knot in her dressing gown. She saw him look down at what she was doing, then raise his eyes questioningly back to hers. She shrugged the dressing gown over her shoulders, letting it pool at her feet, then one by one she unfastened the buttons of her pajama jacket. A tiny murmur escaped his lips as she bared her breasts to him and let the jacket fall to the floor. Then hooking her thumbs under the waistband of the flimsy silk trousers she eased them down over her hips and stepped out of them.

Her skin glowed like burnt amber in the firelight, her coppery hair curled tantalizingly about her shoulders.

"Dear God, have you got any idea just how beautiful you are?" he murmured softly, taking her by the hand.

"Make love to me, Laurence," she said, her voice catching on her desire as she looked down at him.

As their fingers entwined he circled his other hand

around her hips and scooped her toward him, burying his face in the musky scent of her. Then both his hands were on her buttocks, massaging them gently as he pulled her closer. He felt her shudder as he pushed his tongue into the tender, sensitive flesh, and was aware of the way he too was responding.

His fingers grazed lightly over her thighs, barely touching her, yet it was as though he was igniting a thousand tiny sparks inside her. She pushed her fingers into his thick, dark hair, then her head fell back as he took her as far into his mouth as he could. His hands moved to the backs of her legs and he pulled her forward so that she fell onto her knees over him. His mouth was on a level with her breasts now, but after softly kissing each distended nipple he looked up into her eyes.

"Are you sure?" he whispered, circling her waist with his hands. "Is this what you really want?"

Kirsten laughed huskily. "You have to ask?" she said.

There was no answering smile, his eyes were too clouded with love, his lips too bound by the sheer intensity of emotion welling inside him. He lifted her off him, sitting her on the sofa beside him. Then dropping to his knees in front of her he raised her legs up onto the luxuriant patterned silk cushions. With one hand he gently pushed her back so that she was lying down and her entire body was laid bare to his lips. All the time he kissed her, moving his mouth from the velvety smoothness of her navel, down to her thighs, to her toes, and back to the delicious succulence of her nipples, he held on to her hand, squeezing it, caressing it and curling his fingers around hers. It was as though this joining of their hands was every bit as intimate as the one they were moving inexorably toward.

Then he was sitting at her feet, easing her legs apart. Their eyes were locked and they remained that way as he lifted her knees and ran his hands along the insides of her thighs. When he reached her and felt the heat of her burn through his fingertips Kirsten's eyes fluttered closed. She could feel the probing hardness of his fingers as slowly, agonizingly, he pushed them into her; then came the warmth of his breath as he moved closer and closer to her. Then his tongue was there, once again moving languorously across that most sensitive part of her. As though from a great distance she heard herself whimper as his lips closed around her, sucking her gently and drawing every sensation of her body into the very depths of his mouth.

Again he reached out for her hand, lacing their fingers as with his tongue he teased and tormented her. The faint contractions deep inside her were beginning to mount, her feet came to rest on his shoulders, her head was moving from side to side. Her fingers tightened around his, squeezing them and twisting them as he drew her ever closer to the edge. His own desire was a solid, pounding force, the unimaginable depth of his love was like a liquid heat flowing through his veins.

"Laurence," she murmured. She struggled to sit up, but as the pressure of his tongue increased she fell back again. "Laurence," she whispered. "Laurence, I want you." She groaned and sobbed as his mouth moved through her dark thatch of hair. Her legs fell from his shoulders, her breasts rose to meet the descent of his lips.

"Laurence," she said, taking his face between her hands. "I want to see you."

He pulled her up into his arms and covered her mouth with his in a kiss so tender, so intimate and so filled with the immensity of his feelings that Kirsten felt as though her heart was swimming in an entire ocean of love.

"Take off your clothes," she murmured, when finally he pulled back to look into her eyes.

A glimmer of humor leapt into his eyes as, letting her go, he hauled his sweater and T-shirt over his head.

Kirsten lifted her hands to caress the hardened muscles of his shoulders. "Laurence, tell me you love me, please."

"I love you, honey," he whispered, running a finger over her lips. "I love you more than I know how to say." He stood up, and resting one arm on the back of the sofa and the other on the arm behind her, he stooped to kiss her. As he did her fingers moved to his belt, tugging it free of its loops, before starting on the zip below it. In the end, because he was already so very hard, he removed his jeans himself. And as he stood over her, showing her the full extent of his physical need for her, Kirsten drew herself up to her knees and took first one, then the other testicle right into her mouth, massaging them gently with her tongue. But, as she circled her fingers around the stem of his penis and made to draw him toward her, he took her wrists in his hands and pulled her to her feet.

"Honey, I can't hold out much longer," he murmured, draping his arms about her waist and pulling her against his straining erection. "I wanna be with you, right there inside you."

Feeling a surge of near delirious joy Kirsten brushed her lips gently over his, before taking his arms from her waist and drawing him down with her to the floor.

The burning embers of the fire cast dark golden shadows over the splendid nakedness of their entwining bodies, and as Laurence filled her with the whole of his desire Kirsten felt herself being submerged into the realms of an unsurpassable love. He moved slowly, tenderly, holding his entire body against hers, keeping their lips together, rolling and pushing his hips, feeling her hands exploring the taut muscles of his back and buttocks while yielding herself up completely and unconditionally to wave after wave after wave of the most exquisite, most profound sensations either of them had ever known.

CHAPTER TWENTY-THREE

IT TOOK ONLY A FEW HOURS OF BEING BACK IN THE office to show both Kirsten and Laurence how crazy they were to think they could keep their relationship a secret.

"You have to try and control yourself a bit better," she told him at the end of the first week.

"How the hell can I do that when just looking at you gives me a hard on," he groaned, running his hands down over her buttocks.

"Don't exaggerate," she said, wriggling out of the way. "And we've got plenty of time for that in the evenings, so will you at least try to behave like a responsible producer while we're here?"

"I'd be a whole lot better at that if you didn't wear those tight clothes," he answered, putting his hands over her breasts.

"I wore them before but you didn't lose control like this then," she reminded him, sliding her hands into her skirt pockets as he caressed her through her sweater.

"You don't know how close I came," he told her, his

eyes dancing with amusement as he squeezed her nipples and watched the effect it was having on her.

"Laurence, at this rate we'll be going home for an early lunch again," she said huskily, "and it's embarrassing having everyone know what we're doing."

He laughed. "They reckon we're doing it right here," he said.

"Only because you won't let them come in without knocking."

"You want them to catch me feeling your tits?"

She rolled her eyes and laughed. "You're so coarse at times," she remarked.

"How about I remind you of the things you were saying last night?" he offered.

"No, thank you. Now, will you answer that phone."

Turning to his desk he picked up the receiver, listened to what his assistant was telling him, then looking at his watch, he rang off. "I've got an appointment at the bank," he said. "Wanna come along?"

Kirsten shook her head. "No, that's your territory. I've got more than enough to do here. Elizabeth and Jean-Paul are coming in to look at the rushes and rough cut—again! Still, it's not every director who gets the opportunity to put right the things they weren't happy with first time around so I guess I should think myself lucky. See you later," she added as the door closed behind him.

Just like everyone else, she and Laurence were still waiting to see what the press would have to say about their relationship. So far there had been an almost deafening silence. And over the next couple of weeks everything went so smoothly on all counts that they should have known it wouldn't last, and sure enough, only days before they were about to depart for Ireland they learned that County Westmeath was under at least a foot of snow.

Laurence went into immediate action, calling in the heads of all departments and telling them to turn everything around and get themselves ready to shoot in New Orleans the following week. The Irish scenes, he said, would be better in March anyway.

"It seems to me," Kirsten remarked to Helena a week later when they met up in a wine bar on the eve of their departure for New Orleans, "that the entire team has been performing miracles. I can hardly believe how they've got this going so fast. It almost makes me dizzy to think of it."

"It's amazing what you can do when you put your mind to it," Helena smiled. "Anyway, it's real good to see you at last. It's not the same on the phone."

"I know," Kirsten groaned. "And I've really missed you."

"I missed you too. You look terrific. I guess that's what love does."

Kirsten laughed. "Sometimes I feel like I'm about to explode with the sheer joy of it," she said. "He's getting fed up with the way I keep pinching him to make sure he's really there and it's not all a dream."

"So what happened to putting the career first and never letting anything or anyone touch you again?" Helena teased.

"Oh, don't remind me," Kirsten grimaced. "The resolutions we make . . . Still I suppose self-preservation calls for them at times. But you and I both know that no amount of success can ever take the place of love."

"It's pretty good to have both though, isn't it?" Helena commented. "So tell me, how do you feel about going back to New Orleans after all that's happened?"

"I don't know really," Kirsten said, gazing thoughtfully around the wine bar. "I mean, being back with Laurence changes a lot of things, but going over old ground for the reasons we are feels, well, it feels pretty awful actually. I know brooding over Anna's death wouldn't help, but it's horrible to think she can be replaced so easily."

"Only in the context of a movie," Helena said. "You have to think of it that way. It's not real, any of this, and she's not forgotten."

"No, she's certainly not forgotten," Kirsten said, pouring more wine into their glasses. "And there's no point in brooding on what's past, God knows I've got enough to think about for the next few weeks. I'm glad we're starting in the plantation house, though; it's the nearest thing we're going to get to a fresh start. Talking of which, and changing the subject neatly, how are things going with Dermott?"

Helena took a deep breath and stared down at her wine. "Hard to say really," she answered. "We're still seeing each other, but I just don't know if I can bring myself to make a real commitment to him. I want to, but something's holding me back."

"Probably the fact that you don't love him," Kirsten suggested.

"Probably. But I might grow to. I guess it's whether or

not I take that chance. Well, I'm gonna have to if I want kids, 'cause time's ticking on and I don't hold out much hope of meeting anyone else before the child-bearing years run out—if they haven't already."

"Is it really that important to you that you have children?" Kirsten asked softly.

Helena nodded. "Yeah. Now I know I might not be able to I want them more than anything." She gave a wistful laugh. "Isn't that the way of the world? Always want what you can't have." Then for no apparent reason she smiled and reached out for Kirsten's hand.

"What was that for?" Kirsten asked in surprise.

"For being you, I guess. For finding the time to talk about my problems when you're such a big-time director now."

"I'm hardly that." Kirsten laughed.

"But you will be," Helena assured her. "Are Jane and Tom coming to New Orleans?"

"Of course. Laurence wouldn't leave him behind even if Tom wanted, which he doesn't. And what about Dermott? Are you seeing him before you go?"

"I'm going over to his place straight from here. As usual he was pretty pissed off that I was seeing you when I'm going to be spending the next few weeks with you anyway. I wish the hell he'd stop putting me in a position where I feel I have to choose between you."

"I'm afraid I've been guilty of that too," Kirsten said.

"With justification. But sure, I was pissed off about that too. Still, the main thing is that we know we're there for each other now."

It was Kirsten's turn to take Helena's hand. "And that will never change." She smiled.

• • •

It was around one in the morning that Kirsten came awake with a jarring suddenness. All her senses were alert, prickling beneath the surface of her skin as her heart thumped heavily in her chest. She lay very still in the darkness, wondering what it was that had woken her.

Her eyes moved over the shadowy silhouettes in the room, half expecting them to move. There was no noise; even the wind had dropped. Her body was rigid as she pulled herself up. A strange, yet muted panic was rising through her.

"Is anyone there?" she said softly. "Laurence, is that you?"

There was no reply, yet to her horror she realized she could hear someone breathing. Her own breath froze and instantly the gentle rasping sound stopped. Closing her eyes with relief, she gingerly pulled aside the duvet and swung her feet to the floor. Then, lifting her hand she reached out for the lamp and a gentle light filtered into the room. It was exactly as she had left it, her half-packed suitcase on the floor, her dressing gown draped over the armchair, her makeup bottles standing innocently on the dressing table.

Slowly she made her way to the door, feeling the silence as though it were a living presence. Her heartbeats were pounding in her ears as she took hold of the door handle and twisted it downward. It opened without a sound.

The landing was lit by the soft, grayish glow from a streetlight. Everything was still.

"Hello?" she called, then suddenly she screamed as the telephone shrilled.

She turned to look at it. Not since before New Orleans had she had one of the calls with the chilling tinkle of baby chimes.

Her eyes were wide as she moved toward the bed. Something was telling her not to answer, yet already her hand was reaching out for the receiver. As she lifted it she turned to look at the door, terrified someone might come in behind her.

She put the receiver to her ear and listened. There was nothing; the line was dead.

"Oh, my God," she sobbed, dashing a hand through her hair, then quickly pressing the connectors she started to dial.

"Hi, sweetheart." Laurence's voice came sleepily over the line. "I just tried to call you."

"That was you!" Kirsten cried, sinking onto the bed.

"Sure, who else calls you in the early hours?"

"But why did you ring off?"

"You were taking such a long time to answer I thought you'd switched off the phone."

"Oh," she said, a sob of laughter breaking through her relief.

"Are you okay? You sound kind of edgy."

"Yes, I was a bit."

"You want me to come over? It was why I was calling."

"Yes," she said. "Yes, come over. I miss you."

"I'll be right there," he said. "And Kirstie, don't let's do this again, huh?"

"What? Do what again?"

"Spend the night apart."

"No." She laughed. "No, don't ever let's do it again."

CHAPTER TWENTY-FOUR

BEING BACK IN NEW ORLEANS, KIRSTEN QUICKLY DIScovered, was nothing like she had expected it to be. Gone were the sinister feelings of before, though she realized that the fact she was so warming to the city had a great deal to do with seeing it through the eyes of a woman who was in love. And as she, Laurence, and Tom took the first couple of days to explore she became so entranced by the sheer magic of the place that she could almost have wished that there was no movie to shoot and that they could just go on and on the way they were.

While the sets were being made ready, the equipment was checked, and actors were refitted for their costumes, the three of them roamed the French Market buying up spices and cookbooks, fancy knickknacks and painted masks, and gorging themselves on po'boys, jambalaya, and gumbo soup. Tom was enthralled by the street entertainers in Jackson Square and even joined in one of their stunts. Kirsten clicked away with her camera while Laurence protested loudly at being dragged into the stunt himself. They took a horse and carriage ride through the cobbled streets, revisited the captain of the steamboat who remembered Tom from the last time, and joined in the impromptu dancing to a lively saxophonist outside the Café du Monde. At least Kirsten and Tom did; Laurence decided to sit that one out and joined Jane at a table for café au lait and a *beignet.* This was the first time they had managed to persuade Jane to come along with them, and it was only as she and Laurence were talking now that he learned the reason for her reluctance. She had believed that Laurence, Kirsten, and Tom needed some time for themselves and hadn't wanted to intrude.

"But how can you think that?" Laurence cried. "You're a part of the family, Jane. You know that."

Jane smiled and for the first time Laurence noticed that she wasn't shrugging quite so much lately. "I hoped I was," she said. "But I didn't want to presume."

"Presumptuousness is just about the last thing you could be accused of." He laughed. "And this little holiday's going to be over at the end of today so I'm glad you changed your mind and came along."

It was nearing the end of the day when Laurence flagged down a taxi to take Jane and Tom back to the hotel. Tom was so sleepy by then he didn't even protest.

Laurence and Kirsten then strolled hand in hand along Moon Walk, watching the fiery sunset ripple dreamily over the Mississippi.

"I wouldn't have swapped this time for the world," Kirsten said, "but I'm looking forward to getting started again on the movie."

Laurence nodded. "Me too. You know we have your

friend Helena to thank for this break from all the meetings."

"Really?" Kirsten said, looking up at him in surprise.

"Apparently, so Jane tells me. It seems she's been going round telling everyone not to bother us unless they have to."

"Well, that's what I call a friend." Kirsten smiled, resting her head on his shoulder.

The next morning everyone set off early to view the new location for the strangulation scene. Both Kirsten and Laurence had felt it wiser, given the circumstances, to relocate the setting, and now, seeing what Alison and her crew had done to a derelict shack that had once been a part of the slave quarters of a tragically neglected plantation house, all were agreed that the new location was even better than the former one. The shack itself was almost hidden by reeds and brambles and the bayou running alongside it, with its viscous coating of duckweed and shimmering glints of winter sunlight, twisted its way toward the solid mass of swamp trees barely more than half a mile away, where Tom insisted that Jane take him to watch the diamond-backed water snakes slithering into the marshy depths.

They wouldn't be shooting the scene until the end of the week, but already Kirsten could sense an unease creeping into the unit. Not surprisingly it was Elizabeth Bradley who was feeling it the most, so Kirsten went out of her way to try and calm the nerves the actress wouldn't actually admit to.

Kirsten was working in a small room at the back of the plantation house later that day, when Laurence came to join her. She was watching the stunt and effects coordinators who were setting up for the outbreak of the fire. She smiled when she saw Laurence come in, but the smile disappeared when he came to stand so close behind her that she could feel the desire gathering like a storm in her lower body.

"How long do you reckon we've got before they go for the next scene?" he whispered.

Kirsten glanced over to where a dry-ice machine and stacks of books were being carried in through the back door of the house. "An hour? Maybe more," she answered.

Laurence nodded. "That's about what I reckon," he said, and turning away he started back out of the room.

"Cold?" he said, as Kirsten fell into step beside him and drew her fur-lined coat tighter around her.

"A bit," she answered, glancing at him from the corner of her eye.

"I just took Elizabeth over to the slave quarters," he said as they strolled out into the garden, heading toward Kirsten's trailer. "She seems pretty okay about it all now."

"Good. I hoped it would work, bringing her scenes forward. How do you feel about it?"

"I'll be glad when it's done," he answered with an ironic smile.

"You and me both." Kirsten laughed, waving to Jane and Helena, who were sitting on the steps of Laurence's trailer. "Fortunately we haven't had any voodoo scenes leading up to it this time. I think that freaked everyone last time, don't you?"

"Hmm, a bit. By the way, did you get a chance to look over the latest budget report yet?"

"Yes." Kirsten nodded. "It didn't look too bad at first glance, but on a second look . . . We're overspending badly, aren't we?"

"It's serious, but not critical."

"We'll go over it now, shall we? I've made some notes. In fact, there are some other things I want you to take a look at too," she added as they reached her trailer. "The publicity people dropped off some art work earlier and the stills guy wants us to look at some contacts of Elizabeth and Jean-Claude; I think I've got them with me. Oh, and Carrie rang earlier to say that the video of Helena's dance routine has arrived."

"Good," he said, pulling open the door. "But don't show it until we come to pick up the scene again."

"Okay."

Laurence followed her inside and closed the door behind him. "So where's this budget report," he said, his eyes starting to widen as Kirsten removed her coat. She was wearing a much shorter skirt than normal, a black *bustier* that barely contained her breasts and a pair of thigh-high black boots.

Kirsten was still talking as though there was nothing untoward in her attire, and as she hung her coat on the back of the door and started across the trailer, Laurence ignored the stirrings in his groin and barely disguising his smile went along with the charade.

"Here are the contacts," she said, picking up a large

brown envelope and sliding them out. "I took a brief look through earlier and have circled some already—I think these here," she said, handing him one sheet, "portray the right degree of passion." She flicked through the others. "Ah, and here, take a look at these, the humor in Jean-Claude's eyes is terrific."

As he took them she perched herself on the edge of the desk and rested one foot on the corner of his chair. Her firm, smooth thighs were bare and as she leaned forward to watch him leafing through the contacts he was acutely aware of the way her breasts were spilling from the flimsy lace cups.

"I'm not too keen on Elizabeth's costume here," Laurence remarked. "It doesn't have enough color. Did the stills guy blow any up?"

"Only half a dozen," Kirsten answered, straightening up. Her dark nipples were now showing in half moons and Laurence could feel himself hardening. Then, as she turned to pick up the ten-by-eights, her legs parted and he saw instantly that she wasn't wearing any panties.

His eyes were alive with laughter, but his voice was perfectly grave as he took the blowups from her, saying, "Sure, you're right about the expressions here, but there's going to have to be some touching up. See the lines here around her eyes? And the neck. Get him to sort that and we'll take a look again."

Kirsten took the photographs back and put them on the desk behind her, at the same time picking up a wad of color photocopies of the art work. "The originals are out at the production office," she said, passing them to him, "together with the lettering."

"Hmm," Laurence said, looking through them.

"They're a bit yellow, don't you think? Or is that just the photocopier?"

"No, they're yellow. Grant's going to do something about that, but he gave me these just to show the general idea." At that moment her telephone rang and as she leaned across to answer it her left breast broke free of the bustier.

"Yes, he's right here," she said, passing the phone to Laurence. "It's Sonya for you."

Laurence stood up to take the phone, and as he did he drew Kirsten's nipple deep into his mouth and sucked hard. Kirsten's eyes fluttered closed, then suddenly he let her go and started to speak to Sonya, who was relaying the messages that had come in from the UK overnight.

As he listened Laurence turned to sit beside Kirsten on the edge of the desk. But Kirsten got up, and falling to her knees in front of him started to unbutton his jeans. By now Laurence's erection was pounding, but as she licked and nibbled him, then took him right into her mouth, he continued to give Sonya instructions as to how she should deal with his messages.

Eventually he rang off and as he replaced the receiver Kirsten got back to her feet and continued as though nothing had happened. "Okay," she said, "I think we should leave any further decisions over art work and stills until we've talked to Grant and Alison. Shall we take a look at the budget now?"

"Sure."

Laurence moved back to his chair, making no attempt to cover his penis, and Kirsten sat on the desk, this time lifting both feet onto his chair and displaying herself totally.

"I see here that you're still waiting for Alison's latest figures," she said, picking up the computer printout and starting to unfold it, "but she's already warned us of the overspend. Have we had the figures from the effects guys yet?" she said looking up.

"Tomorrow," he said, taking her knees and pulling her legs even wider apart.

"But at the moment it looks like they're under? They don't know it of course, because you told them they had less to spend than we'd allocated. I think we should pour more into Jake's budget, if there's anything—" her voice faltered as Laurence leaned forward to look at the printout and at the same time pushed his fingers deep inside her "—going begging."

She managed to keep going for some time, suggesting reallocations, proposing tighter measures, until he started to circle her clitoris with his thumb.

"Oh, God, don't ever stop doing that," she murmured, letting the printout fall to the floor and lifting her feet to the arms of his chair. Supporting her arched back by resting her hands on the desk behind her, she moaned softly as he removed his hand and put his tongue where his fingers had been.

It was as the first waves of orgasm started to coast through her that there was a frantic banging on the trailer door.

"Laurence! Kirsten! Are you in there?" Alison cried.

"Be right there," Laurence shouted as both he and Kirsten hurriedly made themselves decent.

"Oh, Christ!" Alison gasped, when Laurence threw

open the door, her agitation making her green frizzy hair seem even more outlandish. "You better come quick, both of you. There's been an accident."

"What kind of accident?" Laurence demanded, starting down the steps as Kirsten grabbed for her coat.

"God knows," Alison answered. "It was really weird . . ."

"Who is it?" Kirsten wanted to know. "Are they badly hurt?"

"It's Jake and Elizabeth. . . . They've . . . Oh, God, you'd better come and see for yourselves."

"What's happened to them?" Kirsten persisted.

"I'm not sure. They were on the set alone, everyone was having coffee . . . It seems that Jake was on a ladder doing something or another with a light and he fell. . . . Elizabeth ran to get help and she fell too. . . . Oh, God, I don't know. . . . She seems pretty badly hurt though. But at least she's conscious."

"You mean Jake's not!" Laurence cried.

"He wasn't when I left. There was blood on his forehead, so he must have hit it as he went down."

"Where is he now?" Laurence said, breaking into a run through the gardens.

"Still in the library. Elizabeth's in the pantry place outside. The nurse is there . . ."

When they reached the house it was to find the entire unit crowded into the hall outside the library. Immediately a path opened for Kirsten and Laurence to push their way through. The first thing Kirsten saw when they entered the room was the small pool of blood beside Jake's inert body. Then, as she moved her eyes to watch the nurse she felt a sickening paralysis grip her insides.

The nurse lifted her head, then lowered it again to resume the kiss of life. Laurence and Kirsten exchanged a quick look, both horribly struck by the fact that they had witnessed this scene before.

"An ambulance is on its way," the stunt-coordinator told them. "Seems like Elizabeth has broken her leg."

""Where is she?" Kirsten demanded.

"I think one of the sparks carried her into the drawing room."

Kirsten and Laurence pushed their way out again, both trying very hard to remain calm. Elizabeth was stretched out on a sofa, Helena and some of the other cast and dressers were with her; she looked to be in a great deal of pain.

"It's all right," Kirsten assured her, "the ambulance is coming. What happened?"

"I don't know," Elizabeth said, wincing as she tried to move. "One minute we were chatting while he was climbing the ladder, the next he was on the floor in front of me. I could see he'd hit his head so I went to get help. On the way out I tripped over one of those damned prop machines, and before I knew what was happening I was on the floor myself. I tried to get up, couldn't, fell back against the door, which was why they carried me over here so they could get in to see to Jake. How is he?"

"The nurse is with him," Kirsten answered, glancing at Laurence. Inside she was screaming. This couldn't be happening, it just couldn't. It was a nightmare and any minute now she would wake up. Jake had merely bumped his head and Elizabeth had twisted her ankle. That was all. It would be all right. They could go on with the film—

"Laurence!"

Kirsten and Laurence turned to see Lindon come into the room. His face was horribly pale. "It's not looking good," he said. "The ambulance is here."

Pushing past him, Laurence ran back to the library just in time to see a blanket being drawn over Jake's face.

Numbed by disbelief and horror everyone watched in terrible silence as the medics lifted the stretcher and carried it out of the room. It was only when they had gone that Laurence spotted Detectives Kowski and Greengage watching from the back of the crowd.

"Jesus Christ Almighty," he muttered. "Just what the hell is going on?"

CHAPTER TWENTY-FIVE

THE CORONER'S VERDICT OF ACCIDENTAL DEATH WAS delivered less than twenty-four hours after Jake had been carried from the house. By then both Kirsten and Laurence had been interviewed by the police, and neither of them were left in any doubt that Kowski was deeply unimpressed by what had happened.

Kirsten could hardly come to grips with the fact that she was once again face-to-face with this sinister man. She had thought never to see Kowski again in her life, but his wolfish teeth, elongated cheeks and predator's eyes were right there, swimming before her as he asked her about a death she still couldn't believe had happened. His presence, just like his questions, was as nightmarish as the newspaper headlines that had been faxed over from the U.K.

Kirsten's DP Falls to His Death
New Orleans Police Question Kirsten
What's It All About, Kirstie?
Star Breaks Leg, DP Dies, Kirsten Questioned.

There were so many of them and most all of them were linking her to what had happened in a way that was as terrifying as it was unjust.

When the British press starting swarming into New Orleans Laurence refused to make any comment on what had happened and no one got even close to seeing Kirsten. She remained in their suite where the police came first to interview her, then to tell her the verdict on Jake's death. It seemed to her that Kowski no more believed it was innocent this time around than he did the last. The blow to the head, he told her, wasn't normally enough to kill a man, but in this instance it seemed it had. . . .

"Seemed," Kirsten said to Laurence as soon as the door closed behind Kowski. "He doesn't believe it was an accident, does he?"

"I don't know," Laurence sighed. "It's hard to tell with the cops. They're a real cynical bunch. He was probably just saying it that way 'cause it gives him some kind of kick to do that to people."

"Do you believe it was an accident?" she said, her lovely face pale and anguished.

"I sure as hell wish I knew what to believe." He sighed, shaking his head. "This is just too much of a coincidence, having two deaths on the same movie. Just thank God we were together when it happened and that Alison saw us."

"That's not stopping the press, though, is it? They're trying to make out I had something to do with it."

"I know." His hand suddenly crashed against the wall. "Shit! What is going on here?" he seethed. "Why can't that fucking Fisher woman just leave you alone?"

"Maybe she will once the verdict is made public," Kirsten suggested, though there wasn't much hope in her voice.

"Dermott's flying in later today," he said after a pause. "Did Helena tell you?"

Kirsten nodded. "I wish we could just get out of here and go home," she said.

"There's nothing stopping us doing that," he said, pulling her into his arms.

"But I thought . . . Aren't we going to recast Moyna and carry on?"

He shook his head. "No. We can't do that. I know we only shot a few scenes with her and the insurance will cover, but the cast, at least most of them, are saying that unless their fees are doubled—trebled in some cases—they don't want to continue. Two deaths on the same movie they reckon is a jinx and they don't want to run the risk of any more unless they're well compensated for it. And we just can't afford what they're asking. So I'm calling the whole thing to a halt—"

"But Laurence, what about the completion bond?"

"We'll just have to sort it out once we get back to London," he said.

Kirsten put a hand to her head as it started to spin. "Oh, God, I'm sorry," she whispered.

"Hey, hey," he said, pulling her back. "Will you stop that? It's not your fault."

"But I just know this wouldn't be happening if I wasn't here. It's got something to do with me, I know it has . . ."

"Kirstie, we've got to go with what the police tell us

and ignore what's going on in the press or we're going to end up as crazy as Ruby."

"How is she?" Kirsten asked.

"Not good. The nurse is flying home with her later today. The whole thing's terrified her out of her mind. She's back on her coconut trip, I'm afraid. Said all this was foretold. . . . First the castle, then a woman, then a man. . . . Well, you know how she goes on, you heard it all before. She tried to tell Kowski that some kid inside her pushed Jake off the ladder, but Elizabeth says Ruby wasn't even in the room. No one was except those two."

"What's going to happen to Ruby once she gets to London?"

"My mother's sorting that out. I spoke to her while you were with Kowski."

Had Kirsten not been so numbed by everything else that was going on she might have been surprised to hear that, but as it was her mind was refusing to function much beyond what was happening right now. But then as she recalled what a true friend Jake had been to her she felt the tears sting her eyes.

"God, who would have thought," she said, shaking her head in bewilderment, "while we were all messing around on the set yesterday that in less than three hours he would be dead. It's so frightening. He was so full of life. So kind and uncomplicated. Everyone loved him. . . . No one, just no one would have done this to him. It had to be an accident."

"Sure it was," Laurence said, stroking her hair. "That's exactly what it was and don't you forget it."

• • •

NICE TRY, KIRSTEN, SHAME YOU GOT THE WRONG PERSON. BEING WHERE YOU WERE ISN'T GOING TO SAVE YOU THOUGH, IS IT? NOT WHEN I KNOW HOW YOU DID IT. START COUNTING THE DAYS, KIRSTEN.

As Kirsten stared down at the note great waves of fear were tearing through her. They were back in England now and both she and Laurence had been with Ruby on and off these past forty-eight hours, sitting beside her hospital bed, waiting for her to come out of the blinding stupor she had drunk herself into. Kirsten had just returned home to pick up the mail and get some sleep before joining Laurence at the bank later.

She was still jet lagged and hardly able to think straight, and as she turned and walked into the sitting room, her mind reeling with thoughts chaotic and terrifying, she couldn't even begin to understand what was going on. How could anyone possibly prove that she had anything to do with the deaths when she hadn't even been near Anna or Jake when they'd died. But obviously someone believed she did do it. Either that or they were just doing this to frighten her. She looked down at the note again, a nauseous horror tightening her stomach as she read the words again. But that was it, she decided, someone was trying to frighten her. After all, how many times did she have to tell herself, she couldn't be charged with murders she hadn't committed—that hadn't been murders at all.

Nevertheless, she knew in her heart that she hadn't heard the end of this yet. That the intent behind this note was every bit as menacing as the words themselves, and this time she was going to speak to Laurence about it, to show him the note and ask him to go with her to the police.

Jane was making some lunch for Tom when Laurence got home. He was wondering if he could manage to grab half an hour's sleep when the telephone started to ring. He went into the study to answer it. To his annoyance it was Pippa, just about the last person he needed to speak to right now.

"I've been trying to get you all morning," she said peevishly. "Did you get my messages?"

Laurence looked down at the blinking light on the answering machine. "I haven't got round to playing them back yet," he said, struggling to keep the irritation out of his voice. "I just got in ten minutes ago."

"I take it Tom's with you?"

"Of course."

"Good. I'm at my mother's now. I can be there in fifteen minutes," and before Laurence had a chance to object she hung up.

Replacing the receiver Laurence wandered back down to the kitchen where Jane was trying to coax Tom to eat. "Is everything all right?" she asked when she saw Laurence standing in the doorway watching them.

"Everything's fine," he answered, "that is if you discount the unholy mess we're in. Mommy's on her way over," he added to Tom.

But Tom didn't appear to be listening, he was too excited about being back among his own toys.

Laurence watched him for a while, feeling an absurdly strong need to see Kirsten right now. Then Tom looked up and gave him such a beaming smile that Laurence's heart turned over. "Got a kiss there for Daddy?" he said.

"Can we play with the trains?" Tom asked, as he leapt up into Laurence's arms.

"Sure we can." Laurence smiled. "Let's just eat some of this lunch first, shall we?"

"But I'm not hungry. I want to play with the trains."

"Come on now, Tom, be a good boy, huh?"

"I'll bet my train will go faster than yours," Tom challenged.

Laurence looked helplessly at Jane and knowing that he was about to give in anyway, Jane said, "It's okay. I'll give him something later. But," she added, as Laurence put him down and Tom started for the door, "you've got some tidying up to do before you can play with those trains."

Tom looked back at Laurence. "Do I have to, Dad?"

"Yes, you do. I'll be up in a minute so get to it."

"I didn't realize Pippa was in London," Jane said once Tom had left the kitchen.

"No, neither did I." Laurence sighed. "I hope to God she's not coming round here expecting to take Tom off for the weekend—with all that's been happening he doesn't need any more disruption. Still, I can hardly stop her seeing him, can I?"

"Not really, no," Jane mumbled. Then her eyes came shyly up to his. "Would you though, I mean if you could?"

Laurence sighed heavily. "It'd be a whole lot easier if

Tom wanted to see her. But who knows, maybe this time he will."

Tom didn't though, for as soon as he heard his mother's voice downstairs talking to Jane he shut his bedroom door and stood with his back pressed against it. Laurence was in there with him and felt a lump rising in his throat when he saw the anguish in Tom's eyes.

"Let's hide, Daddy," he pleaded. "Let's pretend we're not here."

"We can't do that, soldier." Laurence smiled sadly. "Mommy's come a long way to see you . . ."

"I don't want to see her."

"Hey, hey. Mommy loves you very much. You got to at least say hello to her."

"I don't want to," Tom declared, his bottom lip starting to quiver.

"It's only polite, son," Laurence said, stooping down to Tom's height. "And she wants to see what a big boy you've got to be since she saw you."

Two fat tears rolled from Tom's eyes. "She'll make me go to Granny and Grandpa Smith's and I don't want to go there, Daddy. I want to stay here with you."

"But you like it at Granny and Grandpa Smith's," Laurence said, pulling him into his arms.

"No, I don't. I hate it there. I want to be here with you. You're my best friend, you said so."

"Sure I am, and you going to Granny and Grandpa's with Mommy isn't going to change that."

"You wouldn't make me go if I was really your best friend," Tom sobbed.

For a while, as Laurence held him, he was at a loss what to do. In the end he held Tom back so that he could see his face and said gently, "How about I go downstairs and talk to Mommy?"

"No," Tom cried, clinging to him. "I don't want you to speak to her. I want you to stay here with me. Please, Daddy, stay here with me."

It was a long hard battle and one that got Laurence so choked up he was finding it difficult to speak, but eventually he managed to persuade Tom to let him go just for five minutes.

Pippa was in the sitting room with Jane, but as soon as Laurence walked in Jane got up and left them alone.

"How are you?" Laurence said, as Pippa walked over to the drinks cabinet and helped herself.

"Fine," she answered.

"And Zaccheo?"

"Yes, he's fine too. Thank you."

There was an awkward silence as Pippa stared down at her drink, unable to meet Laurence's eyes. She'd noticed the instant he walked in the room how very tired he looked, which was hardly surprising considering what he'd been through lately. She was about to ask how Ruby was but stopped herself; her only reason for asking would be to stall for time and there was nothing to be gained from that. So, mustering her courage, she lifted her head and looked him straight in the eyes. "I'm sorry, but there's no point beating about the bush here, Laurence," she said. "I've come to take Tom away with me. I want him to leave right—"

"Hold it! Hold it!" Laurence said. "What do you mean, take Tom away with you?"

"I'm taking him to Italy."

"Like hell you are."

"Laurence, please don't fight me on this," Pippa pleaded, putting her drink down. "It's for Tom's own good—"

"I'll be the judge of what's for Tom's own good," Laurence raged. "You forfeited that right the day you walked out of here."

"I haven't forfeited any rights," Pippa cried angrily. "He's my son. He should be with his mother, especially in light of what's been happening these past months."

"Would you like to make yourself a little clearer on that, Pippa?" Laurence said tightly.

"Two people have died on that movie," she shouted. "How much clearer do you want it? Do you think I want my son around that sort of thing? And if you were any kind of a father you'd see that it was in Tom's interests to be away from you right now."

"Tom's place is right here with me," Laurence yelled. "And if you're trying to accuse me of something here—"

"I'm not accusing you of anything! I'm just telling you that I don't want him around—"

"What you want doesn't feature here, Pippa."

"I'm his mother, for Christ's sake! I only want what's best for him. A home—"

"He's got a home!"

"But for how much longer? What are you going to do, Laurence, when the banks start calling in their loans? What home will you have for him then?"

"I'll find us a home, you don't need to worry about that."

"But I do worry. And so should you. You're already in debt up to your ears thanks to that bloody film and don't think Thea is going to bail you out, not while you're sleeping with Kirsten Meredith. And that's another reason for taking Tom away with me. I don't want that woman anywhere near my son."

"I don't fucking believe this!" Laurence roared. "You knew she was going to be a part of my life again—Christ, you practically pushed us together yourself. You weren't quite so concerned then, though, were you, when you wanted to run off with Zaccheo. No, all that mattered then was you, and what you wanted."

"And right now I want my son. I'm sorry, Laurence, but I'm taking him." As Pippa made to push past him Laurence grabbed her. She gasped. For a moment Laurence thought he had hurt her, but then following her eyes he saw that Tom was standing at the door. "Oh Christ," he groaned.

"Come on, Tom, come to Mummy, darling," Pippa said holding out her arms to him.

Tom just stared at her.

"Come on," she coaxed. "We're going on a nice trip, in an airplane . . ."

Tom's eyes shot to Laurence's and Laurence's heart contracted at the look of betrayal. "Daddy, please don't make me go," he begged.

"But you'll like it where we're going," Pippa insisted.

"No, no, I want my daddy." Tom dashed across the room and threw himself against Laurence's legs.

Laurence swept him up in his arms. "It's okay, soldier, you don't have to go anywhere you don't want to."

"Laurence!" Pippa cried.

Laurence ignored her as he tried to comfort Tom.

"Look, Tom," Pippa said, walking behind Laurence so she could see Tom's face. Tom immediately turned his head. "Tom," she pleaded, "aren't you even going to give Mummy a hug? Please." She was trying to prize his arms from Laurence's neck.

"Pippa, don't put him through this," Laurence muttered under his breath.

"Can't Mummy just have one kiss?" she persisted.

"No!" Tom shouted. "I hate you. I hate you. I hate you."

Pippa's face was stricken and despite everything Laurence felt his heart go out to her. He was even tempted to try persuading Tom himself to give his mother a hug, but he knew that it was only a ploy on Pippa's part to get hold of him. And the last thing Laurence wanted was Tom in the middle of a physical tussle between them. As it was Tom could barely catch his breath he was sobbing so hard.

"I think it would be better if you left now," Laurence said.

Very close to tears herself, Pippa nodded and turned to pick up her bag. "I have to warn you though, Laurence," she said, "I shall be fighting you for custody. I've already spoken to my solicitor and you must know that your chances of keeping him aren't good."

Laurence didn't answer. Tom had heard too much already.

Five days later, after a marathon session with his lawyers, Laurence turned up at Kirsten's looking so exhausted he might fall asleep on his feet.

"How did it go?" she asked, taking his coat and going to pour him a drink.

"Are we talking about the movie or about Tom?" he answered flopping down on the sofa. He smiled grimly. "Either way, about as bad as it could."

"Has she petitioned for custody yet?"

He nodded.

"What does your lawyer say?"

"That it doesn't look good. We're still going to fight it, naturally, but, well, with everything that's happened . . ." He sighed heavily. "The house goes on the market tomorrow."

Immediately Kirsten put down his drink and going to sit on his lap put her arms around him and held him tightly.

"Oh, Kirstie," he murmured into her hair, "you don't know how good it feels to hold you. I love you so much, but if I lose him . . ."

Kirsten pulled her head back to look at him. "You won't lose him," she said firmly. "No one's going to take him from you."

"I wish I could be so certain."

"You could be if you'd just do as I say."

"No, Kirsten," he said breaking away from her. "We've been over this and over it and I'm not going to let you do it. Paul left you this house . . ."

"But, Laurence, I don't need a great big house like this. If I sell it I can give you the money and you can pay off the outstanding—"

"No!"

"Tom needs a home," she argued. "Just think of how much greater your chances will be of keeping him if you didn't have to worry about selling—"

"Kirsten, no!"

"Okay, then look at it this way," she said. "How on earth are you going to buy somewhere else? You're not going to have anything left once they've finished."

"We'll go live with my parents," Laurence answered. "I talked it over with Dad last night. It's what they want . . ."

"Is it what you and Tom want?"

He laughed mirthlessly. "Right now, we don't have a whole lot of choice."

"You could always come here," she said.

His eyes moved to hers. "You've been talking to Tom," he said.

"He wants to come."

"And don't I know it."

"I want you to come too," she said quietly. "Both of you. If *you* want to."

Lifting a hand to her face, Laurence stroked his thumb along her jaw. "Sure I want to come," he said.

CHAPTER TWENTY-SIX

THE PRAM WAS MOVING FAST DOWN THE STREET. HER hands were gripping it so tightly her knuckles were white. Her eyes were glazed; the baby was screaming. Cars sped by, puddles showered her legs, people leapt out of her way. She crashed into a bus stop, dented the pram, jolted the baby, and her album spilled onto the pavement.

Hurriedly she bent to retrieve it, pushing the photos back inside and rushing on. She didn't know where she was going, she couldn't think, the baby was crying so hard she couldn't hear.

Images were dancing before her eyes. Laurence and Kirsten laughing. Laurence and Kirsten loving. Laurence and Kirsten succeeding. The future yawned like a cavern before her, swallowing her into its blackened depths. Fear and resentment burned her heart, desperation whipped her mind. The echoing, sinister sounds of baby chimes rang in her ears, drowning the screams, twisting the sobs in her throat.

She reached the park, wheeled the pram inside, and

sat down on a bench. The drizzling rain soaked her, curious stares incensed her. She was so afraid she was choking on it. She'd killed two people; she was going to kill more. Kirsten, she had to kill Kirsten. She snatched the album from the pram. A frenzied panic blazed in her eyes as she stared down at the mud-spattered pictures of Kirsten. Of Kirsten and Laurence. Of Kirsten and Tom. Of Kirsten and Jane. Of Kirsten's family. . . . But it wasn't Kirsten's family, it was her family. . . . Laurence and Tom belonged to her. . . .

She got abruptly to her feet throwing the album into the pram. It hit the baby's head. She didn't care. Let the baby scream. Let it bleed, let it know pain the way she was knowing pain. She wasn't going to comfort it. No one ever comforted her. . . .

It was past eleven o'clock by the time Kirsten returned home, fighting her way through the raging torrents of wind and rain. It had been a long and tiring week, fraught with tension and fear as the legal processes of winding up the film and preparing for the custody battle ground mercilessly on. Jane especially had started showing signs of strain, which was why Kirsten had taken her off to a movie, just to get her out of the house for a while and perhaps take her mind off things. A few minutes ago Jane had caught the last bus to go off and spend the night with her parents.

Kirsten ran around the corner into Elm Park Gardens, her umbrella buffeted by the wind, her feet drenched by the rain. After what seemed an endless search she managed to dig her keys from her handbag and all but fell in through the door. As she poked her umbrella into the stand she reached out to flick on the light.

"Damn!" she muttered when nothing happened, trying to remember where she'd put the spare bulbs, and picking her way carefully through to the sitting room she attempted to turn on that light. Still nothing.

She'd never been particularly afraid of the dark; power cuts had been so frequent in France she'd got used to them a long time ago, but for some reason the mysterious loss of power in her own house, right here in the middle of London, when the streetlights outside were working, was unsettling.

She turned toward the kitchen, trying to remember where she'd put the candles when suddenly she turned rigid. At first she wasn't too sure what the sound was, but as her ears strained into the silence she was aware of a gentle whirring sound.

Then suddenly a deep, resonant voice echoed out of the darkness, floating around her and settling over her heart in a paralyzing layer of fear.

"Who is it?" she cried. "Who's there?"

"Kirrrr-sten."

"Laurence!" she called, a horrible buzz starting in her ears. "Laurence is that you?"

"Kirrrr-sten."

"Oh, my God," she choked. "Who is it? Who's there?" She was backing across the room, stumbling into furniture, her heart thudding violently through a gale of terror.

"Kirrrr-sten."

The wind and rain beat against the windows, hammered against the door, howled wantonly down the chimney. It was as though she were drowning in a maelstrom of baleful sound. . . .

She clasped her hands to her ears at the very moment that her foot caught on the corner of the sofa. In her panicked state she thought someone had tripped her and screamed as she crashed awkwardly onto the cushions.

She waited, breathlessly, her heart crashing against her ribs, her stomach heaving with sickening dread. Swaying tree shadows careened across the room, a sudden crack of thunder puncturing the appalling silence.

She heard keys in the front door and her every nerve-end jarred. Then as the door banged closed she started to throw herself wildly across the room. "Laurence!" she gasped hoarsely, "Laurence!"

"Kirsten? Kirsten, are you all right?"

"Helena! Oh, my God! Helena, is that you?"

"Of course it's me. Where are you? What's happened to the lights?"

"They're not working. Oh, Helena! Helena!" she cried, throwing herself into her arms.

"My God, what's the matter?" Helena demanded. "You're shaking like a leaf."

"Helena, we've got to get out of here." Kirsten whispered, trying to pull herself together. "There's someone—"

"Kirrrr-sten."

Kirsten stifled a scream as Helena almost jumped out of her skin. "Fucking hell!" Helena gasped. "What's going on here?"

"I don't know. Come on, let's go."

"Not on your life," Helena declared. "Where do you keep the candles?"

"Don't be a fool," Kirsten said, reaching out for the door. "Let's just get out of here."

"But there are two of us and only one of him," Helena whispered. "Come on, follow me."

Steadily they inched their way through to the kitchen where Helena stood guard at the door as Kirsten rummaged in a drawer.

"Oh, thank God," Kirsten gasped the moment she saw Helena's face in the candlelight. Then suddenly a bolt of fear shot through her chest. The drooping black shadows were contorting Helena's features, the eerie, flickering light gleamed horribly in her eyes. For one blinding second the night of the voodoo ritual flashed vividly before Kirsten's eyes.

"Kirrrr-sten."

"Maybe you're right," Helena breathed, "we ought to get out of—" Her voice was choked by a strangled scream as they heard the front door open then close. Footsteps started down the hall. Kirsten's eyes were twin pools of petrified disbelief. Helena reached out for her hand. Kirsten took it, but with the other she started to fumble in the drawer for a knife. Then they heard Laurence swear as he tried to turn on a light.

"Laurence!" Kirsten cried. "Oh, Laurence!" and dashing into the hall she almost knocked him over in the dark.

"What's the matter? What's happened to the lights?" he said.

"Kirrrr-sten."

"What the hell was that?"

"Sssh," Kirsten whispered. "There's someone in here. There's—"

"Kirrrr-sten."

Helena loomed out of the darkness, her face lit by candlelight, and for one ghastly moment, as the point of the knife's shadow plunged into the curling shadow of Kirsten's hair, Laurence half expected Kirsten to slump against him. "Give me that," he growled and grabbing both the knife and the candle from Helena he turned into the sitting room.

"Kirst . . ."

This time the name was cut off halfway through, and Kirsten heard Laurence ejecting a cassette.

"What's been going on here?" he demanded as Helena and Kirsten followed him into the room.

"Oh, God," Kirsten gasped, seeing him holding up the cassette. "What a fool! I should have realized . . . I thought someone was in here."

"Well, obviously someone has been," Laurence stated. "How else did that get on the tape deck?"

Kirsten turned to Helena, a nightmarish suspicion suddenly gathering horror to its heart. "How did you get in?" she asked.

"I've got a set of keys, remember?" Helena answered. "I only used them because I thought no one was in. I was round the corner in the Arts Club and thought I'd beg a bed for . . ." she trailed off as Kirsten started to back away from her.

Suddenly everything was crowding in on Kirsten. So many things that just didn't add up, that had never added up, that she had blinded herself to because she just hadn't wanted to believe it.

"It's you, isn't it?" Kirsten cried, backing up against Laurence. "It's you who sent me that note?"

Helena stared at her, dumbfounded. "What note?"

"Why?" Kirsten shouted. "For God's sake why are you doing this to me?"

"Doing what?"

"The stories in the papers!" Kirsten cried. "All those evil, vicious things that have been written about me . . . Oh, my God! Anna! And Jake! What did you do to them?"

"What the fuck are you talking about?" Helena yelled. "What's she talking about?" she shouted to Laurence.

Laurence was holding Kirsten tightly, aware of how badly she was shaking, that she was nearing hysteria. "Sssh, ssh," he soothed her. "Take it steady now. Just tell us—"

"How could you do it, Helena?" Kirsten screamed. "What did I ever do to you? I thought you were my friend . . ."

"Come on," Laurence soothed her. "Get a grip, honey . . ."

"You don't understand, Laurence. You don't know what she's been doing. You were trying to frighten me, weren't you," she shot at Helena. "With that note! With this tape! Well it worked. I was terrified. Does that satisfy you? Is that what you wanted, or is there more?"

"You're crazy," Helena whispered incredulously. "I didn't send you any fucking note . . ."

"She's lying," Kirsten sobbed, turning her face into Laurence's chest. "Get her out of here, Laurence. Make her go! Please, make her go."

"It's all right, I'm going," Helena retorted. "I'm not staying around here to be abused by a sick mind."

"Leave those keys!" Kirsten screamed after her.

Helena turned back, threw the keys furiously across the room, and stormed out of the house.

Laurence held Kirsten for a long time, stroking her hair and waiting for her to calm down. "Now what is it, honey?" he said at last. "Just what was all that about?"

"I'm not sure," Kirsten said, blowing her nose. "It's all so . . . Oh, Laurence, I should have told you when it started, but . . . you had so much else to think about . . ."

After several false starts Kirsten managed to get out the whole story. She told him about the strange telephone calls, the note that had arrived after Jake's death, the fact that she had thought there was someone in the house the night before they went to New Orleans and how, all along, she had tried to tell herself that all that had happened to her could not possibly be traced to Helena, but when she looked back over the past year she could see now that everything had been moving toward this. "From the time she took me to your party just after I got back to England right up until now, everything's been pointing to her," she said. "Her relationship with Campbell, the broken promises, the stories in the press giving details only she would know. . . . Then tonight," she shuddered, "that voice on the tape . . . I forgot she had the keys, I didn't even know she had any keys, but don't you see, she was probably already in here when I came in. She started the tape, I couldn't see anything . . . Then she *pretended* to let herself in . . ."

"But, honey, it was a man's voice."

"What difference does that make? Just think how many actors she knows. How many technicians who could set it up for her . . ."

"That still doesn't explain why, though."

"Oh, Laurence, all my life people have resented and hated me . . ."

"Hey, come on," he said, hugging her to him and trying to dismiss the horrifying image of Helena standing behind Kirsten with a knife. "No more tears. I'm here, aren't I? And nothing's going to happen to you while I'm around. And this is one guy who loves you, remember?"

"Do you swear it, Laurence? Do you swear that you'll always love me?"

"I swear it," he said, smiling at the uncertainty in her eyes. If only he could wipe away this insecurity altogether, make her more sure of herself and of him so that she'd never doubt, not even for a moment, that this time he really wasn't going to let her down. Or was he? Jesus Christ, he didn't know what the hell he was going to do.

"Jane, what on earth are you doing down here in the middle of the night?" Jane's mother said, turning on the light as she came into the kitchen.

"I couldn't sleep," Jane answered dully, staring down at the dregs of her cocoa.

Amy Cottle eyed her daughter with a mixture of hostility and exasperation, then taking the few steps to the table where Jane was sitting she hoisted Jane's chin up to look into her face. "What have you been crying for?" she demanded.

"Just leave me alone," Jane said, pushing her mother's hand away.

"It's about that child, isn't it?" Amy sneered. "I heard you talking to your father earlier. You think they're going to get rid of you, don't you? If his mother wins custody, you reckon you're going to be out on your ear."

"Just shut up," Jane sobbed. "Shut up and mind your own business."

"Well, I can't say I'd blame them if they did," Amy remarked. "I don't know how that Laurence has put up with having your sullen face around for so long."

"It's not sullen when I'm with them," Jane countered. "It's only you who makes me like this."

"Oh, I see, it's my fault, is it?"

When Jane didn't answer Amy turned to the stove and poured boiling water onto a spoonful of cocoa. "Do you want some more?" she barked over her shoulder at Jane.

Jane shook her head.

Amy turned her prissy face back to what she was doing. "So what's happening over there now then?" she asked.

"They're getting ready for the custody battle," Jane answered.

"His mother'll get custody," Amy stated. "Mothers always do."

"Why don't you just go back to bed," Jane said, fresh tears starting in her eyes.

Amy's whiskery eyebrows shot up in surprise. "If you ask me you're too wrapped up in that family and their affairs—"

"No one's asking you."

"All right, but if you're going to sit here worrying yourself sick over whether or not they're going to get rid of you, then have it out with them. Ask them straight."

"That's not what I'm worrying about," Jane cried, burying her face in her hands.

Amy's glassy eyes gleamed her cynicism. "Who are you trying to convince here? Me or yourself?" She watched Jane steadily for a moment or two. "You've done something to get up their noses, haven't you?" she said. "That's what this is all about. . . . You manage to get up everyone's nose in the end."

"That's not true!" Jane cried, looking up at her mother as Amy got to her feet. "I know you'd like me to think it is, but it isn't. And if you must know, the reason I'm sitting here, the reason I can't sleep, is because I'm trying to work out what I can do to make everything all right."

"You!" Amy scoffed. "You don't have it in you to do anything that takes any guts. You never have. Turn out the light before you go to bed and wash that cup up."

As Amy's squat little body retreated down the hall Jane was watching her, such a debilitating sadness in her heart it seemed to weight her to the chair. Amy never had had any time for her, had mocked and ridiculed everything she did throughout her life. But this time she was going to show her! Her mother was going to find out soon enough just what kind of courage Jane had. She'd change her tune then. Oh, yes, she'd do that all right, in fact she'd regret every scathing attack, every belittling remark, every derogatory word she'd ever uttered about a daughter who wasn't even hers to criticize.

She just needed some more time to think this through, then she would know what to do. . . .

CHAPTER TWENTY-SEVEN

LAURENCE STARED DOWN AT THE NEWSPAPER, RIGID with shock. The words swam before his eyes, all his senses were recoiling from the bitter distortions and slanderous allegations it contained. "Child-Killer Battles for Custody," the headline screamed, and as the real horror of the story that followed began to register, Laurence knew that he would never feel such anger, such hopelessness, or such violence again in his life. Campbell had not only betrayed him, he had done it in the worst possible way.

Six years ago, Campbell had written, Kirsten Meredith had cold-bloodedly slaughtered—*slaughtered!*—her own child as an act of revenge on the lover who had jilted her, the lover she had now so ingeniously lured back into her life and who was preparing to do battle with his wife for custody of his son, a custody he intended to share with the woman who had so callously killed his first child. All the details were there as to how Kirsten had gone about her abortion, making it sound like the premeditated, calculated act of a psychopath. Laurence's stomach churned.

The article went on to say that this wasn't the first time Kirsten had "murdered an innocent child"; there was at least one other occasion that was known of. So was she or could she ever be a fit parent? She had denied two fathers the right to their children, she had used her bountiful charms to beguile Paul Fisher into turning his back on his children, so what would she do if Tom McAllister ever posed a threat to her?

And it got worse. According to unnamed yet reliable sources Kirsten didn't actually want Laurence to win custody of his son. She didn't want another woman's child, in fact history proved that she didn't want a child at all. All she wanted, now that she had Paul Fisher's fortune, was Laurence McAllister. Pippa McAllister had stood in the way; luckily for Pippa she had escaped to Italy. Anna Sage had threatened to come between them, but as everyone knew, Anna—who had borne a striking resemblance to Pippa and who Kirsten had never wanted on the film—had conveniently departed this world in an incident that was still surrounded by mystery. Jake Butler, the same reliable sources claimed, had threatened to reveal what he knew about Kirsten and now Jake Butler was no longer around to tell the story. Where, Campbell demanded, was it all going to end?

Laurence's fist closed around the paper. Fury throbbed in his temples. What in God's name was he going to say to Kirsten when she saw what Campbell and Helena had done? A burning pain closed around his heart as he thought of Tom—he would never win custody now. The pain suddenly intensified, so bitterly and so cruelly that Laurence pushed himself away from the table and moved restlessly about the kitchen.

He snatched the telephone from the wall and dialed Campbell's number. There was no reply. He tried the newspaper offices; Campbell wasn't there either. He dialed Helena's number and got the answering machine. He slammed the receiver down just as Jane let herself in through the front door.

From the look on Jane's face it was plain that she had already read the article. In fact she was carrying the newspaper under her arm, and as she regarded Laurence with fearful eyes Laurence felt a bolt of panic rush through him. Even now he was unable to fully gauge what the repercussions of all this were going to be.

"Where's Kirsten?" Jane asked softly.

"Still in bed," he answered, running a hand over his unshaven chin. They'd been at the police station until the early hours—Jesus, what were the cops going to make of all this now? Laurence hadn't slept well at all; neither had Kirsten. They'd been uptight after the interview. He'd left Kirsten in bed to go out and get the paper and thank God she'd been asleep by the time he got back. But she would have to know sooner or later; there was no way of shielding her from it, though Campbell could consider himself fortunate that Laurence didn't know where he was right now, or both Laurence and Kirsten would be up on murder charges.

Murder charges! Fucking murder charges! This was insane. The whole goddamned world was crazy.

He turned away from Jane and clamped his fists on the edge of the sink, taking a deep breath to try and steady himself. Their whole lives were being blown apart and there was nothing he could do to stop it. Nothing, except get the hell out of here now and take

Tom with him. . . . Tom, the innocent victim in a raging battle that had nothing to do with him. . . .

"Shall I make some coffee?" Jane offered.

Laurence nodded. The muscles in his arms were like rock, the frustration in his heart like an avalanche of relentless, purposeless destruction. He wasn't going to walk out on Kirsten. It was what Dyllis wanted and he'd be damned if he was going to give her the satisfaction. The depth of his love for Kirsten was something Dyllis hadn't reckoned on, but she was going to find out that this was one thing she couldn't destroy. His eyes closed as the muscles in his jaw stiffened. But what about Tom? What the hell was he going to do about his son? Already he could feel his heart breaking apart as he saw Tom's face when he realized that his daddy, his best friend, was sending him away. His daddy had made a choice between him and Kirsten, and Daddy hadn't chosen him. Laurence stopped breathing as emotion lodged in his throat. He couldn't do it to Tom, he just couldn't.

"Here," Jane said, putting a cup on the draining board beside him.

Laurence turned his head to look at her and when he saw the concern and fear in her upturned face he smiled wearily and lifted a hand to stroke her cheek. "It's okay," he said, "it's going to be all right. We'll get through this, all of us, we just have to take it one step at a time."

Jane nodded and smiled uncertainly.

"I'm going upstairs to see Kirsten now," he said. "See to Tom, will you. Try to stop him coming into the bedroom for a while."

"Yes, of course," Jane whispered. "And Laurence, if there's anything . . . well, anything else I can do . . ."

Laurence smiled. "I know."

A while later Laurence was sitting on the bed with Kirsten, holding her hands as she struggled to come to terms with what she had read. When at last she felt ready to speak she was stopped by the telephone shrilling into the room and turned to pick it up.

Campbell's panicked voice came down the line. "Laurence!"

Kirsten handed Laurence the receiver.

"Campbell?" Laurence raged. "Just what the hell . . . ?"

"Listen to me, Laurence. Just listen! I've only just seen the papers. Helena and I have been with the police since seven this morning. We just got back. . . . Laurence, I had nothing to do with that article, I swear it. Dyllis went to print using my name."

"Do you think I'm buying that, you bastard! I don't know what you and Helena are playing at. . . ."

"We're not playing at anything, I swear it. The police questioned Helena after you saw them last night, she's pretty cut up about it. She's got nothing to do with what's going on, I'd stake my life on it. She doesn't know any more than you do."

"Then tell me, Dermott, what the hell was all that about round here last night? And where the hell is the story you told me only three days ago you were going to write about Kirsten setting the record straight? Why isn't that in the papers this morning?"

"I don't know, but you can bet your life that Dyllis is behind it somewhere. But you've got to face it Laurence, she's got to believe herself pretty watertight by now to have gone so far with the allegations."

"And just how did she think she was going to shut

you up? If, as you claim, you had nothing to do with that story?"

"I don't know and I don't think I want to know. I hope I'm overreacting here, but I'm moving out of my apartment. I'll call you again later to let you know where you can reach me. Until then, for God's sake Laurence, please believe me, I'm on your side." And the line went dead.

"Would you care for something to drink, Ruby?" Thea McAllister asked, rolling her eyes at Ruby's bent head.

" '. . . Come hither; I will show unto thee the judgment of the great whore that sitteth upon many waters: With whom the kings of the earth have committed fornication and the inhabitants of the earth have been made drunk with the wine of her fornication.' " Ruby lifted her pale eyes from the Book of Revelation and fixed them on Thea.

"Coffee?" Thea said, not wanting to get into a debate on theological allusion, though she understood perfectly why Ruby had chosen to read her those particular verses.

"Gin," Ruby said, closing the Bible.

"It's a bit early in the day to be drinking gin, don't you think?" Thea remarked, putting the coffee pot down and going to the mahogony and brass cabinet.

"Let's forget my habits and discuss what's really the issue here, shall we?" Ruby retorted. "Did you speak to Laurence yet?"

"No." Thea handed her a glass, then went to sit on the sofa, carefully crossing her legs.

"Well, did you try?"

"Of course I've tried. He won't speak to me."

The muscles in Ruby's tired face seemed to collapse. "No, me neither." She sighed. "So what do we do, go round there?"

Thea's brows arched. "If you want to make a spectacle of yourself, Ruby, go right ahead, but don't expect me to join you."

Ruby's glass hit the table. "What is it with you?" she demanded. "I know you don't approve of me, but for Christ's sake, don't you care what damage this is doing him?"

"Of course I care," Thea answered through gritted teeth; but Ruby wasn't listening.

"I know you all laugh at what that kooky kid told me out there in New Orleans, but even the good Lord couldn't convince me that everything she said didn't come true, 'cause it did. Everything that is, except about the child. Well, I reckon that child's Tom and that's why I'm going to do something about what's going on here."

"But Ruby, you don't have the first idea what's going on here," Thea retorted.

"Don't I?" Ruby said. "Well, maybe that's just where you're wrong. Maybe I been approaching this from the wrong angle. Maybe there's something I didn't see that was staring me right in the face. . . . I came here to see if you would lend me your support, but I can see that between the manicurist and the cocktails you just don't have the time."

"Whereas between the gin and the counseling you do." Thea shot back, replacing her cup on the table.

"I got any amount of time for Laurence." Ruby was

seething, and after downing the last of her gin she gathered up her bag, lit a cigarette, and walked unsteadily out of the room.

Helena looked up as an oblong of flowered wallpaper opened in the wall and Campbell walked into the room. She was sitting with her back against the headboard of the bed, her legs stretched out in front of her, a remote control in her hands. "So," she said, as he took off his coat and hung it on the back of the door, "is she still trying to accuse me of murder?"

"The police have cleared you . . ."

"That's not the point, Dermott, and how do you know they've cleared me? They didn't say that. In fact what they said was to let them know if I was planning any trips out of the country."

"They have to do that. You were on the set both times, and once their inquiries really get under way, *if* they get under way, they'll want to interview everyone who was there."

"Yeah, well," Helena said, throwing the remote control on the bed. "You try having your best friend do something like this to you and see how you feel."

"You try having someone you love lie to you about where she was the night Kirsten found that tape and see how you feel," he retorted, going to help himself from the minibar.

"Well, you know where I was now," she said sulkily.

"I know where you said you were. I just hope you're not lying, Helena, 'cause if you are, the police will find out."

"Jesus Christ!" she cried. "What is it with you? Suddenly Kirsten can't do any wrong, whereas *me,* the woman you profess to love, I'm a liar and a murderer."

"I don't think so." He smiled, going to join her on the bed and handing her a beer. "It would help though if you could remember the kid's name."

"He never told me. It was just a quick screw. I wanted to see if I still preferred young boys, or whether what I had with you was better."

"And is it?" he asked, running a hand along her thigh.

"Don't ask me that now," she said, swinging her legs to the floor. "I don't want to think about it. I've got too much else on my mind."

CHAPTER TWENTY-EIGHT

FOR KIRSTEN THE NEXT FEW DAYS PASSED IN A DAZE. She was wholly aware of all that was going on around her, yet it seemed unreal, intangible, as though she were standing apart from it unable to reach it, unable to stop the storm that would eventually sweep them all from her life.

Outwardly she was responding; her skin absorbed the feel of Laurence's arms around her, her lips smiled at his confidence and words of reassurance, her eyes watched as he played with Tom, tumbling him and tickling him, her ears heard them laugh, heard them calling her name. She went to them, played with them, and laughed too, but inside her heart was numb with fear.

Laurence, Jane, even the lawyers, were all saying that the worst was over. A week had gone by since Dyllis Fisher's article and though many writs had been served there had been no response. Kirsten wanted so much to believe that at last Dyllis was going to leave her alone, but as the date for the custody hearing drew closer the silence was, to her, so ominous it was making her ill.

So far she had managed to hide this from Laurence, shutting herself in the bathroom and running the taps while she leaned over the basin and vomited. Afterward, when she finally found the energy to lift her head, she felt exhausted. Her stomach felt as though it had been pulled from its roots, her breath fluttered and panted in her lungs as her heart hammered the blood back into her veins. She longed to cry, to release at least some of the tension, but she was afraid to. Her eyes looked bruised from lack of sleep, her skin was pale from lack of nourishment. Blinding spells of dizziness descended upon her, pushing her toward a blackness she fought hard to resist. Once she had fallen, sinking slowly, slowly to the floor, watching the walls rear up around her as vivid pinpoints of light flashed before her eyes, but somehow she'd managed to pull herself back from the void before losing consciousness.

That morning, despite her insistence that she was fine, Laurence had called the doctor. Jane had now gone off to the chemist to get the sleeping pills that had been prescribed, though Kirsten knew she wouldn't take them. She hadn't been totally honest with the doctor about her symptoms. Had she been, she knew he'd never have prescribed Tamezepan.

Now, as she walked down the stairs, her dark amber hair shining and clean, her eyes feverishly bright, and her pale face flushed with color, Laurence looked up at her and felt his throat tighten at how very lovely, yet how fragile she looked. The anxiety in his eyes tore at Kirsten's heart. As she reached him she lifted a hand to his face and touched him lightly.

"I love you," she whispered.

"I love you too," he said thickly, drawing her to him. His hands moved into her silky hair, the hardness of his limbs pressed against her bones. She was losing so much weight it was as though she were wasting away before his eyes. He clung to her, afraid that somehow she would slip away from him.

"Kirstie, please stop shutting me out like this," he murmured. "Tell me what's going on in your mind."

Kirsten smiled. "All I think about, Laurence, is how very much you mean to me."

"Then why are you so sad? We're together, we're going to keep Tom, we're getting through this . . ."

"I know," she said, but inside she felt as though she were dying. She longed to tell him that she was pregnant, to see the joy light up his beautiful, blue eyes, to feel his arms squeezing her tightly and laugh at the tears of happiness as they rolled onto his cheeks. But she couldn't do it. Soon, very soon now, it would all come to a head and he would have to leave her. He would have to do what was best for Tom and she couldn't use her own child to hold him when she knew already how difficult it was going to be for him to go. As it was she could hardly bring herself to think about the baby; not knowing what future she would have, where she would end up, or what would become of them was too painful, too frightening to consider. She knew she was behaving like a guilty woman, was losing faith in the justice that would work for her, but unlike everyone else she didn't underestimate Dyllis Fisher. She knew that something terrible was going to happen to her, and as the silence stretched on the more powerless to control the fear she was becoming.

Yet oddly, right now, as she stood there in Laurence's arms, she felt a gentle buoyancy ripple through her. They could be happy for now. They didn't need to think about the future, not yet, and she just couldn't bear to see him hurting the way he was when he was trying so hard to give her hope.

She inhaled deeply, feeling her senses flood with the intoxicating scent of Laurence's masculinity. She slipped a hand under his shirt. The room was so warm, the air so sleepy. They hadn't made love for almost a week. She'd pushed him away, afraid to let him come any closer than he already was.

She turned her head to look up at him. In some ways it was as though she was seeing him for the first time, unable to believe how incredibly handsome he was. It was so hard not to tell him about the baby, so very, very hard, but despite how desperately she wanted to make herself believe in the future, she knew she couldn't tell him—at least not yet. Maybe in another week, maybe by then, with the custody battle behind them, she would have overcome her fears.

"What are you thinking?" he whispered.

Her eyes began to sparkle as she smiled into his and with an ironic lift of his eyebrows Laurence held her against him and stroked her. His love for her was expanding across his chest, throughout his body. For a while there he had been afraid he was losing her. He'd always sworn that he would never let her come between them, but faced with it he hadn't known what to do. She had closed herself off from him and there was no way in. He knew that no matter how long it took he would have kept on trying, but she was here now, returned to him and loving him as much as he loved her.

She moved in his arms, laying her head on his shoulder and lifting her mouth to his. He kissed her tenderly, lingeringly, savoring the taste of her lips, inhaling the scent of her, and feeling it spread a stirring heat through his loins. Her hair was luxuriant in his hands as he bunched it around her face pulling her closer. She unbuttoned his shirt and pushed her hands inside, spreading her fingers through the coarse black hair. He felt the gentle moan of desire vibrate in her throat as he caressed her neck and circled her lips with his tongue.

Kirsten opened her eyes and looked up at him. He looked back. Neither of them smiled, it was as though the depth of their feelings was merging, binding them together, holding their souls in its hands, filling their hearts with a love that surpassed all they had known before.

Very gently, never taking his eyes from hers, Laurence removed her clothes. Their need to join physically knew no urgency, yet it transcended all other needs. Her skin held a longing to be covered by his, as his did to feel hers so smooth and satiny beneath him. Only when he was naked did Kirsten reach out to touch him, running her hands over the solid muscles of his shoulders, his arms, his chest, his abdomen. She caught her lip between her teeth as he brushed his fingers lightly over her nipples. Her eyes fluttered closed, then she felt his mouth come crushing down on hers.

"I love you," he breathed. "Oh, God, I love you."

He lay over her, covering her legs with his, pushing

his arms beneath her and feeling all of her against him. She kept her legs together, loving the way he pushed himself into the moist, soft flesh, yet not entering her. After a while she lifted her legs over his and he guided himself into her.

"Sometimes," Kirsten whispered, "I wish I could take all of you inside me."

He smiled. "You already have all of me," he answered, gently circling his hips as he smoothed the hair from her face.

Kirsten's eyes moved to his mouth and as their lips met she felt her heart rising to her throat. *Don't ever leave me,* she was crying inside. *Please, don't ever go.*

Two days later Laurence was on the phone to his lawyer. Jane was in the garden with Tom making sure that he didn't overhear the conversation.

"Things are looking up," his lawyer was telling him. "I don't want to get your hopes too high, but we could be in with a chance. Apparently the judge isn't too keen on a mother who just ups and walks out on her own son."

"Do you know when Pippa's coming over?"

"Tomorrow, I believe. I've had a request through her lawyer for her to speak to you before going into court."

"Through her lawyer?" Laurence said surprised. "Why didn't she just call me herself?"

"Search me. My guess is she's going to try and persuade you to hand him over without going through all this."

"She can try, but she won't succeed."

"That's what I thought you'd say. I'll call you again when I know more."

As Laurence was replacing the receiver Kirsten came in through the front door. He knew immediately from the way her eyes were sparkling and her lips were red that her meeting had gone well and he felt a lift in his heart to see her looking so happy. "You'll never guess how much they've offered me!" she cried flinging her bag onto a chair.

"How much?"

"A hundred thousand pounds! To write my story! Can you believe it?"

Laurence gaped at her in amazement, then laughing he swept her into his arms. God, did that publisher have any idea what he had done? This was exactly what Kirsten needed to help focus on something other than what was happening now. "I guess this calls for a celebration," he said. "Hang on. You did accept, didn't you?"

"Of course I did. At least I said I'd write the book, but I told them my agent would be in touch to discuss details."

"Agent?"

"You, you idiot. You can do the negotiating for me and take the ten percent. So come on, out with the champagne!"

"I've got some more good news," Laurence said as he popped the cork. "I've just spoken to my lawyer. He reckons our chances of keeping Tom have improved this past week."

"Oh, Laurence!" Kirsten cried, throwing her arms around him. "That's fantastic news. Oh, we'll win, we will, I just know it."

CHAPTER TWENTY-NINE

THE NEXT MORNING LAURENCE, KIRSTEN, JANE, AND Tom were having a noisy breakfast in the kitchen when there was a knock on the door.

"I'll get it," Kirsten said, taking a mouthful of coffee as she got up. "It's probably the postman. And yes, okay, I could start the book at the point you suggested, but I think my idea's better."

"You always think your ideas are better," Laurence declared.

"Because they are."

"Go get the door." He laughed, pouring Tom more orange juice. "We'll talk about it later."

Kirsten skipped off down the hall in her trainers and jogging suit, for one morning mercifully free of the nausea.

"Hi," she said cheerfully to the two men standing in the drizzling rain. She looked from one to the other, then suddenly it was as though everything was slipping from focus. The world was tilting, the menacing sky was swooping down on her, the wet pavements were rearing up at her.

"Good morning, Miss Meredith." Detective Kowski grinned.

Nausea rose in her stomach. Blood roared in her ears.

"This is Detective Sergeant Fulmer of New Scotland Yard," Kowski said as Fulmer pulled his badge from his pocket. "He kinda knows your territory better than me so he's come along to advise."

"On what?" Her broken voice seemed to come from a long way away.

"We got a number of questions we'd like to ask you, ma'am," he answered. "It'll be easier to speak over at the Yard—"

"Oh, my God!" Kirsten muttered. "Laurence! Laurence!"

"What is it?" Laurence said, coming out of the kitchen. Then seeing Kirsten's face he turned sharply to the two men. "What's going on?" he demanded. "Who are you? Kowski! What the hell are you doing here?"

"Pursuing inquiries," Kowski answered, then turning back to Kirsten he said, hunching himself into his collar, "You'll be needing your coat, ma'am."

"What kind of inquiries?" Laurence demanded, claws of fear digging into his chest.

"Concerning two cases of homicide in the parish of New Orleans—"

"Homicide?" Kirsten repeated. She turned to Laurence, her luminous green eyes simmering with terror.

"This is crazy!" Laurence shouted. "The New Orleans coroner—"

"Certain evidence has now come to light," Fulmer interrupted, "that shows the coroner's findings were . . . uh, incomplete. So, miss," he went on, turning back to

Kirsten, "like Mr. Kowski said, if you would get your coat and accompany us . . ."

"Are you arresting me?" Kirsten whispered, putting a hand to her head as though she could stop it spinning.

"We would like your help with our inquiries," he responded tonelessly.

Again Kirsten looked up at Laurence. "Isn't that the same thing?" she said, trembling at the onslaught of panic.

Laurence looked to Kowski for the answer. "It would be in your own interests to come . . ."

"I'm coming with you," Laurence said.

"I don't think that would serve any purpose at this time, sir," Fulmer interceded.

"I don't want her questioned without a lawyer present," Laurence snapped. "I take it she does have that right."

"Naturally."

"Then where are you taking her?"

"New Scotland Yard," Fulmer answered. "For the time being."

Laurence's eyes were blazing. "And what's that supposed to mean?" he demanded.

Fulmer just looked at him, then stood aside for Kirsten to lead the way out to the car.

As Kowski opened the back door for her to get in, Kirsten stumbled. Laurence rushed forward, but Kowski held her.

"It's okay," Laurence heard her mumble. "I'm okay."

Her head was lowered, she didn't turn to look at Laurence, all she knew was that cruel talons of fear were tearing at her heart and pain was throbbing in her head.

Would they allow her to keep her baby, she wondered, hugging herself as bitter tears stung her eyes. *You're innocent for God's sake!* the voice inside her screamed. She took a deep breath. Vaguely she was aware of Kowski talking beside her. He was saying something to Fulmer about a search warrant. They must be talking about her house, but they'd find nothing there. Suddenly she turned rigid, and it was then that the final seal of resignation locked around her heart as she recalled the night she had thought someone was in the house. Something had been planted. Then there was the night she had come home to the tape—and Helena. Something had been planted then too.

Before the police car had even left the street Laurence was on the phone to his lawyer.

"Shit, I don't believe it," Hellerman groaned. "It couldn't have come at a worse time. Your chances of keeping Tom are right out the window now."

"But she didn't do it, for Christ's sake!"

"Maybe not, but clearing her name before Friday's hearing is going to be just about impossible. You've got to face that, Laurence. And even if we could, the fact that she's been taken in . . . Does anyone know? Were there any press hanging about?"

"Not that I know of."

"Good. Keep it under wraps for as long as you can. Now, where have they taken her?"

"New Scotland Yard."

"Okay. I'm on my way. Meet me there."

Twenty minutes later, as Laurence fought his way

through the dense traffic of Victoria, any hope he or Hellerman had of keeping things from the press were dashed the moment he turned on the radio. It had already made the ten-o'clock news.

For over three hours Laurence paced a featureless room at New Scotland Yard waiting for Hellerman, who had joined Kirsten and the two detectives in an interview room. Eventually Hellerman came out and one look at his face was enough to turn Laurence's stomach inside out.

"What's happening?" he asked, feeling as though his voice was being dredged from a bottomless pit.

"Good and bad." Hellerman sighed, shaking his silvery head. "Anna Sage and Jake Butler were definitely murdered. Don't ask me how 'cause I'm not sure I understand it myself. Something to do with the mix of liquid nitrogen and oxygen in the dry ice you use for fog. It kills in a matter of seconds and leaves no trace."

"So how do they know now what it was?"

"They've received information, they're not saying who from yet, but they're going to have to tell me eventually. I'm going to recommend that Ernie Shore takes the case from here. It's not my field and he's one of the best criminal lawyers—"

Laurence winced. "What about bail?" he asked.

Hellerman was taking a mobile phone from his briefcase. "You don't need to worry about that unless she's charged. But if she is, can you raise it?"

"I'll get it," Laurence declared rashly.

Hellerman eyed him skeptically. "If they don't charge

her, then there's a chance we can have her out of here before the end of the day," he said. "But if I were you, Laurence, I'd go back home to Tom."

"Can't I see her?"

"Not yet, no. And to be frank, mate, the best thing you can do now is distance yourself as far from her as you can."

"Are you serious? You think I'm going to run out on her at a time—"

"Be sensible, Laurence. You want to keep your son, don't you? Well, you've really got your work cut out now. You heard the news I take it?"

"Yes."

"Then do as I say. Take Tom to your parents' place."

But for the moment Laurence couldn't see beyond what was happening there. "The dry ice?" he said. "You say it was tampered with?"

Hellerman nodded. "Put me on to Ernie Shore," he said into the phone. He raised a hand as Laurence started to speak again. "Okay, have him call me on this number the minute he gets there. A matter of urgency, tell him."

"But the forensic team checked those machines right after Anna died," Laurence said. "They found nothing wrong with them."

"No. They wouldn't. Apparently once out of a confined space the gas rebalances itself."

Laurence was shaking his head. "But how the hell would Kirsten know about something like that?"

"She probably doesn't, but how's she going to prove it?"

"I thought a person was innocent until proven guilty," Laurence remarked savagely.

"So they tell me. But as far as the police are seeing it right now, Kirsten had a motive for killing Anna Sage. She also had a motive for getting rid of Jake Butler, or so they claim."

"This can't be happening," Laurence cried, dashing a hand through his already dishevelled hair. "It's a fucking nightmare. It has to be. How's she taking it?"

"Pretty well, considering. Still a bit dazed though."

"When will I be able to see her?"

"Laurence, think of Tom, will you? He's got to come first right now."

It cut hard with Laurence to know that Hellerman was right and that there really was no more he could do for Kirsten at the moment, but in the end he had to accept it. Telling Hellerman to call him the minute he heard anything, Laurence returned to his car.

As he drove through the rain-soaked London streets the whole nightmare was running through his mind with a cruelty that made him want to lash out for the sheer madness of it. Who the hell could hate Kirsten so much to want to do this to her? Dyllis Fisher was the obvious answer, but Dyllis wasn't there when it happened. So had Dyllis paid someone to do it? Helena Johnson? Had Dyllis given Helena money to kill two people and make it look like Kirsten had done it? But, Jesus Christ, why? What reason could Helena have to hate Kirsten that much?

Almost missing a red light on Sloane Square he

screeched to a halt, then snatched up the car phone. A few seconds later he had Campbell on the line.

"Laurence, is that you?" Campbell cried through the interference. "Where the hell are you? I've been trying to reach you . . ."

"I'm in the car," Laurence shouted. "Where's Helena?"

"The police have just taken her in."

"Did she do it, Dermott? Tell me, I've got to know."

"The honest answer? I don't know. I don't think she did, but, shit, Laurence . . ."

"What did she tell you about that tape?"

"She said she had nothing to do with it. Do you know yet how they died?"

"Yeah. Something to do with the mix of dry ice. Ring any bells?"

"No. All's I know is that Helena told me Elizabeth Bradley tripped over one of those things when she was going to get help for Jake. It was how she broke her leg."

"That's right," Laurence said, "she did. It set it off." He was racking his brains to remember what else had happened that afternoon. Elizabeth had fallen, the dry-ice machine had tipped over. . . . Hadn't Elizabeth said something about falling against the door? Yes, she had, that was why they had carried her to the drawing room, to get her out of the way so's they could get inside to Jake. Christ, this could mean that Jake's death really was an accident. He'd been shut inside that room, already unconscious, with a lethal mix of chemicals. . . . But why was the dry ice there at that moment? Who was going to be playing that scene? Elizabeth, Frank . . . The camera boys would have been in there, sound, effects, Jesus, it would have killed the whole damned lot of them. Unless . . .

"Laurence, are you still there?" Campbell shouted through the static.

"Yeah, I'm here. Look, Dermott, do me a favor," he said, digging into his pocket for his address book. "I'm going to give you the number of the chief location manager on the movie. Get in touch with him and ask him who was in charge of props the day Jake died. He'll have it there on the schedule. And ask him how many dry-ice machines were prepared for use that afternoon."

"Got it," Campbell said. "Are you going to tell me what you're thinking?"

"That Jake's death was an accident. That someone took that machine from the store in all innocence and put it on the set for rehearsals. In other words, whoever tampered with it probably wasn't expecting it to leave the store when it did."

"Shit," Campbell muttered. "Are you saying that it had been got ready for someone else?"

"That's what I'm saying. That's why I want to know how many machines were primed for use that day. If it was more than one, which it would have been because we were staging a fire, then I'll stake my life on the fact that someone had other plans for that particular cannister. It could well be that it was never intended for use on the set at all."

"Meaning that someone, not Jake Butler, was scheduled for the stygian ferry that day?"

"Maybe," Laurence answered. "I'll call you back in an hour."

By now he had arrived home, but he continued to sit

in the car, thoughts galloping through his head as randomly and anarchically as the rain beating against the windscreen. He was so tense that every muscle in his body jarred. He was so afraid that no reason could break through the disjointed maelstrom of his mind. He had to calm down, he knew, but how the hell he was going to manage it was beyond him. But something wasn't adding up, he knew that both he and Kirsten had missed something somewhere, but for the life of him he couldn't snare it. Everything pointed so conclusively to Dyllis but, he had to ask himself, would a woman in Dyllis Fisher's position really go so far as to plot two murders in order to revenge herself on Kirsten? Sure, it took one hell of a brain to pull off something that could defy even a coroner, and doubtless Dyllis had that kind of brain. What was more, she had Kirsten's neck in a noose now, which is where she'd always wanted it. But he just couldn't make himself believe that she'd put her own neck on the line by trying to frame up something like this. It was too risky, she'd stand to lose everything if she was found out, and she'd have to know that there was every chance she would be. And there it was again, that niggardly suspicion flickering elusively in his mind, that he was missing something somewhere, something so obvious and so vital that it was going to change the face of everything.

He got out of the car and walked to the front door. His head was pounding, his hand barely steady as he inserted the key in the lock.

He closed the door behind him, saw a pile of mail on the table and next to it a well-thumbed copy of the Moyna O'Malley script. And it was then that it hit him—

so forcefully, so blindingly and so repellently that his head jerked back as though the horrendous realization had struck him a physical blow. Ruby!

Ruby and that coconut reading business . . . Her ludicrous jealousy and overprotectiveness . . . The changes in the script just before those two crucial scenes . . . The number of times dry ice was referred to in the stage directions . . .

"Jesus Holy Christ," he muttered falling back against the door.

"Are you all right?"

He looked up to see Jane standing in the doorway of the kitchen.

"I thought I heard you come in," she said in a tremulous voice. "What's happening?"

What was happening? Jesus Christ, just that the world was ending, nothing more than that.

"I'll explain later," he said. "Where's Tom?"

"Asleep."

"Go wake him, we're taking him to my parents." Dear God, how was he going to deal with this? How was he going to face Thea when her animosity toward Kirsten was already something he could barely tolerate?

As Jane started up over the stairs the telephone rang. Laurence snatched it up.

"Laurence, hello there, it's Jim, Jim Cottle."

"Oh, yes, hello. She's right here." To Jane, "It's your father. Don't worry, I'll get Tom. And if your Dad's ringing because he's heard the news, if he's telling you to get the hell out of this mess, then if I were you I'd do as he says."

Laurence dragged himself up over the stairs to Tom's

room. Though panic was driving shots of adrenaline through his body he made himself stop in the doorway and for a long time he simply stood looking down at his son's sleeping face. Of all the emotions that had run amok through his heart that day he knew that nothing, just nothing in the world, could be as powerful as what he felt for that little scrap of humanity. But he wouldn't think beyond that, he couldn't, for the likelihood that he was going to lose him had already become a raw, open wound in his heart.

Around five in the evening, the telephone rang at the McAllister's house. Laurence jumped on it.

"It's like a bloody circus over here," Hellerman grumbled. "Dyllis Fisher's been in, half the cast and crew from that movie of yours—"

"Never mind that, how's Kirsten?"

Hellerman paused and Laurence's heart stopped.

"The news isn't good, I'm afraid," Hellerman said gravely. "They're about to charge her."

"But they can't!" Laurence cried. "She didn't do it! It was Ruby. Listen to me—" He was aware of the exchange of glances between his parents, almost felt the ripple of shock as it went through them.

"Ruby's just left," Hellerman interrupted. "She's been here all day."

"What! Oh, my God, what the hell's she been telling them?"

"I can't answer that, but what I can tell you is that

they found the formula for mixing the dry ice in Kirsten's house. Hang on, just a second."

Laurence could hear Hellerman's muted voice at the other end as he spoke to someone, then he came back on the line. "I'm sorry, Laurence," he said. "They've just charged her. First degree murder on both counts."

It was just after seven o'clock when Hellerman called again to say that Kirsten was to appear in front of the magistrate at ten thirty the next morning. "We'll apply for bail," he said. "I don't know if we'll get it, but I should warn you, the seriousness of the charges makes it doubtful."

"They've got the wrong person," Laurence said, his voice strangled with emotion. "I'm telling you, it was Ruby."

"Can you prove it?"

"No."

Hellerman sighed. "You do realize that even if you're right, Laurence, it won't change the situation as far as Tom's concerned? Even if we could get the charges dropped against Kirsten we wouldn't be able to do it in time for the hearing now."

"I know," Laurence said, unable to keep the defeat from his voice. "How's she bearing up?" he asked.

"Quite well," Hellerman answered, knowing that it would serve no purpose to tell Laurence the truth. Kirsten was sick, even the police were agreed on that, which was why a doctor had been called in just after the charges had been read out.

"If you get the chance, James, tell her I love her."

"Of course," Hellerman answered.

When Laurence rang off he took himself upstairs and lay down on the bed with Tom. His feelings were so near the surface that only with superhuman effort did he manage to stop himself crushing Tom in his arms, as if by doing so he could join their two bodies in such a way that no one could ever tear them apart. Instead, he simply lay there beside him, gazing at his heartrendingly handsome little face and wondering how in the hell he was going to cope with losing him.

After a while Thea came into the darkened room and sat with them. "We've given Jane the night off," she said softly. "Apparently her father called her today and wanted to know what was going on. I thought it was best she go see them so Dad's just driven her home."

"Thanks," Laurence whispered. "I should have done it myself."

"Are you going to speak to Ruby?" Thea asked after a while.

"Yeah. I'll go see her in the morning before I see Pippa."

"Pippa's here, darling. She arrived about ten minutes ago."

It was only then, when Laurence turned to look at her, that Thea saw the tears on his cheeks and reached out for his hand.

"I'm going to tell her to take him," Laurence said, his voice catching in his throat as he turned back to Tom.

"Yes, I guessed as much," Thea said.

"I can't put him through it when I know already that I'm going to lose. You understand that, don't you?"

"Yes, darling, I understand. So does your father."

"The question is though, will Tom?" Laurence said, closing his eyes at the desperate sense of loss that was folding itself with merciless finality around his heart.

CHAPTER THIRTY

SHE SAT ALONE AT AN UPSTAIRS WINDOW STARING out into the dawn. Her face was ashen. Her heart was lead. Beside her the baby lay silently in its cradle. It didn't cry anymore. It hadn't cried for some time. Its skin, once so warm and soft, was now cold and cracked. The downy lashes were brittle and matted.

She had no idea what she was going to do now. She couldn't think, her mind was as motionless as the photographs she held in her lap. She didn't look at them. Her neck was rigid, her head wouldn't move.

Somewhere, not too far from here, fates were being sealed and hearts were breaking. A chasm of devastation cleaved open inside her. It was as though it was squeezing away her soul, emptying her body and making her a void. Soon she wouldn't exist anymore. Even the shell of her skin would disappear.

She lifted a hand to the window, as though to reach out to the rising sun. Her fingers stabbed against the transparent wall between her and life. Breath fluttered into her lungs; it kept alive the red hot pain of her heartbeats.

Purple clouds were fusing over her mind, blotting her thoughts, absorbing them in terrifying confusion. The violence of her fear animated her limbs, twitching them, stiffening them, and causing a demented sob of laughter to gurgle in her throat. She had lost Laurence just as surely as he would lose Kirsten and Tom. But it needn't have been that way. If Kirsten hadn't come back into their lives they wouldn't be suffering the way they were now. Kirsten didn't belong, she was an outcast, a pariah, the victim of a deadly revenge that had brought devastation into all their hearts. But in the heat of hatred and resentment she knew a love so deep and transcending, a need so powerful and consuming that it fueled an agony beyond healing.

Her wide eyes stared out at the distant trees. Their bare branches stood like arteries against the bloody sky. They were like the veins of her mind, brittle and jagged, forlorn and devoid of everything beautiful. She felt their urgency for nature's loving hand—for them it would come, but for her there was nothing now, nothing at all. . . .

She looked down at the photograph she was holding. As her eyes drank in the incredible beauty of Kirsten's smile her heart twisted cruelly. She could save Kirsten, but she wouldn't. Kirsten was going to pay for the sin of her beauty, she was going to pay for the denial of her children's lives, for the destruction of families, and for not loving those who loved and needed her so much. . . .

Her head fell forward as burning sobs tore at her throat. The calmness in her mind was so brutal, more brutal even than the torment. It forced her to see the eroded edges of her sanity, the danger of her desperation. It blinded her with what she had done, of how she was able to govern herself with a rational, humble mind—a mind that could explode into a chaos so bitter and so destructive it knew only the pain and unfairness that had entrenched itself in her soul. She wasn't loved, had never been loved, never would be.

She knew nothing of Dyllis Fisher, yet all this time she had been Dyllis's accomplice. But then Dyllis was calling in a debt, Dyllis with her power and her glory, was exacting the price of betrayal, so why shouldn't she? She would make no confession. Kirsten must stay where she was and reap the rewards of not caring for someone who loved her so much she would kill for her. . . .

The next morning, just after nine thirty, Kirsten was ushered out of a back door of New Scotland Yard, bundled into a waiting car, and driven to the magistrate's court. James Hellerman and Ernie Shore were waiting for her. An hour later, after bail had been set for a less staggering sum than expected, Hellerman drove her home.

When they arrived he went in with her. She looked pale almost to the point of exhaustion, but on the whole she seemed better than she had the night before. It was the surprising turn in events that had come just after nine o'clock that morning that had given her this temporary revival in spirits and an unthought-for freedom. The voice on the tape had been identified—it belonged to the very man who was now giving evidence. In light of that it had taken Ernie Shore very little time to convince the magistrate that Kirsten could be precisely what she was claiming to be—the victim of an unscrupulous conspiracy. In fact, as they'd left the court, Shore had been laughing, so confident was he that they would soon get all charges against Kirsten dismissed.

How much Kirsten had taken in of what was being said was hard to tell, but a little color had returned to her cheeks and unless Hellerman was greatly mistaken there was the tiniest flicker of hope in her eyes. As yet none of them knew who the man giving evidence was, but Kowski himself had gone along with the other officers to escort him back to New Scotland Yard immediately after the results of the voice test were known.

Now, as Kirsten went through the mechanical process of lighting a fire, Hellerman offered to fix her something to eat. She smiled, told him she wasn't hungry, and continued with the fire until the flames were roaring spiritedly up the chimney.

"Do you think," she said finally, "is there any chance that I might be cleared before the custody hearing tomorrow?"

Hellerman's sun-weathered face showed the compassion and admiration he felt for this woman whose prime concern, despite all she was facing herself, was for the man she loved. "It's doubtful," he said.

"How's Laurence?" she asked.

"I haven't spoken to him yet today," Hellerman answered, "but he was pretty shaken up last night. He's worried about the custody hearing tomorrow, naturally, though his main concern right now is that you're all right."

"Tell him I am, won't you? Tell him not to worry about me at all. I'll be fine."

Not long after that Hellerman left and Kirsten huddled in a blanket to stop herself shivering. If only she could speak to Laurence, just to hear his voice might calm her a little, but she knew that she had to stick to what the lawyers had told her. It helped to know that the police were now starting to believe that she had had nothing to do with the murders, that they were, perhaps, getting close now to who had actually done it. What a relief it had been to receive Laurence's message last night, when he'd asked Hellerman to tell her he loved her. She had been terrified that he was blaming her for what this would do with regard to his custody of Tom.

But she had to face the fact, just as Laurence would have to, that Pippa was going to take Tom away. Were Tom her own child Kirsten couldn't have loved him more and the thought of losing him was tearing her apart. But God only knew what it was doing to Laurence. Nothing could ever make up for the gap he would leave in Laurence's life, not even the baby she was carrying.

As Laurence drove through the streets of South London his mind was concentrated rigidly on the task ahead. He wouldn't allow himself to think about the meeting with Pippa last night, that was something he'd have to deal with later. For now he had to sort out in his mind exactly what he was going to say to Ruby.

The car phone rang. It was Hellerman telling him that Kirsten was home. Straightaway Laurence dialed Kirsten's number. "I was just starting to panic," he said when her voice finally came on the line.

"I was in the shower," she said. "How are you?"

"I'm doing just fine. How about you?"

"Better now. How's Tom?"

As a lump rose in Laurence's throat he found himself unable to answer.

"Laurence? Are you still there?"

"Sure. Tom's okay."

"Where are you now?"

"On my way to Ruby's.

"Hellerman told me what you told him. . . . Laurence, are you sure about this? I mean—"

"No, I'm not sure," he interrupted. "That's why I want to speak to her before I speak to the cops. Kirstie, did they tell you exactly how the murders were done?"

"Not really, though they did tell me what dry ice does to you."

"Which is?"

"Apparently, when you inhale it it hits the muscle that controls the larynx first, so you can't shout. It happens in seconds. The next muscles to go are the leg muscles so you can't move, and within less than a minute you're dead. It can only happen in a confined space and as soon as you let more oxygen into the room it ceases to be lethal. . . . Kowski says it would take a physicist to work out something like that . . ."

"Or an effects guy, a props guy, a scene hand, anyone who works with the stuff. Or a writer who makes it her business to research what she does to the point of actually carrying it out. Anyway, I guess we're going to find out soon enough and all that matters to me is that you're where you are. You sure you're okay?"

"Sure. Still a bit numb, I suppose, but better now I've spoken to you."

"Go see if you can get some sleep," he said, wondering if he should tell her what was in his mind. In the end he decided he had to. "Sweetheart, I want you to lock all the doors. I don't want to scare you and I'm pretty sure there's nothing to be scared of, but don't let's take any chances."

"What do you mean? Are you saying . . . ?"

"I'm saying that I think Jake's death was an accident. That there was every chance that particular cannister of dry ice had been made up for someone else."

"Laurence, you're frightening me. Are you saying that someone might come here to try to . . . ? Maybe I shouldn't be here. Maybe I should go out—"

"Yeah, maybe you should. Go over to my parents. Call yourself a cab right now and get yourself over there. My father's here with me, but Thea's there with Tom and Jane."

"But . . ."

"Please, Kirsten, do as I say. We're almost at Ruby's now so I'm going to ring off. I'll call you again later."

"Okay. I miss you."

"I miss you too."

As Laurence pulled the car to a halt outside the mansion block he gazed up at the tobacco-stained windows of Ruby's apartment. His father was silent beside him, neither one of them was relishing what they had to do. If they were wrong there was no calculating the hurt they were going to cause her, but if they were right . . .

"I guess we should start by finding out if she's still at home," Don said.

Laurence turned to look at him.

"It's been over half an hour since you called to tell her you were coming," Don explained. "Kirsten's release has been on the news since then."

"I, like the Lord our Savior, ask the Lord our God to forgive you, for you know not what you doeth," Ruby declared solemnly. "Deliver unto me a cross and I shall bear it through the streets of London whereupon you may crucify me for sins I have not committed."

"Ruby," Laurence said tightly, "let's just quit talking in riddles, shall we? If you know who killed Anna and Jake then for God's sake tell us."

"I'm telling you," she said. "It's just like the coconut kid said, it's the child within us all. The one who goes unnoticed, the one we all take for granted, the one you have allowed to mother and smother your son . . ."

Laurence's face was starting to freeze. His father started to speak, but Laurence put out a hand to stop him. What Ruby was saying was insane, crazy, it was so goddamned ludicrous he wanted to strangle her for even suggesting it. But even as shock and denial ground disbelief into his heart he was remembering a telephone call he had taken just the day before when he'd returned from New Scotland Yard. "Jesus Christ Almighty!" he murmured, then pushing his way past Ruby he snatched up the phone and started to dial.

"What is it?" his father cried. "What—who are you talking about, Ruby?"

"Mary fucking Poppins," Ruby answered. "Who else?"

CHAPTER THIRTY-ONE

IT HADN'T BEEN KIRSTEN'S INTENTION TO FALL ASLEEP right after she'd spoken to Laurence, it was simply that the moment she'd put the phone down she'd felt so suddenly weary that she just hadn't had the energy to stand up. Deciding to give herself a moment or two to gather her resources she'd sunk back on the bed and the next thing she knew almost half an hour had gone by.

Now, as she struggled to her feet, she was hoping that the rest of her pregnancy wasn't going to be as taxing as these early weeks, for even though it didn't seem she was destined to spend them in prison, she didn't much relish the idea of spending them flat on her back either.

Suddenly she turned to look out of the open bedroom door to the landing. In the same instant that she heard the noise again she recalled Laurence's warning her either to lock the doors or go to his mother's.

"Oh, my God," she breathed, praying that she was mistaken, that the noise had come from outside. But no, there was definitely someone moving about downstairs and whoever it was didn't seem to care that they might be heard.

Maybe, she thought, they didn't realize she was in here. If that was the case then perhaps she could close her bedroom door and call the police without them knowing she'd done it.

She started toward the phone, then jumped back as it suddenly shrilled into the room. To her amazement after two rings it stopped then she heard Jane's voice downstairs saying hello.

Immediately Kirsten relaxed and only then did she realize how furiously her heart was beating, that her entire body had broken out in a sweat. She waited a moment, then hearing Jane replace the receiver, she went into the bathroom to brush out her wet hair.

A few minutes later, still wearing her toweling robe, she tripped lightly down the stairs feeling stronger than she had done in days. By now though she was getting used to her energy only coming in short bursts so she was glad to think Jane was there, if only to help a pregnant old lady out to the taxi when it came.

"Hi," she said, seeing Jane standing in the doorway of the kitchen. "You gave me quite a fright just now, I didn't hear you come in. How did you know I was home?"

"I heard it on the news," Jane answered.

"Of course. Who was that on the phone?"

"Just my dad ringing to see if I'd got here all right. I told him I was coming round."

Kirsten nodded and wondered why Jane continued to stand in the doorway as though. . . . Kirsten's head went to one side, curiously . . . as though she were barring the way. "Are you all right?" she asked.

"Yes, yes, I'm fine," Jane said, her protruding teeth

baring in the nervous giggle Kirsten hadn't seen in weeks. "How are you?"

"Right at this moment it's hard to put into words," Kirsten smiled, lifting a hand to stroke Jane's cheek. To her surprise Jane flinched, almost as though she'd expected Kirsten to strike her. "Are you sure you're okay?" Kirsten said, looking at her closely.

"Yes. Yes, I'm fine," Jane repeated.

Kirsten shrugged, then turned into the sitting room. As she picked up the bellows to liven up the fire she was wondering if Jane was responding to the possibility that Kirsten might have killed someone. Kirsten sighed, watching a fountain of sparks fly up the chimney. What was she going to say to put Jane at her ease?

She had already drawn breath to call out to Jane when she turned to look over her shoulder and found Jane standing so close to her that the air was expelled from her lungs in a breath of surprised laughter. "There you are," she said. "I thought you'd gone into the kitchen."

Jane looked at her, her pinched, pale face as motionless as her staring eyes. "Why did they let you go?" she said.

Kirsten blinked. Then suddenly her stomach heaved. "Oh, Christ," she muttered, and clasping a hand to her mouth she ran past Jane and into the downstairs bathroom.

"Sorry about that," she said, coming out a few minutes later still watery eyed and slightly breathless. "It must be the food they gave me yesterday."

Jane was standing in the hall, watching her with that same deadened expression.

Kirsten smiled awkwardly. "Shall we have a cup of tea?" she said, waving an arm toward the kitchen.

"Why did they let you go?" Jane repeated.

"Well," Kirsten said, eyeing her curiously, "mainly because I didn't do it. And because they've identified the voice on the tape."

"Whose voice was it?"

"I'm still not sure yet. Jane, at the risk of repeating myself, are you sure you're all right?"

Jane turned away, walked into the sitting room, and picked up a bundle of blankets.

"What have you got there?" Kirsten asked, going in after her.

Jane cradled the bundle to her meager chest, lowering her head so that Kirsten could no longer see her face. Kirsten was on the point of repeating the question when she heard footsteps on the stairs and turned round.

"Tom!" she cried, seeing his little face peeping over the bannister.

"Jane bought me a new train," he said. "I've been playing with it."

"Have you?" Kirsten said, feeling a strangeness in the air she couldn't quite comprehend.

"Want to play too?" Tom offered.

"Um, uh, yes," Kirsten answered.

"No," Jane said as Kirsten started toward him. Her voice was muffled by the blankets, strangled by tears.

Kirsten paused.

"Don't, Kirsten, please," Jane begged, lifting her head to look at Kirsten. Kirsten looked back, perplexed and oddly unnerved by the intensity of feeling that was making Jane's normally bland face almost unrecognizable.

After a moment she turned to Tom. His wide blue eyes moved anxiously between Kirsten and Jane.

"Jane, you're frightening him," Kirsten said softly.

"Tom, go upstairs and play with your trains." Jane's thin, choked voice held an unexpected note of command.

Tom looked at Kirsten.

"Go on, sweetheart," Kirsten said. "I'll be up in a minute."

Obediently Tom turned round and climbed back up the stairs.

"Jane, what is going on?" Kirsten demanded. "What's happened to you? I've never seen you like this before."

Jane looked at her for a long time, then suddenly something in her seemed to fracture and to Kirsten's amazement she could see an unsteady emotion beginning to surface. "You don't care what's happened to me," Jane sobbed. "You don't care about anything except yourself and Laurence."

"But that's not true. Of course I care about you," Kirsten insisted.

Jane was shaking her head, jerking it backward and forward almost as though she didn't know what she was doing. "No, no you don't. You want to get rid of me. I heard you telling Laurence—"

Kirsten's head was starting to spin. "You must have misunderstood—"

"No, I understood," Jane interrupted. "I heard what you said. I was there in the room when you said you felt as though you'd stepped into Pippa's shoes. You didn't mind taking Laurence and Tom, but you didn't want me."

"Oh, God," Kirsten groaned. "You did misunderstand . . ."

"No! You never had any time for me, you never held me the way you hold Tom . . ."

"But Jane, he's just a child."

A hot color was flooding Jane's cheeks, her teeth were bared in a quivering grimace of heightening emotion. Tears flowed from her eyes as mucus seeped from her nose. "He's not your child though is he?"

To Kirsten's amazement Jane raised a hand as though to strike her. Kirsten caught it, squeezing the frail bones in her grip.

For a moment Jane's eyes bored into hers, then quite suddenly the fight seemed to leave her, and pulling her hand free she sat down on the sofa with her bundle of blankets. "Sssh, sssh," she said soothingly, "there's no need to cry. Mummy's here."

A curl of unease twisted through Kirsten's gut. "Jane," she said, moving tentatively toward her.

Jane raised her head and Kirsten stopped, arrested by the inexplicable sadness that was now suffusing the pale gray eyes. "Do you want to hold him?" Jane said.

Kirsten stared down at the bundle Jane was offering. Jane's delicate fingers pulled open the blankets. The instant Kirsten saw the tiny face a hand flew to her mouth to stifle the scream as she recoiled in horror. "Jane, for God's sake, what is this?" she gasped.

"He's just a baby," Jane answered.

Kirsten's heart was pounding. She lowered her eyes again to the huge staring blue eyes, the cupid bow mouth, and the hideous black cracks that were fracturing the lifeless white face.

"Sometimes I used to pretend he was yours," Jane said. "I pretended that you'd lied to Laurence about the abortion and that I was looking after him for you."

A sob of disgust and fear erupted in Kirsten's throat. How could Jane have harbored this kind of madness and no one ever have noticed?

"Here, take him," Jane offered again. "He's a very good baby."

Kirsten started to back away. "I don't want to hold him," she said. "He's not—"

A feral rage contorted Jane's face so suddenly and so terrifyingly that Kirsten reeled back as though she'd been struck. Jane ripped away the blankets, swung the baby into the air, and hurled it savagely against the wall. "Then I don't want him either," she screamed.

Kirsten watched in horrified disbelief as the fragile body smashed into a thousand pieces, and tiny fingers and toes scattered over the floor.

As the final remnant of porcelain came to rest Kirsten lifted her eyes back to Jane. Jane's grief-stricken eyes were fixed sightlessly ahead, her hands pressed together in her lap.

Long minutes ticked by before Jane's head suddenly jerked toward Kirsten. "I know you got rid of the baby, I know you did it to punish Laurence for leaving you," she cried, "but I didn't want you to be like that. I wanted you to be kind and care about him."

Kirsten's head was throbbing. So many horrifying thoughts were looming from the corners of her mind that she couldn't make herself think straight. The baby chimes on the phone . . . the tape . . . What the hell was it all about? Why was Jane so tormented by an abortion that had happened so long ago, that had been nothing to do with her?

"He had the most beautiful mother in the world," Jane cried, beating her fists on her lap, "but you didn't want him. You didn't care about him . . ."

"If he'd lived I would have," Kirsten said, so stunned she hardly knew what she was saying.

"No. No, you wouldn't," Jane cried, shaking her head vehemently. "You never wanted him. You never wanted any children, it was why you got rid of me too. I was prepared to forgive you, in the beginning . . . I did forgive you. And I loved you. . . . But you never loved me."

"Jane," Kirsten breathed, "I don't understand what . . ."

Jane's gray eyes were glittering, her lips a tight line of resentment. "Why did you tell everyone you got rid of me!" she said. "Why did you tell them I was aborted when you knew it wasn't true?"

Kirsten looked at her, so shocked that nothing in her could respond.

"Well, say something!" Jane cried, saliva oozing between her teeth as her cheeks quivered with frustration.

"I don't know what to say," Kirsten answered. "I don't know what you're talking about."

"Liar! *Liar! Liar! Liar!* You know who you are. You know who I am and what I am to you, so stop all these lies, Kirsten . . ."

"Jane . . ."

"Jane? Is that the name you chose for me? Or did you let someone else choose it? How well did you know me when you let me go, Kirsten—when you gave me to strangers? Well enough to name me? Did you ever feed me . . . ?"

"In God's name, Jane, what are you talking about?"

"Stop pretending!" Jane screamed, leaping to her feet. "You're my mother! You know you are, so stop lying!"

Kirsten's eyes darted toward the stairs. She was so stunned that for the moment the only coherent thought in her head was that Tom shouldn't hear any of this. Why in God's name had she brought him here?

"Why did you tell everyone you'd got rid of me?" Jane raged on, her face strained with bitterness. "Why did you tell them you had an abortion when the truth was you gave me away? Your own child, a defenseless baby not even a year old and you gave me away. Why, Kirsten? Why did you give me away?"

"Jane," Kirsten whispered, "I'm not your mother."

"You are! You are, you are! Was it because Laurence left you?"

"Jane, please listen to me. I'm not your mother."

"Stop lying! You're my mother. Look at me, can't you see the resemblance? I look like you."

"Jane, you're nothing like me and even if you were, it's just not possible—"

"It is! You're my mother and Laurence is my father! We're a family!"

"Oh, God," Kirsten groaned, burying her face in her hands. "Jane, please believe me. I'm not your mother. I can't be your mother because I've never had a child. Never, do you hear me? And even if I had, that child still couldn't be you."

"Why?" Jane cried, her brilliant eyes gleaming the

challenge. "Why couldn't it be me? Because I'm not pretty enough?"

"Oh, God, Jane, what do I have to say to convince you?"

"You can admit to the truth, that's what you can do. You can admit that I'm a part of you, that you carried me in your womb—"

"Jane! I've never carried a child beyond three months, but even if I had, it could never have been you. You're too young. I was fifteen when I was pregnant, I'm thirty-seven now and you're only twenty-two."

"You see, it adds up."

"No, it doesn't! You're not allowing for the other six months I'd have had to carry you. I'd have been sixteen by then, well and truly sixteen. But even so, Jane, I had an abortion."

"No, it's not true," Jane said, banging her fists together. "It can't be true. You're my mother, I know you are. . . . And Laurence is my father."

"Jane, I didn't even know Laurence then . . ."

Jane's nostrils were flared, her teeth were clamped together, and her eyes glittered manically as she stared sightlessly into the fire. "Laurence is my father," she whispered. "I know he is. And you are my mother." Her eyes came up to Kirsten's. "Please say it's true," she begged.

"Oh, Jane, I can't . . ."

"Then let me prove it."

Kirsten took a breath as she pushed her fingers through her hair.

"I've got the pictures," Jane declared, tears of desperation spilling onto her cheeks. "I can show you. I've got them here," and before Kirsten could stop her she had run into the kitchen and picked up her album.

"Here," she said, offering it to Kirsten. "Here are all the pictures of when you and Laurence got married. When you had me . . ."

Not knowing what else to do Kirsten took the album. Jane came to stand beside her and Kirsten could feel the trembling of her slight body. "See here," Jane said triumphantly as Kirsten turned to the first page. "There you are on your wedding day."

Kirsten's heart contracted as she looked down at the photograph that had had Pippa's face cut from it and her own glued on beside Laurence's.

Excitedly Jane turned to the next page. "See here," she said, "this was when I was born." And there was a picture of Kirsten, one that Laurence had taken six years ago, with a tiny black and white snapshot of a baby stuck to it. Fleetingly she remembered Jane once telling her that Laurence had kept the photographs in the attic of his Kensington home. Obviously this was where Jane had got them.

On the next page was another photograph from the same era, this time of Kirsten and Laurence together, and added to it was a picture of the baby Kirsten now recognized to be Jane. Around the picture of Jane were the same scissored edges as before. There were more, many more, and as Kirsten went through them, despite the fear mounting inside her, she felt as though her heart was breaking. It seemed that the only pictures Jane had been able to find of herself were those of when she was less than a year old and those that Kirsten and Laurence had taken when they were in New Orleans. There was nothing in between.

"So you see, it's all there," Jane said, tearing her eyes from a photograph of Kirsten, Laurence, Tom, and herself that a waiter had taken for them at the Café du Monde and gazing beseechingly into Kirsten's face. "We're a family. I know you don't want me, I know you're trying to get rid of me again, but Laurence won't let you."

Silently Kirsten closed the album, put it down on the coffee table and turned to take Jane in her arms. As she held her she felt Jane's fragile body start to convulse.

"That's it," Kirsten soothed, stroking Jane's hair as the sobs tore painfully through Jane's chest and her scalding tears soaked Kirsten's shoulder. "Let it all out. Come on now, no one's going to hurt you."

After a while Jane pulled away. She sat on the sofa, hugging her spindly knees to her chest. "You always said you would talk to me, but you never did. I used to call you up so I could hear your voice, but then I was too afraid to speak. Sometimes I said your name, but whenever I did you hung up on me." Tears were flowing freely down her cheeks; her tiny body was shaking. "I just wanted you to love me, Kirsten," she sobbed. "I wanted you to be a part of our family, just me, you, Laurence, and Tom. I even killed Anna so that she wouldn't come between us all."

Jane started to cry again. Kirsten stared down at her hardly able to think. It wasn't credible; Jane could never have done something like that, yet Kowski's voice was ringing in her ears. 'It would take a physicist to work something like that out,' Kowski had said, and Jane's father was a physicist, had tried to encourage Jane to become one too, had taught her chemical formulas. . . . Kirsten's head fell forward as she thought of Anna, saw her body being carried from the set—the innocent victim of a madness that had been festered by an unimaginable loneliness and a need to be loved. . . . A madness that was at last surfacing through the layers of buried emotion and destroying the poor, tortured mind that harbored it.

"What about Jake?" she whispered.

For a moment or two Jane didn't answer, then her voice came, almost as an echo, from the depths of a bottomless pain. "I didn't mean to kill him," she croaked. "I liked Jake, I didn't want him to die." She raised her head, blinked as though clearing her vision. Her pale skin was mottled, huge tears still rolled down her cheeks. "It was supposed to be you," she said, staring absently into the fire.

Kirsten looked at her.

"I loved you, Kirsten. I loved you so much, why didn't you want me?"

"Oh, Jane, I did," Kirsten said, going to kneel in front of her.

"No. You didn't care about me. You just wanted me to go. No one ever wants me. No one's ever cared about me—"

"I care about you, Jane."

Jane's desperate eyes searched Kirsten's face. "Do you?" she said.

Kirsten nodded, but though her heart was churning with pity all she wanted was to get Jane out of the house.

Above all, she had to protect Tom. She wondered if she could contrive a reason for going upstairs. She could use the phone in the bedroom to get help.

She looked down at Jane's colorless face. For the moment she seemed calm. Carefully Kirsten got to her feet.

"Don't leave me," Jane whispered as Kirsten reached the door. "Please, don't leave me."

Kirsten turned back to see Jane's crumpled body huddled on the sofa. "I won't be long," she said gently.

Jane's gaze returned to the fire. Kirsten walked to the bottom of the stairs. She was on the point of going up when she heard Jane move. She turned round, saw Jane coming, and put out her arms. Suddenly Jane's hand whipped out from behind her back and the poker crashed brutally down on Kirsten's wrists.

Kirsten cried out, snatched her hands back, gasping at the excruciating pain. Jane lifted the poker again. Kirsten ducked, the poker slammed against the bannister.

"He's my father!" Jane cried. "You're trying to take him away, but I won't let you."

"Jane, please," Kirsten choked, clutching the stair rail and trying to pull herself up. It was strange how, despite the reality of the pain, she still couldn't make herself believe this was happening.

"He loves me! He cares for me! Why don't you? You're my mother! Why don't you love me?"

Kirsten started to speak, but suddenly her head snapped back as the poker crashed toward her face. Somehow she managed to duck out of the way and stagger into the kitchen where she fell against the sink.

"Laurence won't want you if you're not beautiful,"

Jane said, coming in after her, and to Kirsten's horror she snatched a knife from the wall.

"Jane, for God's sake, please stop this." Kirsten choked on the words, backing up against the sink, but there was an inhuman energy flowing wildly from Jane's eyes and Kirsten could see there was no reaching her. As Jane lunged, Kirsten twisted herself away, but Jane grabbed her hair and dragged her head back so far that Kirsten clutched on to the sink to keep herself up.

As the knife plunged toward her face Kirsten let go of the sink and dropped to the floor. The knife cut through the air, but already Jane was lifting it again. Kirsten rolled away, throwing herself under the table, so panicked and shaking so hard it was as though every part of her was bound in paralyzing knots of terror.

She watched helplessly as Jane flung the chairs across the kitchen. Then everything went silent. She could see Jane's legs, standing at one end of the table, unmoving. Briefly she turned her head to see if the way was clear to the door, but when she turned back she saw Jane start across the kitchen as though sensing her intention.

"Kirstie, why are you hiding under the table?"

At the sound of Tom's voice Kirsten's head came up. "Oh, my God," she muttered, starting across the room. "Tom! Go! Go back upstairs." But Jane already had hold of him.

"Jane, he's just a baby, for God's sake let him go!" Kirsten cried, her heart freezing with terror.

"It's all right, Tom," Jane was saying, as she dragged him into the sitting room. "No one's going to hurt you. You just be a good boy now."

"Kirstie!" Tom wailed, trying to look back over his shoulder.

"Jane! Let him go!" Kirsten shouted, but as she came up behind her Jane spun round, lashing out with the knife.

Kirsten gasped as it sliced into her shoulder. Tom struggled to break free, screaming Kirsten's name, but Jane wrenched his arms behind him and held the blade to his throat.

"This is the baby you want!" she sobbed. "But he's not yours. You can't have him. He's mine and Laurence's. He's not yours!"

"Jane, don't do this to him," Kirsten begged. "You love him, you can't— *Jane!*" she screamed, as the point of the blade sunk into Tom's tender flesh.

The whole of Tom's body was shuddering with sobs.

Jane's tormented eyes held Kirsten's. "You're all going to be together," she said. "You're going to have everything you've ever wanted and I'll be alone. No one will care about me. . . . But why should you have everything? Why should Tom have so much love when I never had any?"

"Jane," Kirsten pleaded, her voice shrill with panic, "can't you see that if you do anything to Tom you'll break Laurence's heart. If you love him, Jane—"

"Daddy!" Tom whimpered.

Jane looked down. Kirsten seized her chance and slammed her bunched fists into the side of Jane's head. The knife flew across the room as Jane crashed against the back of the sofa, and grabbing Tom's hand Kirsten fled to the front door.

"I want my Daddy! I want my Daddy!" Tom gulped.

The front door was locked. There were no keys. "It's all right, darling." Kirsten was panting as she hitched Tom under her arm and ran as fast as she could up to her bedroom.

She slammed the door behind her and hefting Tom onto her hip dashed to the phone. The line was dead.

"Oh, no," she muttered under her breath, realizing that Jane must have disconnected it.

"I don't want Jane to be frightening anymore," Tom sobbed.

"No, sweetheart, neither do I," Kirsten mumbled, looking frantically around the room and wondering what to do next. Then realizing there was no lock on the door she ran into the bathroom.

Still holding Tom she turned on the tap and put a facecloth under the running water. Then putting his head back she dabbed at the cut on Tom's neck. To her relief it was no more than a scratch. Not so the one on her shoulder, and as she stared down at the gaping flesh she felt a terrible, nauseating fear rush through her. What the hell was she going to do now?

She lowered the lid of the lavatory seat and sat down, holding Tom tight. She must make herself think. There was a way out of this, there had to be, but dear God how much easier it would be if Tom weren't there.

Suddenly she stiffened. The creak of a floorboard, the soft tread of footsteps. Jane was coming up the stairs.

Kirsten's head was pounding. Even after all that had happened she still couldn't accept that it was Jane, the Jane they had known—at least thought they'd known—who was doing this.

"Kirsten! Kirsten!" Jane called.

Tom buried his face in Kirsten's neck and clutched her tightly.

"Tom? Where are you, Tom?" Jane's voice was as normal as if they were playing hide and seek.

"I think you must be in here," Jane said, and Kirsten knew she was at the bedroom door.

She listened, every nerve in her body clenching with fear, as Jane's footsteps drew closer.

"Yes, I think you're in here," Jane said, and both Kirsten and Tom jumped as Jane rattled the door.

Kirsten tried to look down at Tom, but his face was still pressed against her neck. "It's all right, sweetheart," she whispered, smoothing his hair. "It's going to be all right."

CHAPTER THIRTY-TWO

LAURENCE ACCELERATED ACROSS THE HAMMERSMITH overpass, his foot jammed flat on the accelerator as he careered perilously from one lane to the other. He was aware of the police sirens behind him, and glancing in the mirror saw the blue flashing light weaving furiously through the traffic. He geared down to give himself more power. The car screeched in protest, another driver bumping his car onto the pavement to clear the way. The lights ahead were turning green, and pressing his hand on the horn Laurence blasted his way through the sluggish traffic.

Of all the times for his goddamned car to have broken down this couldn't have been a worse one. He'd have been at Kirsten's by now if he hadn't had to go through the rigmorole of borrowing a car from Ruby's neighbor and having to explain the urgency. He'd tried calling Kirsten from Ruby's, and to his horror Jane had answered. She'd said no more than hello before hearing his voice, then ringing off and disconnecting the line. He'd left his father at Ruby's to contact the police and keep trying Kirsten's number.

As he attempted to force his way through red lights, ignoring the hoots and fury of other drivers, he saw the police car bump up onto the pavement, swerve around the filtering traffic and screech to a halt in front of him. He didn't even wait for them to get out of their car, instead he leapt from his own, ran to meet them, and explained who he was and what he was doing, thanking God for the publicity surrounding Kirsten's arrest, which meant that one of the officers recognized him.

Within minutes they were once again speeding through the streets of London, this time with the police car in the lead, and one of the officers shouting frantically into his radio to get reinforcements to Elm Park Gardens as quickly as possible.

Laurence came back to be with Kirsten in hospital as soon as he had settled Tom at his parents'. Thea was mortified that she'd let Jane take Tom out earlier—to a birthday party, Jane had said apparently—and as appalled at Jane's duplicity as they all were. Tom himself seemed quiet, withdrawn but basically okay. Jane had been arrested at Kirsten's house as soon as Laurence let the police in: It turned out that the police were already on to her, the key witness Hellerman had mentioned being none other than Jim Cottle, her father. He'd grown more and more suspicious of Jane's behavior in recent weeks, and the final straw was when the police played him the tape and he recognized his own voice saying Kirsten's name. Jane had obviously taped him in some unguarded moment and used electronic techniques to distort the voice, but not so distorted that Laurence didn't also recognize it as Jane's father's voice, just after Ruby made her startling revelation. "It's a cruel irony when you think that her parents' treatment of her must really be responsible for her insanity."

Kirsten was amazed at how calm she was when all she wanted to do was scream with the pain and shock of what she and Tom had gone through. Suddenly she remembered. "Oh God," she groaned, "how could I have forgotten? It's the hearing tomorrow. Laurence, you must go home. If Pippa wins, this could be your last night with Tom."

"It won't be," Laurence said.

Kirsten drew herself up, looking at him curiously. "What do you mean?" she said. "Has something happened?"

"Yes, but it can wait."

"I'd rather you told me now," she said, an uneasy sensation starting to gather at the pit of her stomach. Oh, dear God no. Please let her be reading this wrong. "Laurence?" she said, as he got to his feet. "Laurence, what is it?"

"I told you, it can wait."

"No," she said shaking her head. "I want to know now."

He turned around and when Kirsten saw the look on his face a debilitating numbness started to creep into her heart. "Laurence, tell me, please."

"There's nothing to tell," he said.

"Laurence! Don't lie to me. Something's happened and I want to know what it is."

"Kirstie, you've been through enough for one day. . . . We'll talk about it tomorrow."

"No! How the hell do you think I'm going to sleep knowing that you're holding something back from me. I want to know now. . . . Whatever it is."

"Kirstie, don't make me do this. For your own sake . . ."

"Oh, God, Laurence, you're frightening me. What's happening to Tom? You said you saw Pippa? Did she say something?"

"Yes, she said something."

"Then what!"

"She's decided that Tom should stay here in England," he said, unable to meet her eyes.

"But that's fantastic, isn't it?" Kirsten said uncertainly. "Aren't you pleased?"

"Yes, of course I am. It was what I wanted. Well, you know that . . ."

"But?" she said.

At last he turned to look at her and reaching out to take her hand he sat down gently beside her. "Kirstie, you know how much I love you, don't you?" he said.

"I thought I did." She breathed uneasily, her eyes darting between his.

"I do. I love you, Kirsten, and I don't ever want you to doubt that."

"Then why am I starting to?"

His head fell back. "Oh, God, I don't know how to tell you this," he groaned. "Not now, not ever."

"Laurence, please," Kirsten whispered, feeling the numbness in her heart turning to ice.

"Pippa's agreed to let me have custody . . ." he said. "But not quite the way we wanted."

"Then in what way?"

"She wants to come back. She wants us to be a family again."

For a long time Kirsten just stared at him. She could sense the pain struggling its way through, but for the moment all she knew was the incapacitating shock that now, after all they had come through, she was going to lose him anyway. In the end she gently extracted her hands and said, "Then that's what you have to do."

"Oh, God," he murmured. "I shouldn't have told you, not tonight . . ."

"It's all right," Kirsten said calmly, but deep down inside she knew it wasn't. "If that's how you get to keep Tom, then that's what you must do."

"I love you, Kirstie. I'll always love you."

She smiled shakily. "I think you should go now," she said.

"I'm not leaving you tonight . . ."

"Laurence, please. I . . ." Her voice faltered, but mustering her courage she tried again. "I think it would be best if you did. Please, don't argue. There's no point dragging this out, it'll only be more painful for us both. Laurence *please*," she said, as he started to argue again. "You've made your decision, I understand the decision, but I want you to go."

She turned away, so desperate to cling to him, to beg him to stay, and so filled with pain at the knowledge that for the second time in her life she was losing him while carrying his baby that she couldn't look at him anymore. For one fleeting moment she almost told him, the words were there on her tongue crying out to be spoken, but she stopped herself. She couldn't do that to him. She loved him too much to want to see him so torn apart by the agonizing choice she would force on him.

A few minutes later she heard the door close behind him and at the sound of it she knew that her whole life was breaking irreparably apart.

CHAPTER THIRTY-THREE

"WHERE IS EVERYONE?" LAURENCE ASKED, WALKING into the sitting room and finding only Pippa.

"Your parents have gone to some function at the American embassy," Pippa answered, putting aside the manuscript she was working on.

"And Tom?"

"Upstairs. Sulking."

Instantly Laurence's face darkened. "Why?"

"Why do you think?"

"Did you smack him again, Pippa?"

"As a matter of fact, yes. He deserved it. He was so bloody rude to me. . . . Where are you going?" she cried, getting to her feet as Laurence turned to leave the room.

"To see to Tom, where do you think?"

"Laurence! We've got to present a united front on this. He's getting out of hand and you know it."

"What he's getting is smacked," Laurence said tightly, "and I'm not siding with you on that, Pippa. You can't expect to walk back into his life and have him behave as though nothing has happened. He doesn't trust you. He's afraid you're going to leave him again—"

"Bullshit! He's afraid he's never going to see Kirsten Meredith again, that's what he's afraid of."

"Of course he is. He loved her, Pippa, and he's going to need some time to deal with it."

"He's had over a month now. How much longer does he need?" she snapped angrily.

"How much longer do you need?" Laurence countered.

Pippa turned away.

"Look," Laurence sighed, letting go of the door and coming back into the room. "This hasn't been an easy time for any of us, but I thought we agreed that Tom should come first."

"He does," Pippa said miserably. "It's just that I get so hurt when he talks about Kirsten and what she would and wouldn't let him do."

"I know," Laurence said, putting a hand on her shoulder. "But you've got to be patient, Pip. He's just a child and all he can see right now is a mother who's always angry with him. . . ."

"Always?" Pippa said, turning to look up at him.

Laurence nodded. "Pretty much."

"I do love him, you know that, Laurence, don't you?"

"Sure I do. You just got to convince him of that. And smacking him isn't the way."

"But what am I supposed to do when he's so defiant and throws those godawful tantrums the way he does? Do I just let him get away with it?"

"No. But don't hit him. Try to reason it out with him and *tell* him you love him."

Pippa tilted her head to one side and brushed her

cheek against his hand. "You still miss her too, don't you?" she said softly.

Laurence swallowed hard. "Yeah," he said. "I miss her."

"Are we doing the right thing here, Laurence?" Pippa asked, her eyes shining up at him the same way Tom's did whenever he was unsure of something.

"I don't know," he answered, dropping his forehead onto hers. "I wish to God I did."

"I want it to work," Pippa whispered. "And I know you're doing everything you can, so I guess it's for me to try a bit harder, hmm?"

"I guess so," Laurence said, folding her into his arms. As he gazed up at the ceiling he was trying hard to suppress the resentment that was flooding through him. If only she would admit it wasn't going to work, if only she would give up and go back to Zaccheo where she really belonged. Neither of them were happy and neither of them truly believed they could be, but until Pippa was ready to give up there was nothing he could do. Perhaps if Tom was willing to go with his mother it might make things easier, but as it stood, there was no way in the world Tom was going to let go of his father—he felt safe and secure in Laurence's love and Laurence couldn't even begin to contemplate doing anything to shatter that.

But, dear Christ, he missed Kirsten. Not a minute of the day went by when he didn't think about her and long to pick up the phone and speak to her. He'd stuck by his promise not to call because he'd known it was her way of handling things, but it was tearing him apart. He was so afraid of what might be happening to her, how she was dealing with this separation. He knew she'd do everything she could to pull herself through, but what he didn't know was whether, ultimately, she had the strength. She'd suffered too much in her life, was too vulnerable, too dependent on the love she had for him—as he was on the love he had for her. They shouldn't be apart this way, they needed each other in a way that he and Pippa never had and never would.

Lately his sleeplessness had become constant and his inability to make love to Pippa was, he was sure, soon going to become permanent. He wanted only Kirsten, his entire body and soul ached for her in every way imaginable.

He was due to start work on a new project the following week, but his heart wasn't really in it. With Kirsten he could have gone to Hollywood and with Kirsten he guessed he could make just about anything work. But all the dreams they had shared of a great future together had turned to ashes the day Pippa had asked to come back. And now the fear that Kirsten's life was falling irreparably apart haunted him night and day. He didn't want to break his promise, but he knew that sooner or later he was going to pick up that phone because he just had to know if she was all right.

Hearing the front door close and his parents' voices in the hall, Laurence let Pippa go. "I'd best go see to Tom," he said.

Pippa smiled sadly. "I'll come with you," she said. "And then, Laurence, I think we'd better talk. We've got to sort something out here, something that's going to work for us all—but I think you already know what the answer is."

"Do I?" Laurence said.

"Yes. You want her back. You can't stop thinking about her. . . . Neither can Tom. And if she can make you both happier than I can, then perhaps I should go back to Zaccheo and leave you two to get on with your lives."

For long moments Laurence looked down at her, then putting an arm around her shoulders as they turned to walk from the room and trying to hold back the euphoria, he said, "At least we tried." Dear God, how he wanted to go to the phone right now and call her, to tell her he loved her and ask her to take him back. But Pippa was right, they had to talk first and sort out just what her relationship with Tom was going to be.

Smiling distantly to herself Kirsten looked down at the letter she was holding and read it again. It had arrived that morning along with a letter from her lawyer telling her that Dyllis Fisher had been persuaded to resign from the newspaper, to hand over the reins of her power to someone of a more stable disposition. Kirsten had thrown that particular letter away. She wanted to hear no more of Dyllis Fisher. As far as Kirsten was concerned the bitter need for revenge that had driven Dyllis was not going to be what drove her. That was all a part of the past now, and the only pleasure Kirsten could feel in Dyllis's downfall was relief to be free of her.

The other letter, however, Kirsten had kept and read

several times already that day. Each time she did she could only marvel at the cruel way life played these little tricks, reminding her of all she'd once dreamed of and letting her know that now it would never be. She wondered if Laurence had received the same letter, but reminding herself that she mustn't think that way, she put the letter down and ran up the stairs to continue packing.

Since she'd made the decision to leave, to take herself back to France and bring her baby up in the depths of Provence, she had felt much better. They would be happy there, the two of them, safe and secure and as unlikely to cause Laurence any more pain as they were to be discovered by the press. Paul had left her well enough provided for so that she need never work again, but she would fulfill the contract she had with the publisher and write her book. That wasn't going to be easy, she knew, but she'd take her time over it and only write when she felt up to it. And maybe, one day, she would feel the need to go out into the world again and take on the challenge of getting her ideas on the screen. But for now that ambition had left her. Whether it had gone with Laurence or whether it was because she wanted her baby to come first she didn't know, and what did it matter? She was getting her life sorted out, she was coming through, and though she missed him every hour, every minute of the day, she reminded herself constantly that in time the pain would ease. In time she would hold his baby in her arms and give it all the love in her heart.

For a moment she stopped what she was doing and sat down on the bed. She knew she was going to cry, was willing to let the tears come. The doctor had told her that bottling up her emotions the way she had been was no good for either her or the baby. It hadn't been easy at first, but now she sometimes wondered if she would ever stop. And as the terrible voice of denial started to cry out inside her, trying to turn her back from a future without Laurence, she took the picture of him from beside the bed and hugged it to her.

Eventually she dried her eyes, got up and went into the bathroom to splash cold water on her face. It was all right, it really was, it was just that sometimes the memories stole over her and made it hard to be strong. She loved this house, had known such happiness here, that she was dreading leaving it. But she could always come back, she reminded herself. There was nothing in the world that was making her do anything she didn't want to do and right now she really did want to leave. She needed to sever the bonds that still tied her to Laurence, to remove herself from the temptation to call him and tell him how much she still loved him. In her heart she knew that his suffering was as great as hers and to do that to him would only make it worse.

Walking back into the bedroom she continued with her packing. She wished desperately that she had someone to talk to, someone with whom she could share all that was in her heart, maybe then the burden wouldn't seem quite so great. She knew it was madness to blame herself for all that had happened, that in coming back she had brought only pain and misery to those she loved, but it was difficult not to. In her bleaker moments she saw herself as someone who carried bad luck with her, who was in some way tainted by the hand of misfortune and passed it on to the lives that touched hers. But thinking that way served no purpose, and besides, gloomy thoughts would make for a gloomy baby—or so she told herself.

As she snapped one suitcase shut and opened another she was wondering whether or not to call Helena before she left. It would be so good to hear her voice, to see her even and be able to apologize for all the hurt they had caused each other. It had been over three weeks now since Helena had left a message on the answering machine. Had she not been pregnant Kirsten would have called her long before now, but she didn't trust herself to see Helena and not tell her about the baby. If she did that, then there was no doubt in her mind that Helena would go straight to Laurence.

However, now that the flight was booked for the following morning, her packing was all but complete, and it was too late in the evening to ask Helena to come over, there was little chance she'd do more than say how sorry she was and wish Helena good luck for the future.

She looked across at the telephone and almost laughed at the bolt of nerves that began agitating her stomach. Maybe she should call Laurence too. They should say good-bye; that way the break would be cleaner. In fact, now she came to think about it, to disappear without a word the way she was planning would hurt him immeasurably. So yes, maybe she should call him; she didn't have to tell him where she was going, but she could at least let him know that she was all right.

The bedroom was in such chaos that she decided to go downstairs and use the phone. When she reached the landing she stopped. Was this really such a wise thing to do? They'd made a pact not to contact each other and though she longed every day for him to break his promise . . .

She started as the telephone rang. Instantly she wondered if it were he. Allowing the hope to gather in her heart, she ran toward the stairs.

She didn't even see the little toy train that she stepped on, neither did she see the packing case at the bottom of the stairs. It all happened so fast that all she knew was the blinding dagger of pain that shot through her head just before the ringing stopped and she was swallowed into the swirling realms of darkness.

CHAPTER THIRTY-FOUR

THEA LET HERSELF QUIETLY INTO THE ROOM AND closed the door behind her. Helena looked up from where she was sitting beside the hospital bed, her fingers curled around Kirsten's.

"How is she?" Thea whispered.

"Still sleeping."

Thea walked to the bed, leaned over, and brushed a loose strand of hair from Kirsten's face. "Thanks for letting me know," she said.

"Have you told Laurence?"

"No. Not yet."

"Will you?"

Thea smiled down at Kirsten's pale face. "He tried to call her last night," she said. "There was no answer. . . . Well, we know why now. Thank God you got to her in time."

"Helena?" Kirsten croaked.

"Yes, I'm right here," Helena said turning back to her. "How are you feeling now?"

Kirsten was blinking, trying to clear her vision. "I'm not sure. My head hurts. . . . Where am I?"

Helena smiled. Obviously Kirsten had still been too dazed when she regained consciousness earlier to register anything Helena had told her. "In the hospital," she answered.

"Why? What happ—" Kirsten stopped and as she squeezed her eyes tightly closed Thea left the room to find the nurse.

"Lie still," Helena admonished gently, as Kirsten tried to lift herself up.

"Who was in here?" Kirsten asked.

"It was—" Helena stopped herself, any reference to Laurence might not be wise right now. "Just a nurse," she said.

"How did I get here?"

"By ambulance. I came round, last night. I thought it was time we patched things up." She laughed shakily. "Talk about leaving it until the eleventh hour. Anyway, I knocked and knocked. . . . I could see the lights were on so I knew you were in. . . . I was terrified you might have— Well, you know. So I ran next door to use the phone. The police broke the door down and the ambulance brought you here."

Kirsten was shaking her head and smiling, as though silently chiding herself for having caused so much fuss. "Thank you," she said, tightening her hold on Helena's hand. "I don't deserve you as a friend after the way I treated you."

"It's me who doesn't deserve you," Helena whispered. "But we'll leave that for another time."

Kirsten looked down at their joined hands then lifted her head and smiled. "It wasn't deliberate," she said. "I know you think it was. . . ." She swallowed hard on the lump rising in her throat. "I would never have done anything like that, not when . . . not when . . ."

"It's all right," Helena said soothingly as Kirsten's eyes filled with tears.

"Helena, tell me, please. . . . The baby . . . is it all right?"

"Baby?" Helena repeated.

"Oh, God," Kirsten said, closing her eyes as fear pushed her heart into her throat. Surely that would have been the first thing they'd do, check if the baby was still alive, and if they hadn't mentioned it to Helena . . .

"Helena, please, you have to find out for me."

"Find out what?" Helena asked.

"Whether or not I . . . I lost the baby when I fell."

"Oh, Christ," Helena groaned. "You mean you're pregnant. Oh, God, Kirstie . . . I'll go and fetch the doctor right away. You just stay right there. Don't worry, it'll be all right. I promise you, everything will be all right."

When the door opened a few minutes later the doctor came in alone. Kirsten took one look at his expression and covered her face with her hands.

Later in the day Helena brought Kirsten fresh clothes to travel home in. She wasn't at all sure that the doctor would release Kirsten, but after he had checked her over earlier Kirsten had been so insistent that she was all right to leave that Helena had thought it wise to bring the clothes, if only to humor her.

When she walked into the room she found Kirsten sitting on the side of her bed looking . . . Helena blinked. She looked almost goddamned radiant. Of course her cheeks were still pale, so too were her lips, and the edge of the scar where she'd hit her head on the packing case showed vividly just beneath her hair line, but her eyes were shining so brightly they were very nearly dazzling.

"For someone who's just tried to top herself you look like you just won the pools," Helena remarked.

"I didn't try to top myself," Kirsten retorted. "And maybe I have won the pools. At least, in a manner of speaking."

Helena eyed her skeptically.

"Oh, Helena, you should see your face." Kirsten laughed. "I'm all right now, honestly. They wouldn't be letting me go home if I weren't."

"But I've never seen such a quick recovery. And are you sure the doctor said you could leave, because I'm warning you, I'm not being an accomplice to anything he hasn't agreed to."

"If you don't believe me, then go right ahead and ask him yourself. We had a long chat this afternoon," she pulled a face, "I have to spend the next couple of weeks taking it easy, but on the whole he thinks we'll both be all right. Oh, Helena," she said as an unsuppressible emotion flooded from her heart. "I just can't believe it. . . ."

"Hey." Helena laughed, taking Kirsten in her arms as tears started in her own eyes. "Come on now, that baby's sure to be all right. After all he's come through and still he's hanging on . . ."

"He?"

"Okay, she. What does it matter just so long as it's all right."

"It doesn't matter one bit." Kirsten laughed, using her fingers to wipe away the tears.

"Why the hell didn't you ring me?" Helena said.

"Why didn't you ring me?" Kirsten challenged.

Helena gave a wry smile. "Now that," she said, "is a long story and one I'm not particularly proud of. But we'll save it, shall we, until you're out of here and back on your feet."

"Okay. But tell me what's been happening to you?" Kirsten smiled. "How are things working out with Dermott?"

Helena's eyebrows arched comically as she pulled up the corners of her mouth. "We got married," she said. "Two weeks ago. He bulldozed me into it, but I'm kind of glad he did."

"Oh, Helena, congratulations," Kirsten laughed, putting her arms around her friend.

"I guess we're destined for the divorce courts, at least that's what I keep telling him, but I reckon we might rub along all right together. He's not a bad sort of jerk as jerks go."

Kirsten was laughing. "Did you have a honeymoon?"

"Not yet and to tell you the truth I don't want one. At least I don't fancy what he wants very much."

"Why? What does he want?"

"Brace yourself. He wants to take a nice slow train ride from anywhere to anywhere just so long as it's slow and just so long as he can get off whenever he wants. Me, if I had to suffer that, I'd push him off just for being a dickhead, but I don't guess we'll be going anywhere until we get some money together. He's hoping for a real bundle out of Dyllis's newspaper for using him the way she did, but in the meantime he's as broke as I am."

"But haven't the lawyers paid you for the movie yet?" Kirsten said.

"Sure they have, but we've got to live on something till Dermott gets what he's calling his inheritance."

"I'll tell you what." Kirsten laughed. "I've rented a cottage in Provence. I should have been going this morning. . . . Well, I can't now, at least not for another week or so, so why don't you and Dermott go there?"

Helena was shaking her head. "You think I'm running off and leaving you now?" she said. "Someone's got to look after you and make sure you rest up and that's just what I'm going to do. I've already told Dermott I'm leaving him for a fortnight. . . . He's threatening to come too, but don't worry . . ."

They both looked around as someone knocked on the door, and the smile faded from Kirsten's lips as Thea put her head in.

"Thea?" she said, feeling a painful lurch in her heart.

"How are you feeling?" Thea smiled.

Kirsten's eyes darted to Helena. "Better," she said. "Yes, much better, thank you," but Helena could see the haunted look that had come into her eyes. Obviously Kirsten was thinking that she, Helena, might have told Thea about the baby.

"It's all right," Helena whispered, "no one knows. I haven't breathed a word."

"Are you well enough to receive a little visitor?" Thea asked.

Kirsten's eyes widened with uncertain delight.

"He's right outside," Thea said. "Shall I get him?"

"Yes," Kirsten said, starting to laugh. "Oh, please yes."

Thea opened the door, popped her head out, and said, "Okay, put that back and then you can come in."

Kirsten was already crying by the time Tom flung himself into her arms. "Kirstie!" he shouted. "I've just had a go in a wheelchair!"

"Have you?" She laughed through her tears. "And what was it like?"

"Brilliant. You ought to give it a go."

"I will," she said, holding him so that she could look at him and kiss him some more.

"I've got a present for you," he declared.

"You have?"

"Yep, I did a painting of you. I put it up on my wall at home, but Granny said you might like to have it. So I brought it with me."

"Then where is it?" Kirsten laughed.

Tom looked up at Thea, suddenly confused. "I forget the next bit," he said.

It was Kirsten's turn to look at Thea in confusion. "I think he must have left it in the car." Thea laughed. "I'll go and get it." At the door she turned back, and catching Helena's eye, signaled for her to come too.

"So," Kirsten said to Tom when they were alone, "what have you been up to?"

"Oh, lots of things. But I missed you, Kirstie. I even cried because I missed you. Mummy got angry with me, but Daddy said it was all right to cry. He told me a secret. He said that he cried too because he missed you."

"Did he?" Kirsten whispered shakily. "I miss him too."

"Didn't you learn yet how to keep a secret, Tom?"

Just the sound of his voice was enough to make Kirsten's heart tighten so painfully that as she turned to see him standing at the door she felt an uncontrollable rush of tears lodge in her throat.

"Hello," she said, swallowing hard as she tried to smile.

"Hello." His eyes were dancing mischievously, but Kirsten could see the concern and instantly felt her cheeks color. Did he, too, think she had tried to kill herself?

"Did you bring in my painting, Daddy?" Tom asked chirpily.

"It's right here," Laurence said, putting it on the end of the bed. "A pretty good likeness, huh?"

Kirsten felt a bubble of laughter rising from the very core of her heart as she looked down at the awkward spindly limbs, the fiery bush of hair, and smiley face. "You're so clever," she said to Tom, squeezing him.

Laurence came to sit on the bed beside them and lifted a hand to run it over Kirsten's hair. "I love you," he whispered. "If anything had happened to—"

"It's not what you think," Kirsten said. "It was an accident, I promise you."

His eyes were looking deep into hers.

"I swear it," Kirsten said, and at last he started to smile.

"I tried to call you . . ." he said. "Last night . . ."

"You mean that was you?"

"Yeah. Or I should say it was us," he added, chucking Tom under the chin.

"I dialed the number," Tom said proudly. "I know it off by heart now."

"And what were you calling about?" Kirsten asked, looking at Tom.

"We were ringing to ask if we could come home," Laurence answered.

Kirsten's heart stood still. She hadn't heard him right, she couldn't have. . . .

"Can we, Kirstie, please? Can we?" Tom begged.

Kirsten turned her eyes to Laurence. "I don't understand," she said. "What about . . . ?"

"We're getting a d-i-v-o-r-c-e."

"And c-u-s-t-o-d-y?"

"Mine. She's not going to fight it now. I'll explain later, when old big ears here is out of the way. So what do you say, can these two guys who love you come home?"

"Why are you crying, Kirstie?" Tom said, his own chin starting to wobble. "Don't you want us to come?"

"Of course I want you to come, silly," she said, hugging him.

Laurence waited until she let Tom go, then turned her mouth to his and kissed her softly. "There's something else I want to ask you," he murmured.

"You mean about the letter? Did you get one too?"

Laurence looked baffled. "What letter?"

"Never mind. I'll tell you about it later. What were you going to ask?"

"As a matter of fact I was going to ask you to marry me."

"Oh, yes!" Tom cried triumphantly. "Oh, please, Kirstie, say you'll marry us. Please."

Both Kirsten and Laurence burst out laughing. "How can I possibly refuse," she said, ruffling his hair.

"Oh, yuk! Not more of them, Daddy," Tom cried, pushing Laurence away as he tried to kiss him. "Come on, let's go home."

Laurence looked at Kirsten. "Are you sure you're well enough?"

"I'm well enough," she smiled. "In fact I've never felt better in my life."

"So," Kirsten said, looking up as Laurence came back into the bedroom after the third attempt at putting Tom to bed, "what happened with you and Pippa?"

"With me and Pippa not very much," Laurence said, taking his brandy away from her and putting it down. "With Pippa and Tom, plenty."

"Meaning?"

"Meaning that they just couldn't get along," he said, sitting down beside her and pulling her into his arms. "She never was cut out for motherhood, she'll admit as much herself. Oh, she loves him all right, but she just doesn't know how to handle him. In so many ways she's like a child herself; she wants all the attention, all the praise. . . . Not that she isn't prepared to give it, she's just better at taking it. She came back because she thought it was the right thing to do, and because she truly did want us to work as a family, but it didn't take long for us to see that it was going nowhere. She's still in love with Zaccheo and with him she can be a free spirit, never have to take on any responsibility she doesn't want to and never have to play second fiddle to a child. She missed Zaccheo more than she'd admit. . . . Then Tom started getting on her nerves. . . . They started to fight, there were tears every night. . . . It was pretty bad all round."

"Poor Tom," Kirsten smiled. "Anyway, he seems happy enough now and what I want to talk about is us. . . ."

"You want to set a date for the wedding?"

"Get your divorce first." She laughed.

"That's not going to take too long," he said, lifting her chin and kissing her softly on the lips. "God, it's been a rough road, Kirstie, but having you here at the end of it . . . Did you ever wonder, sometimes, if love was measured against pain?"

"Yes, I've wondered. Maybe that's why it's been so hard for us."

He smiled. "The deeper the pain, the harder the struggle, the greater the love?"

She nodded and her eyes closed as he leaned forward to kiss her.

"Okay," he said, before reaching her, "what was all that about a letter?"

"It's right here." Kirsten laughed, reaching across to the bedside table. But unable to contain her excitement she decided to tell him herself what was inside. "It's an offer from Columbia to talk to us about *Moyna O'Malley* or any other ideas we might have for movies. They want us to go out there as soon as we can to meet with them."

"I don't believe it," Laurence said, scanning the letter. "It's what we always talked about. . . ."

"Well, now you've got it."

"We've got it," he corrected her.

"Uh—uh." she shook her head. "You'll have to find someone else to boss around, I'm afraid. You see, I'm not going to be available."

"Well, I'm sure as hell not going without you," he declared.

"Too right you're not. We're all going." She grinned. "All four of us."

Laurence's smile started to fade as he looked from her eyes to her mouth and back again.

Kirsten nodded. "We're going to have a baby."

Still Laurence just looked at her. "Oh, Christ, I don't know what to say," he murmured. "Kirsten, oh, God, Kirstie, are you sure?"

"Of course I'm sure."

"Then just thank God it turned out this way. I'd never have been able to live with it, you having my baby and me not with you. But it would never have come to that, I'd have been there. I wouldn't have let you down, not a second time."

"I know."

Once again his eyes were studying hers and she could almost read his thoughts before he spoke them. "How long have you known?" he whispered.

"I just found out today," Kirsten lied, knowing that it would only hurt him to think she'd known all along and had tried to spare him. "So," she went on, "I thought I could write my book and look after Tom while you're talking big ideas and big bucks with the big guys."

He was still gazing at her, looking as though he wanted to say something but wasn't too sure what. "I'm going to find a way of telling you how much I love you," he said hoarsely, "I just got to figure out the words."

"Who needs words?" she smiled, "when we've got so many other ways."

"You sure you're up to that?" he said.

"Oh, I'm sure," she said.

It was in the middle of the night, when they were making love for the second time, that the bedroom door opened and Tom walked sleepily into the room to find Kirsten sitting astride Laurence.

"Can I play Humpty Dumpty too, Daddy?" he said, rubbing his eyes.

Kirsten looked down at Laurence, who groaned when he saw the laughter spring to her eyes. And sure enough, wrapping a sheet around her, Kirsten rolled onto her back and swept Tom into the bed with them. Still, Laurence decided, he was man enough to concede defeat on this occasion, 'cause there were going to be plenty of other chances for them to play their version of Humpty Dumpty. And, he guessed, wrapping them both in his arms, tonight was a night when the three of them—four of them—really should be together.

HarperPaperbacks *By Mail*

Read These Steamy Novels of Money, Power, and Passion From SUSAN LEWIS

OBSESSION

Corrie Browne always dreamed of leaving the quiet village where she grew up. After her mother's death, Corrie's search for the father she has never known leads her to London. There she begins a career in television and a search for the love that could bring her to the heights of passion, or to the depths of betrayal and heartbreak.

STOLEN BEGINNINGS

Marian Deacon and her cousin, Madeleine, are closer than most sisters. Marian is the responsible one, while Madeleine is carefree—and irresistible to men. Everything changes when Paul O'Connell, a handsome, enigmatic writer, lures both women into his life. Marian falls in love, but it is Madeleine who makes an easy conquest.